DUMP AND CHASE

Nashville Assassins: Next Generation

TONI ALEO

Editing by: Lisa Hollett of Silently Correcting Your Grammar

Proofing by: Jenny Rarden

Cover Design: Lori Jackson Design

Photo by: Sara Eirew

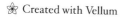 Created with Vellum

❧

When I met Jessica and Heather, it was at an author dinner in DC about four years ago. They were a delight, both so funny and gorgeous in their own ways. They are huge Blue Jackets fans, and the hockey love runs deep. We hit it off from the beginning, and we clicked. They got me and I got them. They told me that my books brought them together as best friends, and to this day, they are still best friends. I'll never forget when Jessica looked at me and begged me for Aiden. At the time, I couldn't even fathom Aiden being grown and needing a story. Now, though, I'm incredibly proud of the book she asked for.

Heather and Jessica are not only my beta readers but also two of my closest friends. Two women I know cheer for me on a personal level and a career level. In this world, I need that.

So this book is for you two.
I am grateful for you.
I love you.
Here's to many more years of books that will bring us closer.

CHAPTER ONE

SHELLI

I CAN'T SEEM TO CATCH MY BREATH. EVERY SINGLE FIBER OF MY being is vibrating with nerves. I feel the tension everywhere. My chest, my arms, my legs—I'm pretty sure my ass is shaking with excitement. I can't believe I'm here. I'm really here.

In Aiden Brooks's apartment building.

When Chris, my buddy, passes me a bottle of tequila, I take a long pull before passing it back, shuddering from the bitter liquid. I need it, though. I need the liquid courage to get me into this building. I run my hand down the long platinum blond braid of my wig. I didn't want to wear my wig from the show, but Chris was in a rush to get here. We came straight from the theatre after our last performance. I washed my face free of the dramatic stage makeup, but I wish I'd had time to take this damn wig off. Chris convinced me it didn't matter one way or another.

Being here, though, I find that it does matter to me. With each step I take, I regret my decision not to change. To be me, instead of the character I've played for the last six months. Not anymore, though, and as much as I want to be sad that my part in our show is over, I'm not. I had every opportunity to re-sign for another six months, but I decided not to. I'm done. I'm going home, and I am so damn excited.

I haven't lived with my parents full time since I was sixteen. I know most girls wouldn't be complaining, but I really do love my mom and dad. My siblings are okay on a good day, and I enjoy being with them. I miss them constantly, and I'm finally ready to go home. I need the distance from New York, I need to figure out who I am, what I want, and what my future holds. I am done with Broadway.

I know my mom is sad I'm quitting, but I don't like who I am becoming here. I don't feel happy, and I'm not living my life to my fullest. I feel like I'm just going with the flow, doing whatever my castmates do, and I don't want that. I don't want to develop a drug habit. I don't want to sleep around or get drunk every night. I don't need that stuff. I was good with who I was before I was exposed to this world. Don't get me wrong. It's been great, and I've made wonderful memories. The standing ovations have been intoxicating and the money has been awesome, but this doesn't feel like my path anymore.

I want something more. I just have no clue what that is yet.

Tonight, though, I don't have to worry yet about what the future holds. It's my last night as a New Yorker, so I'm going to make it the best night ever. Because tomorrow, I head back home to my new reality. I want to say I'm scared, but I'm not. I'm stoked.

I bite my lip as I climb the stairs to the entrance with Chris. As animated as always, he is talking with his hands. "Are you sure you've gotta go?"

I don't even look at him as I nod. He's taller than me, way taller, and good-looking to some. I knew the moment I met him, though, that he would only be a friend. He didn't get that memo, and he has begged me daily to date him. I don't see him as boyfriend material. Even with his blond hair, green eyes, and beautiful jawline, he isn't who I want. He isn't the one I've been crushing on for most of my life. Which is probably why every guy I've ever met has not been boyfriend material. But now is not the time to evaluate that.

"Yeah, I'm ready for a change."

"You're turning your back on your art. You were made for the stage. You're Elli Fisher's daughter, for fuck's sake."

I smile at the use of my mom's maiden name. I'm not sure anyone really remembers Elli Fisher. Even though she was one of the most amazing performers of her time, I don't even think my mom misses her. Not once Elli Adler made her mark on the world as one of the best owners and general managers for the Nashville Assassins. My mom started making a name for herself when she was the youngest owner in NHL history. She's always been ruthless and makes bold moves. She was one of the first owners to sign a woman and play her on the ice. She makes trades like no other, and she loves her players as if they were her kids. She's absolutely phenomenal, and if I can be half the woman my mom is, I'm winning.

"I hear you, but I want more."

"More? What's more?"

"I don't know yet," I admit with a smile. "But I'm going to find out."

He rolls his green eyes, every bit annoyed with me. I know he wants me to stay so he can get me to fall in love with him, but that won't happen. Not when my sights have always been set on one guy in particular.

The stairs into the lobby are endless, it seems, but when I see the elevator, my heart stops. I clear my throat. "So, he's here? Aiden?"

Chris chuckles. "Yes. Why would we be going to a party at his house if he weren't here?"

I shrug as he pulls out a card, sliding it into the slot before the doors open. "You have a card?"

Chris flashes me a grin. "Aiden and I are good friends."

I know this. Ever since Chris found out I had a thing for the Rangers' center, he likes to rub it in my face that he knows Aiden. It's crazy that in the two years I've known Chris, this is the first party he's taking me to. I don't know if it's because I'm leaving or if he really thought he was going to get in my pants and make me fall for him so I'd forget Aiden.

If it's the latter, he's so very, very wrong.

"Do you want another hit?"

I glance over to where Chris is lighting up his blunt. I shake my head. "No, I'm good."

I should have taken a bigger hit before, but what the hell. I do take the bottle of tequila, though, and swallow one more gulp as the elevator takes us up to the top floor that is apparently Aiden's penthouse. My heart rises into my throat with each floor we ascend. Chris takes the bottle from me as I pull up on my belt loops. The pants I'm wearing are a bit too tight, squeezing my waist and cutting off circulation to my legs, but they make my ass look really thick and big. I almost didn't wear the crop top I stole from my cousin, but I want to impress him. Problem is, Amelia, my cousin, is a small, though she wears a medium so her breasts don't show underneath. Because I'm a solid large on top, it's easy to say my breasts are peeking out the bottom in a way that would make my mom cringe.

But my mom isn't here. Aiden is, and I want him to notice me.

I've known Aiden my whole life. There are pictures of him holding me when I was a baby and from every year at my birthday. He was such a big part of my life; he even babysat my little brothers when my sister Posey and I had hockey tournaments. Our families have always been so close, and I've been infatuated with him forever. I still remember the moment I knew I'd never want anyone else but him.

He came to the house in a badass Willie Nelson tee. I was learning the chords to "Georgia on My Mind," and I wanted to gush to him that I was learning to play Willie Nelson's version, but I was nervous he wouldn't think I was as cool as he was. He was letting his hair grow long, and he had a faint mustache on his lip. He was downright gorgeous—unfairly gorgeous—so much older than me. He never even noticed me. I was just one of those Adler kids. Even when I begged my mom for a Willie tee because I wanted him to see me, to see that I loved Willie too, he didn't.

He never noticed. It was like I was invisible to him.

In his defense, though, he was older and so busy keeping up with his grades and his skills on the ice. He never dated much—yes, that may make me a stalker for knowing that, but his mom always bragged about how he was so driven. He graduated early, went to college, and didn't even finish the year before the NHL wanted him. He is absolutely amazing, and all I want is for him to see me.

To want me.

When I moved to New York, I was convinced our paths would cross. Surely, right? Nope. Never. Even when our moms tried to set us up for a group dinner, we were just too busy. It annoyed me so much because all I wanted was a chance. Once I was eighteen, I knew he couldn't see me as a little girl anymore. But I never got the chance.

Until now.

When the doors open, my heart is in my throat as I take in what's before me. The party is in full swing, but I can't ignore the spectacularness of the penthouse. It's all glass. There are absolutely no walls, just glass looking out over the New York skyline. I wonder if Aiden walks around naked in here? Not that anyone would be able to see him; we're so high up. The black furniture is sleek, modern, and ostentatious art hangs on the walls. A piano sits in the corner, the bench being used right now as a chair for a few girls, and I'm curious if Aiden plays.

"Whoa."

"Yeah, it's pretty awesome," Chris says as we walk farther in. "He's swimming in money."

Of course he is. His entry-level contract was one of the highest salaries ever for a rookie. Reason being, everyone wanted him. And I mean *everyone*. He had his pick of teams, but he chose the Islanders. Mom didn't have the salary cap for him, so the Assassins weren't an option, which, of course, bummed me out. But then I moved to New York, he was traded to the Rangers, and things were supposed to change.

They didn't. Though, maybe now they will.

I look around the party, hoping to spot him. I notice many of the Rangers' players, along with some very gorgeous women. Puck bunnies, of course. I've been around this sport my whole life; I know them when I see them. My dad played in the NHL for close to fifteen years. With my mom being an owner, it's easy to say I live, breathe, and sleep hockey, and if I'm honest, I wouldn't want it any other way. I love the sport.

A massive TV sandwiched between two stunning guitars captures my attention. From where I am standing, I'm pretty sure they're Gibson electrics, and I want so badly to go over and check them out. When Chris's hand grips my wrist, I look over to where he is pointing.

And there he is.

Aiden Brooks.

In all his gorgeous glory.

He stands taller than the group surrounding him. A mixed group of beautiful women, hockey players, and businessmen. He wears a black bomber jacket with a white tee underneath it. Even in his jacket, his shoulders are massive, while his waist is trim. His dress pants are tight on his thighs and low on his waist, but they are loose around his ankles. He's barefoot, looking every bit like a Greek god. His gray eyes are spectacular from where I stand, with his long lashes kissing his cheeks every time he closes his eyes. While his dark brown hair is up in a messy ponytail, wavy pieces fall along his temple from where they've come out of the elastic. His chin is covered in thick, coarse hair, but I can tell his jaw is so chiseled and strong.

When he smiles, the world stops and all the air rushes out of me audibly. His teeth are so white, his face is so bright, and this all seems unreal. I move my hand to my other wrist, pinching myself hard. I can hear Chris laughing, but I don't care.

"He's expecting you."

I shake my head. "No way,"

"Yeah, I told him you were coming."

My stomach swirls. "Really?"

"Yeah," he says with his easy grin. "Are you going to go say hi, then?"

I nod, though I don't move. I hear my cousin Amelia in my head. She always teases me for never having the balls to go up to Aiden. But not today.

I inhale deeply, licking my lips as I watch him walk away from the group he was with. He moves through the crowd with a grin, a cup in his hand. He stops at a group of guys, and they each take a shot before his laughter fills the room. Over the music, over all the conversations, I hear him. He slaps hands with his friends, even nods at a girl who has her eyes on him. I assume he's going to go to her, but he doesn't. He steps to the side and pulls out his phone as he leans into the wall, taking a sip of his drink.

I know this is my chance.

My legs are moving before I even realize it. My heart is so loud, I can't hear anything but it thudding in my chest. The way he's leaning, his shirt has pulled up a bit on his stomach, showing off a naughty sliver of skin that makes my mouth dry. I swallow hard as I weave my way through the crowd, my gaze locked on him, hoping he doesn't move. When he looks up, his eyes land on me, and good Lord, his eyes are hooded. The air is knocked out of me, but a grin moves across my lips.

This is it.

Aiden nips at his bottom lip as he slowly tucks his phone into his pocket. "Hey."

"Hi," I whisper, and his lips curve even more. "How are you?"

"I'm really good now that you're here." He takes a long sip of whatever is in his cup before licking his lips as he lowers the cup to his hip. "You came with Chris?"

I nod, but I can't feel myself doing it. I feel as if I'm on autopilot, I'm so lost in his gray eyes. "I did."

He pushes off the wall and takes a step toward me, towering over me in the sexiest way. Almost like a lion stalking its prey. His lips are so wet as he gazes down at me with those naughty, hooded eyes.

"You're really fucking beautiful."

I think I just died. Aiden Brooks just called me, Shelli Adler, *really fucking beautiful*. And not just beautiful. *Fucking* beautiful.

I mean, he's isn't wrong.

I have my dad's eyes and my mom's beauty. But knowing that about myself doesn't mean my face doesn't flush with color and my lips don't curve into the brightest smile. Because it's him. The guy I've crushed on for most of my life. He thinks I'm beautiful, when I thought he never even saw me. "Thank you."

He looks me up and down, his eyes poring over me like the sweetest syrup. "Usually, Chris's friends aren't this gorgeous."

The way he says friends is weird, but that's neither here nor there. Aiden Brooks is looking at me, and I swear he sees me. He really sees me.

"Thanks...?"

He grins, and Lord, he is so charming. A simple grin has my heart fluttering in my chest. "That's one hell of a compliment. He's brought a lot of girls through here."

"This is my first time." Well, no shit, Sherlock! He knows this. Why the hell did I say that? I'm such an idiot!

He reaches out, taking my hip in his grip. I look down at his hand as my body burns with fire from his touch. I have wanted to feel his hands on me for as long as I can remember. I look up at him, wide-eyed, as his white teeth blind me. "Believe me, it won't be your last."

I blink, and when my eyes open, it's just in time to see his lips coming for mine. His hand moves to the middle of my back, pushing me into him as his lips capture mine. It's like a siren is going off in my head as I fall into the kiss, my hands sliding up and around his neck to hold on for dear life.

Because Aiden Brooks is kissing me.

CHAPTER TWO

SHELLI

I WANT TO SAY MY HEAD IS SPINNING FROM HOW QUICKLY AIDEN gets me into his bedroom, but if I'm honest, it's just him. He smells absolutely phenomenal. His scent is somewhere between that right-off-the-ice smell and woodsy. If an ice rink were in the woods on a cold winter day, that's how I would describe Aiden's smell. I don't know where he got his cologne, but it makes me want to ice-skate right now.

Well, maybe not right now.

Aiden slides his large hands down my back, cupping my ass as he lifts me into his arms with ease. I wrap my legs around his narrow waist as my mouth moves with his. He tastes like tequila and lime. His lips feel so damn good against mine. He rakes his teeth along my bottom lip, biting ever so softly as I gasp into his mouth. He open-mouth kisses me with desperation, leaving me absolutely breathless. Has he wanted me for as long as I've wanted him? What's stopped him? I mean, we could have been doing this for years!

When his tongue duels with mine, I feel like I'm floating. I have been with my fair share of guys and I have no problem admitting that, but none of them have kissed me like Aiden Brooks is kissing me right now. When he falls on top of me on the bed, I squeeze his hips as he cups my jaw, his tongue sliding against mine. I push his jacket down his arms before reaching for his shirt. I pull it up and off him, only parting to get the shirt off. I run my hands down his taut chest, and I want to look at every single part of him, but then his mouth is back on mine. A deep moan rumbles in his chest, and soon I'm dripping with want. I'm sure there are some things to be said, but I've been dreaming of this moment since I was old enough to know what sex was, and there is no way I am ruining it with chitchat.

He wants me. I want him. Let's do this.

When he sits back on his heels, he lifts me so that I'm in his lap, our mouths never stopping. His kisses are demanding, unrestrained, and I almost can't keep up. It's like he's devouring me, and never have I felt so wanted. I feel him through my jeans, and my heart jackhammers in my chest. He's so thick, so long, and Jesus, I want to taste him. I tear my mouth from his, and when he whimpers in the sexiest, most manly way, I swear I almost come.

"Well, that was really hot," I tease. His teeth flash at me as I move out of his lap, my knees landing on the bed on either side of him.

"I have never done that before. You taste really good."

"I could say the same about you," I admit as I reach for the button on his slacks. "But this is what I really wanna taste."

His eyes are hooded, dark, like the sky during a nasty tornado warning in Tennessee, as he watches me unleash his cock. I tear my gaze from his and look down at the swollen girth in my hand. He's enormous, but I didn't expect anything less. With my ass in the air, I take him into my mouth with no hesitation at all. I grip his base as I bring my lips up his velvety smooth skin. He slides his hand down my back, pulling at my shirt as a desperate moan leaves his lips. Holy crap, he makes me hot.

I run my tongue over his head, along the ridge, and down the shaft before dipping my tongue in his hole. He jumps in my mouth, his moans getting louder with each lick I take of him. When he cups my breast, I lean into his hand. His fingers tweak my nipple, and thank God I didn't wear a bra. Damn thing would be in the way. I move my tongue along his shaft, taking him deep into my mouth with gusto.

I feel his fingers at the button of my jeans as I continue my work on his cock. I want him to come. I want to hear my name on his lips. Taste him. I want to watch him as he loses control. Dreams are nothing compared to reality in this case. He must have gotten frustrated with the button on my jeans because he just cups my center, squeezing it as I continue to move up and down his cock with ease. I can feel him pulsating, and soon he is jerking up into my mouth, coming hard.

I open my eyes, needing to see him, and as I thought, the dream is nothing compared to the reality of watching Aiden Brooks come. His eyes fall shut, and his lashes kiss his cheeks sweetly. His face is full of color as he parts his mouth, and a hard moan leaves his swollen lips. His grip on my pussy tightens as I suck him dry. He lets his head fall back, and when he shakes it, my eyes widen.

Was it not good?

"Holy fuck, I like you," he moans as he lifts his head. I rake my teeth along his cock as I sit up, looking over at him.

"Oh yeah?"

"Yeah, I've never met a mouth so damned dangerous."

With that, he captures my mouth, such heat in his kiss, I feel it all over. In my nipples, my pussy, my fingertips, down my back, along my shoulders, my stomach, my toes, everywhere. I feel him everywhere. His fingers tangle in the bottom of my shirt as he pulls away, looking down as he lifts it. He cups my breasts with both of his hands before meeting my gaze once more.

"I swear, I don't usually say this, but man, you're gorgeous."

Heat explodes inside me. "You're pretty gorgeous yourself," I say with a wink, and he grins. I reach up, undoing his hair so that it falls in his gorgeous face. "I've always wanted to do that," I whisper.

"Yeah?"

"Yeah," I confirm as he pushes me back on the bed, and I laugh as he covers my body, kissing me almost immediately. Our limbs tangle, as do our tongues, while I hook my legs over his waist. He tears his mouth from mine and drags it down my jaw, nibbling and licking almost every single inch of me. When he trails his mouth down my neck, I lengthen it for him. My eyes drift shut as he runs his tongue over my collarbone and squeezes my breasts.

I'm drunk with lust as he runs his tongue down the center of my chest and around the curve of both of my breasts. When he captures one of my nipples in his mouth, he takes the other in his fingers as he sucks and tweaks. It's so much at once, and I feel my orgasm building in a way I've never felt it build before. I lift my head, wanting to watch his torturous mouth on me, but then he's there, his eyes burning into mine.

He takes my breath away.

Dark tendrils fall into his face and mine. He moves his lips slowly against mine, not kissing me but slightly touching mine with his. When he rises up on his knees, I watch as he yanks at my jeans, pulling them down my legs and then tossing them over my shoulder. His eyes darken as he yanks down my thong but not all the way. It gets caught on my toe, but I don't think either of us cares or notices.

With such tenderness, he kisses down my belly before running his tongue down into the molten hot crux of my thighs. He pushes my knees apart and into the bed as he laps his tongue against me. It feels totally amazing. He dips the tip of his tongue between my lips, and his name comes out in a harsh moan. His fingers bite into my thighs at the sound, and when he finds my clit, he's ruthless. I almost come off the bed, arching so high as he devours me. His tongue is wild inside me, probing and licking every single part of me. He drops to his elbows, opening me up and then flicking his tongue against my clit until I'm screaming so loud, I'm sure the other partygoers can hear me.

But I don't care.

When I come, I come so hard, I feel like I was knocked into next week. My heart is in my throat, and I'm pretty sure I can't move. My legs are trembling, and my heart is knocking so hard it hurts. Aiden kisses my thighs, my hips, before dipping his tongue into my belly button. I open my eyes and take in his gorgeous body. I couldn't see it well earlier, but now, with the moon shining in on us, he's spectacular. He's rippled with muscle. Such defined shoulders, thick biceps, and a set of abs that could wash nine loads of laundry. He has those crazy dips at his waist that I've read make girls stupid, and I can now confirm that's a fact.

I feel dizzy.

He must have been looking me over also, because when our eyes meet, we both seem pretty damn satisfied. He takes me by the back of my knee and pushes it up against the mattress. He grips his engorged cock, and my eyes widen when I realize what he is doing. I press my hand into his rock-hard stomach, and our eyes meet again.

"Whoa, buddy. Where is the condom?"

He draws his brows in. "I'm clean."

"So? I don't know that, and you also don't know that I'm clean—though I am."

He looks so offended. "Usually, the girls Chris brings don't make me wear one."

Now, *I'm* offended. "Well, I'm not like these other girls you keep bringing up."

He blinks, and I narrow my eyes. "You're sure the hell not."

He bites his lip as one side of his mouth quirks up. It's so charming in a way that hits me right in the gut and makes it easier for me to ignore the fact that he keeps mentioning all these girls Chris brings. I'm gonna have to ask about that. I forget all about that though when Aiden lies across my stomach to rummage in his bedside drawer. I watch as he rips a condom from the pack and then sits back on his haunches. He tears the condom package with his teeth before sheathing himself with the rubber.

When he looks back down at me, heat has crept up his neck into his face. "How do you like it?"

I lick my lips. "How do you mean?"

"Hard, slow. Tell me what you want." He moves his fingers up my leg, wrapping them around my knee.

The side of my mouth lifts as I run my hands down his arms. I've never had someone ask me that. "How do you want it?"

"I just want you," he says roughly, and then he pushes into me in one hard thrust. His appreciative groan is loud, matching my own moan as he falls on top of me. I let my eyes fall shut, digging my head into the bed and making my shoulders lift off the mattress. I press my breasts into his thick, hot chest as he pulls out of me and pushes back in, harder this time, taking my breath away. He grips my hips in his hands, shifting them up, and goes deeper inside me, filling me completely. His knees are under my ass as he starts to pound into me, my lust-filled cries echoing off the walls of the room.

"Hell, I love your ass."

I thought things were too hot for me to laugh, but I find myself giggling. I open my eyes as he licks at my breast. "Want to hit it from behind?"

He lifts his head, his hair falling into his eyes. "Yes. Yes, I would."

"Be my guest."

I don't even get to take in my next breath before he has me on my stomach, lifting my hips so that he can enter me from behind. I didn't think he could go deeper, but he does, his hips slamming into my ass with each thrust. He molds my ass with his hands as he continues to thrust into me, each jerk pushing me forward into the headboard. Since I don't want to hit my head, I hold on to it as he continues his massive pounding.

It's glorious.

When I feel his hands in my hair—or, more accurately, my wig—my hands come up to stop him, but all that does is push me forward into the pillows.

"Oh, it's a wig?"

"For the love of Pete." I reach up, pulling off my wig and the cap and letting my hair out of its low bun. "Yeah, I didn't have time to do my hair."

I hear the fake crown on the wig hit something, and I assume he just threw it on the floor. When I look over my shoulder at him, he's grinning. "I bet you're still hot."

"Can't see me?" The room is dark, but I can still see him in the light of the moon.

He shrugs. "Not really, but it's okay. I know what I've got."

"And that's a good thing, I guess?"

"A real good thing. If I weren't so lazy, I'd go turn the light on."

When he starts to move into me again, I smile. "Well, thanks."

He smacks his hand hard against my ass and I cry out, but I love it.

He continues to slam into me, each thrust harder than the one before, and I can't get enough. I feel my orgasm building, I feel my body getting tight, but before I can come, he slams into me, jerking into me with his release.

"Wow. Couldn't wait for me?"

He trails kisses down my back, squeezing my ass as he chuckles. "No one has ever said that to me."

"Well, you may be some hotshot hockey player, but I like getting mine just as much as you do."

He takes me by the jaw before he smothers my mouth with his. When he pulls away, he's breathless. "Next time. Promise."

I fall into the pillow as he removes himself from me. A smile sits on my lips as I hear him walking, and then the light from the bathroom fills the room. The room is spinning a bit, and I realize I might be a little more drunk than I realized. Or maybe I'm drunk on Aiden.

He is absolutely perfect.

The water starts to run as I rub my nose into the pillow, feeling completely and utterly spent. When the light switches off, I squeeze the pillow in my arms as he falls into the bed. I'm not sure if he wants me to leave, but I'm not ready to go. Pretty sure walking is going to be a challenge.

He reaches for a bottle of water and holds it out to me. "Thirsty?"

I take it from him, taking a long swig. "Thanks."

He nods and takes one too. He lets out a long breath and falls back into the pillows before he pulls the sheets over us. It feels so natural. So perfect. I almost ask why he didn't ask me out earlier. Why he didn't tell me he wanted me. I totally would have been on board. So on board. Think I've been on board since I was eleven.

When he snakes his arms around my waist, our limbs tangle as he lays a soft kiss on my nose. "A nap and then round two."

I grin against his top lip. "What about the party?"

He squeezes me. "The party is right here."

My heart flutters. "It's a pretty banging party."

"It really is." He kisses my nose again and then my temple. "That was incredible."

"It was."

"Don't leave, okay?"

"Okay," I agree, and I feel like I'm about to explode.

"So, sorry for not asking earlier—" I look up at him, the shadows hiding his beautiful eyes. "But what's your name?"

I blink.

A cold feeling fills me as my heart sinks.

He doesn't know who I am?

"I know it's shitty, but Chris didn't tell me your name. He usually tells me the names of the girls he brings for me to hook up with."

"For you to hook up with…" I say slowly.

"Yeah. You knew that, right?"

Now, anger explodes inside me. "Yeah," I lie as I close my eyes. I feel tears gather behind my lids as I ask, "So, you don't know who I am?"

He furrows his brow, perplexed. "Am I supposed to? Like I said, Chris failed me this time." He presses his lips to my top one. "I'm really sorry. It's fucked up, I know. Please tell me your name."

It is fucked up. It's fucked up that my friend made me think Aiden knew who I was. That he wanted me. When, in reality, he had no clue. I was just another girl for him to fuck.

I press my lips together against his as I close my eyes. "It's Grace."

"Grace," he mumbles as he kisses me once more. "What a beautiful name for an angel."

I lean into the kiss, even though I know I shouldn't. I should storm out of here. I should tell him to go fuck himself. Yet, I stay, using my middle name so that I'm not completely lying to him. I don't know why I care, but I do. As pathetic as it sounds, I wanted this. I wanted this moment with him. While I want him to know it's me, there has to be a reason that he doesn't. That reason starts and ends with Chris, and I'll deal with him tomorrow. But tonight, I want this moment. I won't ruin it with the truth.

That he just had sex with me, Shelli Adler.

The girl he has always known…but sees right through.

CHAPTER THREE

AIDEN

MY PHONE IS VIBRATING ON THE BEDSIDE TABLE, BUT THERE IS NO way I'm moving.

Not when I'm snuggled into the most perfect tit I've ever had the pleasure of having in my mouth. My bedmate's legs are tangled with mine as my arm rests lazily against her waist. She is so soft. A bit thicker than I'm used to, but one night with her, and I realize I've been missing out. Hell, Chris has been holding out on me. He should have brought her in at the beginning of our little arrangement. I've never felt this satisfied in my life, and man, I want more.

I can still hear my phone vibrating, but instead of answering it, I move my hand along her skin. I grip her ass as I run my tongue along the curve of her breasts, and a soft moan leaves her sweet lips. Her head is above mine on the pillow, so I can't see her face, and her hair is wild around us. It's so long, so dark with streaks of blond. I don't know where that wig went, but I'm glad it isn't her real hair. I like the brown better. I just wish I had gotten a good look at her face.

We went at it all night in the dark, and I regret that. I wish I had turned on the lights. I want to look at her, admire her. I was pretty far gone last night. With the NHL All-Star break, I'm able to let loose, have some fun. It's the first time I regret not being sober when I had sex. I feel like I didn't give her all that I could, but she seems pretty satisfied.

Fuck, I know I am.

I wonder if I can convince her not to leave. To stay for the day. I don't have anything to do, and I wouldn't mind rounds six and seven with her. Maybe make it to round ten. I owe Chris for this one. He never disappoints. He brings me some really great girls who keep quiet about our time together, but he went above and beyond with her. As much as I hate depending on someone else to get me a girl, I can't trust myself to pick them. Seems every girl I find and fuck tries to screw me over. Wants me to fall in love, take my money, and make me theirs. When I refuse, they come up with some bullshit story and go to the media. I love to fuck, don't get me wrong, but I always make sure to respect the girl. I don't do anything they don't want to do, yet I've been pegged as some kind of womanizer. Hence the reason I have to depend on a friend to bring me someone to fuck. I refuse to allow another woman to make more fucked-up allegations. I refuse to embarrass my mom and dad any more than I already have.

I don't know why I'm thinking of that when I have this spectacular beauty in my arms. I kiss the side of her boob and then her ribs. Just as I'm about to run my tongue across her ribs, I notice her ink. I pull my brows together when I realize it's the Nashville Assassins logo. The Assassin with the skyline of Nashville on his shoulders. It's the old-school logo, the one my dad wore for most of his career. I'm a bit taken aback by it. Usually, the girls I get hooked up with are Rangers fans or don't know a stick from a puck, but she must be an Assassins fan. It's actually kind of cool since Nashville is my hometown and I watched my dad play for them almost my whole life. His jersey hangs in the rafters of the Luther Arena. I have always dreamed of playing there professionally, but it hasn't happened yet.

One day.

I kiss that spot on her body as the sun shines in on us. Just as I'm about to wake her to ask her about it, my phone starts to go off again.

"Is that your phone?"

I kiss the underside of her boob. "Yeah, ignore it."

"What time is it?" she asks, her voice raspy and sexy.

"I don't know. Don't care. Please don't move."

She ignores me, and when she reaches over me, I suck her nipple into my mouth. The breathy giggle that leaves her lips awakens my cock in seconds. "Shit, it's nine. I've got to go. And it's your agent."

She drops my phone on my chest as she untangles herself from me.

"He can wait. Where are you going?"

She moves quickly through the room, picking up her clothes. Her hair is still in her face, and I want to brush it aside so I can see her features. I go to get up, but she holds up her hand. "Don't. If you get up and come anywhere near me, I won't go. And I gotta go."

My mouth goes dry as I watch her dress quickly. Her body is a wonderland, and I am nowhere near done with her. As she pulls her hair up into a big messy bun, I say, "But I don't want you to."

She shakes her head. "I have to." When her eyes meet mine, I cock my head. She blows her hair out of her face and sends me a sweet grin. "I had fun."

I blink a few times because there is something familiar about her. "I did too. Please stay."

"I can't," she says, and she bites her lip. "Have a good life, Aiden."

And then she's out the door.

I hop out of bed and run to the door completely naked. She's fast, and by the time I reach her, the elevator doors are closing. That sweet smile is still sitting on her lips, and fucking hell, she's beautiful.

"Bye."

What the hell just happened? Usually, I have to kick a girl out when we're done, but she basically hightailed it out of here on her own. But that's not the part that is bothering me the most. I think I know her. But from where? I can't place her. Maybe she's one of Chris's actor friends. Maybe I've seen her onstage. Though, that doesn't seem right. Weird.

Either way, I want to see her again.

I head back to my bedroom and reach for my phone in the sheets to see it's ringing once more. Again with my agent. I ignore the call and notice that my mom and dad have called many times too. What the hell is going on? I should call them back. But I go to Chris's text thread instead.

Me: Dude, after making me wait a month, you hit the jackpot with her. Can you send me her info? I NEED to see her again.

He doesn't answer me back. Not even those three dots pop up, but then, it is early. When my phone starts ringing one more time, I hit answer, and the voice of my agent, Joey Brown, carries over the line.

"What the fuck, Aiden? I've been calling you all morning!"

I fall back in my bed, looking up at the ceiling as I cup my balls. "Sorry, man. Busy night and late morning."

"Whatever. Listen, she did it."

"Who?" I ask, bringing in my brows.

"Elli Adler."

The name of the owner of the Assassins makes my heart stop. I have known Elli Adler for as long as I can remember. She has always been a pillar in my life. My family is close with hers, and I grew up babysitting her sons when I wasn't watching my own siblings. She has wanted me on her team since I went into the NHL, and I want to be on her team, too. It's my dad's team, and I want to be just like him.

"What about her?"

"She offered the Rangers the Assassins' next three draft picks and two prospects for you." When he pauses, my heart stops. "The Rangers accepted. You're an Assassin now."

My heart suddenly goes dead in my chest. Surely I'm still drunk. "Seriously?"

"Seriously. She wants you in Nashville by tomorrow. Dude, you've wanted this. Sound excited!"

I am, I really am, but holy shit, I never thought this would happen. I've wanted to play for the Assassins since I started playing. When I was younger and my dad would take me to the rink, I would imagine I was an Assassin in my way-too-big number twenty-two Brooks jersey. I would score the winning goal in game seven for the Stanley Cup. I've dreamed of this my whole life, yet my thoughts are consumed by the girl who just ran out on me.

"Aiden! What the hell? I thought you wanted this?"

I cover my face with my hand. "I do, man. I'm shocked."

"It's a great thing. You're going home."

Home. I'm going home. To play for my dream team.

Don't get me wrong. I've enjoyed New York. I've had the best time here and made some really great friends. Problem is, New York isn't Tennessee. It's insanely busy, things are always moving, and I feel like I never get a chance to breathe. When I go home for holidays or the summer, I feel complete. I feel calm. I've been homesick for a really long time. I miss my mom and dad, my brother and sisters. I wonder if they know I'm coming back.

I've loved playing for the Rangers and, before them, the Islanders. They're great teams, but they're not the Assassins. I didn't grow up pretending to be a Ranger. I was always an Assassin. When I would score in high school or even college, I wouldn't hear the Rangers' goal song; it was always the Assassins'. Everything has always been the Assassins for me. I was bummed when I didn't get drafted by them, but my dad insisted I go where the money was. I was *the* rookie. Everyone wanted me, and when people are flashing boatloads of money at you, it's real easy to put aside that childhood dream. Especially with my dad promising that one day I would play for the Assassins. That day is now.

I've been itching for a new start after everything that's happened, and this is it. This is my new start, and by the grace of God, it's at home. Where my love of hockey began. After having the best sex of my life, I have to say, this morning is probably one of the best. Man, I wonder if I can see her again before I leave.

Grace. I really want to see Grace again.

CHAPTER FOUR

SHELLI

"GRACE. I TOLD HIM MY NAME WAS GRACE."

I'm facedown in the pillow, feeling like the cheapest whore in Bedford Park.

My cousin Amelia tsks at me on the other end of the line. "Wow. You are not living up to my mom's name. She would be very disappointed."

I roll over, covering my face with my hands. My phone is now lying on my chest on speakerphone. "Please. Aunt Grace was no saint."

"True. But still, Shelli. What in the world?"

"I don't know," I groan, running my hands over my nose and mouth. "I got swept up in the whole thing. He was looking at me—like, really looking at me—and I thought he knew who I was. I thought he fucking saw me."

"I told you to let go of that crush a long time ago." I can hear the disdain in her voice. "He wasn't interested in you, never has been. Like you've said many times, it's as if he doesn't even know you're there. Why in the world would you think, after ten years of being ignored, he finally sees you and wants to bang?"

I press my lips together. "Because I was looking mighty hot and my boobs were showing from under your 'Trix aren't just for kids' shirt?"

"I knew you stole my shirt!"

I let out a long breath. Amelia is more my sister than my own sister. We're very close, which is crazy since Amelia's three years older than I am, and my sister, Posey, is only ten months younger. But Posey is just a different kind of girl. She's brilliant and athletic. While I am somewhat athletic, I have more of a creative brain. She has to know all the facts and how to apply them. She makes thought-out decisions. I jumped into bed with a guy I've been infatuated with and who has ignored me for ten years because I thought he knew who I was. I didn't even ask. Posey would have asked, made sure he was with the right person, and questioned his motives.

We're different. Obviously.

But Amelia has always been my better half. We love the same things, we get excited about sparkly stuff, and we love being together. I'm pretty sure I annoy the shit out of Posey, and she sure as hell annoys me with her dry sense of humor. I love her, but she isn't the person I tell everything to.

"I just wanted him so bad."

"And now you're just a little notch on his bedpost."

"Shit, I'm a huge notch. I made him squeal."

"Nice." She sounds impressed, and my lips curve.

"It was," I agree, but then my grin falls. "I just thought it was happening. I thought he saw me in a different light. It was so perfect. He was more than I ever could have imagined. He felt so good, and I felt good. I don't know. It sucks."

"Yeah, it does, because I'm telling you, your imaginary Aiden is nothing like real Aiden. He's actually a real manwhore."

I shake my head. "He isn't. He's a twenty-seven-year-old dude in the NHL. They live for the speed on the ice and the fastness of the girls. He got a bad rap with everything that happened, but I'm telling you, he isn't that guy. He's a good guy."

"Always making excuses for him."

"I'm not. Normal single men in their twenties want sex and only sex. Not everyone is like Prince Chandler."

Amelia laughs, and it fills me with such joy even with how low I feel about myself right now. Her laugh is so happy and carefree. It's refreshing to hear her like this. After a nasty and disastrous first marriage, she found Chandler Moon. Her Prince Charming. Her forever. I can't help but be jealous of how great he is to her and how much they love each other. He wanted her from the moment he met her. He was ready to lay down his life for her and make her his. As much as I hate admitting it since it sounds so childish, I want that. I want that epic love story. The one with the dramatic declaration of love that is the beginning of my forever. Every time my mom and dad get a little drunk on their end-of-the-week wine, their story almost always comes up.

First and foremost, my aunt Victoria is an asshole. She's a money-hungry whorebag who kissed my dad to make my mom break up with him. She did it for my grandma, who didn't want my mom to be with my dad. Don't know why—my dad is basically the best person to ever walk this earth, but my grandma didn't like him, which is probably the reason I've never met any of those people. I have my dad's family, and that's it. My mom always says, "Blood doesn't matter if they hurt you." In her case, it's true. She has more friends she would give her left tit for than anyone in her own family. Can't blame her, given how everything went down.

After my aunt kissed my dad, Mom broke up with him because she thought my dad wanted her sister. Mom had some insecurities going on then, but she's way better about it now. Probably because my dad tells her daily that she is gorgeous.

Swoon. I want that.

Not the point, but after my aunt kissed my dad, my parents broke up for a couple months, and when my dad saw my mom with another guy at his hockey game, he lost his shit. He busted the glass of her box by shooting a puck straight at them. He had the hardest shot in the league for seven years. He's so badass. But he was letting her know he wasn't over her, nor did he want to let her go. She ignored it because she was upset, but when she found out what my aunt did, she went on the ice and sang to my dad after not singing for years. When I get really sad, I find the video on YouTube and cry. Because they're now living happily ever after.

I want that.

Or even a guy who looks at me the way Chandler looks at Amelia. Like she holds the world in the palms of her hands. Instead, I have sex with a guy who doesn't even know who I am—when I've been totally infatuated with him my whole life.

Wow. I'm a winner.

"Speaking of Chandler," Amelia says, pulling my attention away from my thoughts. "Can you swing through here on the way home?"

"I don't know. Dad is coming to help me take everything to be shipped, and then we're supposed to fly home, I don't think Carolina is on the way."

"Can you take a detour?"

"Why?" I ask, sitting up and checking the time. My dad should be here any minute. "I was going to come next month."

"I know, but I need to talk to you."

"Um, Am, we're on the phone, and guess what, our mouths are moving—"

"Oh my God, shut up. I mean in person."

I shake my head. "Again, guess what." I hold up my phone and hit the FaceTime button. When her face appears, a look of pure annoyance on her features, I can't help but smile. I've always thought my cousin was stunning enough to be a model. But instead, she uses that lean, toned body of hers to flip over stuff. She's been a gymnast since she could walk, but now she's a coach, and I can see all over her face how happy that makes her. "Holy crap. We live in a world where we can be face-to-face!"

"I hate you."

"I know," I say with a grin. "What's up?"

She's moving through the house and ends up in the bathroom. How I know is because I just helped her paint that bathroom when she moved in with her boo thang. A little grin sits on her lips as she holds up a stick. I squint at the phone as I try to figure out what she has.

"What the hell is that?"

"A pregnancy test."

My heart stops. "No way."

"Yeah," she says slowly, and unchecked excitement shows on her face. "I know it's crazy and superfast, but we're really thrilled."

"A baby? You're having a baby?"

"I am," she says, and soon tears are running down her face. "A little Amelia or Chandler."

Emotion clogs my throat. "Am, that's absolutely amazing."

"Right? I can't believe it."

"I can't either. I'm so happy for you," I gush. And I am happy, but crap, she's young. They've only been together like six months. But then, who am I to judge? When you know, you know, and Chandler is the one for her. "Was it planned?"

She scoffs but with a dreamy look on her sweet face. "Not at all, and I was scared Chandler would be upset, but he wasn't."

"Because he's perfect."

She gives me a wide grin. "He is." But then her grin falls. "Even though he somehow set the kitchen on fire."

I snort. "No."

"Yes, he was cooking me some eggs, and I don't know how, but the cabinets are all burned."

Most people would be annoyed, but Amelia just looks blissful. Like she thinks it's adorable that her dude just burned up their cabinets. "He's insane. Keep him out of the kitchen. He can't be burning down the house with my—" I pause. "Wait, what is the baby to me? My second cousin? I hate that."

She mirrors my disgusted look. "Me too! No, you're its aunt."

"Yes, aunt," I agree with a grin. "Have you told your mom?"

She shakes her head. "Not yet. We're gonna wait to tell everyone. You're the second to know, after Chandler."

I grin. "I'm special."

"You are," she agrees, and then she sets me with a look. "Which is how you should be treated. Don't be slumming it with assholes who thought you were brought there to be a booty call."

I let my shoulders fall. "I don't make the best decisions."

She grins. "You don't. Has Nico been calling?"

Nico Merryweather, the goalie for the IceCats and one hell of a gorgeous man. We had a little thing going. It was mainly sex, and we had fun. With me living in New York and him in Carolina, I knew it wouldn't work. I didn't want it to work because he wasn't Aiden. I've kept all guys at arm's length because I wanted Aiden. Now that I've had him and know that he has never and will never notice me, I should probably move on. Even so, Nico isn't for me. He's too obsessed with himself to care about anyone else. He just likes having sex with me. He should. I'm good at it.

"We text, but nothing worth talking about."

"He told Chandler he's gonna get you back."

I laugh. "We were never together. Just banging."

She rolls her eyes. "He's a sweet dude."

"He is—for someone else. Not me," I say, but then there is a knock at my door. "Hey, my dad is here. I'll call you later."

"Okay! Love you."

"Love you! And my baby!"

She grins as she waves, and I wave back while I get up off the bed. I hang up as I jog toward the door, excitement rushing through me. Time to ignore what I've done and get the hell out of New York. When I throw the door open, my dad is standing as tall as ever in front of me.

Shea Adler is my hero.

At 6'3", my dad is a brick wall. The years have been good to him, with only a few wrinkles here and there. A nice dusting of gray is in his hair and sprinkled throughout his beard. But his blue eyes are as bright as ever, and his grin takes up his whole face. He reaches for me, and I go to him without any thought. As we hug, tears fill my eyes. I just saw him at Christmas, but I miss him the most. When I'm with him, I feel like I can do anything.

"Hey, baby girl," he says, putting me back on my feet. I'm so excited to see my dad, I don't even notice my brothers standing behind him.

"Oh! Hey!" I exclaim as I hug each of them. My twin brothers, Owen and Evan, are spitting images of my dad. Built big, with dark black hair, bright blue eyes, and ready to smash anyone into the boards. They are identical twins, so sometimes it's hard to tell them apart. But Evan does have a scar beneath his eye from where Owen hit him with the blade of his stick. I've never been so thankful for my brother getting hurt since it makes it easier for me to figure out who's who. They're defensemen for their high school and play on the same line. It's kinda scary to see them on the ice together. I wouldn't want to play them. Quinn, the baby of the family, looks just like my mom. He's small, a little thick, with green eyes and dark hair. He doesn't give two shits about hockey, but he loves soccer. Dad says it's okay as long as he plays something; he has entirely too much energy not to.

"Hey," Quinn says, hugging me tightly. "Ready to go home?"

"I am."

Owen hooks his thumb behind them, where another ginormous guy stands. I've never seen him before. I raise a brow as he says, "This is Maxim. He's our billet boy. He's sleeping in your room."

I look up at my dad, but he holds up his hands. "We'll take care of it at home."

Maxim gives me a shy grin, and I wave. "Hey, I'm Shelli."

"Maxim," he says with a very thick accent. "Nice to meet you."

"You too," I say, even though I forgot he existed. He went home for the holidays, so I didn't meet him, and he plays for the Bellevue Bullies. He will move out of my room once I get there, though.

My dad slaps his hands together. "Ready to blow this shithole?"

I laugh as I tuck my phone into my back pocket. "You love New York."

He shrugs. "It's all right, but I don't want my baby here. I want her home." He gives me a sweet grin as he looks around. "All right, boys. Let's get to work."

At once, they all start to pack everything up. It doesn't take long before I'm standing in a bare studio condo. We're leaving my furniture in case one of us needs to use the place in the future. Dad bought me this place when I got the lead in my first play. Now, I'm leaving. I thought I'd be sadder, but I'm not. I'm ready to go.

"So we'll hit up the shipping spot and then go to lunch to kill time."

I turn back around from grabbing my purse. "Why are we killing time?"

"Your mom is having lunch with the GM of the Rangers."

Just the mention of the New York Rangers puts me on edge. "What for?"

"You didn't hear?" Owen asks, a funny look on his face.

"Mom made a blockbuster trade to get Aiden home," Evan says, giving me the same look. Almost like they're disappointed I didn't know already.

But what they don't know is that the acid from my gut is currently eating away at my heart.

"Aiden who?"

Owen laughs. "Aiden Brooks, dude. Come on. You know who!"

I was worried it was that Aiden.

Shit.

"Yeah, he's actually moving back home today too," Dad says. "I asked if he needed help, but he said he's good."

"I can't wait to see him on the ice!" Evan says, super pumped.

"He's gonna kick ass. It's so awesome," Owen agrees.

Dad nods. "Yeah, he should help bring the Cup home."

Home.

My home.

Aiden is coming home to Tennessee.

Well, isn't that just peachy?

CHAPTER FIVE

AIDEN

"WHAT DO YOU MEAN?"

I'm standing by the gate I just walked out of. I should head to the front of the airport where my family is waiting, but when I turned my phone back on, there was a text from Chris.

About Grace.

"She doesn't want to see you again. She's pretty pissed at me, actually."

"Why?" I ask incredulously. "We had a great night."

"I may not have been up front with her on the conditions."

My blood runs cold. "What the fuck do you mean, Chris?"

"No, dude, I promise. She won't ever say anything. She's solid, but she was pissed that I basically made her a call girl and didn't tell you who she was."

"Oh, well, that was a dick move."

"Probably, but in my defense, it was getting her back for all the times she rejected me."

"And now you're a double dick," I say, and I'm not joking, though Chris laughs. "But nevertheless, she has to want to see me."

"Nope. She said she didn't want anything to do with you. That if I gave you her name and number, she'd file a lawsuit against me. She's kinda crazy, I'm finding out."

"Well, in her defense, you did actually try to turn her into a call girl and deliberately kept her identity from me," I say simply. "I think that's shitty, and she has every right to be upset."

"Well, fuck. I was just doing what you wanted."

"No, I want girls who know the score and want me anyway."

"She wanted you! She's just pissed it didn't play out like her little fantasy."

"Fantasy?" I ask, confused. "Dude, I don't like this. Just give me her info so I can talk to her myself."

"Can't. She kinda scared me and threatened to beat my ass, so I'm washing my hands of this."

"You're kidding me."

"Nope. You've moved, so why does it matter?"

"It matters 'cause I want to talk to her. Get to know her."

"Yeah, I can't help you."

"Can you give me her last name? I'll find her myself."

Chris lets out a long sigh, and I realize I'm getting nowhere. "Sorry, bro. Can't help you."

When the line goes dead, I throw up my hands, a curse falling from my lips. When an older lady side-eyes me, I press my lips together. "Sorry. News I didn't like."

I even shake my phone at her, but she raises her brows. "You're entirely too handsome to be using that language, son."

I nod, a grin covering my face. "Yes, ma'am, you're absolutely right. Can I help you with those bags?"

"Well, my goodness, yes, please. It's a long walk to baggage claim."

"I know, and for some reason, I always come in to the gate that's the farthest."

She grins, her crinkled eyes making my heart swell. "It does always seem that way."

I reach for her suitcase, and she takes my arm. By the time we reach baggage claim, I learn she is here to see her granddaughter be born. She lives in Manhattan with her husband, who is coming in at the end of the week. Their daughter is married to a country singer. Not that she'll brag who he is. I wait for her to get her bags, and then I help her out to the car that is waiting for her.

"If you've got yourself a rich son-in-law, make him hire someone to help you with your stuff," I tease, but she flashes me a big smile.

"But if I did that, I wouldn't get to enjoy having such a handsome man to come to my rescue." When she winks, I feel my face burn with color before she gets in her car. When she waves, I wave back, just as I hear my name being screamed.

"*Aiden!*"

I turn at my sisters' united voices. They run toward me with wide grins on their faces, and my heart about explodes out of my chest. I haven't seen them in months, and I swear they've gotten taller. They both run into me full force, but I catch them in my arms, hugging them tightly. Being the oldest, it was my job to make sure they were always taken care of when my parents were busy. Because of that, I love them way more than a normal brother would. Asher, my nineteen-year-old brother, is completely over them, finds them annoying, but I don't. I think my siblings are amazing. Even his weird self.

Stella Ann is almost eighteen and such a diva, it's scary. She does her makeup like Kylie Jenner, even though my mom loses her freaking mind. Stella thinks she's one of the Kardashians, though. Without the ass, of course. She's built like a string bean, which she says is good since she wants to be a model. Drives my mom crazy. I think it's funny. Stella's already been featured in some local photography—for good reason too. She's absolutely stunning. She looks so much like my mom...if my mom wore a whole palette of makeup and shorts way too short. I can still hear my mom screaming at Stella to change her shorts.

Scary, I tell you.

Emery, my fourteen-year-old sister, well, she's...Emery. There is no other way to describe her. She's absolutely insane. She's quick with her mouth, does what she wants, and if you don't like it, oh well. She's gonna do it anyway. If I thought my mom and Stella fought, it doesn't even come close to Stella and Emery. Emery isn't disrespectful—she's actually very smart and very talented on the lacrosse field—but sarcasm gets her in a lot of shit. Add in the fact that she thinks Stella is an idiot, and it can be very loud in my parents' house.

And somehow, I'm living there until I can find a place I like.

But I don't mind. I've missed them. I kiss them both on the cheek as they cling to me.

"I've missed you so much!" Stella gushes as she holds me.

"Me too. I cleaned your room today. For real, Aiden, I missed practice for you! I even polished all your awards."

I grin as I put Emery to her feet. "You didn't have to do that."

"I wanted to! I'm hoping you'll never leave."

I scoff. "Oh, I'm leaving. I can't handle you two plus Mom and Dad. You four will kill me. Why do you think Asher left so quickly?"

That puts grins on their faces because they know it's true. Asher turned eighteen and hightailed it out of the house as fast as he could. I thought he would stay in town to go to school. Nope, he went to California. He's wicked smart, though, and has a full ride to UCLA. I thought I would be the one the girls would look up to, but Asher's got me beat.

Kind of hate him for it.

"So, how long will you stay with us?" Emery asks, wrapping her arm around mine as Stella does the same to my bicep. They carry my bags, which is totally backward, but I don't mind.

"Just until I find a place. I'm stuck at the moment since Elli wanted me here so quickly and all."

"Yeah, I think we're going by there before we go home."

I make a face. "Why?" Not that I don't want to. I love the Adlers, but I want to go home. I'm tired. Flying sucks.

Stella lets out a long breath before bringing in another. "So, she has chickens."

"Chickens?"

Emery nods. "Nine of them."

"Who?"

"Mom."

"Why?"

"Because she wants to be all healthy and stuff. So she makes us eat the eggs from the chickens, but what she didn't realize would happen was that those things lay enough eggs to feed an army. So now we are distributing them to Elli because Mom has her on this healthy eating craze too."

"Healthy eating craze?"

"No processed foods or carbs."

I make a face. "Holy crap. I'm not gonna make it without Pop-Tarts."

Emery scoffs. "If I can, you can."

"I'm not as strong as you," I complain, and she beams up at me.

"Oh, hush. You'll be fine."

At the sound of my mom's voice, I look up and am immediately in awe of her. I'm pretty sure she hasn't aged at all. She's as stunning as always, in a power suit and ass-kicking heels. I let go of my sisters to wrap my mom up in a hug. It's been way too long since I've seen all of them.

She kisses my cheek hard, hugging me tightly. "Oh, my baby."

I squeeze my eyes shut as I hold her. She always calls me her baby, and even at twenty-seven, I'm okay with it. My mom was all I had for the first part of my life. It wasn't by my dad's choice or anything. Mom thought she was doing what was best for me. My dad wasn't all that great when she left him, and I get it now. I understand why. I'm pretty sure all that is why I don't rush into relationships. My mom always knew that my dad was it for her. If she didn't have him, she wouldn't waste her time with anyone else. I think I've applied that to my life. The most important thing is hockey—and hockey only. If I need someone to keep me warm, I find someone for the night. I'm good with that.

A hand grips my bicep, and I open my eyes to see my dad pulling me to him. Like my mom, he hasn't aged either, in my eyes. They both look how they did when I was younger, just a little bit grayer and with deeper laugh lines. My dad holds me tightly in a backslapping hug.

"It's good to have you home."

"I'm excited to be home," I say as I pull back, looking at the family I haven't been able to spend much time with in the last ten years.

Hockey has stolen me from them, but they all understand. It was my dream, a dream they all supported.

"Was it a good flight?"

I nod as I take a step back. "Yeah, a little long, but I watched movies."

"Is everything packed?"

"I paid someone to pack all my stuff. It should be here Friday."

Mom nods. "We'll store it in the garage until you get a place."

I shake my head. "No, it's too much. I paid for a storage unit. Hopefully I can find something before long."

Dad nods. "We will. I've got a real estate agent on it. We've all used her."

When Dad says "We've," he means the whole Assassins team. If one Assassin does something, the rest always follow. It's such a family mentality. I love that about my team. "Great. I hadn't had time to look for one."

"I got ya," Dad says, smacking my back before picking up my bags and throwing them into the back of his Lexus. "Like my new wheels?"

"Fancy," I tease as I open the doors for my sisters and my mom.

"Such a sweetheart," Mom says before climbing in. "But hurry up. We gotta get to Elli's, and then we have plans for lunch."

"My favorite restaurant?" I ask, hoping to God it's Hattie B's, and she nods.

"Yes, even though it's full of the gluten and so many carbs."

"Thank God," my dad, Stella, and Emery all say under their breaths.

I chuckle. "Mom, what are you doing to my family here?"

"Trying to save their asses from cancer and death. The food is trying to kill us!"

Everyone is rolling their eyes and shaking their heads. "Dad, didn't I tell you to keep her away from those Netflix documentaries?"

Dad scoffs. "I try, but she watches them at work."

I grin as I lean back, my sisters cuddling into me. I feel so complete, I almost forget the fact that Grace has blown me off. *Almost.* I really don't get it. We had a really good time. When we weren't having sex, we talked hockey. There aren't many girls who can spit out stats like they're reading from a book. She knew the game, she loved it, and she enjoyed talking to me about it. So quick with her mouth too. If she didn't like something, she let me know. I don't know... It was fun. I wouldn't mind exploring her a lot more than I was able to.

I'm lost in my thoughts, though Stella and Emery haven't stopped talking since we left the airport. Even so, I can almost taste Grace on my lips. Totally inappropriate while I'm sitting with my sisters, but I can't help but think of her. I'm craving her. I want to see her again. I need to call Chris again. A little pressure and he'll crumble like a fortune cookie.

When we arrive at the Adlers' house, I'm surprised by how excited I am. This is my new GM's house. The woman who brought me home. Also, it holds one of the greatest hockey players of his time—well, besides my dad. Shea Adler is a beast. Even now, the dude is amazing. We talk weekly, and I look forward to our discussions. Usually, they're about hockey, but then sometimes we talk about life. He's just a good guy.

Once I'm out of the car, my mom hands me two dozen eggs from her chickens, and I roll my eyes. "Why am I carrying these?"

"I don't trust the girls, and we have some already."

I make a face. "How many chickens do you have?"

"Nineteen."

I look back at Emery disbelievingly. "What? I thought it was nine."

She shrugs.

"Jesus," I say under my breath as we head up the driveway of the massive house the Adlers own. With how many kids they have, they need this big ol' house. I've grown up with this family, and it's weird being back. Not that I haven't been by in the last ten years, but it's mind-blowing that I can come over whenever I want and it will be totally normal.

Because I'm home.

Man, what a feeling.

After knocking on the door, my dad pushes it open. "Be decent! The Brooks family is here."

Shea's booming voice answers back. "I'm completely naked in the kitchen."

My dad squeals as he runs through the living room like a kid. I enter after the girls to find the house is quiet, which is totally not how the Adler house runs. Usually, it's loud as fuck, but then I notice the boys are outside playing hockey. "Ooh, Mom—"

She cuts me a look like I'm ten. "Come say hi first before you go outside."

"I was going to," I protest as I follow behind them. I notice the girls go outside, and I'm totally jealous. I want to play hockey too.

"Where did the girls go?" Elli asks as I enter.

"You know they went out there to see Evan and Owen. Oh, and *Maxim*," Mom says, drawing out his name. "Stella is convinced she is going to get him to go to the dance with her, and Emery just wants to beat up Owen."

A grin pulls at my lips. My sisters are insane.

"Oh, Shelli! It's so wonderful to see you!" my mom gushes.

I come around the corner just as Elli's gaze falls on me, and her face lights up. "There is my center."

"Hey, Elli. Shea."

"Hey, bud," Shea says, and then my mom turns to me, her arm around...

I swear, it's like being hit by a Zamboni.

No. No. No.

It's her.

Mom and Elli are grinning, as if the girl who is standing between them isn't the one I just fucked not even forty-eight hours ago!

"Aiden, you remember Shelli, don't you?"

Shelli *Grace* Adler. How do I know this? Because when Elli is mad, she uses her kids' whole names. Oh my God. Shelli's in a cute little shirt and a pair of jeans, and her hair is up in the same messy bun she left my penthouse in. Her eyes are as bright as I remember them. I mean, it wasn't even that long ago that I was staring into them and watching her come all over my cock. She may appear confident and sexy as fuck, but I can see the worry in her eyes. How did I not put two and two together?

Alcohol. Lots of alcohol.

But then it dawns on me.

I had sex with my new boss's daughter.

Shea Adler's daughter.

Oh, fuckety fuck, he's gonna kill me.

And then, the next thing I know, I drop the eggs.

CHAPTER SIX

AIDEN

"Aiden!"

I can't even care that there is egg all over my overpriced shoes. Or that my mom is yelling at me and everyone is staring at me like I killed the chickens instead of just dropped some damn eggs. My heart is in my throat, and I feel like I'm about to have a panic attack. What the hell did I do? And why do I still find her utterly irresistible? I don't know how she can make a pair of jeans look naughty, but she does. Those lips are still dangerous as fuck, but she looks like a damn angel. But for the love of God, she's like, ten? Wait, she's legal, right? Oh fuck, I'm going to die and go to jail all at once.

Whelp, there goes my career.

"What the hell is wrong with you?" Mom complains as she moves to clean up, Elli right there with her, but I'm staring at Shelli, and she's staring at me. Her eyes are wide, full of worry and anxiety but also a bit of rebelliousness. A slow grin pulls at her lips and—wait, did she do this on purpose?

Is she out to ruin my life?

And not in the good way like she did in my bed.

I tear my gaze from hers, my heart pounding as I drop down to help clean up the mess. "Sorry. My hands slipped."

"Hope you don't do that on the ice. Shit, babe, maybe you made a bad trade," Shea jokes and Shelli laughs. Everyone does.

But I'm still processing what I did.

Fantastic sex. With my boss's daughter. Who I think is still a minor.

Crap.

"Sorry, Elli," I mutter, and she grins as she pats my bicep.

"No biggie. I know she's gorgeous," she says with a wink before standing. "She has that effect on me all the time," she teases as she throws the eggs into the sink.

"Yeah," I mutter as I glance over at Shelli, who is watching me. "I didn't think you were old enough to have a...?"

Elli waves me off. "I know. I can't believe my baby is twenty-one either. Mind-blowing, right?"

I almost drop to my knees and cry. Shelli, though, she just grins. "Crazy, huh, Aiden?"

I narrow my eyes. "Yeah. Wow, you've grown up."

"Yup. It's good to see you."

"Yeah, you too." I'm glad I'm only going to die when Shea finds out. I don't think I'm made for jail; they don't have an ice rink.

"It's so wonderful to have both our firstborns home! I think this calls for a party to celebrate the both of them!" Elli gushes as she wraps an arm around Shelli's waist.

But Shelli rolls her eyes. "Mom, that's silly."

"No, it's not," she argues. "I love parties. You hush."

"I doubt Aiden would want a party. He'd hardly recognize anyone."

Oh, she's got jokes.

"Oh, he'll fit right in. He'll love it!" Mom says, and I want to die.

I don't want to be anywhere near Shelli.

But then I also want to smash my mouth to hers and smother her in my arms. Feel her hot body against mine and breathe in her breath. I feel like I'm holding my own breath as I keep stealing glances at her. She is fucking stunning, but this can't happen. It's bad enough I slept with her once; I can't do it again. Our families are so intertwined, I'm going to see her more than I should, and that can't be good. Shit. I need to make sure she doesn't tell anyone.

Fuck me.

"Great. I'll plan something for the end of the week!" Elli smiles broadly.

Shea and my dad roll their eyes, but Mom and Elli look excited. Shelli, well, she's staring at me as I stare at her. I always observed her from afar when she was growing up. She was so much younger. I guess I didn't notice that we only have seven years between us, but still, that's a lot of years. I do remember the first time I noticed her, though.

She was sixteen and wore a little bikini one hot summer day. We were celebrating something, and her ass was hanging out of her bottoms in the sexiest way. Since I knew she was younger, I looked the other way. I knew I had to. But don't get me wrong... I've always thought she was beautiful.

Shelli takes after her mom in all the right ways and has her dad's blazing blue eyes. Her face is that of an angel, with a Cupid bow's mouth and a dainty little nose. Her eyes are naturally narrowed in such a sultry fashion. Her hair is long, and it used to be super dark until she put those highlights in. She's thick in all the right places, and my mouth is dry as I stare at her...remembering what we did in my bedroom. Shit, I want to do it again, but I know I can't. I need her to keep her mouth shut, and I need to stay away from her. Things are changing for me, and I can't have anything else get in the way of furthering my career.

"So can you run home and get me more eggs? Do you have time before your lunch?"

I look over to my mom as she nods. "Yeah, I'll run home real fast, leave everyone here."

Elli nods. "Great! I wanted to talk to Aiden."

Mom looks at me and grins. "Ha. You're in trouble, and you haven't even hit the ice yet," she teases, but of course, I'm in full panic mode.

Did Shelli tell her mom that I smashed her from behind and pushed my cock down her throat?

Oh God.

"No! Don't look worried, Aiden. I just want to chitchat."

I don't believe her. "Ha. Yeah, I know," I choke out.

My mom laughs before kissing my cheek. "I'll be back. Lucas, are you staying?"

"Yeah, I'm gonna go play with the kids and Shea."

She rolls her eyes. "Bunch of children."

"They are," Elli agrees before looping an arm through mine. "Shall we?"

"Sure," I squeak, and for the love of God, I haven't squeaked since I was in high school. Elli just laughs, and I don't miss the sneaky little grin on Shelli's face.

She's out to kill me!

As we head out of the kitchen, I feel my body shaking with nerves. Elli is animated, talking about how excited she is to have me on the team, but I'm looking around the house, taking in all the photos of her family.

Of Shelli.

How in the world didn't I know who she was? I have seen her face for years—I know her. Yeah, I haven't seen her in a couple years, but it's Shelli Adler! I know her. She was just all over the NHL Network and Twitter for decking some dude in the face. She had her own hashtag! #SlapshotShelli is what they were calling her. I thought it was hilarious, yet I didn't put two and two together when she was in my arms. Under me. When I was in her... Oh, fuck me.

I'm never sleeping with anyone else unless I see their ID.

We enter Elli's office, where there is a pristine black desk, teal walls, and black accents. The walls are covered with photos of the teams that have played since she took over. Her chair is a wingback covered in teal velvet, and when she sits in it, she looks regal as hell. She's wearing sweats, and I'm scared shitless of her.

"So, are you excited?"

I nod as I lean back in one of her black guest chairs. "Yeah, I am." *Though, at the moment, I'm freaking out.*

"I am too. I feel good about this trade. I feel damn good about you. We haven't had the Cup in Nashville in a long time. I'm ready to bring it home."

"Me too."

"Which is why I brought you here. I believe in you."

"Thank you. That means a lot to me, Elli. Honest."

She smiles a sweet smile that almost makes me feel better, but then I feel the *but* coming on. "With that being said..." she starts, and I brace myself. "We do need to discuss something."

"Okay?" Here it comes. I feel it. I'm dead.

She leans on her hands, her eyes like green lasers burning into mine. "Do you know I've been trying to get you on my team for almost five years now?"

My lips curve at the side. "No, ma'am. I didn't know that."

"I have. I've wanted to bring you home for a very long time."

"I'm honored, Elli, really. That means a lot to me."

"I know you're one badass player. You're an amazing center, your passing is beyond compare, and your shot is a gift from the hockey gods."

"Thank you," I say, feeling pretty damn good about myself.

"You remind me so much of your father. He was a gritty player and fast. You mirror his game, and we need that on our team." I smile, and before I can say anything, her smile falls. She speaks again. "Do you know why I was able to acquire you the way I did? If the Rangers had been smart, they wouldn't have let you go. You aren't even in your prime yet."

I press my lips together and look down, a disappointing feeling taking over. It's the one I get when I know someone is going to bring up the past. "Unfortunately, I think I do know why."

She nods slowly. "The incident from ten months ago is still heavy on the GM's mind—"

"I know," I say, holding up my hands. "But the allegations were thrown out, and I had the chance to sue her, but I chose to close the book on the situation altogether."

"They were thrown out because you had a wonderful lawyer."

"Yes, but they weren't true," I stress, my eyes pleading with her. "I would never do that to a woman. She was stalking me and trying to extort money from me."

She looks down at her desk as she holds her palms up at me. "I believe you, which is why I put you on my team." When she looks back up at me, I swallow hard. She does believe me, I see it in her eyes, but I know that the Rangers weren't too happy with me. Even though I hadn't done what that girl said. "Either way, their loss is my gain. But I do have some restrictions."

Oh, this is gonna be great.

"You will keep your nose clean. You will not tarnish my team's name. I am not naïve... I know what it's like for you guys. Girls throwing themselves at you and living life in the fast lane. Shea did it—hell, your dad did it. But now, it's time to slow down. Settle down, if I can be so bold. You're almost thirty."

I make a face that causes her to laugh. "I'm only twenty-seven."

"Almost thirty." I don't agree, but she goes on, "If the lady you want to hook up with is crazy, get rid of her. Be selective. Know what you are doing and with whom. Do not get involved with someone who can ruin your career. Do you understand me? You will not only disappoint your parents again, but me, and I don't do well with that. You were raised right. You know how to act. You are too damn talented to be fucking up off-ice. Do you understand me?"

I nod slowly, though I don't hesitate to agree. "Yes, ma'am."

"Good. We are so glad to have you home, and I'm so thankful and excited to see you play for my team. But please hold my words in that thick skull of yours."

I swallow hard as I look down at the floor, inhaling deeply.

Do not get involved with someone who can ruin your career.

She doesn't know about Shelli. Okay. Good. Because that girl could ruin my career. As much as I want to trust that Elli does believe me and knows I wouldn't ever be guilty of the allegations that were made against me, I also know she wouldn't want someone accused of that to be with her daughter. Especially with how special Shelli is. I just gotta make sure no one finds out. I gotta make sure Shelli keeps her mouth shut. For both our sakes.

And I gotta resist her.

For my sake.

CHAPTER SEVEN

SHELLI

"What are you doing?"

I throw my sister a dirty look and hold my finger to my lips. "Shh."

She rolls her eyes as she leans on the other side of the door that leads to our mom's office. She has her resting bitch face on lock, while her unruly, curly auburn hair falls down her shoulders. Her eyes are wide and round like my dad's, but they're a gorgeous light hazel color that I swear only she can pull off. They're so pretty. She has super thick shoulders and thighs, while her waist is very trim. I've always been thicker than her because I like candy, but my sister is thick because she hits the gym hard. She's a beast.

"You know you can't hear anything, right?"

"Well, not when you're talking!" I whisper back at her.

"They can't hear us either."

"I am going to kill you," I warn, and she scoffs.

"I wish you would try," she snaps at me, rolling her eyes. "What are you even doing? Who's in there?" She presses her ear to the door and then gives me a dry look. "Oh, come on. Really?"

"What?" I ask innocently.

"Still into Aiden? That's pathetic."

"You're pathetic," I throw back at her as I walk past her. "Still living at home when you have every opportunity to move out."

"Um, Shelli," she says, and I look over my shoulder. "You're living at home now too, after making buttloads of money on Broadway, and still obsessed with a dude who will never want anything to do with you. So, really, who's pathetic?"

I glare. I want so badly to throw in her face that Aiden did want me—and had me—but that isn't a good idea. I don't want anyone knowing. My actions toe the line of whorebagish... Okay, they don't really toe, but I'm not ready to accept the reality of my actions. So instead, I do what any mature adult would do when her sister pisses her off.

I flip her the bird and try to kick her.

She smacks my leg away as I stick out my tongue and head down the hall to my room. I don't realize she is on my tail until I go to shut the door and she stops me. "But for real, why don't you get a place?"

I shrug as I turn, shooting her a look. "Why does it matter?"

"You made Mom and Dad move Maxim. That's unfair. He was comfortable here."

I fall back onto my bed. My room hasn't changed at all. It's still all pink and full of lace. My bed has a canopy of lace, while my walls are full of Broadway posters. I hold up my hands. "I think he may have been relieved to leave my Pepto-Bismol hell."

She growls. Like actually growls. "No, he likes the view of the lake."

"He has that upstairs in the bonus room."

"Yes, but that eliminated the space for the boys' games."

I roll my eyes. "Oh my God, the boys have to play games in their rooms. I bet they're suffering so much."

She glares. "I'm just saying, you're selfish. You don't need to live at home."

"Nor do you. You can live in the dorms."

"I don't want to."

"Well, I don't want to either! Jeez, what is your issue—" I pause, and then I laugh. "You have a thing for Maxim, and with me taking my room back, you don't share a bathroom with him. Do you peek in when he is showering, you stalker you?"

Her face turns bright red. "Shut up."

"Does he brush his teeth with just a towel on?"

"For real, Shelli—"

"Aww, Posey and Maxim sitting in a tree—"

"Shut up. I don't like him."

"Yes, you do! Hmm, he is hot, and that accent..."

"Shut it, Shelli."

"You know Stella has a thing for him."

Her brows furrow as her lips press together, pure annoyance on her face. "So? I don't care."

"I beg to differ," I sing. "Does he know you like him? Wait, where are you going? Don't leave! We can have girl talk!"

But she's gone, hightailing it out of my room.

Mission accomplished.

She's so dramatic.

I shouldn't tease her, though. She hasn't ever openly liked a guy before. Probably because I'm an asshole and tease her for it. But she's so cute when she wants to kill me. Man, I wonder what my mom is talking to Aiden about? She has no clue about us. No one does, minus Amelia. She'd never tell since I hold all her secrets too. Man, he looks so hot. I didn't realize how hot a guy in a suit could make me until Aiden Brooks walked in with his arms full of eggs.

Mmm...

I fall back on my bed just as my mom yells my name. I cover my face as I holler back, but when she doesn't answer, I know she wants me to come there. I get up and head down the hall. While the house is quiet, it's a madhouse outside. My brothers are so damn loud. I'm almost into the living room when a hand comes around my bicep and pulls me into the bathroom. Next thing I know, I'm looking up into one hell of a gorgeous face.

"We need to talk," Aiden demands. "Like A-S-A-P."

"Who actually says 'A-S-A-P'? No one. That's weird. Just say 'asap.' It rolls right off the tongue."

"I'm not joking."

"Fine. What's wrong?" I ask. I try to back up, but the half bath is just that, half the size, and Aiden is huge. He takes up most of the room, and I didn't realize how big he was when I was on top of him. He's wearing a button-up that is straining at his shoulders. The shirt is tucked into his dress pants in a sophisticated way, and even though he smells like eggs, he's still hot as fuck. His long hair is wavy along his shoulders, and I want so bad to run my fingers through it. I didn't do that when we were together. I was too busy trying to devour him.

"You know about what."

"Sorry, I don't."

"You're going to make me say it."

"Sure," I say simply. "You're the one who has the issue."

"You lied to me," he says, holding his finger up at me.

I push it away as I pull in my brows. "I didn't."

"You said your name was Grace."

"It is."

"It's your fucking middle name."

"Still my name."

"You knew hooking up wouldn't be a good idea."

"I didn't know any such thing. You're the one who jumped me like a cat in heat."

His face fills with horror as he holds up his hands. "Because I thought you were there for sex!"

I shrug just as my name is called once more. "Maybe I wasn't, but it doesn't mean I didn't want it."

I pull the door open, but he slams it shut with his hand, glaring down at me. "You can't tell anyone."

I shrug. "Already have."

He widens his eyes. "Why? Who? Do your parents know?"

"Are you okay? You look stressed."

"Shelli, stop playing around. This is serious."

"It's nothing. We fucked, and that's that. It's over. Relax." I pull at the door, but he shuts it once more.

"We need to talk this out. We need to make sure we have our bases covered."

"Lord, was that your first time? Excuse me, my mom is calling me."

I yank the door open, and this time, he lets me go. My heart is in my throat, and I can't believe I just spoke to him like that. I was so aloof. Not the least bit affected by him.

I think I might pass out.

Before doing so, though, I find my mom and Fallon waiting for me in the living room when I enter. "Hey, sorry, I was in my room on the phone," I lie, but Fallon waves me off.

"I have an offer for you."

"I love offers," I say with a grin, and behind me, I feel Aiden coming into the room. Fallon's face lights up at the sight of her pride and joy, while my mom looks hesitant. I don't know what her meeting was about, but I don't think it went well. "What's up?"

"Well, your mom says you need a job."

I scrunch up my face as I look back at my mom. "I do?"

"You know the rules. You go to school or work when you're under my roof."

Stupid rules. I don't have to work. I'm good. "I couldn't sign up for school. I waited too long."

"Exactly, so I guess you'd better get a job."

"Wow. Maybe I should move out like Posey said."

Mom gives me a dry look as Fallon laughs.

"But maybe I should know the job first."

Fallon grins. "I think you'll love it. We need a pianist for our bar. I figured since you're home, a fantastic singer and piano player, it would be great for you."

It would. It would be fun too. I love playing, and I heard that Fallon's new wine bar is pretty amazing. She sold her space in the arena to branch out, and she's doing great with it while running her winery too. She's a busy lady. "Yeah, I would love that, actually."

"Great. Can you start tomorrow?"

"Yeah... Wow, thanks."

"Of course. Come in at five so we can discuss everything."

"Sounds good," I say, and then I hug her tightly. "Thank you."

"Anytime."

Mom gives me a look. "Not moving out, then?"

"Not at the moment," I say as she wraps her arm around my neck. I hug her tightly, just as Fallon does the same to Aiden. The only difference is Aiden swallows his mom in his arms, while my mom and I are basically the same height.

Maybe I am pathetic, because I am super jealous of Fallon being held by Aiden.

"Isn't it wonderful having them home?"

"So wonderful," Fallon agrees. "Even though I think he's gonna find a place and move out as soon as possible. The girls scare him."

Aiden tries to smile, but he looks stricken. "They're fine, but I'd like my own place."

So his call girls can come over. I roll my eyes, and he narrows his at me.

"I hear you. I thought she'd want her own place, but she misses us," Mom says, kissing my cheek.

"I've been gone for, like, ever. I want to be home."

Mom beams. "She's a saint. My sweet girl."

I don't miss the way Aiden scoffs a bit as he stares at me. Fire flares inside me. He knows how un-saint-like I can be, and his eyes are full of irritation and anger. I know he wants to speak to me, but I have nothing to say. He didn't know who I was. And while I knew exactly who he was, I don't have anything to say to him at this point. He didn't want *me*; I was just there, and that's fine. I know he is stressing and probably scared shitless I'll tell my parents. But the thing is, I'm an adult. I sleep with who I want, and I don't feel even the least bit sorry for his anxiety. Maybe next time, he'll find out who he is sleeping with first.

Maybe I hope it will be me again...but maybe I don't.

One thing is for sure. Aiden Brooks is nothing to me.

Another thing that is for sure... That is a total fucking lie.

CHAPTER EIGHT

AIDEN

I KNOW LUTHER ARENA LIKE THE BACK OF MY HAND.

I have been roaming these halls and hiding in lockers since I was six. It was awesome. I broke my fifth bone here after falling off the Zamboni. I broke my first stick and I think also a skate blade. I can't remember, but I love this place. It was honestly a second home for me. Man, if it isn't great to be back. I thought when Elli demanded I come home so quickly, I would be joining practice. But unfortunately, everyone has been on break until today. She brought me in to meet with her, the coaching staff, and then the personal trainers. While it wasn't really what I wanted, it's been a great couple days.

When I'm not home with my family.

My sisters are on a whole other level. I now truly understand what Asher meant when he said he had to get out of there. Those two girls fight like cats and dogs and are ruthless. Emery set fire to Stella's newest makeup palette because Stella ate the last bowl of Emery's favorite cereal. I wish I were lying, but I'm not. Nope, I watched my youngest sister take my other sister's makeup, put it on the grill, squirt it with lighter fluid, and set fire to it.

I'm gonna start to pray for the dude who decides Emery is the one he wants to be with, because she's gonna kill that guy if he does her wrong.

Emery is crazy, while Stella is just loud. She isn't violent like Emery, but she cries about everything. My mom isn't fair, my dad doesn't listen to her, Emery is trying to kill her, and apparently my presence there is no longer adorable. She hates me too. Hormones, man, they're a bitch in my house.

Then my parents are on my last nerve too. They've insisted on going condo shopping with me, but they hate everything I look at because it's not close to them. That's the point. I want to visit, but I don't want to be close enough that it's a daily thing. I love my mom, but if she bitches one more time about how I eat, I might scream. My dad is so engrossed in his audiobooks, he doesn't even hear the madness.

He may be a genius.

Because of all that, I am more than ready to go to practice. I'm actually excited to meet my team and get started. It's a great group already, and I hope I fit in just right. I want to add to the team. I want to make Elli proud. My family. I want to be proud of myself. I haven't felt like that in a while.

As I stand in front of my new locker with my name on it, I smile while I dress. The greats have all been in this room. My dad, Shea Adler, Karson King, Jordie Thomas, Phillip Anderson, and Tate Odder, to name a few. Tate, who is also my uncle, is the goalie coach here. Usually, the guys who retire from the team find their way back into the organization. It really is one big old family.

Across from me is my captain, Jayden Sinclair. He went to my alma mater, as did all his brothers. The Sinclair brothers are household names in the NHL. There are three of them, and they were all drafted one right after the other. Jayden is a hell of a player, strong, and smart. I'm excited to play *with* him rather than *against* him.

Beside him is Markus Reeves, one of the grittiest players I've ever met. He knocked me on my ass last year, and I swear I still have a bruise. The most badass goalie in the league, Jensen Monroe, dresses four spots down from me. He was actually the first to greet me, along with Vaughn Johansson. Man, I hope I get to play on his line. He has one sick-ass shot. The resident older guy, Benji Paxton, sits beside me, and he's been real nice.

"You need anything, bud?"

I shake my head. "No, thanks."

"I played with your dad. It's kind of surreal to play with you too."

I laugh. "Yeah, talk about trippy."

His laughter is refreshing. He's the oldest guy on the ice, but the dude is a beast. Says it's the way he eats that keeps him playing. He probably eats that no-carb shit my mom is trying to preach. As I look around the room, there are a lot of faces I've played against, and it's weird to be on their side now. I didn't realize I was nervous until I started to dress. What if these guys think I'm a dick? I'm actually a delight, I feel. Well, unless you ask Shelli Adler.

I'm pretty sure she thinks I'm an absolute twatwaffle. Damn it, I am so pissed at her. She acted all blasé with me in the bathroom. She didn't even seem at all interested in me or even affected by me like I was her. It was taking everything in me not to capture that rebellious tip of her chin and kiss the shit out of her. I don't know what the hell her deal is, but I need to know she isn't going to tell anyone. And also, I want to know what the hell changed from that night to now. I know I was good, and she was good, so why wouldn't she want me now? Not that I *want* her to want me, but it would be nice to know she's craving me like I am her.

I need help.

People start to file out as I tape up my socks. The guy beside me, Wesley McMillan, taps my skate with his stick. "Nice to have ya, Brooks."

His voice is thick with an accent I don't recognize, but I send him a grin nonetheless. "Thanks, bro."

He heads out, and once I am done, I rush out so I'm not the last. That would be weird. Once I hit the ice, though, I'm not ready for the emotion that comes over me. I have watched games in this arena my whole life. I have sat in our box and watched my dad raise the Cup above his head three times, the last time being his last game. I swallow hard, the lump in my throat a little overwhelming as I look up to see the number twenty-two jersey hanging in the rafters. I've been number twenty-two my whole life, just like my dad, but since his number has been retired with the Assassins, I went with twenty-three. A new number for a new start.

For my start.

As a Nashville Assassin.

Wow. What a feeling.

I take a deep breath as I start around the rink, warming up with the rest of the guys. Once everyone has hit the ice, we take a knee as Coach Townes blows his whistle. He's the fourth coach of the Assassins franchise. Elli pulled him up from our AHL team, and so far, things are going pretty damn good. He's young and he's smart. He wants to make things happen, and I've admired his game from afar. Now I get to play with him.

"Welcome back, boys," he says in his deep tenor. "First off, I want to welcome our newest center, Aiden Brooks, to the team."

I hold up my hand in an awkward, dorky wave and say, "Thanks. Excited to be here."

"Us too," he says with a nod. "Do you have a nickname you go by?"

Before I can even speak, Tate decides this is the perfect time to open his mouth. "Boogie Butt. His aunt has been calling him that since he was a baby."

Kill me now.

The guys all chuckle as I silently die inside. "Thanks, Tate."

Tate laughs, and Coach nods. "All right, well, I'm a thirty-one-year-old man, and I will not be calling you that."

"I appreciate that."

"So to celebrate Boogie Butt's return," he says, pausing for the laughter. And I can't help it, I chuckle along. "Let's do some drills. BB, we're gonna try you out with McMillan and Johansson. Let's go."

BB. Boogie Butt. Fan-fucking-tastic.

Once Coach blows the whistle, everyone is up and getting into position. I skate to my line and watch as the center before me gets the puck and passes it to his right before the right winger sends it to the left wing for the shot if he has the opening. Once it's our turn, I start off passing it to my left since I'm left-handed. Johansson passes it across the ice to McMillan, who acts as if he is going to take the shot but instead sends it back to me for a beaut of a goal. A simple tap in that is pure perfection.

In this moment, I know for a fact, I'm home.

"I LIVE OFF MUSIC ROW."

"Really? Where?" I ask as I wash my balls.

Wes is in the shower next to mine as he says, "It's closer to the Gulch. Broadstone?"

"I haven't looked that way. My mom is trying to keep me close to her."

He laughs. He's a shorter dude, but he packs a punch. He ran into me playfully when I scored, and he knocked me over. Like, clear on my ass. He reminds me of one of those *GQ* models with the perfect hair, even after wearing a damn helmet. "My mom did the same, but then I got traded and made her stay back in Montreal."

"Nice," I say. Though, I'd never ask my mom to stay back. I just wish she'd give me a bit of space...and carbs. I need some bread, damn it. "Can I come check out your place?"

"Yeah, I think there is a space above me, like directly above me, that is coming up for sale in a week or two."

"Really?" I ask, but then that means that I have to be a part of the Stella and Emery madhouse for a bit longer. Plus, I'll need to get a fridge for my room for beer and ice cream. I can hang if I get the fridge.

"Yeah, Willy's girl is moving in with him, and she lives there," he says, pointing to one of our forwards, William Bacioretty.

Willy turns, looking over his shoulder as he washes his pits. "Yeah, she'll be out tomorrow, I think. You can come check it out for sure. I didn't know you were looking for a place, or I'd have offered. My girl is nervous about selling."

"For sure, dude. If I can come check it out today, that would be awesome."

"Yeah, I'll call Caitlin after I get out."

"Appreciate it."

Wes nods. "Hey, come by my place afterward. We'll have a beer."

"I'd appreciate that," I say as I shut off the shower. I head out to get dressed just as Wes and Willy do. We trade numbers once we're dressed, and I'm pretty happy when I have an appointment to do a walk-through with Caitlin and Willy later that afternoon. All goes well, and I could be out of the no-carb zoo, also known as the Brooks household, in no time.

I pull out my phone to text my mom when Wes says, "You dating anyone?"

I shake my head as my mom asks what time she needs to be there. "Nope. Got a lead for me?"

He smiles. "The pickings are great here. Lots of honey-sweet females."

"Just what I want—" Before I can even finish, Wes pulls me to the side with more force than I expected. I glance up to see what the hell is going on, and I find myself looking down into a familiar pair of sparkling blue eyes that have been haunting me for the last four days. Her hair is in a high ponytail, and by God, she's only wearing a black sports bra and the tightest yoga pants I have ever seen in my life. Not much of her stomach shows, just enough to remind me that my tongue has been in her belly button. I suspect she just got done working out, because her face is blotchy with red spots.

She looks fucking delicious.

"Sorry about that, Shelli," Wes says with a grin. "He's new."

"No problem," she says as she goes to walk around me, but I step in her way.

"I need to speak to you."

Wes's brows pull in, and I point my finger to him. "I'll call you."

"See ya."

But Shelli is walking past me. "Don't have anything to say."

I step in front of her once more. "No, seriously, we need to speak."

She looks me up and down, and she seems bored. "If I let you speak, will you leave me be?"

I should very much leave her be, and I will—once we talk. "Yes."

"Great," she says, and then she opens a door to her left. When the door shuts behind her, I realize it was the door to the hallway that leads to the ice. I forgot how all the rooms lead to one another. She leans on the wall, pulling her leg up under her as she crosses her arms, making her breasts even plumper than before. I don't get why she is acting as if she doesn't have time to talk to me. I've known this girl her whole life, and she's always been pleasant. Where is all this hostility coming from? We had a damn good time.

With her lips pursed, she demands, "Talk."

I swallow hard, my mouth going dry. *Focus, Brooks.* "Listen, what we did can't ever happen again."

She shrugs and laughs softly. "Okay?"

"I'm just making sure you know this."

She glares. "Oh please, don't you worry. I'm not asking for it."

I narrow my eyes. "Well, you weren't saying that last week."

"Because I was lied to. I was told that you were expecting me, that you wanted me, and that I was in for the night of my life. All of that was false," she snaps, her eyes a little crazy as she looks up at me.

I blink. "We had a great night."

"Great is a stretch. Maybe okay. But sure as hell not the night of my life. The night of my life would include the guy knowing who he's fucking."

I really hate how offended I am. Why am I so pissed? Good. She didn't like it, so she won't want me again. This should be a good thing. My hands slam into my hips as my voice rises. "That's not my fault. As soon as you realized I didn't know you, you should have stopped everything."

She lowers her brows, her eyes narrowing to slits. "I didn't even get two words out before you had your tongue down my throat."

I hold out my hands as I gawk at her. "Because I thought you were sent for sex."

With a disbelieving look, she yells, "Maybe next time ask, dumbass!"

"Whoa!"

"Whoa what? You used me."

"Um, I didn't force you into anything. If I remember correctly, you were basically humping me."

"So, because I like sex, it's okay not to make sure you're with the right person? Yeah, you didn't force me into anything, not that I'd ever accuse you of that, but you sure didn't slow down enough to find out who I was. Or, hell, to make sure I came at all."

I glare. "You came plenty of times. And you knew who I was the whole time, so what was your end game? Trying to get knocked up by me? Trap me?"

Her laughter fills the room. "I'm barely twenty-one years old. I'm not trying to get pregnant. Remember I'm the one who demanded the condom? Also, why would I need to trap you? Maybe you've heard of my family? In case you've missed the memo, I'm not hurting for money, buddy. I'm not like those whores you're used to. Maybe you should learn about the girls you go to bed with. Ha! Wait, who am I kidding? You don't even take the time to learn their names."

She makes me stabby. "You knew who I was. When you found out I didn't know, you should have told me, but you said nothing. Why not? You had every chance! You trying to ruin me?"

Something flashes in her eyes, yet she laughs, and it absolutely sets me on fire. "No, Aiden. I am not. I wanted to sleep with you, and that was it. But a bit of advice..." She leans in, and I hold my breath. "Next time you decide to fuck some girl who walks up to you, ask for her name and maybe volunteer to wear a condom."

"Hey, don't blame me for liking it without a condom. It's a different sensation, and I get off faster."

"Faster?" she asks incredulously. "You get off faster than that? Thank God I made you wear one."

My jaw actually drops. "Whoa. That's bullshit. You were satisfied."

"Hardly." She pushes off the wall. "But that's neither here nor there. We did it, it's done, move on."

"I am ready to move on."

"Really? Seems to me you're trying to blame someone else for your bad decisions. If anyone is trying to ruin anyone, it's you. You're sabotaging yourself."

"I am not."

"Dude, there were red flags left and right about that night. You are so self-absorbed, you didn't even realize you were fucking the girl you used to babysit. Maybe you need to reevaluate your life and stop obsessing over what we did."

Who the hell does she think she is? "You were wearing a wig!"

"A wig doesn't change my face."

"I was drunk!" I yell back, and then I point at her. "And if there were red flags, why was my cock in your mouth, then? You weren't pushing me away. Better yet, you were pulling me in. You sure as hell didn't leave afterward. You stayed and fucked me all night. You wanted me. Don't deny it."

"I wanted to fuck, and you were there."

"You could have fucked anyone, and you chose me."

She shrugs so nonchalantly. "I mean, you ain't ugly."

Do not be turned on by that country charm. Too late. Unable to come up with anything else, I yell, "You're lying!"

She presses her lips together, her sparkling blue eyes burning into mine. The hall seems smaller than it is. I don't know what it is, but I feel like she is taking up all the space in the room, all the air. She's maybe five-five; she's little yet a huge presence at the same time. She holds her hands out. "What do you want? Want me to promise not to tell my mommy and daddy? Don't know if you know this, but I'm an adult. I fuck who I want, and I do it without telling my parents."

She gives me a tight little condescending grin, and I glare down at her. "Good to know."

"Sure is. Maybe try it," she tosses at me as she pushes off the wall.

"Don't worry about me," I sneer, glaring at her.

"Never do." And somehow, she's right there.

"Fine," I throw at her sharply.

"Fine," she throws back with just as much sass.

But neither of us moves. My eyes are held hostage by hers as we both breathe in and out hard and fast. She's so freaking pretty, it's annoying. I want to yell at her for being so defiant, but then I want to kiss the hell out of her too. Her lips part and, of course, take my attention. When she licks them, I go hard—everywhere. I am burning all over with anger, and I'm unsure if it's really my anger or my need for her. I have never been accused of not satisfying my partner in bed, and it drives me crazy that she is claiming I didn't. I made her come so many times, I can't even count.

"You loved it with me."

She snorts. "You're delusional. But don't worry, Aiden, I won't tell anyone. I'm just as embarrassed I slept with you as you are about sleeping with me. So, have a good life."

I can't admit to her that I'm not embarrassed at all, and I shouldn't be as upset as I am that she's embarrassed to have slept with me. I'm a fucking great lay. So I go on the defensive. "Oh, I plan on it."

"Good for you," she says offhandedly. "Maybe you should plan to ID your next fuck too? Do you need rubbers? I can send some over."

I swear the space between us is on fire. For such a little thing, she is setting me aflame. "You're pretty obsessed with my sex life. Want a repeat?"

"Repeat that disappointment?" She smirks. "Please. I'm good."

"You're so full of it. You were screaming my name."

"Well, since it was the only name that was known at the time, I figured, what choice did I have? Didn't want you to forget it too."

"Wow, you got a smart fucking mouth." A beautiful, sexy, smart mouth, but no need to tell her that.

The most cunning grin spreads across her pouty lips before she shrugs and says ever so calmly, "Yeah, well, you're a jackass. So, go fuck yourself very much."

She then flips me off with both hands before kicking the door open and heading through it.

"Real fucking ladylike. Your mom would be so proud!" I yell as the door shuts with a thud. I cover my face with my hands and shout out in annoyance, "Damn it!"

One thing I can't deny is that she frustrates the ever-living fuck out of me. She may also turn me on beyond belief. I'm so hard, I can't even see straight. Yeah, I must stay away from her. But hell if I don't want to prove her completely wrong and make her scream my name. Then I'll scream her name, over and over again. Jesus, this has the potential to get complicated. Thankfully, I am a grown man who can control himself just fine around infuriating, sexy, gorgeous, sassy-mouthed little minxes like Shelli Adler.

Damn it, I may be in a smidge of trouble.

CHAPTER NINE

SHELLI

"WHO DIED?"

Amelia's question should make me laugh, but it doesn't. I wipe my face free of the stupid tears that fall as I shiver. I try to put my arms in my jacket as Amelia watches me on FaceTime, but I'm shaking so badly with anger and cold that I'm struggling. Only I would run outside in only a bra in the middle of the fucking polar vortex! God, I'm so stupid.

"No one," I snap as I finally get my jacket on and zipped. "I'm just pissed."

"At me?"

"No," I grumble as I turn the heat on blast in my mom's Ford F-150. Some would say my mom has small-girl syndrome with how big this truck is. But then, the big metal beast does make me feel unstoppable. Well, that is, when I don't think of Aiden's dumb face.

"Posey?"

I roll my eyes as I cuddle deep into my coat, covering my face and feeling pretty pathetic. "No."

"Okay, you gotta give me more. I can't just stare at you and keep guessing. You're gonna get pissed and yell at me."

She knows me so well. I don't even want to admit what is wrong with me. I feel so pathetic, so sad. I am Shelli Fucking Adler. I have been the lead in six Broadway productions since I was sixteen. I am smart, I am hilarious, and damn it, I am beautiful. How dare some *boy* make me feel less? "Stupid Aiden Brooks."

I peek out of my coat to see her eyes widen. "Oh. Oh shit."

"Yeah, oh shit is right!" I yell, slamming my arms down on the seat as I let my head fall back. "He's such a prick!"

"I mean, I don't think too highly of him right now. He's made you cry. You never cry."

My lips tremble as I wipe away another tear. I think the last time I truly cried was when my uncle died of cancer. Just thinking of that day makes the tears roll faster. I miss him. He was like a second dad to me. Real situations make me cry. The occasional movie gets me, but I *do not* cry over guys or frustrating circumstances. Amelia does, but she's more emotional than I am. I was always told, "You don't cry. You rub ice in your wound and keep moving on." Thinking about those words now, they make absolutely no sense. Ice would hurt the wound more. My dad is insane—how am I just realizing this? Ugh. It's like a pinball game in my head, a million thoughts a minute. But none of that matters; Aiden made me feel literally worthless.

"I'm so mad. I want to kick him. Straight in the balls."

Amelia flinches. "I would highly oppose that. You've already been to jail once for assault."

I roll my eyes. "I didn't even hit him that hard."

"You broke his nose."

"He deserved it," I grumble as I sit back, shaking my head. I want to say I learned from punching Amelia's ex-husband in the nose and then kicking him square in the boys, but I didn't. I'd do it all over again if I had the chance. After all the emotional and physical abuse he put her through, someone needed to put him in his place.

Chicago had it right. He totally had it comin'!

It all seems like eons ago. Amelia is happy, and I know that douchecanoe isn't ruining her vibe anymore. Not when she has Chandler. Not when she's pregnant. Not when she feels totally and utterly complete. I'm not jealous of her. I'm so unbelievably happy for her, but I am a bit salty. I want to be complete. I want to feel good. I want to feel like I am doing something right.

"I just don't get it. Everything was so perfect when he kissed me. Even when I knew he didn't know who he was with, I was good. I lived out one hell of a fantasy, and it was great. But then he goes and ruins it all. He's obviously so embarrassed by the fact that he slept with me. He doesn't give two shits about my feelings. He's so worried about his pride and my mom finding out, he doesn't care that he is putting me down or making me feel like I was just another fuck."

Amelia's eyes widen, and I see tears forming. "Shelli, I love you. You know that, right?"

I nod slowly. "Yeah. Why are you crying?"

She wipes her cheek. "'Cause I'm pregnant and emotional. You're hurting, so I'm hurting."

My bottom lip puckers out. "I love you too."

"But, honestly, Shelli. You *were* just another fuck. You gotta remember that."

My lip puckers out more. "But I wanted to be more." A sob rips through me. "See, this is why I should have stopped myself from going there. This is why I've never gotten the balls to talk to him before. I care more for him than just a fuck. I always have. Everyone else, we bang, I move on. But Aiden is different. He's always been different. Only now, he's just another asshole."

"I'm pretty sure I told you that," Amelia reminds me, but I shake my head. "He isn't boyfriend material."

"But that's the thing, I wasn't out to make him my boyfriend. I just wanted him to enjoy me, respect me—"

"Wait... That fucker didn't respect you?"

I roll my eyes. "Whoa, momma bear, yes, he was very kind. I mean now. He's being a dick because he's scared. Because he knows all I have to do is tell my mom and I'll ruin him. I thought he knew me... And I think that's what hurts too. I've always been nothing to him. It stinks. I'm a really awesome person."

"You are," she stresses. "Way better than that dude."

"See, and that's where I struggle. My crush of over a decade just blew up in my face. He should have just stayed a crush."

"That would have been for the best, I think."

I close my eyes as my tears leak out. "I feel so stupid."

"Don't."

"Why do I still want him?"

I open my eyes to Amelia shaking her head. "Because I think it's gonna take more than a week to get over a ten-year crush, Shell."

I swallow past the lump in my throat as I wipe my face. "I really thought something was going to happen. I thought I would rock his world, and he'd want me. Why doesn't he want me, Am?"

Tears are falling down her face as she gazes back at me. "Because he doesn't see what an amazing—"

"He's never seen me. It's like he's fucking blind."

"Well, how can he see you with all that hair in his eyes?"

I pout. "I can't laugh right now."

"Fine. He's a dumb boy."

"He is," I insist as I shake my head. "But he's actually brilliant."

She rolls her eyes. "He can be book-smart but dumb in common sense."

I shrug as I sniff. "Yeah. I just wish that I didn't care. That he meant nothing to me, the way I mean nothing to him."

"It's gonna take time."

"I guess," I say, blowing my nose and clearing my throat. "I don't have a plan either."

"A plan?"

"Yeah," I say, rubbing my eyes. "Like, you're a hotshot gym coach, and you're pregnant, getting ready to marry the love of your life, and I'm nothing."

"Wow, okay, changing gears," she says, nodding. "For one, shut up. You are more than nothing, and you know it. And two, I want to rip Aiden's face off for making you feel like this!"

"No, it's not him," I protest, shaking my head. "I've been feeling like this since I decided to leave New York."

"I thought you wanted to go to school?"

"I do, but for what?"

She shrugs. "Music?"

"See, you don't know, and I sure as shit don't know. So, what am I doing? I'm singing in a bar because my mom won't let me sit on my ass and spend the money I already made."

She snorts. "Aunt Elli was always so weird about that. My mom didn't care."

"Or she didn't want to raise selfish, entitled, little assholes. Though, the boys are skating that line."

She laughs. "You know you're okay, right? It's only been a week."

"A week longer than I planned to not have a plan. Posey would have already had a plan."

"Posey's already planned out her life," Amelia adds, and I nod. "It's okay. You'll figure it out."

I just don't feel that way, though. I feel lost.

When I look up, I see my mom.

With Aiden.

She walks with him, laughing as he talks with his hands, looking so damn excited. It was his first day. I'm sure he is thrilled. He looked great out there, like one of the guys, when I peeked out before starting my workout. But that's him; he belongs on the ice. They could throw him on any team, and he'd adjust. He's one hell of a player.

My mom sees me, and she tilts her head to the side. "Mom is coming, and I'm about to get the third degree 'cause my face is beet-red and tear-streaked."

"May the force be with you."

"Thanks."

"But really, Shelli, you're okay. Don't let that dumbass get in your head."

I nod before blowing her a kiss. I hang up as my mom starts for me. Aiden stands there watching, a stricken look covering his handsome face. Damn it. I didn't want him to see me like this. I wipe my face as I watch my mom get into the truck. Her brows are raised and almost in her hairline. Her auburn hair is up in a high and tight bun, while her makeup is flawless. She's wearing a pantsuit with heels that are so high, I don't understand how she walks in them.

But that's my mom—a masterpiece.

"Shelli baby, what's wrong? Why are you crying?" she asks as she wipes my face with the back of her hand.

I move away from her hand, taking a shuddery breath. I tell my mom a lot of stuff most daughters wouldn't. She knew when I had my first kiss and when I lost my virginity. I used to tell her all the time how in love with Aiden Brooks I was, and she would just laugh, thinking I was so adorable. I never told her about the drug use in New York, but she knew I drank. Even before it was legal for me. She knew about the men I'd slept with, she even knew about Nico, but there is no way in hell I can tell her about Aiden.

As much as I would like to wear his penis as a necklace right now, I don't want to ruin his career.

I wipe my face free of tears as I shake my head. "I'm just feeling a little lost."

When I look at her, she is eyeing me. While it's not the whole truth, it is part of the emotional breakdown I am having. "How so?"

"I don't know. I thought coming home was the answer, but I'm worried that it wasn't."

She nods, her emerald eyes searching mine. "Do you regret leaving the show?"

I shake my head. "Not at all. I wanted that. I *needed* that. But now that I'm home, what am I doing? I can't go to school yet, and when I do, what am I going for? I just feel lost, unsure, and I hate that feeling."

I don't know how my mom does it, but she gathers me up and brings me into her lap. The steering wheel is making for a tight fit, but I don't think either of us cares. She kisses my temple, and I smile as she taps my hands. "You can do whatever the hell you want to do. Do you want to study music?"

I shrug. "I don't know. I thought I did, but what am I going to do? I did the performing thing. I don't want to do it again."

"Okay... Would you like to write? Teach?"

"I don't know."

"Honey, what do you want?"

"Mom, I'm literally telling you I have no idea," I deadpan, and she laughs before kissing me again.

She moves the baby hairs out of my eyes before taking my chin in her hand. "You know what I always thought you'd do?"

"Stay on Broadway?"

She shakes her head. "I knew you'd get sick of it and come home. You love Nashville."

"I do."

She gives me a small smile as she wraps her arm around my shoulders. "I always thought you'd take over from me."

I bring my brows in. "Huh?"

"As the GM for the Assassins."

I blink. "Seriously?"

"Absolutely. There is no one else I can even think of to take my place."

I hold up my hand, counting off my siblings. "Posey, Owen, Evan, Quinn? Especially the boys."

"Why? 'Cause they're boys? My uncle had the choice of boys over me, and he chose me."

I don't think my heart is beating. "Are you serious?"

"Yes. Shelli, what team leads the league with goals per game?"

"IceCats."

"Who's the leading scorer in the league?"

"Jude Sinclair, but Jace Sinclair is right there coming up behind him."

Her eyes are bright as she asks, "And who has the most wins as a goalie?"

"Nico Merryweather."

"Who is the newest rookie they think will draft first right now, just by his numbers?"

"Mikel Ladervont."

Her eyes shine with pride. "I don't know anyone else who can answer as quickly as you do. We can talk hockey for hours, honey. The sport is your jam."

"It is."

"So can you see why I feel you'd take my place perfectly?"

I look down at where she's holding my hands. "I mean, yeah. But I never thought you'd give it to me."

"Well, you thought wrong."

It all is overwhelming. "But you're not giving it to me now, are you?"

"Not at all. I want you to live a bit. Have some fun," she says. "I know you took the job with Fallon, but I was really hoping to get you on board with the organization. You'd start out at the bottom as an intern. Work your way up."

"Really?"

"Yes, if you want it."

I think that over. This would be a dream job for me. To be like my mom? To run the Assassins one day? To make bold moves and win Cups? When I was growing up, I would follow my mom around the arena and act just like her. I mirrored my dad on the ice, but I wanted to be powerful like my mom. I wanted to walk into a room and have everyone look at me with respect. I know I'd be starting from the bottom, and that could be tough but, in the end, rewarding. Do I really want it?

"Hell yeah, I do."

She winks at me before kissing my temple. "That's my girl. And that's your plan. Now you feed it, and you work toward it. You'll get there just like you got the lead in your first show."

I grin widely as I wrap my arms around her, hugging her tightly. It all seems so unreal but also so perfect. It's exactly what I want, exactly who I want to be.

I have my plan. Now I just have to get over Aiden.

CHAPTER TEN

AIDEN

"I LIKE IT."

I grin over at my dad as we head back to the house. We just finished touring Caitlin's place, and I put in an offer on it. She said she's gonna accept it, so looks like I'm gonna have a place sooner rather than later. "I loved it. It's not as great as my New York pad—"

"Or as expensive."

I chuckle as I nod. "Yeah, but that place was sick."

"And expensive."

We share a laugh before he directs his attention back to the road. The plan is to drop him off and then head to get Stella from work. I need to buy a car. I just haven't gotten around to it. Dad hardly uses his truck, so I've been driving it. I definitely didn't need one in New York. "What are your plans tomorrow?"

"Nothing with a side of nothing. Oh, wait. Emery has lacrosse at four."

"Nice. Can you go car shopping with me?"

He flashes me a grin. "Don't want to go with your mom?"

I groan. Loudly. I love my mom. Like to the moon and back. She is the best woman I know, but I thought I was going to kill her today. Or hell, this whole week. Every place we look at, she finds something wrong with. Or what she thinks is wrong, when really, I don't give two shits if my door is adjacent to a stairwell. I don't care. I just want a place. Living on my own for so long has spoiled me. It's quiet, and I don't have to worry about being a witness to murder.

As we walked through Caitlin's place, Mom was in a mood. Everything was bad.

"Well, honey, you obviously wouldn't be able to walk naked through here. Everyone would see."

"Aiden, baby, this is way too expensive."

"It's too far from the house."

"The bedroom is bigger than the living room."

I happen to disagree. I like my bedroom big. That's where the magic happens.

"She was insane."

"Well, in her defense, she could have gone without the 'magic happens' comment from you." I snort as he shakes his head. "In her head, you don't have sex."

I don't know what to say to that, so I just change the subject. "I love the place."

"It's nice. She'll come around. She just doesn't want you to leave. But we understand. Stella and Emery are hard to live with."

"They're not that bad," I say, but even I cringe. "They're loud, *so loud*, for being so small."

He laughs. "Our house has always been loud. It's our normal."

I smile, remembering my childhood. I was almost eight when Asher came along. I was so excited to have a brother, but what I got was a genius who didn't have time for me and my hockey. He's brilliant and way smarter than I am. The girls arrived, and I thought to myself, heck yeah, I get to be that protective older brother. For Stella, for sure, I was. But Emery... Sometimes I think she could protect me.

Not that I would need it—well, maybe if Shelli Adler ever came after me.

I don't know why, but seeing her in the truck, crying, did something to me. I got this pain in the pit of my stomach, and I still haven't been able to shake it. I don't know what was wrong, or even why I cared, but I sure didn't like seeing those tears falling down her cheeks. A part of me feels like maybe I put them there, and I *really* don't like that. Though, I doubt I did. She obviously has no time for me and doesn't even care in the slightest. She made that very clear. But what bothered me was when she said I was embarrassed by what we did. That isn't the case at all. I enjoyed her, immensely, and still would love another round. But it can't happen. I'm just now clearing my name, starting a new chapter. And pissing off Elli Adler isn't on the agenda.

I still can't stop thinking of Shelli, though.

When the truck stops, I look up to see we're in the driveway of our house. Shit, I must have spaced out. I unbuckle my seat belt, ready to scoot over to drive, but my dad hasn't moved. He glances over at me, lets out a sigh, and then looks out the window at our home. My dad bought this place before he even knew about me or had run into my mom again. He bought it because he wanted a big house for a big family. Over the years, he's had renovations done, but it's our home.

His dream.

When he clears his throat, I pull my brows together. "You okay, Dad?"

"I need to talk to you."

Well, fuck me. This doesn't sound good. "Okay?"

"You're not seeing anyone right now, are you?"

I lick my lips as I look away. "I mean, since I've been home, no, I haven't seen anyone."

His jaw clenches, but he doesn't look at me. "I heard you earlier. At the rink."

My whole body goes cold. "Heard me?"

"With who I am pretty sure was Shelli Adler, but I can't and won't let you confirm or deny that."

"Oh fuck," I mutter under my breath as I cover my face. "Dad—"

"No," he demands, and when he looks at me, breathing isn't an option. I'm knocked back about twenty years to when I decided to steal a candy bar from the gas station. Dad told me I couldn't have it. I wanted it, so I took it. Not only did I get my ass handed to me, but I also had to apologize to the gas clerk. Dad even made me go clean for the guy for a month. I have never felt so small since, until now. "I did not raise you to talk to women like that. To belittle them, to not take ownership of your actions, or to disrespect them."

I press my lips together, a little taken aback by his accusations. "I didn't realize—"

"You did," he insists, his eyes dark and angry. "I would never talk to your mother like that. We get into some heated fights and she can be in the wrong, but I never would have made her feel like she was nothing but a fuck when we were dating."

I didn't do that... Did I? "But I'm not dating her."

"Exactly, which makes your actions ten times worse," he snaps, and I feel like he's two seconds from taking off his belt and beating me with it. "You didn't know who was around, and you were yelling about what you two did, and that's wrong. You treat her with respect."

"You heard her, right? She wasn't very nice to me."

"Because you were a jackass from the rip, Aiden. She had to jump on the defensive and hold on to her pride since you were trying to drag it through the fucking mud."

I look away, biting the inside of my cheek. "It's all just a unique situation. She lied to me—"

"Or you were too drunk to know what was going on. I don't know what the fuck is going on with you. But, boy, I suggest you get it together. The drinking and the girls, son... You need to pump the brakes."

I shake my head. "Dad, it's the life—"

"I don't give a shit. I get it. Fast and hard, that's how we do things. But there comes a time when it gets old, and you need to realize your actions can ruin you. Not the girl. *You*."

I look back at him as his eyes burn into mine. "I know for a fact that everything that woman last year claimed about you was an utter lie. I know you wouldn't do those things to anyone. You have two young sisters I know you wouldn't want that to happen to, but listening to you talk to that girl today in the hallway, it made me think maybe I was wrong. Maybe you don't have any respect for women—"

"That's untrue, so fucking untrue. I respect women—I was raised by you."

"But I wasn't there, and all you knew was your dad wasn't there for your mom. So all I can think is this is my fault."

I throw my hands up. "Damn it, Dad, no. It's nothing like that. I truly respect women, I am kind, and we have a good time. The problem is, I don't know those other girls or want to know them. The thing with Shelli—"

"For the love of God, do not use her name. I will not be involved in this. Because when Shea Adler and her twin meathead brothers come to kill you, I want to be as surprised as everyone else. You are so damn lucky I was the one to hear all that go down and not him, Elli Adler, or, hell, your mom."

I press my lips together as my heart sinks. "I know. I wish you hadn't heard it either."

"Shit. Me too," he sighs. "Not the light I wanted to see my son in."

Guilt rakes over me. "It's different with her because I know her. I've known her my whole life, and I thought she was trying to get one over on me or something. I don't know. It's not like I won't ever see her again. She's everywhere! Her mom is my boss, Dad. Things got heated, and yeah, I took a shot at her pride. But hell, she demolished mine. We had a damn good time, and she kept taking low blows at me—"

"I don't give a fuck if that girl kicked you in the dick and called you a pussy. You don't make women feel small. There are enough jackasses in this world who do that. Society does it. Everyone is always out to hurt women, and fucking hell, you will not be one of them," he insists, and I've never seen such heat in his eyes. "If you overheard someone speaking to Stella like that—because let's be honest, if that happened to Emery, she'd just kill them—how would that make you feel?"

I bite my top lip between my teeth as the rage rattles my body. "I'd want to rip him limb from limb."

"I would too," he says simply. "Is that how you'd want your sisters treated?"

"No, but I also hope my sisters wouldn't be dumb enough to wear a wig and not tell the dude they're hooking up with who they are."

"Well, I'd hope your sisters wouldn't be involved in an escort service either."

"Dad, you make it seem so bad. I was protecting myself," I stress. "I had a friend who would bring girls in who wouldn't say anything, and we'd have fun. It's not that big of a deal."

"It's pathetic and sad. I never had to have—"

"Because no one was trying to get a fucking payout then, Dad," I yell, at my wits' end. "I was burned bad. All I'm trying to do is play hockey and bang when I want."

"Have you thought about doing it the old-fashioned way and finding someone you trust to be with?"

I let my head fall back. "Dad, I don't want to *be* with anyone."

"And why not?"

"Because I'm good by myself. I don't have to worry about anything but hockey. I don't have to feel anything. I can just fuck and move on."

"Isn't that lonely?"

"No, 'cause no one out there is worth my time," I say, and I don't know why emotions have to be involved. "I don't ever want to feel what Mom felt when she didn't have you."

He narrows his eyes as he holds my gaze. "But what about how she felt after we found each other? How she feels now? How I feel? There is more to life than fucking and hockey."

I shake my head, completely done with this conversation. "Listen, I'm sorry. I will never speak to a woman like that again. I don't want this to be something that comes between us. So before something is said that will hurt the other, let's let it go."

He doesn't want to be done. Pretty sure my dad could go another round or two with me. "I'm sorry, Aiden. I am. I still hold guilt from that time without y'all. But I thought after the years you've watched me love your mom and keep her on the throne she deserves to be on, it would erase what I did. What she did. She didn't have to keep you from me, but I'd fucked up enough to make her do so. So, I get it. I do. And I don't blame anyone but myself, but I don't like the way my boy is acting right now."

When I see the tears flooding his eyes, I have to look away.

"If it's my fault, I'm sorry. Truly, I am. But if this is you being a pigheaded little fuck because it's easy, get it together."

"Dad, I love you, and I don't blame you or even hold resentment for you," I say to him, and I don't. My mom did what she did, and my dad had issues all those years ago. It all worked out in the end, but I'm still cautious. "I just don't want to hurt like she did. Nothing is worth that."

He throws his hands toward our home. "Yeah, it can suck. It can hurt, and it can knock you on your ass. But when it's right, when it's true, you get all that. A partner, someone who loves you even when you feel worthless. Kids who idolize you, and a pretty fucking great life."

Once more, I have to look away to keep my own emotions in check.

"You are the best thing that ever happened to me, Aiden James. Hands down, the best thing. I will never love anyone the way I love you, but you need to grow the fuck up."

He gets out of the car, and I heave a big sigh. "I love you, Dad. I do. I don't blame you for what happened."

He shakes his head. "Show me that with your actions. Do better."

I swallow hard.

"And while I'm at it, don't be a dumbass. Wear a fucking condom."

"Kill me now," I mutter, but apparently my overbearing father is not done.

"Also, apologize to her."

"Who? She who must not be named?" I ask incredulously. "She wasn't very nice to me either, and I don't hear her apologizing."

"Yes, be a man and apologize for how you spoke to her." Just as he goes to close the car door, he shoots me a dark look. "And don't use cute little Harry Potter terms to try to ease my anger. I'm pissed at you, even if I can still see you fighting hippogriffs at six years old. You're a great guy, Aiden, but grow up."

He then slams the door hard, and I just sit there as I watch him go into the house.

The house he turned into a home for us.

Because he loved my mom and me more than anything in this world.

It all seems so inconceivable. I just don't understand what he wants from me. But above that, how in the hell am I supposed to apologize to Shelli?

CHAPTER ELEVEN

AIDEN

As I drive to Mom's wine bar, Brooks House, my dad's words play over and over again in my head. I hate when he is mad at me. My mom always says I have that first-child syndrome, where I aim to please everyone. For the longest time, I didn't agree with her, but it's moments like these when I feel she may be right. I don't want my dad to be mad, and if I'm honest, I don't like how things went down with Shelli either. I don't like how any of it went down. The sex, I liked that a lot, but I don't like that I didn't know who I was sleeping with. And I sure as hell don't like that I may have hurt Shelli's feelings.

As much as people want to believe I don't care, I do. I don't like hurting people; it's not my jam. Which is why I keep feelings an arm's length away. Things go bad when you actually start caring about someone. I've always had a soft spot for Shelli Adler, so it's easy to see why this is a fucking shitshow. Our lives are too intertwined, and I don't want her to hate me. Though, I think that ship has sailed, and she's the captain of it.

When my phone rings, I pull it out of my pocket. My brows shoot up when I see it's my brother, Asher.

"About time, I've only called nine times in the last week."

My brother's deep chuckle fills the car when the Bluetooth connects. "I knew why you were calling, and since you used to ignore me when our sisters would drive me crazy, I figured I'd hit ya with the same treatment."

"Rude," I accuse, and he laughs. "You know they're insane."

"I know, dude. I don't get how Mom and Dad had such amazing, civil, handsome sons and then those two."

"Emery set fire to Stella's makeup."

Asher doesn't even laugh. "Dude, I watched her pick up a TV and toss it at Stella. That's when she had to start going to therapy. She's still going, right?"

"Yeah, but I don't think it's doing anything."

"Because the cure is getting her away from Stella. Those two are insane. They hate each other but love each other at the same time. It's some weird, sister shit. I don't get it."

I grin as I turn off the highway. "I don't either, but it is what it is."

"It is."

"How's school?"

"School, man—I'm kicking ass and taking names."

"Nice. You don't miss us, do you?"

"Nope," he teases. "I'm happy out here. Thinking about staying after I graduate."

"Really? That's surprising."

"Yeah, I love it."

"That's awesome, dude." I mean it. Whatever makes the guy happy.

"How about you? Love being home?"

"Eh," I laugh. "I thought I'd enjoy it more, but it's only been a week and Dad already lit into me."

"No way. His golden child prodigy? Never!"

"Ha. If you asked him, I'm the mud on the bottom of his shoe right now."

Asher's laughter falls off. "Wait. It's not about that bullshit from last year, is it?"

"No," I say quickly. "He says I need to grow the fuck up. His words, not mine."

"Damn. What did you do?"

Even with the eight years between us, Asher has and always will be my best friend. He's the yin to my yang. He's totally different, but he gets me. And while I have no clue what he's talking about when he gets all smart on me, I'd die for the dude. He's a good brother. Great, even. When everything happened last year, I didn't call my parents first. I called Asher. So spilling the beans on my situation with Shelli is easy enough.

"So. Wait. Sorry." He laughs when I'm done telling him, and then he takes in a deep breath. "Dude, you slept with Shelli Adler?"

"I did."

"You know that's bad, right?"

"Depends how you look at it. We had a great time, but the Adlers will kill me."

"Exactly!" he yells, and then he laughs again. "I'm so jealous. She's so damn hot."

"I didn't know it was her."

"Yeah, I don't know how you didn't, because I would know Shelli Adler a million miles away. She's stunning. Don't you follow her on Instagram? I mean, holy fuck, she's gorgeous."

"No, because for the longest time, she was ten."

"She is not ten, dude. I mean, she's *a* ten for sure. Jesus, she posted this picture of herself in this black dress... I swear, if she bent over...ass for days."

"Wow. Do you have a thing for her?" I ask, and I'm confused by the knot in my chest. I don't like that he's talking about Shelli that way.

He scoffs. "Have you seen her? Everyone has a thing for Shelli Adler. She's gorgeous."

"We need to move on. You're pissing me off," I say, getting more annoyed. "But Dad says I was an asshole to her and I need to apologize."

Asher tsks at me. "You do know our parents fucked you up?"

"Wait, what?"

"For real. Look at me, Stella, and Emery—we don't have these issues because we only saw Mom and Dad after they got together. You saw them before and during, so you're all scared to feel something, which is why you sleep around like you do. Why you won't allow yourself to actually get close to someone."

"What's your point?" I ask, bored. I heard this not even ten minutes ago.

Asher laughs. "My point is Shelli scares the fuck out of you because she knows you, and you know her. Feelings could happen in a snap, and you don't want that. You don't know how to handle what you're feeling, so you just turn into a jackass."

"That's bullshit. I'm not feeling shit because nothing could ever happen—even if I wanted it to. She's her, and I'm me. My career could be ruined."

"Likely excuse."

"What does that mean?"

"Means until you get your head out of your ass and realize there is more to life than just fucking around, you'll always be like this. Your career wouldn't be ruined if you had a meaningful, loving relationship with her."

There is a knot in my throat. "Are you high? I told you to be careful with those brownies out there."

He laughs. "Seriously."

"That will never happen, and there is nothing wrong with me. I'm good."

"You're lonely. You've never been in a relationship—"

"And I don't want to be in one with her, that's for damn sure."

"Or you really do, and you don't like the way that makes you feel."

"What the hell? You know nothing!"

He scoffs. "I've been in a committed relationship for nine months. I know a thing or two. It's pretty cool."

My eyes narrow. "You're still with that chick?"

"Jasmine. Yeah, it's nice."

"No, that's dumb. You're gonna break up and then feel like shit."

Asher laughs. "Please tell me more about how Mom and Dad didn't fuck you up?"

My face scrunches up as I pull into Brooks House. My mom and dad's history has nothing to do with me. Yeah, I saw it all go down. I still remember the nights my aunt would hold my mom as she cried.

Mom always felt like she was failing me because I didn't have a dad. I was curious. I wanted a dad, but I loved my mom, I loved my aunt, I was okay. But then my dad came along, and I learned what it was like to be great. Dad completed us. But even so, I never forgot the way my mom would cry. Or how mad she would get at him. He'd hurt her, and she'd hurt him too. Yes, I've seen them be the happiest they've ever been, but the pain is there. Guilt. I don't want that.

"I don't like you right now."

"I bet you don't even like yourself right now," he says. "You're not an asshole, Aiden. I get it... It's weird to feel something other than the need to fuck, but don't be a dick just because you don't know how to handle it."

"You act like I'm in love with her or something."

"Or something," Asher says simply. "I think, for the first time ever, you can't get someone out of your head, and you don't like it. I just heard you rant over a girl for more than ten minutes for the first time in our lives. I think that means something."

"I think you don't know shit," I snap, and he laughs. "I have more important things to do and worry about than Shelli Adler. I have a new start, and I'm not ruining it by getting involved with someone who, *hello*, doesn't even like me."

"Whatever you say," he says offhandedly. "But when you guys hook up again—and believe me, you guys will since she is still very much into you, because if she weren't, then she wouldn't have jumped on the defense so quickly."

"She hates me."

"Whatever, dude, but remember, don't be a dick. Don't be that guy."

He's on something. Probably those hippie-dippie brownies or something. "I gotta go."

"Great talk!"

"Yeah, whatever."

I hang up on his laughter as I get out of the truck and lock it up. Asher has no clue what he is talking about. Do I think about Shelli? Of course I do. She's hard to forget. The things we did in bed, the way we touched, and then the way she looked at me with that defiant little tilt of her chin? Not even the pope could forget that. She's unforgettable. But that doesn't mean I want to shack up and make her mine. I'd love to sleep with her again, but it wouldn't be smart. I've already made some bad choices—no need to make any more.

Though, man, if there is anyone I want to make bad choices with, it's her.

That wasn't a smart thought.

I shake my head as I head inside my mom's wine bar. It's a really upscale joint in Nashville's Gulch. The place is packed like always, and the ambiance is pretty damn sexy. Mom wanted it to be as if you were sitting in a fancy barn illuminated only by candlelight. She succeeded hands down, and this was just voted one of Nashville's most romantic spots. The food is supposed to be pretty damn good, and the wine is, of course, perfection. Tables are everywhere, some for four, some only for two. There are booths around the perimeter of the room and a huge bar in the middle of the floor, right beside the stage that holds a piano. There is someone setting up, but my sister immediately steals my attention.

"Hey, the girl replacing me is running late. Take a seat at the bar. I'll be done soon."

Then she's off again. She's been working here since she was sixteen. She started off as a hostess, but when she turned eighteen, she became a waitress. She makes damn good money and loves it. I think she'll be the one to take over for Mom when the time comes. For the longest time, we all thought Asher would, but he wasn't interested in Mom's wine empire the way Stella is. She loves it. Can't blame her either. Mom's business is great.

As I sit at the bar, a glass appears before Stella winks at me. Then she's off again. From the looks of the stellar red in my glass, I assume it's merlot. I take a big sip, and I am impressed with myself when I'm right. Go me. I take another sip just as Stella appears in front of me behind the bar.

"Mom told me to tell you that Elli had to push back the party. She wanted to wait till y'all had a two-day break. I think that's in a week or two, I don't know," she says quickly as she pours four wide-mouth glasses. "Call Mom."

"I'll get right on that," I say since that party is the last thing I want to deal with right now. I look around the bar. "This place is poppin'."

"Oh yeah, it's a good night. Wish Mom would let me work past eight. She's killing me."

"You're a baby, Stella."

When she flips me off, I grin as she rushes to deliver her drinks. The crowd gets a little sexier after eight, which is why Mom doesn't like Stella here then. I get it, but Stella doesn't. She just wants to work. I lean back in my chair as a beautiful melody comes from the stage. I lean on my elbows so I can see, and I don't expect what is before me.

In a tight black dress that hugs her thighs in the most delectable way, Shelli moves her fingers along the keys as she sings like an angel. I don't know the song, but I also don't care. It's stunning. She's stunning. Her hair is down over her shoulders in big wide curls, while her makeup has been applied to accentuate her eyes. Not that her blue eyes need it; they shine no matter what. When she hits a high note, her eyes shut, her lashes kissing her cheeks, and she captivates me.

For the love of God, how am I supposed to ignore this girl?

"Oh, let me get that." I don't even pay attention to Stella as she playfully wipes my mouth with a rag. "You're drooling, bubba."

"Shut it."

"She's pretty amazing, huh? I love listening to her."

"Yeah," I say as I watch people drop money in her tip jar. I knew Shelli sang; I remember when we were younger and all she did was walk around with her guitar. She was talented even then, but it's nothing compared to now. Her voice stops the room, or at least me. It's beautiful and belongs on a real stage. Just like that, all the pieces fall together. That was how she knew Chris; she was on Broadway.

Maybe I do need to grow up. If I had been paying even a bit of attention, I would have put two and two together. Then none of this would have happened. Then I wouldn't have seen her crying in Elli's truck. I still don't know if that was about me, but I have a feeling it was.

"Everyone loves her here. She makes more money than I do, I swear it."

"With a voice like that, how could she not?"

"Right? So talented."

So beautiful.

I can't take my gaze off her. Shelli opens her eyes, looking out into the bar as her voice carries, stealing everyone's attention and stopping conversation. Her voice has an edge to it, but it's soft and magical also. It's not only her voice that has me breathless, it's the way she sings. With such beautiful emotion, it's impressive. It's as if she is the song herself. It's amazing to witness. She's spectacular, but I could tell that before I slept with her.

If the need to apologize wasn't great before, it is now. I don't want her to be mad at me or even hate me. I don't know why, but I can't have that. Problem is, I don't know how to apologize. I hardly ever have to, but I know I need to now. Not because my dad said to but because I want to. I lift up my glass and take a long sip as the napkin falls from where it clung to the base of my glass. I watch it fall, and then the idea is there. I place my glass down and reach for the napkin before stealing a pen out of the jar in front of me. I write quickly on the napkin and then glance back at the stage. She's still singing as if there is no one in the room. My heart is in my throat as I get up, heading toward the stage and folding the napkin in my hand as the distance between us closes.

Her gaze locks with mine, and everything stops. With a shaky hand, I place the napkin on the sleek black piano before I bite my lip. She doesn't stop singing, nor stop playing, but her eyes stay locked with mine, sending jolts of heat through my body. I want nothing more than to capture that mouth with mine and never stop. Her lips are so plump, so beautiful.

Shit... Asher may be right.

CHAPTER TWELVE

SHELLI

IT'S AS IF I'M ON AUTOPILOT.

Aiden's eyes are like gray thunderclouds as he walks toward me. Or better yet, walks like he's having sex. He's just so smooth, so sexy. I'm usually not into guys who are always so damn G*Q*ed out—nice suits, perfect hair, and expensive shoes. But all the times I've seen him since New York, he's been just that, and I've been insanely turned on by him. It irritates the fuck out of me that I allow him to do that, but then, my body has not caught up with my brain. And if I'm honest, my brain is the only smart thing at the moment.

Because this heart of mine is still one hundred percent yearning for Aiden Brooks.

It's so annoying.

Especially since I'm pissed that I cried over him. How pathetic do I have to be to cry over some dude who doesn't even want me? But then he's walking toward me like that, and I feel like I'm the only thing he sees. My breath catches, but I keep on singing a soft version of Julia Michael's "Issues." I didn't think I would love this job as much as I do.

It's such fun doing songs my way. I love it, and the money is great. Plus, I start my internship at the Assassins on Monday, and I'm stoked.

My life seemed to be getting on track, but then Aiden started for me with that spark in his eyes.

With his gaze intent on mine, he slides a napkin toward me. That's it. Just the napkin, and then he walks away. Of course, I want to end the song right now and read it, but I still have another verse. As I sing, I watch him sit back at the bar and sip his wine. He's watching me, those eyes ever so dark, with no cares that he's staring at me. He's utterly divine, and his suit fits him perfectly. His hair is down, curly around his face. He just shaved, and I know if I were near him, he'd smell delicious. He runs his finger along the mouth of his glass, and shit, it almost makes me forget the words to the song!

It reminds me of when he touched my mouth with those fingertips.

I finish the last note, and the room fills with the sounds of clapping. I love it here. It's easygoing and I feel good, but right now, I'm on the edge of my seat as I reach for the napkin.

My breath is gone once I read what he's written.

I'm sorry,
-Aiden

I blink. Then again. And then I squint at his handwriting. Irritation rattles through me as I glare at his napkin. If I were still ten, I would smell it to see if it smells like him, but now I just want to ball it up and throw it at him! Is this some kind of pity apology? When I snap my gaze up to find him, I see him walking out with his arm around Stella.

Oh, hell no.

"I'll be back in five!"

I get up quickly and run as fast as I can in heels toward the exit. The cold hits me as soon as I push the doors open. I regret not getting a jacket first, but for some reason, when it comes to this guy, I don't make good choices. I don't see him at first, but then I catch him as he's opening the door to the truck for Stella.

"Aiden!"

He whips his head toward me as he draws in his brows. I hear Stella ask, "Who's that?"

He shakes his head. "Don't worry about it. Stay in the car." I stomp toward him as he shuts his sister's door. "Yeah?"

I hold up the napkin. "What is this?"

He looks at the napkin and then at me, his brow still furrowed. "Shelli, it's cold as hell—"

"Answer me!" He glares, looking every bit as frustrated as I feel. He then shrugs out of his jacket, and I snap, "I don't want that."

"I don't care," he says flatly. He steps to me, wrapping his jacket around my shoulders as his eyes bore into mine. He doesn't step back like he should. His eyes stay locked with mine as he says, "It's an apology."

"You think you're cute? This is not cute!"

He shrugs. "It's a little cute."

"Not cute!" I insist, and he shrugs. "You don't have the balls to talk to me?"

"I didn't know how to approach you."

"Why?" I ask, my heart in my throat.

"'Cause I don't."

"That's dumb! I'm approachable!"

"Yeah, as approachable as a ravenous lioness," he scoffs with that stupid little charming grin of his.

Oh, he infuriates me! "Again, not cute."

"Hey, that was clever."

"Ugh! Aiden, why are you apologizing?"

He narrows his eyes before he slips his tongue out to lick his lips. The simple motion drives me absolutely foolish, of course. "I don't know of anyone ever asking *why* when someone apologizes."

"Um, in this situation, it's warranted! It seems real out of the blue, when not a couple hours ago, you didn't look the least bit apologetic."

He shrugs. "I don't like how things went down."

"Why? Because you saw me crying? I wasn't crying over you," I snap, and his gaze darkens.

"Never said you were."

"Just seems funny that now you're apologizing after you saw me crying."

"You crying has nothing to do with this apology. I felt like shit when you walked away anyway."

"But you had no problem saying I wasn't being ladylike."

"Because I was pissed, and you weren't."

"So?"

"So..." He shakes his head. "What do you want from me, Shelli? I'm trying to apologize—"

"I want it to be real. I want it to be truthful."

His face twists in confusion, and I feel stupid. *Why am I out here?* He isn't supposed to matter. "I am being truthful. I mean it. I thought about you all day. It was wrong how things went down. We both said things we shouldn't have, and it escalated."

"Whatever."

"Can you just accept my apology? Please?" he asks firmly. "Listen, I suck at this kind of thing. I don't apologize for things because I don't usually feel guilty, but I feel wrong about earlier. I never should have spoken to you the way I did or made you feel less than your worth—"

I scoff, even if my heart is pounding like a motherfucker. "I know my worth, and you made me feel nothing!"

He blinks twice and then nods. "Good, I'm glad. I wasn't out to hurt you. My anger got the best of me."

"I find that hard to believe."

"Why?"

"Because your anger has been getting the best of you since you saw me at my house."

He licks his lips once more, slowly nodding. "I don't know how to talk to you because I'm still upset with how it all went down."

"And you think I'm not?"

He shakes his head. "Shelli, seriously, you could ruin my life."

"But I wouldn't," I stress. "Yes, it wasn't ideal how we ended up in bed, but it's done."

"You're right. But still, it's sort of a mess, and I don't want this hostility between us. Our lives, our families, are too intertwined for it to be like this."

"Like you care," I say, and I hate the emotion that's taking over.

He narrows his eyes, and I can see the annoyance on his beautiful face. "I get it, I was a dick. But come on, cut me some slack here."

"Why? I'm just another—"

His hand gripping my wrist stops me. "No. I do care. And, yeah, maybe at the time you were, but that all changed when I found out who I had slept with."

"Because of my mom—"

"Yeah, and because of you."

I look down at my hand in his hold as fire courses through my whole body. "Oh."

"I'm really sorry."

I don't know what to say, so I just shrug. "It is what it is," I say simply.

"No, it's more." I look away as his thumb moves to my palm, pressing gently. "On a totally different subject, and this goes against my better judgment, you look really hot tonight."

"Oh wow, whiplash," I say as our eyes meet.

"Yeah, I know," he says softly, his thumb gliding up and down my palm. "As much as I know this can never happen, I can't keep from telling the truth."

"Oh?"

He grins, that heart-stopping, slap-your-momma kind of smile. "Truth is, you're stunning, and you're still talented as all hell. Like, wow."

Now, against my better judgment, my lips curve. "Well, thanks."

"So, you accept my apology?"

Oh yeah, I'm supposed to be mad. I move my wrist out of his hand. "I don't want to wear your dick as a necklace any longer."

"Hey, that's progress." He gives me a smirk.

"I guess, for us, it is."

"Yeah," he agrees. "I am sorry, though."

"I hear you."

He nods as he steps back. "I'll see you around, Shelli."

"Yeah."

He turns without another word, walking toward the truck with such swagger. I watch as he gets in, and then I turn on my heels to head inside. When I cuddle deeper into his coat, I turn to run it back to him, but he's already driving off.

With a wave and a sexy little smirk to boot.

That plan for getting over Aiden... Yeah, that's gonna be a real bitch.

CHAPTER THIRTEEN

AIDEN

I slam my body into the Canucks' defensemen, fighting for the puck. The bastard has it caught between his skate and the boards like a fucker. He knows if I get it, I'm scoring. I poke my stick at it, using my hip to push him, but he outweighs me and isn't budging.

"Move, fucker!"

"Fuck you, you pussy!"

I use all my body weight to push him off just as Wes grabs the puck and passes it to Sinclair. I go to rush the net, when the guy I was just in the corner with shoves his stick in between my skates. As a result, I'm eating ice. I wait for the whistle, my bench waits for the whistle, but nothing.

"Son of a bitch! Ref, you blind?"

"Play on, Brooks!"

I hear the thunk of puck on pad, realizing Sinclair has shot. I scan the ice, seeing the puck where Wes just threw it up the boards to Reeves. He cradles it as he moves in, passing it to Sinclair, who returns it back. I skate around my man, trying to screen the goalie. I get jabbed in the back by the goalie a few times as we try relentlessly to score. Wes shoots, he hits the damn post, and when the puck hits my blade, I'm convinced this is a goal. Top shelf, yes, baby. Come to Daddy!

But the damn goalie gloves me.

"Fucking hell!"

"Not today, you fairy-looking bitch!"

I glare at the goalie. "I don't look like a fairy! My beard grew in —try it!"

Asshole. That should have been a goal. I should have gone lower. Damn it. I skate to the bench while our next line comes on. As I go in through the door, Coach is yelling, "Good shot, BB. Great pressure. Keep shooting. You'll find the back of the net."

I could kill Tate—honestly. I thought BB would have fallen off by now, but nope. It's been two weeks, and it's stuck. Lovely for me. I lean on the boards as I watch our defense fight off their forwards. The Canucks came to play tonight. They're up by one and giving us a run for our money. I squirt some Gatorade into my mouth as I take in lung-filling breaths. I feel as if I'm flying, and it's been like that since my first game on Assassins' ice. I love it here. The crowd is electrifying, the ice feels like home, and knowing my family is up in the box watching me is so overwhelming I almost can't handle it.

But I am.

In the seven games we've played, I have nine assists, and I've scored three goals in just the last three games. None on home ice, though. I'm itching for a goal here. I want to be the reason the goal song plays and the lights go nuts. I want to hear the crowd yell for me like they did for my dad for so long. I want to hear the announcer call my name and number. It's something I've been waiting for since I was a kid. But like Coach said, it's coming. I can feel it. I'm one of those streaky players. When I get hot, I get hot. And right now, I'm hot.

Since I joined the Assassins, we're six, one, and one. I am stoked for those numbers. Elli is pretty pleased, and that makes me happy. I want to keep my boss happy. Especially when I can't stop thinking about her daughter. I made the mistake of going on Shelli's Instagram, which Asher had told me about. Big mistake. I've been up countless nights, whacking off because she's so damn hot. She's possibly the most beautiful woman I've ever seen. I want her so damn bad. Which is so damn bad. So bad. But I can't control my lust for her, which is why I have done everything in my power to keep clear of her.

But if she doesn't stop posting pictures of herself working out in those barely there shorts, I might lose my damn mind.

"One!"

Ah, my line. I jump over the boards as I rush to where the puck was thrown into their zone. I go center ice, waiting for them to bring the puck in. The defensemen tries to pass it up the middle, but Wes is there, catching it on his blade. I rush forward as he does the same, catching the Canuck on a change. He passes it to our linemate, Hoenes, who takes it in. I rush the goal, and we have a two-on-one. The defensemen lays out so that Hoenes can't pass to Wes. But he can pass it to me.

When he does, I'm ready, and I shoot it so damn hard, I fall to my knee, waiting for that red light.

When it lights up, my heart stops.

Goal.

The crowd goes wild as my teammates come and wrap their arms around me. Emotion takes over, and I feel it in my throat as I hug my teammates hard. When we break apart, I look around as I skate to the bench to slap hands with the rest of my teammates. Everyone cheers me on, and when I round the corner, Sinclair is there with a puck.

"First goal at home as an Assassin."

I take it from him and grin. "Thanks, man."

I go over the boards and hand it off to Ryan Justice, my trainer. "I'll put it up."

I nod as I lean on the boards, and I swear I can hear my mom screaming. But then it's all drowned out when the announcer's voice fills the arena.

"An Assassins goal!! Scored at 12:52, by number twenty-three, Aiden Brooooooooooooookkkkkksssss!! That's his twenty-ninth goal of the season but his first as your Nashvilllllllllllllllle Asssssssssaaaaaaaaaasssin!"

Yeah, I'll never get used to that.

"Dude, there is this waitress here—holy mother of sweet baby Jesus, she is gorgeous."

I didn't know that most of the guys go to Brooks House after all the home games until Wes asked me to go. I also didn't know they all eat for free. Seems like something my mom would do. She doesn't let them drink for free because she's no fool.

Since I love the penne here, that's what I got, but Wes went with the lasagna to go with the tall beer he ordered. He isn't a wine drinker —in fact, I've noticed that most of my teammates aren't, so I'm the only one with a glass. We're all excited, celebrating our win, and I'm having a good time. It's my first night out with the guys since joining the team.

Problem is, it's hard to pay attention when Shelli Adler is singing.

Boon Hoenes leans over me and nods. "So hot. The one with the long brown hair, right? Brown eyes?"

Wes shakes his head. "No, you mean chocolate-cake eyes. I mean, they're such a rich brown, it's unfair. She's stunning."

Willy nods. "Yeah, she is. But isn't she like eighteen? In high school?"

Wes grins. "Hey, she's legal."

My brow perks. "What's her name?"

"Stella," Wes says dreamily. "Stella fucking gorgeous face."

I snort along with the guys as I shake my head. "That's my little sister."

Laughter comes to a complete stop as everyone looks from Wes to me. I just grin at him. But then Wes gets up. "Excuse me, I'm gonna go jump off a bridge."

I grab him by the shirt and pull him back down as everyone laughs. "Dude, I didn't know."

I grin over at him. "It's cool, but she's young. How old are you?"

"Twenty-two."

"Oh, I thought you were older."

"No, I'm just mature. Bad childhood."

"Got it," I say with a nod. "Still, stay away from her."

"Ten-four," he says with a salute, and we share a grin. "She is really gorgeous, though."

I only nod in agreement as my gaze drifts back where Shelli is singing some Taylor Swift song. The only reason I know that is because it's all Emery listens to. I happen to think Shelli sings the song better, but I may be biased. She's striking. Her hair is up in a bun, but little tendrils fall down the sides of her face. Her neck is on full display, and I want so much to suck her skin right beneath her ear.

Jesus.

I swallow hard as I admire her short little dress. It's a bold red that makes her skin look delicious. Her black, red-soled shoes are high and dangerous, but it's her voice that has me in knots. She's so talented.

"The only thing I don't like about this place..." Boon says, and I glance over at him. He's a funny dude. Real big, but fast. I thought he'd be a defensemen, but he's actually one hell of a shot. He's taller than me, with dark brown hair and hazel eyes. He has an insane beard, with a jagged scar running along his cheek and brow. He got into a nasty fight when he was younger, and that's the result. He's a cool guy, and we click. Our line—he, Wes, and I—is doing big things. "There aren't enough single girls here. There's just a whole bunch of couples."

"Hey, some of the waitresses... Never mind," Wes starts, and I laugh.

"We can head out, hit up a club or two," I suggest, and everyone nods.

"Yeah, I gotta call Caitlin. I told her I wasn't going to be out late, but I'm not ready to head back. Maybe she'll want to come out," Willy says as he gets up and takes out his phone.

Boon looks over at me. "Can we dump him as a friend? He's boring when it comes to partying."

I laugh as Wes sets Boon with a look. "Hey, Willy is awesome. He's just in love. You know how that is."

Boon shrugs. "Yeah, turns you into an idiot. It's all about the girl. What they want. You don't matter. It's fucking annoying."

Wes scoffs. "Says the guy who just got out of a three-year relationship."

"Hey, I learned the error of my ways and got out."

"She left you," Wes says dryly. "You cried for a month."

Boon shoots him a murderous look. "I don't cry."

Wes snorts. "Fine, you leaked from your eyes in a very manly way."

Boon nods. "Thank you."

"Why did she leave you?" I ask, and he looks to me.

Boon's face sort of changes, and he shrugs. "She wasn't happy. Didn't like the life. She wanted me home, and I couldn't be there. I wanted to play. She asked me to choose, and I went with my first love. Hockey."

"Don't blame you."

"But that's an asshole move. She never should have asked," Wes says then with a furrow of his brow. "This is our dream. Our life. No one should ask us to give it up."

We all nod in agreement as I take a sip of my wine. My gaze, of course, ends up on Shelli as she finishes the song. She loves hockey as much as I do. She'd never ask me to give... *What the hell am I thinking?*

I start coughing from the wine going down the wrong pipe. Shit, I'm going to die. I put the glass down as Wes slaps my back. "Told ya. Wine is dangerous. Stick to beer."

Boon tips his glass to me as I hack up my lung. "Yeah, leave the classy side and slum with us."

Laughing and coughing don't mix, and soon I'm in a fit. Everyone is looking at me funny, but all I hear are sirens in my head. Why the hell did I think that? What the hell is wrong with me? I hate Asher. This is his fault. I don't know what is going on, but Shelli is more dangerous than I thought. I know this. I've got to remember this!

"Hey, guys. Great game tonight."

I look up to see Shelli standing there in all her beautiful glory, and I'm still coughing a bit. Her jacket is over her arm, along with a jar full of money. From beside me, Wes flashes her a winning grin. "Thanks, Shelli. Did you watch?"

She nods with a "come on" look. "Of course. I messed up three songs 'cause I cheered when y'all scored." God, her country drawl is so damn sexy. Her eyes fall on me. "Great goal from the slot."

My throat is dry. "Thanks," I rasp, and her eyes flash with something treacherous. I feel it all in my gut, and I don't know what the hell is wrong with me, but I need to remember.

This. Can't. Happen.

No matter how much I want to lift that skirt of hers and bury my face between her legs.

It. Can. Not. Happen.

Willy comes up beside her, wrapping an arm around her as he squeezes her tightly. "Great set. I love that Elton John song."

"Thanks," she gushes, and I love the pink of her cheeks.

"Hey, so Caitlin said it's cool. She isn't going to meet us. She's not feeling up to it."

"Cool," Wes says, getting up. "Hey, Shell, what you got going on?"

"Heading home, I guess."

"We're gonna go barhopping. Wanna come?"

No. No! Don't invite her!

Her gaze shifts to me before she looks back at Wes. "Yeah, that sounds like fun."

"Cool. Ready?" Wes asks, throwing a hundred on the table. "Someone is paying for my drinks at the next place since I paid for them here."

"I got you," Shelli says with a wink, shaking her tip jar.

He laughs. "Yes, drinks on the boss's daughter!"

Shelli's eyes flash to me, and I look away. I shouldn't go, but if I don't, it would seem like I'm not going because of her. While that *is* the reason, I don't want the guys knowing that.

And I don't want to hurt Shelli's feelings.

Why do I care about her feelings? What is happening to me?

After gathering our things, we make a game plan to hit up the bars down in the Gulch. We decide to leave our cars and walk, even though I feel it's too cold for Shelli out here. She's wearing the shortest of skirts, and I don't want her to freeze her ass off. It's a great ass; it needs to stay there.

"Okay, let me go put my stuff up," Shelli says, and she starts for her truck.

The guys just stand there, and it irritates me. "Is someone going to go with her?"

Wes makes a face. "She's going right around the corner."

"Assholes," I grumble.

I reluctantly run to catch up with her. She looks surprised when I fall into step with her. "Oh, hey. I'm only going to be a second."

"Yeah, I didn't want you walking alone. Are you sure you want to walk? Maybe we should drive."

She makes a face as she unlocks her door, throwing her jar on the seat before pulling out the money. "It's all within walking distance. I'm fine."

"I don't want you to freeze."

Her lips tilt. "I'm fine. I have tights on."

And I want her out of them. Now.

"Yeah, I guess."

She flashes me a grin before shutting the door and tucking her money between her breasts. It's hard to breathe watching her hand cram between those two sweet mounds before she stuffs her key in there too. "Is that a safe place to put that?"

She shrugs. "I don't have pockets, and who's going to be reaching between my boobs?"

Me. I would.

"I can hold them for you." Her brow perks, and I shake my head. "I mean your key and money."

"I'm good," she says with a little grin.

I swallow hard. "Yeah, um, you got your ID?"

"Ah!" she exclaims, going back into the truck. She leans over the seat, and that dress of hers rides up, leaving me breathless. When she leans back, she smiles up at me. "Got it."

"Great."

But it's not great.

It's far from great, because I'm going to die before the night is over.

CHAPTER FOURTEEN

AIDEN

We catch up with the guys and head to the first club. It's as loud as ever, but Willy knows the bouncer and gets us a nice little spot in VIP. The club is a swanky one I hadn't been to before. It's new. The Spot has everything from go-go dancers to one badass DJ. The music is pumping, and it's hard not to notice the little shake Shelli does with her hips. I fall back into the seat, trying to ignore her, but it's hard. Wes dances beside her as the music vibrates around us. I want to push Wes out of the way, but I'm sure that would blow the cover I'm trying to stay under.

When the first round of drinks comes, Boon calls the two of them over, and Shelli sits beside me as she takes the shot from him. We all cheers before we shoot back the bitter liquid. Tequila. Ugh. That was my one and only shot for sure. Tequila is not my friend. It's all I was drinking that night when I went to bed with Shelli. Being drunk might not be my jam anymore. It took sleeping with my boss's daughter to realize that. My dad would be so proud.

I lean back in the booth as Wes takes Shelli's hand again and they go back to dancing by the rail. They're laughing, having a great time, and I'm sitting here, pissed the fuck off. Wes reaches out and moves some of her loose hair back behind her ear, and then they both start laughing. As if it's some kind of joke. Why does he get to touch her like that? When he takes her in his arms, dipping her back, her laughter carries to me and turns my stomach with anger. I don't know why the hell I'm getting so fucking pissed, but I am.

"Bro, you need a drink," Boon yells over the music before passing me a beer.

I shake my head. "I don't drink beer."

"Oh yeah. You're the tooty-fruity type. Let me order you a...what was it? A mer-lot?" he pronounces it like *a lot,* and I can't help it, I laugh.

"Merlot," I say, pronouncing it correctly for him. "But I'm good."

"I'm not getting it for you," he says as he waves down the waitress obnoxiously. "I'm doing it for Wes, so that you don't get up and rip off his head to piss down his throat."

I give him a blank look. "What are you talking about?"

"Oh. Wait, are you not feeling her?" he asks, nodding toward where Shelli and Wes are now salsa dancing. It makes my blood boil with how close his hands are to her ass. I don't understand these feelings. I don't need that kind of headache. I don't even need to care, but for some really annoying reason, I fucking do.

"Not at all," I say as dryly as I can. "I just think he's stupid for doing that with the boss's daughter."

Boon looks over at them, his head tilting before he looks back at me. "I don't think he cares, and I wouldn't either. That girl is fire."

He's absolutely right.

Boon flashes me a grin that shows his two front teeth missing. He forgot his falsies but, eh, I don't think he cares. When the waitress comes back, he pulls her into his lap and she giggles, kissing his cheek. I guess they know each other, or they will know each other by the time the night is over. I glance over at Shelli, and her hair has come down. It's falling like a thick, beautiful curtain along her back, swaying as she laughs.

"Shots!"

Willy comes over with a tray, and Shelli drops down beside me. She goes to hand me a shot, but I shake my head. "I'm good."

She eyes me, but Boon takes my shot. "Shit. If he isn't going to shoot, I will!"

Everyone laughs, but Wes looks toward me. "You done?"

"Gotta make sure you idiots get home."

"Aww, BB turned into our DD," Wes teases. I flash him a playful dark look as everyone chuckles and teases me.

"BB?" Shelli asks, and then she glances over at me. "Oh, boogie butt! That's awful. Who told them that was your nickname?"

Her eyes are sparkling with excitement. It's hard to be upset with her. Though, I have no right. She is nothing to me. She's just really hot, and it's pissing me off that someone else is touching her. "Tate."

"So rude!"

"Agreed."

She takes the shot, shaking from the aftertaste. She then takes a long pull of her beer.

"Better slow down there, Adler."

She looks back at me. "I know how to handle my liquor, BB."

Her grin is hypnotizing, and soon I'm smiling back at her. "My apologies."

She takes another long pull, and I admire her profile. It's so round, sweet. Like a cherub's. When she glances back at me, I look down at my hands.

"So, are you excited for our shindig tomorrow?"

I snort. "So excited."

She laughs. "Right? It's gonna be so embarrassing."

"Absolutely." I then lean in and chuckle softly. "Remember that party my mom threw for Stella, and she made me dress up like a damn fish?"

Shelli's face lights up as she giggles loudly. "Flounder!"

"Not funny."

"So funny! You had to wear those blue tights!" Her laughter is intoxicating as she leans back, shaking her head. "You were the grumpiest Flounder ever."

"You would be too if you were seventeen in a fish costume."

She snorts. "But you were so adorable."

I shake my head. "Whatever. I looked stupid."

She leans into me, her chin in her hands. "I didn't think so."

I'm lost in her blue depths. "You and Wes a thing?"

Why did I ask that? Why in the hell did I ask that?

Her brows furrow as her lips twist. "Wes? Wesley?"

"Yeah," I somehow say, and am I not in control of my lips? What the hell?

"No," she laughs and shakes her head. "We're very good friends. We've known each other since pee wee travel hockey. He's more a brother than anything."

Oh. "Cool."

"Why?"

"Just wondering."

"Wondering why?"

I shrug. "You two seemed mighty close."

"We were dancing."

"Closely."

She eyes me. "Why does that matter?"

"It doesn't," I say with a shrug. "Just making an observation."

Her lips curve into the most sinful smile I've ever seen. It's not only her lips that hit me straight in the gut—no, her eyes are dark and full of everything naughty. "Seems to me that observation was made out of a bit of jealousy. Do you not like me dancing with Wes?"

"I don't care. You do you."

She leans on her hand again, her eyes locking with mine. "You're an awful liar."

I scoff, rolling my eyes. "I'm not lying."

"Mmm-hmm," she says, her lips pursing. "Would you like to dance with me, *Aiden?*"

She says my name so slowly and with so much heat, I choke on my tongue. "I don't think that would be smart."

"Who cares?"

Her eyes are challenging mine, leaving me completely breathless. I want so badly to wrap my arms around her and move against her.

"Shell, come on. This is my jam!"

She doesn't even look to where Wes is calling her. Her eyes are on me. "Last chance."

"I don't think it's a good idea."

She shrugs. "Your loss."

And then she gets up, shimmying to Wes. In that tight skirt, I can see her ass jiggle. She's right, it is my fucking loss. I sigh deeply as I reach for the bottle of water Boon ordered for me. I lean back in the booth, and I'm thankful for the dark shadow cast over my face.

Because I'm watching Shelli Adler move in ways I wish she'd only move for me.

As the night flows on, so does the alcohol. We hit up three more clubs before I start to notice this party is getting a little out of hand. Willy left about an hour ago to go home to Caitlin, while Boon is dry-humping anyone who will let him. He's completely toasted, and I'm wondering if I should get him out of here. Wes was dancing with Shelli, but now I have no clue where he is. I've kept Shelli in view, and she hasn't stopped dancing since we got here.

I'm watching Boon stumble into a chair when Shelli falls beside me in the booth I'm sitting in. She leans into me, her mouth coming close to my ear. "I'm really drunk."

My lips curve. "Are you now?" She leans back laughing, and I grip her wrist so she doesn't fall out. "Wow, you are really drunk."

"I am."

I mutter a curse under my breath. I move to get up, but she clutches my wrist. "Don't leave me."

"I'm gonna get Boon and see if I can find Wes."

"But don't leave me," she says as she stares up at me, eyes half lidded. I can see her eyes floating in tears, and I want to groan. Great, she's a crier when she's drunk.

"I'm not," I promise, and then I look up to see Wes coming toward me. I point to him. "How drunk are you?"

He holds up his hands, moving them up and down, like he's weighing his answer. "I might be."

"That's not a unit of measurement."

"Fine. A lot."

"Ha!" Boon laughs. "Like mer-lot!"

The peanut gallery, ladies and gentlemen.

"Great. Give me your phone."

He hands it over as he sits down beside Boon. I notice the bouncers watching us, and I know we gotta get out of here. I sit on the arm of the chair, and Shelli's head falls into my lap. I move my hand over her hair absentmindedly as I use Wes's app to request an Uber.

"Nice. It's already outside." I get up and grab Shelli's jacket before putting it on her. "Guys, come on." I then look down at Shelli and say, "Come on, angel. Let's get out of here." She takes my hands, and I pull her up into my arms. She's so much shorter than me, and when she tips her head back, I can't help but look down at her.

"You called me angel?"

I smile. "Yeah, I guess I did."

I wrap my arm around her waist and then follow my two buddies out. Thankfully, we all make it outside without any assistance from the bouncers. After a long argument with Boon and Wes about leaving their cars back at Brooks House, the Uber finally drives off with them in it. I promise to take them to get their cars tomorrow. It's all good, and I'll text my mom so she doesn't tow them. We're only a block from Brooks House, but I'm unsure Shelli will make it.

"You good there, Shell?"

"I think I might puke...or pass out," she mumbles, and she looks a little green.

"Fantastic," I mutter as I lift her into my arms with ease. I can feel her skirt riding up, so I put her back down, much to her dismay.

"But I don't want to walk."

"Hush you," I murmur as I take off my jacket, which, luckily, she returned to me earlier, and wrap it around her waist. I then pick her back up, satisfied knowing no one will see her ass. She wraps her arms around my neck and cuddles her face into my chest as I head toward our cars. She smells like tequila, smoke, and absolute perfection. She drives me wild. Problem is, I'm unsure what I am going to do. I don't think I can take her home. What the hell would I say to her parents? Plus, it's almost three in the morning. They're probably sleeping. There is really only one thing to do.

When we reach my car, I hit the unlock button for my brand-new

Fiat Spider and open the door. I slowly lower her into it and then buckle her seat belt. When I go to make sure the belt is over her chest correctly, she opens one eye.

"Hey."

"Hey."

"You're super hot."

I chuckle as I pat her thigh. "You too, but don't throw up in my new car, please."

"You should kiss me."

Yup, I knew I was going to die tonight. "No can do, angel. When I kiss you, I want you to know what's happening."

"Eh, knowing shit is overrated. If you knew it was me, we wouldn't have had some really great sex," she mumbles, awakening every fiber of my body. "God, we were so hot that night."

My lips curve as I pat her thigh once more. "We sure were."

"We should do that again. Here," she says, and when she starts to lift her skirt, I stop her.

"Shelli, stop. Rest."

She groans but then passes out again, thankfully. I shut the door and rush around the car, taking a quick peek at her car to make sure it's good. Once in the driver's seat, I start the car as I text my mom really fast. When she doesn't answer, I'm thankful. I put the car in drive and head toward my place, which is only four minutes down the road. I'm not sure if this is the right idea, but I really don't know what else to do. I can't leave her in her car, and I don't want her mom knowing she was out drinking with me and the guys.

When we reach my condo, she's snoring loudly. It's so cute, I can't help but grin. After parking, I get out and then help her out. I learn very quickly that walking is not an option for her. "I told you to slow down."

"Shh. You can't control me."

I've never heard truer words.

I snort as I lift her up in my arms. I carry her to the elevator and hit my floor before leaning back on the wall. She's cuddled into my chest, looking so small and perfect. Her hair falls along her rosy cheeks, and her mouth is parted sweetly. When the elevator dings, I tear my gaze from her and step off before turning left down the hall. I dig the keys out of my pocket and open the door before kicking it shut behind us. I don't pause to turn on lights or anything. All the boxes are against the walls, so hopefully I won't fall.

I push open my bedroom door with my hip before carrying her to my bed. My room is bare, but at least there is a bed and a dresser. I lay her down slowly before pulling the covers out from under her. She stretches all her limbs as her head falls to the side, her mouth still wide open.

What a sight.

I shake my head as I unbuckle her shoes, throwing them onto the floor once I get them off her. How she walks in these deathtraps is beyond me, but man I love watching her in them. I pull the blankets up her legs and over her torso when I remember her ID, money, phone, and keys are in her bra. I don't want her key to stab her, but I also don't want to touch her boob. But I also don't want her to get cancer from her phone so close to her boob. So reluctantly, I reach into her bra.

Jell-O, a warm bowl of Jell-O, not Shelli's boobs.

Thank God, I get her phone first and then finally her key. The other stuff can stay in there.

I set her things down, but then I see her phone flashing with a text. It's Elli.

Shit.

Mom: You coming home tonight?

She sent it at twelve.

Shelli doesn't have a password, so I open her phone to the text.

Me: Hey, sorry. It was loud in the club. I'm staying the night at a friend's. I left my car at Brooks House.

Elli writes back right away.

Mom: Too much to drink?

Me: Yeah, sorry. I'll be home in the morning.

Mom: It's okay. Just remember to text me earlier next time. I've been worried.

Me: I'm really sorry.

Mom: I love you. Be safe.

Me: I love you and I am safe. Promise.

I swallow hard at the promise I just made in Shelli's name.

As I set her phone on the nightstand, I look down at her and know that it's true.

She is safe because she's with me.

I hook her phone up to the charger and then glance back at her once more. She's just so pretty. I trace her lips with my fingers before a smile comes over my lips. As sweet as she is, she's wild as all hell. She danced the night away and flirted relentlessly with everyone but me. Mostly because I was sulking in the corner. I wanted her to flirt with me. I wanted to be on the receiving end of those luscious lips.

Now, she's in my bed. Again.

And I'm going to sleep on the couch.

CHAPTER FIFTEEN

SHELLI

I'VE GOT COTTONMOUTH LIKE A BITCH.

My head is pounding.

And, ugh, I gotta pee.

As I smack my mouth, I sit up slowly and look around. The room is bare, with a lot of boxes by the bathroom, and a dresser is on the wall opposite the bed. This bed is huge too. I look to my left, and there is my phone and a tall glass of water. I reach for the water and gulp it quickly. I don't finish it, thankfully, because I notice two white pills.

"Oh, praise God."

I take the pills even with my mom nagging in my head that I shouldn't take strange pills. *Sorry, Mom. I've done worse.* But the real question is, where the hell am I? I put down the glass and reach for my phone. I open it to find no texts or even calls. That's so weird; my mom should be losing her mind since I forgot to text her. I open her thread to find someone has already texted her.

Me: I love you and I am safe. Promise.

Well, that's good to know. Maybe I'm at Wes's? I go to get out of the bed, but then my phone rings. I look down to see it's Amelia.

"Hello?" I ask in a hushed whisper since I don't want anyone to know I'm awake.

"Why are we whispering?" she whispers, and I close my eyes to shield them from the sunlight.

"I don't know where I am."

"I'm sorry, what?"

"I went out last night, got shitfaced, and now I don't know where I am. I'm in someone's bed, and my panties are still in place."

"You live a sketchy life, Shelli Grace Adler."

I scoff. "No, I just don't think things through."

"Who did you go out with?"

"The guys...and Aiden."

She tsks at me. "Are you at Aiden's? Are you sure your panties are in place?"

I nod as I lift my skirt again. "Totally, and I don't feel like I had sex. Oh my God, I sound like such a whore. I am never drinking again."

"I agree with that statement."

"So, I do sound like a whore?"

"Well, maybe not a whore, but definitely someone who doesn't make terribly thought-out decisions."

"I'm not Posey!" I snap, and she laughs. "God, I can't believe I don't know where I am."

"What in the world were you doing? Why did you get so drunk?"

I shrug. "I don't know. I was trying to impress Aiden. He told me to slow down, and I wanted him to be impressed with my drinking skills."

"You know how ridiculous that sounds, right?"

"I am aware, thank you." I hear movement behind the door. "Someone is here."

"Probably the person who lives there," she says dryly.

"I'll call you later."

"Please do, so I know you're alive. Plus, I'd love to know whose house you're at. The suspense is killing me."

"You and me both, sister," I say before I hang up quickly. I move my hands through my hair and pull it up into a bun with the hair tie at my wrist. I hope I look okay. Not like a hungover, drunken mess. Oh! There is a bathroom. I head toward it, and I notice that a towel and a toothbrush have been laid out. Yeah, this has to be Wes's place. Only he would go out of his way to make sure I'm comfortable. We did the same for him when he would come to stay with us when we were younger. A little grin sits on my face. That's really nice of him. I brush my teeth and then clean my face free of my makeup. Once I look presentable, I head out and then to the bedroom door.

I pull it open just as someone knocks on it.

That someone being Aiden.

"Oh!"

He jumps in surprise as he takes a step back. His gaze moves along my body so damn slowly before he says, "I was coming to check on you."

"Oh, I'm good," I say quickly, and of course, I'm practically knocked on my ass by how hot he is. He's wearing some basketball shorts and a fitted purple Assassins tee. His hair is in a high ponytail, and he has the sexiest five-o'clock shadow on his angular jaw. "Why are you here?"

His brows quirk. "I live here."

"Oh," I say slowly as I look around. Everything is in boxes, but in the corner is a sleek black piano that I remember from New York. Yup, this isn't Wes's place. "You brought me here?"

"I didn't want to take you home and wake your parents."

I nod. "Did you text my mom?"

"Yeah, and you really should put a password on your phone."

"Yeah, I'm lazy," I say softly as I twist my fingers together. I didn't expect this from him. He made it very clear he didn't want anything to do with me last night. No matter how hard I flirted, he rejected me left and right. I don't know why he brought me home or even cared to leave me water or aspirin. Heat and something else flush through me in abundance as I gaze up into his face. His lips are parted, his eyes kind, and it reminds me of when we were younger. When he used to be the oldest of everyone, making sure we were okay. He was always nice when he didn't have to be. Really, I shouldn't be surprised he was the one to take me home. Yet I am, especially after everything that's happened. "Um, thanks for taking care of me."

"No problem. Listen, I had to take Wes and Boon back to their cars, and we grabbed yours too."

Oh. He wants me to leave. Duh. "Oh, nice! Thanks. I'll get out of your hair."

I turn on my heels and feel him watching me. "You don't have to. I made some food."

I shake my head. He's just being civil. "No, it's cool. I've overstayed my welcome. I'll go."

"It's not like that at all," he says as I quickly grab my stuff, yanking my phone off the charger before heading back toward him. "Really, I'd like—"

"I gotta get home. I have to help set up the party and stuff and then shower. And yeah, I gotta go." I move past him and notice my key on his bar. I grab it and see a plate of bacon. "You cook?"

He moves a piece of hair out of his face. "I'm the oldest of four. I had to feed those heathens."

"I didn't think you cooked."

"I do, and you should stay."

Before he even finishes what he is saying, I shake my head. "I really can't. Sorry." I grab a handful of bacon, and then I see the French toast. I take two pieces and make a sandwich. "For the road."

He looks annoyed. "Of course."

"Yeah, so um..." I say, walking backward. "Thanks again."

"Like I said, it's no problem."

I flash him a grin. "Yeah, thanks."

I reach for the door and pull it open, but my name from his lips stops me. "Hey, Shelli."

I look over my shoulder at him. "Yeah?"

He looks unsure and, damn it, super adorable. "I had fun last night."

Shit. I press my lips together. "Did we sleep together?"

He scoffs, shaking his head. "No. We don't have to sleep together to have fun. I meant at the club."

"Oh," I say softly, my face warming. "You hardly spoke to me."

He shrugs. "I don't know. I didn't know how to act."

I squint at him. "Like yourself?"

He chuckles softly. "Yeah, I'll try that next time."

I squish up my face. "Probably didn't help I was so drunk. Sorry. I feel like an idiot, drinking like that."

He shrugs. "Hey, we were having fun."

"You're not hungover."

He smiles. "I don't think drinking is my jam anymore."

"No?"

He slowly shakes his head, his gray eyes bright today and set on me. "Nah, last time I was drunk, I slept with a girl who deserved way more than I gave her."

My heart jumps up into my throat as our gazes stay locked.

I open my mouth and wait for something to come out. Something witty and maybe a bit sassy, but all I hear is my phone ringing. I tear my gaze from his to look down at my phone. "It's my mom."

His lips quirk at the side, and heat swirls in his eyes. "Guess you'd better answer."

"Yeah, see you later. Thanks again."

"See you," he says as I go out the door. When it shuts, I lean on it as I answer my mom.

When, really, all I want is to go back in there and have breakfast with Aiden.

❦

IT'S AS IF MOM AND FALLON WANT TO RUIN MY LIFE.

Or kill me with embarrassment.

All around the living room are blown-up pictures on easels of Aiden and me as kids through the years. There is a picture of me in a swim diaper as Aiden sprays me with water. There is one of him and me playing hockey. There is another of us at one of the Cup finals and then just random photos. It's mostly him, and in them, I'm staring at him like the love-sick child I was. There is even a photo of us when I was just born. He's holding me close to his chest and grinning down at me like I'm the sweetest little thing in the world.

Pathetic thing is, I wish he'd look at me like that now. I still can't believe he brought me to his home last night and took care of me. It's something the Aiden I grew up with would do. But the Aiden I've been dealing with lately...I wouldn't expect that. I'm pretty sure when he gets here, though, and sees this pitiful display, he'll stay real clear of me. If a normal, sane person came over, they'd think this was an engagement party instead of an "Oh! Our firstborns are home!" celebration. It's outrageously idiotic and so humiliating.

But I guess no one notices. The party is in full swing. Everyone is here. Past and current Assassins. It's good to see Erik and his wife, Piper, with their two kids. Katrina is as stunning as Piper, with her glass-like blue eyes, and Dmitri is huge. Phillip and Reese are here too, and Flynn and Sawyer are as tall as Phillip. It's kind of crazy. I grew up with all these people, and we're all old now. When Jordie Thomas comes through the door with his wife, Kacey, tight in his arms, I grin.

"Kace!"

Kacey, who is whoa-pregnant, waves as we hug tightly. I used to work out with her all the time, but then she got pregnant and decided to take a break. I grab her belly as Ella, their daughter, runs past us to go play with the other kids. "He's gonna be here soon, right? Like real soon?"

"A week or two," she gushes as Jordie, her magnificent husband, kisses her temple. He's got the sexiest beard I've ever seen, and he's all rugged and rough. He also just celebrated ten years clean. It's amazing, and we're all still so proud of him.

"I think she'll pop next week," Karson King, her brother, says as he comes in with his younger daughter, Rose, on his back, his eldest, Mena Jane, running in and around him to get to the backyard. His wife, Lacey, walks with their son, Braden. "And who has a kid damn near ten years after the other is beyond me."

Kacey gives him a dark look as Lacey laughs. "It's called a surprise."

Jordie holds up his hands, waving them. "Surprise!"

Everyone but Kacey laughs, and I hug her once more. "Either way, you're gorgeous as always."

"You're a good girl, Shelli."

Soon my mom's voice is carrying through the room, and they walk toward her. I go to shut the door when Jayden Sinclair blocks me. "Whoa, coming in."

Baylor, his wife, comes in first and grins happily at me. "I can't get over how pretty you are! Welcome home."

I hug her and then Jayden. "Thanks! Where are the boys?"

"We left them with my brother Jude and his wife, Claire. They're practicing since they should be getting their new baby soon. I think the adoption is almost final. Right, Bay?"

Baylor nods. "Almost. We're so excited for them!"

"I am too, but they should have come. I love Claire. She used to watch me."

"It was a surprise they came in. They didn't want to impose."

I wave her off. "Tell them to come if they want! Bring your boys. We have plenty of food and drinks."

Jayden grins. "I will."

I once again try to shut the door, but again, someone blocks it. "Are we not welcome?"

Ugh. Benji Paxton. While Aiden was my for-real crush, Benji was the guy everyone was in love with. He is by far the nicest and kindest man I've ever met. "Of course you are!"

He hugs me tightly. "I cannot believe you're twenty-one and we're having a party welcoming you home from being on Broadway. You've done big things, Shelli."

I beam up at him. He's so much hotter with his dusting of gray. "Thanks, Coach," I say with a wink, and he grins. He helped coach the pee wee hockey team I played on with his daughter Angie.

"Where are Angie and Lucy?"

He shakes his head. "They're off in Kentucky, doing tours for college. They left me with the twins," he says, and just like that, their twin eight-year-olds, Max and Ryder, run past me. "I'm not sure the boys'll be alive before those two get back. Charlotte's with Autumn and River this weekend for some peace and quiet. I'm jealous."

I laugh as I pat his arm. "You're silly. Go have fun, grab a soda. The boys will be distracted for a while."

"Great. Good seeing you. Welcome home."

"Thanks," I gush, and I watch as he walks away. Lucy Paxton is one lucky woman. I let out a long sigh before I go to shut the door once more, and again, it's blocked. "That's it. It can stay open for—"

My words fall off when I see Aiden gazing back at me. He looks delicious in a pair of fitted maroon slacks and a black button-up. He wears an adorable maroon bow tie, and his hair is down, curly and luscious. "Oh."

He tips his lips up at the side. "Hey, Shelli."

Fire fills my gut in seconds. "Hey."

"You look really good," he says, and my heart jackhammers in my chest. I'm just wearing a simple maxi dress, but under his gaze, I feel like I'm in a ball gown.

"Thanks. You too. I like the bow tie."

He grins as he reaches into his pocket. "You left this."

He hands over my ID and money, and I sigh with relief. "I thought I'd lost them!"

"Nope, they were in my bed," he says, and when our gazes meet, both our faces are flushed with color.

He swallows hard, and I look away. "I thought I had tucked them in my bra well."

"Yeah, I didn't feel them when I grabbed your phone and key."

I look up at him with a sneaky grin. "You grabbed my phone and key?"

Aiden's face reddens even more. "In the most respectful way," he promises, and I flash him a wide grin. "I really didn't want you to get stabbed by your key or get cancer from your phone. But I didn't feel your other stuff, and I wasn't digging. Didn't trust myself."

He didn't mean to say that last part; I can see it all over his face. But for me, it sets butterflies free in my belly. He coughs. "Yeah, I'm gonna go find my mom."

He walks past me, but I reach out, taking his wrist without really thinking. Heat runs up my arm as our eyes meet. "Thanks again."

He turns his hand so I lose my grip and then laces his fingers with mine, his thumb moving along the back of my hand. It takes my breath away. In a low, very dangerous voice, he says, "It was a pleasure."

He squeezes my hand and then walks away. He doesn't get far before everyone is on him, welcoming him home and telling him how proud they are of him.

Me, I can't move because I just realized there might be no getting over Aiden Brooks.

CHAPTER SIXTEEN

SHELLI

THE PARTY IS IN FULL SWING. EVERYONE IS DRINKING, LAUGHING, and having a great time. I walk through the living room, chitchatting and enjoying everyone's company. It's almost like a party from when I was younger. The team family is here, and it's nice. I thought this was going to be awful, but it's actually kind of fun. I pick up cups as I head toward the kitchen. For some reason, I always need to clean when there is a mess. I don't know why, but it drives me crazy. With over fifty people in the house, it's gotten messy in a hurry.

As I gather things, I head to the kitchen, passing by Aiden. While I haven't talked to him the whole time, I always know where he is. I don't know if it's some kind of sixth sense or what, but every time I look around, I see him. Man, it's hard to act like he isn't the most gorgeous thing in the room.

And he's standing with some very fine men. Even in their late forties, they're hot as all hell. I can only hope my future husband ages like these men have. While some are rocking that hot dad bod, some are still fit as ever. Like yummy Benji. I'm still so jealous of his wife, and he's more than twenty years older than me. Hmm, maybe I need help with my older men thing. I don't even know where it comes from.

Probably my ridiculous crush on Aiden.

I bite my lip as I drink him in. He looks so good in those damn pants. His ass is so tight. I'd bounce a quarter off that sucker in a heartbeat. A sneaky little grin pulls at my lips at the thought of doing just that. Or seeing it again. I sigh deeply as I hear my mom's voice.

"Shelli, honey, come in here."

I stand up, throwing a paper plate in the trash before I head to where my mom is standing by the piano with Karson King, Fallon, and Aiden. I twist my fingers together as I rock back on my heels. "Yeah?"

"Karson never got to see you on Broadway."

I glance to him. "Sorry?"

He laughs as Mom smacks my hand playfully. "So, sing for us."

My shoulders fall. "Now?"

"Now," she says with a grin.

"Shelli, please do *Frozen*," Emery begs, and Mena Jane nods eagerly.

I want to groan, fall on my face, and die. "Please do not make me."

"I love *Frozen*," Aiden says, and I glare.

"Oh, you do?"

"Biggest fan ever. Especially for Elsa. She's hot."

My mom laughs. "That's who Shelli played."

His eyes widen in mock surprise, but when he looks back at me, there is nothing but heat in those gray eyes. "No way."

Fallon shakes her head. "I told you that you should have gone."

"Yes! She had this awful white-blond wig. She didn't even look like herself," Mom says, and the look that comes across Aiden's face irks me.

"You don't say. A wig, hiding someone's identity."

I glare. "Yes, but anyone who knows me, knew it was me."

"Well, of course. It's your eyes." Fallon cups my jaw. "So blue and so pretty."

I almost stick my tongue out at Aiden, but Emery pulls me to the piano, and I laugh as I sit down. I move my fingers along the keys, and soon the melody to a song from the popular Disney movie starts. "For the First Time in Forever" is my all-time favorite to sing. I know more people are fans of "Let It Go," but "For the First Time in Forever" is where the magic is. As my voice carries, singing both parts, all the kids gather around. Soon, they're singing along, even the adults, and it feels just like it did onstage. I get that rush of excitement, that tingling feeling in my gut, and I feel good. There is no pressure on being perfect either; I can just do it because I love it. When I finish, the room erupts, and all the girls ask for more.

"Oh guys, I'm so *Frozen*ed out."

"Then sing something else," Emery begs. "Anything."

I smile as I think of what to do next. I bite my lip as I look up, my gaze finding Aiden's. His lips are tilted in a sneaky grin, and I wonder what he's thinking. Is he thinking of that night? I am. Soon my fingers are moving again, playing the beautiful, stunning melody to the candle-light mix of Cascada's "Everytime We Touch." It's one of my favorite songs, and when my voice fills the room, a hush falls over the crowd. The lyrics flow out of me, and I feel each word in my soul. When I look up, Aiden is leaning on the piano, a peaceful look on his face.

Does he know I'm singing for him?

My eyes fall shut as I hit the high notes, and when I strike the last key, my voice carries on. Everyone claps once more, and I stand up, bowing obnoxiously. "And now, for the next show, Aiden will be outside doing stick and puck tricks."

Everyone laughs, but I notice Aiden doesn't. Instead, he's staring at me like it's the first time he's seeing me. It brings on such a rush, one greater than the one I felt when I was singing. I swallow hard as I walk around the piano toward the kitchen for a beer. I reach into the cooler, and when I turn, he's there.

"Oh."

"I really like listening to you," he says, his body so big next to mine.

I'm a tad bashful as I gaze up at him, popping the top off my beer. "Thanks."

"That song was beautiful."

"It's one of my favorites."

He opens his mouth, and I don't know what he is about to say before my mom yells, "Aw! Look, they're finally standing beside each other. Kids, turn and hug. Let me get a picture."

I look back at my mom. "No way. You're gonna blow it up and add it to the rest of that embarrassment out there."

"So? That's the point," Fallon says as she holds up her phone. "Do it now. We supplied beer."

I glance up at Aiden, and he looks uncomfortable. "Mom, he doesn't want to hug me. We're like—"

"I don't mind," he says then, pulling me in close to his chest. His hip presses into my hot center as my hand comes up on his chest. I look up at him as he looks down at me with those naughty hooded eyes of his.

"Oh."

"Aw! You two look like a couple," Fallon gushes. "Isn't that sweet?"

"It is. Remember when Shelli had the biggest crush on Aiden?"

I go cold. "Mom, oh my God, take the picture."

"Yes! She used to write in her journal and chase him around. She was so cute," Fallon laughs. "Aiden had no clue she was so in love with him."

"Hey, two feet between you two. What are you doing?" my dad barks. And please, anyone, kill me.

"Dad! We're taking a picture!" I yell, and he shakes his head.

"No way. He's a boy," he says sternly, and of course, Aiden takes a good step away from me. This is awesome.

"Yes, Dad, and I touch boys. Hell, I've kissed boys—"

"Ah! Elli, make her stop. The angina!" My overdramatic dad grabs his chest with one hand and the counter with the other.

Mom sets me with a look. "Really, Shelli. You know he can't handle that."

"I'm twenty-one! Have you had the talk with him?"

Dad's eyes widen before he looks back at me. "What talk?"

"Nothing, sweetheart," she says, waving him off. But then she glares back at me. "I haven't had time."

"Mom! It's been damn near six years!"

She points to my dad. "The angina, Shelli."

"Oh my God, you guys are insane. What are you going to do when I get married and have kids? Do you know where kids come from? Sex, Dad—"

"Angina! Elli! Angina!"

"For the love of Pete," Mom complains. "Why do you mess with your father like that? Is this because I said you had a crush on Aiden?"

I throw my hands up. "I did not!"

"Oh, you so did," Lucas adds. "Didn't I see her write 'Shelli Brooks' on her skin as a tattoo?"

Mom laughs while my dad bends over the counter as if he's having a heart attack. "She did! It was so cute. But, honey," she says, going to my dad. "It's okay, she is a good girl. No boys."

I can't even look at Aiden right now. I am completely mortified. I turn on my heel and head out of the room in a huff. I hear my mom and Fallon laughing and trying to call me back, but they can all go to hell. Who brings up something from ten years ago? Especially when the guy is right there! And I slept with him like a month ago! No one has respect for me in this house. I head down the hall to my room, going in and slamming the door behind me. I feel the tears burning in my eyes, but there is no way I will let them fall. So what? He knows I had a crush on him. Doesn't mean anything.

When I hear a TV, I walk into my bathroom and through it to see that it's in Posey's room. I go to turn it off when I realize there are people watching it.

Posey and Maxim.

In bed, watching TV. Mighty close.

Posey looks at me with wide eyes and looks back at the TV as she yells, "We're just watching TV."

"Yeah, I know. But I'm gonna shut my door. It's loud."

She nods quickly as she tries to put space between Maxim and herself. Maxim, though, is fully engrossed in the movie with no cares that I am there or how close Posey is. She's two seconds from strad-dling him. Does he really not realize my sister digs him? What an idiot.

I shut her door and head back into my room. I don't even want to go back out to the party. Not only did Aiden hear all that, but he saw how ridiculous my dad acted. I'm twenty-one. What does he expect? This is entirely my mom's fault. She was supposed to talk to my dad about me having sex after I lost my virginity. If Aiden didn't see me as a kid before, he sure as hell does now. I knew this party was going to be a shitshow.

When there is a knock at my door, I glare it at. "Go away."

It cracks open, and Aiden's head pops in. "Does that apply to me?"

I cross my arms over my chest, looking away. "Yes."

"Well, that's rude."

I roll my eyes. "What do you want?"

"Hey, I did nothing here. I was just trying to take a picture." I hear the door shut again, but I refuse to look at him. "Your dad is terrifyingly funny."

I scoff. "He's an idiot."

The silence stretches between us until, finally, he says, "So that's why when I kissed you, you didn't stop me."

I press my lips together. "I don't know what you're talking about."

"That night," he says, and when I see his outrageously expensive shoes, I close my eyes. "I couldn't figure out why you'd let me kiss you if you knew me, but you thought I was returning feelings you had."

"Could you not say that out loud? It makes me sound totally tragic."

"Is it true?"

I bite the inside of my cheek as I look up at him. His eyes are full of gentleness, leaving me breathless. "Is what true?"

"What I said?"

How the hell do I get out of this situation? I look away as I shrug. "I don't know."

"Shelli."

I lick my lips as I glance back up at him. "Yeah, I thought you knew who you were kissing and that you wanted me because maybe you liked me too."

"So, you like me?" His eyes are a tad playful, but he's serious.

"I may have at some point."

He moves closer, his hands gripping my hips. "And now?"

His head is dropping to mine, and slowly I tilt mine back. "Maybe."

Before the word can even escape my lips, his take over mine.

And I'm flying.

I wrap my arms around his neck as his go around my waist, holding me so close, I can feel his heart jackhammering against mine. He runs his tongue along my lips, and I instantly open for him, wanting the kiss to deepen. Because he knows who I am—and he wants to kiss me. The kiss is hot, wanton, and I want to wrap myself around him and not let go.

But, of course, there is a knock at my door.

"Shelli. Honey, come on out."

My dad's voice has us separating like two naughty teens caught trying to cop a feel during a movie.

Aiden's eyes are wide as I clear my throat. "I'm coming."

"Is the door locked—" Dad starts, but then he is coming in. I push Aiden back into my closet and kick off my shoe real fast. There is a loud bang from Aiden's body hitting the wall, but I play it off.

"Damn, I didn't mean to kick my shoes off that hard."

Dad looks at me, and I lean into the closet, rubbing my foot in my hand. "What are you doing?"

"Changing my shoes," I answer quickly.

He eyes me. "Your lipstick is smeared."

I cover my mouth. "I need to reapply it. I always mess it up when I'm singing."

"Oh, that's right. Are you okay? I'm sorry that your mom mentioned your little crush on Aiden. I don't think he cares. It was a cute thing about you when you were younger. He's way older, so he doesn't care."

I swallow hard. "Dad, I don't want to talk about this."

"It isn't like he would date you, honey. He's in his own world. Don't be upset."

"Dad, please stop."

He sighs deeply. "Fine, come on. Let's go get a beer, ignore your mom together."

"So I can drink without the angina acting up, but boys are out of the question?"

He looks at me dryly. "Yes."

I roll my eyes. "Let me change my shoes."

"You don't need them. Come on," he says, and then he grabs my wrist, but I pause.

"My lipstick."

He moves his thumb along my bottom lip and then gives me a warm smile. "As beautiful as ever."

I lean my head on his chest. "Thanks, Dad. Let's get out there."

Before you find the boy in my closet.

CHAPTER SEVENTEEN

AIDEN

I LEAN MY HEAD OVER THE BACK OF MY COUCH AS I EXHALE HEAVILY.

I run my hand over my bare chest and down into my open slacks. I can still feel Shelli's mouth on mine. I can also feel the sting of pain in my elbow from where she shoved me into the closet. For such a small girl, she sure does have some power. But damn if she isn't exquisite. The dress she wore today fit her perfectly. Even though it was flowy, her ass was unstoppable. The neckline dipped down in the front, showing off those perfect breasts of hers... Hot damn. There is something about her hair that makes me want to wrap it around my fist. I want to tip her head back, take her mouth with mine, and never stop.

I can't believe I kissed her. I don't know what got into me. Especially in her parents' house. It's like I wanted to get caught. That's not like me, but I couldn't resist. Her lips were so pink, her eyes so blue, and something about the fact that she thought I was returning feelings that night did something to my chest. I don't know. She does something to me.

When my phone rings, I look at it where it's vibrating on my coffee table. It's Asher. I lean forward and answer it before bringing it to my ear. "Hey, bro."

"Hey, how was your party?"

I scoff. "A fucking shitshow."

"I figured. I saw the pictures."

"It was so embarrassing."

He laughs. "Well, I had to call and say how adorable you and Shelli are. I mean, goodness me, you two need to be on a magazine," he says in a higher-pitched voice.

"You done?"

"Yeah, I guess. But for real, the picture was cute."

I bring in my brows. "Where did you see it?"

"Mom's Facebook."

I pull my phone away from my face, hitting speaker so I can look through Facebook. I go to my mom's page, and there it is—a damn good picture of Shelli and me. Like a lot of the other photos displayed in the house today, she's looking up at me so sweetly. This time, though, I'm looking down at her. Our moms were onto something; we do look like we're together.

"Well, that's a cozy pic."

"Very much so. Anyone who doesn't know you two would think you're together."

"That's what Mom and Elli said," I say as I save the picture. I'm not sure why I'm doing that, but I want it. "I kissed her tonight."

"No way. Tell me more," he teases, and I laugh.

"You're such a jackass," I accuse, and he laughs along with me. "I don't know what happened, really. Elli and Mom were saying how Shelli was in love with me when we were younger, and it all came together. That was why she didn't push me away when I kissed her in New York. She thought I was returning her feelings."

Asher clicks his tongue. "Damn, that's awful. No wonder she wasn't nice to you. You embarrassed the shit out of her."

"Yeah, I think that's why I kissed her this afternoon."

"Or you kissed her because you like her."

I shake my head. "I mean, I've always liked her. She's cool."

"Yeah, but I think you might have developed a little crush yourself."

"No way. I don't do that."

"Before. But maybe Shelli is different."

"Eh, I don't know," I say, leaning on my knees and moving my hand through my hair. My fingers get caught in my curls, but I welcome the pain. It's better than this ache I have in my chest. What the hell I'm aching for, who knows, but it's there.

"You know, every time we've talked, it's been about her."

"No, I called you about Dad."

"And that led into Shelli. Might need to wake up there, buddy, and notice what you got."

"I got nothing. I haven't even spoken to her. I kissed her, and then she pushed me into the closet and left. It felt like she avoided me the rest of the night."

"Probably because she likes you still and is scared you don't feel the same and that you think she's just a fuck."

My face squishes up. "Where the hell are you getting this shit from?"

He laughs. "When you left for New York, I had to deal with Stella and all her drama. Believe me, I know way more about girls than I want to, but in a way, it helps with my own relationship."

"Good for you," I grumble as I let my head fall back once more.

"You should call her."

"I don't have her number."

"I do," he says, and then my phones dings. "I sent it to you."

I close my eyes. "What would I even say?"

"'Hey, pretty lady, how's it going?'" he says in an even deeper voice.

"You're a really big dork, you know that?"

He scoffs. "Yeah, but at least I'm getting laid all the time and I don't have to have anyone set it up for me."

"Wow. Low blow."

"Yeah, you're right. But so am I." I laugh as he chuckles. "Call her."

"Eh, I don't know. I need to unpack."

"So call and do it while y'all chat."

"I don't even know what we'd talk about."

"Life? How our moms are out to embarrass the hell out of both of you."

I laugh. "Yeah, I don't know."

When a knock comes at my door, I look at it, confused. "Someone's at the door."

"Oh. Well, usually when that happens, you answer it."

I shake my head as I get up. "Bye, jackass."

"Bye."

I hang up, throwing my phone on my couch as I button my pants. I reach for the door, and when a pair of blue eyes meets mine, I can't seem to find my next breath.

Shelli gazes up at me, her eyes wide as she twists her fingers together. Her eyes move down my body as she takes in a deep breath, her lips parting. "I don't know why I'm here."

"I didn't ask," I say almost automatically. I don't care why she's here; I need to kiss her. I reach for her as she reaches for me, and our mouths meet in a heated assault. I slowly walk backward, pulling her with me before she kicks the door shut. I slide my hands down her back to her ass, cupping her sweet mounds in my palms. She arches into me, her tongue prodding my lips for entrance. I don't hesitate in deepening the kiss. She tastes like something sweet, an orange or something. I gather her dress in my hands before pulling it up and over her head. She stands in front of me in nothing but a thong and a barely there bra. I shake my head as I drop to my knees, kissing down her breasts as I unhook her bra. The cups fall, and I take one of her nipples in my mouth while my fingers tweak the other one.

Her sighs are soft and precious. She moves closer, her fingers tangling in my hair as I move to her other breast, taking that nipple in my mouth. I bite her softly, and the cry I'm rewarded with makes me harder than a frozen puck. I kiss along her stomach as I yank her thong down her thighs. Without another thought, I bury my mouth between her thick thighs like I've wanted to for days. She's wet for me, slick, and I want it all. I want her. She bucks against my mouth, her cries getting louder and much more aggressive as I sneak my tongue between her lips, finding her taut clit.

I suck her pussy in my mouth, open-mouth kissing it like there is nothing in the world I'd rather be doing. If I'm honest, there isn't. She tastes so damn good, perfect even, and when I lift her leg, throwing it over my shoulder, her body vibrates against my mouth. She holds on to my shoulders as I eat her ruthlessly. I can't get enough, and I want her to scream my name. I need her to scream it. I open her up with one hand and hold her ass with the other before I flick my tongue against her clit, fast and hard. She starts to rotate her hips against my mouth, and when she comes, she stills as my name falls from her lips in almost a whisper.

"Aw, come on. I know you're louder than that," I tease as I lap up her release. I kiss her thighs, her hip bone before dipping my tongue in her belly button. She leans against me as I slowly lower her to the floor. Now on her back, she gazes up at me as I stand, pulling my wallet out of my pants. I open it, getting a condom before throwing my wallet to the floor and tearing open the package quickly. I watch her. Her body is speckled with red marks, and a flush spreads down her chest as she gazes up at me. I undo my pants and kick them off. I shove my boxers down before sheathing myself with a shaky hand.

"Look at you, remembering a condom."

I wink at her. "There is no way I wouldn't be prepared for you."

"Or anyone else," she says, her eyes dark as they hold mine.

"I haven't wanted anyone but you."

Her lips tip up. "Well, that's a very hot thing to say."

"It's the fucking truth," I say before I drop to my knees, grab her by the back of hers, and pull her to me. She giggles as I direct myself inside her, and then the giggles stop as the most beautiful moan leaves her naughty mouth. I push into her to the hilt, and she wraps her legs around my waist. I fall against her, my hands on either side of her as I take her mouth once more. She squeezes me with her hot pussy, sending wild chills through my body. I can't get enough of her kisses, but I also want so badly to come inside her.

I lift up, thrusting into her with more force each time. She holds on with her legs but props herself up with her elbows to meet my mouth once more. She draws the kisses out of me—her mouth is so damn dangerous, it has me on the edge. I tear my mouth from hers. "You keep on like that, I won't be able to wait for you."

She flashes me a sexy little grin. "Let me be on top."

"Yes, ma'am," I say as I pull out of her, but she's already pushing me back onto the floor. My legs come out from underneath me as she straddles me, taking my cock in her hand before she positions it for her sweet spot. When her ass hits my thighs, I feel my eyes roll to the back of my head.

Hot. Fucking. Damn.

She starts to move her sweet pussy up and down my cock so slowly, my toes start to curl. She's so tight, so fucking hot, and I can't handle her. She presses her hands into my chest, and her head falls back as she gyrates her hips up and down, her ass smacking against my thighs. I grip her ass, spreading her cheeks as she cries out, her pussy squeezing me. I dig my fingers into her ass as I thrust up into her, my release right there. I open my eyes just in time to see her come, her face flushed, her eyes squeezing shut as she shatters on my cock.

I've never seen anything more beautiful.

I follow almost immediately, jerking inside her as she falls onto my chest. Her hair covers my face as I bring my arms around her waist, holding her against me as our hearts beat in time. All I see is stars behind my lids, but my body is on fire against hers. I move my nose along her hair, drawing in her scent before whispering, "Hey."

I feel her smile against my chest. "Hey."

I find myself smiling back. "Well, I'm glad you didn't know why you came over."

She kisses the middle of my chest before lifting her head to look at me. "I knew damn well why I came over."

Her lips curve, and her face is so beautifully flushed that my heart skips a fucking beat. I thought that was a saying, but I swear I feel it. I cup her face before pressing my lips to her bottom one. "I knew too."

"I know," she says against my lips. "So, shall we take this to the bedroom?"

"If you want."

"Oh, I want to."

"Me too."

She sits up before getting up to her feet, standing stunningly naked in front of me. "Maybe you'll scream my name this time," she says with a wink.

"Oh, angel, there is no way I won't."

When she flashes me that sly grin, I notice the ache in my chest is gone.

It doesn't mean anything.

But I notice it's gone.

As if it's been replaced.

With Shelli's fire.

CHAPTER EIGHTEEN

SHELLI

I LIE ON AIDEN, MY FACE ON HIS THICK, STRONG CHEST AS HIS HAND strokes up and down my spine. His other hand holds my ass, his fingers biting into my skin. Our legs are tangled together, and his lips are in my hair.

I feel absolutely amazing.

My body is humming with all the tenderness and affection he gave me the night before. We didn't go at it like we did that first night; this time was different. We did it three times and then slept. He's a cuddler, and I find that adorable. Even if it is like sleeping with a volcano, there is no way I'm breaking apart from him. Maybe I'm a cuddler too. With the right person.

"You have no tattoos?" I ask, kissing his pec.

"Nope," he whispers, his voice low and raspy.

It makes me wet in all the right places.

"Why not?"

"Scared to death of needles."

I grin. "But your dad has a ton."

"True. I don't think you remember this—you were a baby—but I broke my arm. They shoved this fucking needle the size of the earth in my arm, and it ruined me."

I try not to giggle, especially with how fast his heart is beating. "That's unfortunate. You'd be hot with them."

"Shit, I'm already hot."

"Oh Lord, tuck the ego back in, Brooks. I wasn't taking a hit at it."

He kisses my hair as he squeezes my ass. "I like yours."

"My ego or tattoos?"

"Both."

I lift up my head, lightly pressing my chin into the middle of his chest as I look up at his gorgeous face. His hair is all over the place, and his eyes are all dark and sultry. "Well, thanks. The Assassins one is my favorite."

"Mine too, but that butterfly on your ass is quite nice."

"It's on my thigh."

He raises a brow. "All I see is ass, baby."

I roll my eyes, but then he lifts up, capturing my mouth with his. I lean into the kiss, needing it. Wanting it. Craving it. When we part, he kisses the side of my mouth and then my jaw before nuzzling my neck. I bite my lip as he rolls us over, hugging me close to him. I hook my leg over his hip, and he grabs it, squeezing my thigh in his large hand. He runs his tongue up my neck and down my jaw before softly biting my chin.

With his nose against the side of my mouth, he whispers, "I thought you were mad at me last night."

I glide my lips along his forehead. "No, I was embarrassed."

"Because of your dad?"

"Yeah," I say softly. "I thought you would think I was pathetic."

"I didn't. I know your dad. I know you. He's a nut."

I smile. "Yeah, but he's annoying sometimes."

"Aren't all parents?"

I kiss his eyebrow as he gathers me close to him. "Did you want to talk to me?"

"You're the only one I wanted to talk to, Shelli."

"Then why didn't you?"

"I don't know."

I want to roll my eyes, but I don't want to ruin this moment. He's so unsure of himself when it comes to me. If he would just communicate what he is feeling or thinking, things would be a hell of a lot easier. "Were you scared of my dad?"

He sighs. "Shelli, I'm terrified of your parents. I don't even know what we're doing, to be honest."

I swallow hard as I trail my fingers along his chest. "Why do we have to know? Why can't we just enjoy what we have?"

He gathers me closer. "I don't want to hurt you."

"Then don't."

His eyes burn into mine. "I don't know what I'm doing."

"No one said you had to."

He kisses my nose. "Okay."

"Okay," I say softly, kissing his top lip.

"I hate to say this—"

"No, don't!" I complain, and he smiles against my lip.

"I gotta go. I have to be at the rink in thirty minutes."

"Ugh. Can't you call out?"

He bites my jaw again. "While it is optional, I want to make a good impression."

I nod. "Yeah, I guess."

"Plus, my linemates are going."

"Fine."

"Don't hate me."

"I don't," I draw out as I grab his jaw in my hand. "But if I had balls, they'd be blue."

His face lights up with laughter. "I can relieve you when I get back."

"Really?"

"Yeah."

"So, you want me to wait?"

He kisses my top lip. "Yeah."

"Okay," I say as my face breaks into a grin. He wants me to stay!

He kisses me once more before rolling off me. "There's food in the fridge. I should be back after lunch."

"Okay."

He looks back at me as he gets up, grabbing some clothes. "Don't judge me. I'm going to shower at the rink."

"No judgment, but I'm showering here."

He nods. "I think your toothbrush is still under the sink."

"Cool," I say. Oh my God! We sound like a couple. A sweet, adorable, sexy couple.

After he dresses quickly, he comes back to the bed, beckoning me to him. I rise up on my knees as he takes me by the back of the head, his fingers threading into my hair before he covers my mouth with his. His lips feel absolutely amazing against mine, and my whole body feels as if it's on fire from within. Like it always does when he touches me. He pulls away, his eyes burning into mine. "I'm really glad you're staying."

"Me too."

"But if you leave, text me."

"I'm not."

His lips quirk. "Then I'll see you in a bit."

He smacks my ass, and I giggle as I sit back on my haunches. "Bye."

"Bye, angel."

And the whole "angel" thing is probably as adorable as his cuddling! I fall back on the bed as I stretch my arms over my head, feeling spent. I don't want to move. I'm pretty sure no one could ever take this grin off my face. When he shuts the door, I let out a long sigh. Aiden just left, but he wants me to stay. Here. To wait for him. I never in my wildest dreams thought this would happen. I wanted it to happen, but I truly thought he was going to leave me in the fuck zone for a while. But not after last night and this morning.

Nope, we're heading straight for relationship-ville. *Eek!*

When my phone rings, I reach for it off the nightstand to see that it's my friend Nico. My lips curve as I answer. "Hey you."

His rugged voice fills the line. "Hey there, beautiful. How's it going?"

"It's going good. How about you?"

"Real good if you say you'll have dinner with me tonight."

My brows pull in. "We don't play y'all until tomorrow."

"Chandler and I came in a day early to have dinner with Amelia's mom since she can't be here with the new coaching job. Plus, a bunch of the guys like hanging out in Nashville."

"Well, it's the best city, so duh."

"Agreed, and it holds the hottest girl I know."

I grin widely as I roll onto my back.

"So, what do you say? Dinner tonight?"

I lick my lips. I don't know what Aiden would think. It's not like we've said we're exclusive, but I don't want to mess up that possibility. "I gotta work tonight."

"After, then. Late dinner. Maybe take you back to my place."

I grin. "I done told you many times now, that's over. We're friends."

He groans loudly. "One more time."

"That's what you said last time!"

"I mean it. One last time, and then I'll never ask again. I miss you, Shell. So damn much."

I roll my eyes. "You miss the way I give head."

"So fucking bad."

I laugh. "No, Nico. Plus, I'm kinda seeing someone."

"Ugh. That lucky fucker."

I giggle. "He is," I say, and then I bite my lip. "Let me tell him I'm having dinner with a *friend* tonight and see how he takes it."

"Fine, but know I'm terribly jealous."

"You shouldn't be."

"But I am. See you tonight. Send me the address of the bar you're working at."

"Will do."

We hang up, and I exhale heavily. In another world, another place, Nico would be a great guy to be with. But he isn't the guy I want. Great lay but terribly self-absorbed. He only likes me because I can tell him how great he is on the ice. I shake my head and get out of bed, passing by all the boxes of Aiden's stuff as I head to the bathroom. There are more boxes in here, and it makes me itch. I hate clutter, and I know Aiden's been here long enough to unpack. I don't know what he is waiting for, but it's driving me nuts.

I brush my teeth and then shower quickly. I put on my dress from last night without my bra and panties. I have some workout stuff in the truck I could go get, but I would like to be naked when he gets home. Work him as hard as he worked it on the ice. I need food, though. I ignore the boxes as I walk to the living room, but then I'm met with more boxes. The need to scratch my itch gets greater. Why hasn't he unpacked? He has been so busy, but why haven't Fallon or Stella and Emery come over to help? Maybe he hasn't asked.

Then an idea dawns on me.

I can unpack his stuff and have it done before he gets home. I remember how he had his place decorated in New York. I can do this, no problem. I can also cook a great lunch. He would love it. It would blow him away, and he'd have no choice but to fall head over heels in love with me.

I'm a great lay, a great cook, and my organization skills put Marie Kondo to shame!

⚜

I'M FRYING CHICKEN WHEN AIDEN COMES THROUGH THE DOOR. Music blares from the speaker in the kitchen, 5SOS singing their latest banger. I only had short shorts and a bra in my bag, but I doubt he'll mind. I sure didn't mind because it was easy to get his unpacking done. It took me a moment to get started since I had to find his tools and then develop a system, but once I began, no one could stop me. I grin over at him as he drops his bag to the floor, his eyes not on me but everywhere else. I turn off the music and shut off the stove as I hold out my hands.

"Surprise."

He still isn't looking at me. Aiden's eyes are locked on where I hung his two badass guitars by his piano. In the middle is that weird art he likes, but it does bring the whole area together. I put together his bookshelf that I'm pretty sure he got from IKEA. Damn thing took an hour to assemble. I put his books on it, along with a bunch of pictures of his family. Everything is exactly where it was in New York.

"Before you think I'm weird, I pay real close attention to detail."

He swallows hard. "You don't say." Aiden finally looks at me. "So, you were bored?"

"No, I wanted to do this for you," I say, coming around the bar. "I love this kind of stuff, and it bugged me you hadn't unpacked. I don't like clutter."

"I haven't had time."

I wave him off, trying to ignore the furrow of his brow and the way his lips are pressed together. "I get it. I totally don't mind." I go to him, kissing his mouth. "Hey."

His eyes meet mine, and I don't think he likes what I did. But he hasn't seen the closets yet. "Hey."

"Come on," I say, lacing my fingers with his. We walk into his office, and I show him where I stored the boxes in case he still needs them. I unpacked all his memorabilia from his years with the New York teams, and then I cleaned up his computer area and hooked everything up. "It's all ready to use."

He doesn't say anything, just looks around as I take him to the spare bath. "I didn't really do much in here but hang the shower curtain and store the toilet paper. I also bought these little beige hand towels, but if you don't like them, I can take them back."

He blinks as he steps out and heads to his room.

"Oh! I can't wait for you to see the closet," I gush as I walk past him and head to the closet. I open it with my hands out. "Amazing, right?"

He walks in, his eyes wide. "It's all separated by color?"

"Yes and no. So these are all your suits, and I think I matched the right shoes with them on this side, and then here are all your regular clothes, in order by color. Then back there is all your workout gear. In the drawers are underwear and socks. All your shoes are up on the racks, but I can move them down here."

He doesn't say anything. He just turns to look around the room. "I'm not supposed to think it's weird that you remember my place back in New York, right?"

"Right. We are ignoring that."

He swallows hard again. "Okay."

"I unpacked all your bathroom stuff and put it away," I say, moving my hand toward the bathroom, but then I start out the door. I feel as if I'm rambling, and if I am, it's because he doesn't seem very impressed by my amazing organization skills. My mom says I'm a genius, and I need Aiden to realize that before I start feeling like a weirdo. I bite the inside of my cheek and try to ignore the warning signs in my head that Aiden has decided I'm a freak. "I put away all your kitchen stuff, but I noticed you only had plastic plates—which, you're almost thirty, you need real plates. I went to Pottery Barn and picked out this gorgeous set," I say, going over to the bar and holding up one of the plates. "It's a housewarming gift." His brow is still furrowed, and his arms are now crossed over his chest. I lick my lips to keep from freaking out. "I made my mom's famous fried chicken and mashed potatoes for lunch. I know you like her sweet tea, so I made some. I know it's not very health conscious like your mom has been cooking, but I figured, why not?"

"Thanks, I guess."

"You guess?"

He shrugs as he looks around. "It's just a lot."

"A lot?" I ask, breaking down each syllable.

He meets my gaze and nods. "You unpacked my whole apartment, and you remembered what my other place looked like. That's weird."

"I thought we weren't discussing that."

"Shelli, it's hard not to. I didn't expect this. I thought you'd be waiting for me naked and we'd go at it some more. Not for you to completely unpack and cook for me. I didn't ask you to do this."

I bite the inside of my cheek as my heart pounds in my chest. "I know. I did it to be nice."

"It's weird."

"It is not!"

"Shelli, you put away my underwear. Bought towels for my bathroom. It's all very intimate."

I make a face. It is, but I'm not admitting that. "It's not like we don't know each other. We grew up together. It's different for me. Maybe after a first date with a girl that you don't know, yes, this would seem way out of line. But I helped pack you to move you to New York. I know you."

He holds his hands up, moving them around his head frantically. "Wait. What first date?"

Now my brow is furrowed. "Last night."

"We had sex."

I am pretty sure there is steam coming out of my ears.

"Shelli, come on. Don't look at me like that."

"Like what?" I sneer.

"Like you're about to throw that plate at me."

I let go of the plate and take a step back. "Tell me something, Aiden. What are we doing?"

"What are we doing?" he asks incredulously. "You said we didn't have to know what we're doing!"

"That was when I thought you liked me."

"I do like you."

"Then why are you being weird?"

"Shelli, we fucked last night, and I thought we would today. Thought we'd order in and then go at it some more. But I come home to this madness—"

I blink back the tears. "Madness?"

"Yeah, it's a lot to digest. No one has ever done this for me."

"And if it were Stella or your mom who did this?"

He makes a face. "They're my family. You're you."

"Which is?" I ask, and his mouth just opens, no words coming out. I see the panic in his eyes. I want to feel sorry for him, but the proof is in the pudding. "That's right—just a fuck."

I blow out a breath and walk around the bar as he says, "Shelli, that is not true."

He tries to grab me, but I move out of his grip. "Fuck you, Aiden Brooks."

I need to get out of here. I grab my phone and my keys.

"Shelli, please, stop. Calm down."

I whip around. "Do not tell me to calm down. You've hurt me twice now, Aiden. I'm done."

"I'm not trying to hurt you. Please, take this in from my point of view."

I shake my head and walk toward the door as he calls my name.

"I don't want you to leave. Let's talk about it."

"Talk about what? I can open my legs for you, but I can't help you with your place. Cool. I know where I stand, but I'm better than that—"

"That's not fucking true. Calm the hell down and talk to me!"

I glare. "Go find someone else to open her legs for your uncool, man-bun self who's scared of tattoos so you don't even work in the cool, long-hair dude kind of look! Shave your stupid head to match your bare skin! Asshole!"

His eyes widen as I slam the door shut, and I swallow back the tears. I rush down the hall and pray he doesn't chase me.

Thankfully, he doesn't.

And it hurts.

When I get to my truck, I text Nico that I'll meet him at Brooks House, even against my better judgment. Knowing me, since I'm butthurt right now, I'll probably go to bed with him just to feel better. It's pathetic and sleazy, but I feel shitty. Why doesn't Aiden want me? His place looks amazing, and I cooked damn good food. I get that this would be weird if I were some new chick, but he's known me since I was born. Surely he knows how I like stuff clean.

But then, does he even care to know me?

I'm about to pull out of the space when my phone starts ringing. I look down in the hope it's Aiden, but of course, it's not. It's my mom.

"Hey, Mom."

"Hey, can you do me a favor and pick up the boys at two thirty? I have a meeting."

"Yeah, that's fine."

"What's wrong?"

"Why are boys stupid?"

She pauses. "I don't know, honey. I'm pretty sure it's your father's fault, but what did they do?"

I let my head fall to the steering wheel. "No, I mean boys in general. Not Owen and Evan."

"Oh, that's a relief," she says on a sigh. "I don't know, honey. I didn't even know you were involved with anyone."

"I'm not anymore."

"Well, that doesn't sound good."

"I just don't get it," I say, shaking my head. "I bought a beautiful plate set for his ass, and he basically called me weird."

She whistles. "Oh, honey. You don't buy a guy plates. It always goes bad."

I make a face. "What? Why?"

"I don't know. I did the same for your father when we were dating, and he got all weird on me. Something about he liked his white plates. I don't know, honey. Guys are strange when it comes to their stuff. It's something to do with their bachelorhood. I don't get it, but they want their things left alone. Now, when they fall in love, that's when you swoop in and take over. That's what I did. Now, Daddy loves anything I buy."

I know she said it to be funny, but I'm so mad. "He didn't even have plates, Mom! He just moved in to a new place, and I remembered what his old place looked like, so I did it all while he was at work this morning. I thought he would be impressed by my awesomeness, but he was all freaked out."

"How long have you been dating him? Not too long, right?"

"No, but I knew him in New York."

"Are you two in a relationship?"

I make a face. "Nope. Guess not."

"Oh, well... I mean, I can understand why he'd be freaked out. It does seem like something you would do in a relationship."

I close my eyes. "You don't know all the details."

"Tell them to me, then."

"I can't, Mom. I don't want to talk about it."

She pauses, and I know she's annoyed. "Why did you do it?"

I shrug, even though I know she can't see me. "I wanted to make him happy. Take a little of the work off him since he's so busy. Plus, I love organizing stuff."

"I know, but honey, was it your place?"

I bite my lip. "I don't know. I think I wanted it to be."

"Exactly," she says softly. "I think you may have rushed into this, romanticizing the situation. And when he freaked, you got your feelings hurt."

"Because he was an asshole and didn't even want to admit that we have something going on. It's all just sex for him."

"Oh, baby, sometimes that's all it is."

"I know that," I snap, and I glare at my steering wheel. "I just wanted this to be different."

"Maybe you should talk to him."

"I don't want to. It's all over anyway. Fuck him."

"My goodness, Shelli Grace. Don't hold back what you're feeling."

I roll my eyes. "I gotta go, Mom."

"Okay, baby. But it's all right. It will work out if it's supposed to. You're smart, beautiful, successful, and kicking ass at your internship. You're gonna have my job in no time."

I don't even smile. "Thanks, Mom."

"Chin up, sweetheart."

We hang up, and I shake my head. My mom would be embarrassed with how I acted up there in Aiden's place. I sounded so immature in his condo. But in my defense, he's an asshole. My mom always told me when I was younger and a boy would hurt me, "Stupid boys make you say stupid things."

Aiden Brooks is a stupid boy.

But then, am I a stupid girl? Did I rush into this and romanticize the situation? My mom doesn't even know what happened, but she may be onto something. I wanted to make him happy. I wanted to impress him. But he hurt me. I thought I was doing something nice, helpful, but he made me feel like a freak.

A fuck.

Why does that hurt so bad?

CHAPTER NINETEEN

AIDEN

Since watching Shelli walk out, I've felt like utter shit.

Her eyes were filled with such pain and anger that I can still see them even hours after the fact. I didn't want that look on her face, and I sure as shit didn't want to be the one to put it there. It all freaked me out, though. I didn't expect to come home to her unpacking and organizing the way she did. I thought she'd lie around and be lazy until I got back. I thought we'd spend the day in bed until she had to go to work. I never thought she'd work her ass off to unpack me. I know I should have been appreciative, and I am since I haven't had time to do it, but it freaked me the fuck out.

My mom or even Stella or Emery, sure, it would be totally normal for them to come and do it, but not Shelli. It's something a girlfriend or spouse would do. I don't know how many times I saw my mom do things for my dad growing up. She was always there for him, doing the little things and the big things. It felt like Shelli was being there for me in that way, and it rattled me.

But I never meant to hurt her.

I don't get what the hell is wrong with me when it comes to her.

I'm not a dick, but for some reason, I can't seem to express what I'm feeling. I could have handled that so much better. I could have told her that it felt very girlfriend/boyfriend, and I don't know if I'm ready for that. In all reality, I know I can't have that with her, which is why I think I keep pushing her away, when really, I want her. I want her so bad. I want her all the time, but I can't seem to say that without being a dick first.

She scrambles me. She makes me feel things I've never felt, and I don't like that. I like my life the way it is. I play hockey, and I fuck when I want. It's a good life. But since that night in New York, she's all I want. As I held her last night, I couldn't think of anywhere I wanted to be more. She felt so damn good in my arms. She felt so fucking right, and when I walked away, I missed her. So why can't I say that? Why do I continue to say stupid shit that hurts her?

I honestly don't even know why I've come to Brooks House. I want to talk to her. But if I were her, I wouldn't want to talk to me. She'll probably tell me to fuck off, but I have to try. I have to apologize. I don't want this to end. I just need to tell her what is going on in my head. Problem is, I don't know what that is. It's a fucking shitshow up there right now. I want to try, but what if I mess it up? What if I hurt her more? What if her mom fires me and her dad puts me six feet under? Why is this so hard?

Why do I want her so much, when I know it won't work?

Even knowing that, I still find myself walking into Brooks House. I hear her voice the moment I step inside, and it gives me a fluttery feeling in my gut. I head to the bar, sitting at the front so that I can see her, but I know she can't see me. I don't want to upset her while she's singing. I just want to talk to her when she's done.

Beautiful as always, she wears a long black dress that dips down so far in the front, I get a great view of the side of her boob. Her hair is down, bone straight, except the top is pulled up in a little topknot. She's wearing some makeup, but it's her red lips that make it so there is no room in my slacks. She has her eyes closed as she sings, her lips right on the mic, while her fingers move along the keys with certainty.

So stunning.

She finishes with flair, and the room cheers for her. When she stands up, I hold my breath as I watch her grab a guitar. She sits back down, her lips coming to the mic. "This is my last song for the night." A few people complain, loudly, and she grins. "I know, but don't worry, the bar has some great music to play for y'all. Anyway, I heard this song today, and with where I'm at right now, I feel it applies. So sit back and enjoy."

Her fingers start to move over the guitar just as her voice fills the bar. A hush falls over the room as she sings. I love how her eyes close, how her lips stay on the mic as she sings. She plays the guitar way better than the piano. It's almost like she's just breathing instead of picking the right chords. I want to play with her. The song is dazzling, something about not wearing makeup on Thursdays. When she sings that she only wants to feel beautiful, my heart stops. Doesn't she know she is absolutely exquisite?

Did I make her feel like she wasn't beautiful? God, what is wrong with me?

Once she finishes, she stands up while everyone claps. She takes a bow and says, "Good night, everyone."

She puts her guitar in its case, and I get up, ready to go to her. But then I pause. A really tall guy stops at the stage, and when she sees him, her face lights up. She wraps her arms around his neck, and he hugs her tightly to him. When he kisses her, *on the mouth*, my stomach drops.

What. The. Fuck.

She pulls back and gives him a disapproving look. He says something, and then they both just laugh. He takes her hand in his, kissing it before lacing his fingers with hers. She leans into him as they walk toward a booth. When they sit down, I realize I am glaring at them. I have never felt this kind of anger in my life. Even when I got suspended last year after the allegations, I wasn't this mad. No, I feel as if I'm about to morph into the Hulk.

I'm pretty sure I know the guy. He's huge, with long, dirty-blond hair and an ugly mug. He looks so familiar, but I can't place him. He looks at her like she's the only one in the room, and that pisses me off. That's what I want to do. That's what I *am* doing. Who the hell is this fucker? When he reaches over, cupping her face, she grins as she leans into his hand.

And then I'm moving.

I almost fall out of my chair, I get up so fast, and all I see is red. I feel like I'm stomping toward them, and if I am, I don't give a fuck. I don't know what she's doing, but it isn't right. As I come to their table, she turns and sees me. Her brows pull together as she moves back, crossing her arms over her chest. I stand there, staring at her as she does the same to me. You could cut the tension with a knife.

"Yes?" she asks, all sassy and fucking hot. Her chin is up at me defiantly, and her eyes are narrowed.

"What the hell are you doing?"

She scoffs. "That's none of your business."

"It is because you were with me just hours ago."

She nods. "Yup, and you told me I was just a fuck. So it doesn't matter what I am doing and with whom. So, bye."

"Shelli, I didn't say that—"

"Maybe not outright, but you meant it. Now, if you'll excuse me—"

"Fuck that," I say, my eyes burning into hers. "I never meant that. I was overwhelmed. Let me talk to you."

"No."

"You're serious? What the hell?"

"I was doing something nice for you, and yeah, maybe I stepped over the line. But even so, you don't tell someone they're just a fuck."

"Shelli, I didn't say that—"

"You implied it!"

I look to ugly-mug guy. "Does that make sense to you?"

He shrugs. "I don't give a shit. I'm hoping she's done with you so we can get together."

"Really, Nico?" she sneers. "Shut up."

"So what, you're with him?" I jerk my thumb toward the guy.

She laughs. "None. Of. Your. Business."

"It is my business—"

"It is not," she says simply.

"Bro, believe me, we're something, but she doesn't want it."

I ignore him. "Answer me. Are you with him?"

"Maybe," she says, and I don't miss the smug grin on the fucker's face.

"I want to talk to you," I insist, and I feel like I'm coming out of my skin.

With her eyes burning into mine, she says, "I have nothing to say to you."

"Shelli—"

"I'm enjoying dinner with someone who wants to spend time with me, so please leave."

She looks away, and I glare. "I do want to spend—"

"With clothes on, Aiden. Goodbye."

"Shelli—"

But then the guy stands, and damn it, he towers over me. "Listen, dude, she doesn't want to talk to you."

"I will knock your head off your fat neck if you don't get out of my face," I warn, and he laughs.

"She doesn't want you."

"Shut up, Nico!" she yells, pulling him down into his chair. "Just go, Aiden."

I look over at Shelli, but she won't look at me. "Fine."

I sulk out, my body vibrating with anger. I don't get how she can jump from me to someone else so damn quickly. I can't even think of another female right now, yet she's out fucking some dude like she didn't just have sex with me and rearrange my house! Talk about mixed signals.

Once I'm outside, I take out my phone, shaking as I dial Asher's number. When he answers, I say, "She's here with someone else."

"Okay? What did you think would happen when you basically made her feel like shit for doing something nice for you?"

"It was too much at once."

"Yeah, but girls are girls. She's always been Miss Clean Up. Don't you remember when she was like nine and started that cleaning business to make money for her singing lessons? She likes that kind of stuff."

"It's weird."

"Sure, but she was trying to do something polite. Was she a little overzealous? Sure, but that's Shelli. She's a big personality with a huge heart."

I cover my face. "What the fuck do I do?"

"Sulk?"

"I should go back in there. Force—"

"Aiden. No. Give her some space."

"I don't want her with someone else."

"Should have thought about that before you basically told her she was just a fuck."

I cover my face. "I didn't say that!"

"Dude, you did."

I shake my head as I close my eyes. "What do I do?"

"Give her time and then call her."

"And say what?"

"You're a sorry bastard," he says, and I hear the annoyance in his voice. "You can't treat people like that and expect them to want to be with you."

"She deserves more than that."

"Yeah, so grow up and be that—or let her go."

"Wow. That was a very Dad thing to say."

"Well, I learned from the best. So did you. So get your head out of your ass and do right by her, or leave her alone."

I swallow hard. "It just all freaks me out."

"That's love—"

"Whoa. No need to bring that word into this."

"You're pathetic," he says under his breath. "Relationships are hard. They're scary, but they can be great. If you really like her, like I assume you do, get over yourself and tell her that."

"I should go back in there."

"No, you need to go home and sleep it off. I can hear it in your voice. You're too emotional right now."

"I am not."

"You are. Go home."

Maybe he's right. I really want to go back in there, demand she talk to me because I want to work this out. I need to apologize, but she probably won't even hear it.

Because even though she has a big heart, she can also hold a grudge.

I FEEL LIKE SHIT.

I didn't sleep well. I wasn't hungry when we went for our pregame meal, and my nap wasn't good. I feel so fucking off. I wanted to call Shelli so many times last night. I wanted to go to her house, to beg her to listen to me, but I knew it would do no good. She's stubborn, and I was an asshole. I don't blame her for being upset, but I sure as hell blame her for moving on to some jackass without even a second thought. I don't know how she can be so ready to move on after all we've been through.

Probably because you're a moron, you fucking idiot.

As I skate around, playing with the puck while I warm up, I keep going over and over again everything that's happened. I could blame my parents for my poor communication, but truth be told, it's me. I don't know how to express what I'm feeling when it comes to anything more than sex. I've never had to, and now it's biting me in the ass. I just want to talk to her. Tell her what is happening inside my head, and maybe she'll forgive me.

Or she won't.

While it would be for the best if she completely blows me off, I don't want that.

I want her.

The crowd is cheering us on, welcoming us, but I can't even hear them. I'm too in my head. I shoot mindlessly, and I know this is not good. I can't play like this. I gotta put all that to the side. It is what it is. I'll call her after the game and ask her to come over. She'll say yes or no, and that's my answer. Right now, I gotta win this game.

We're playing the IceCats, and they're on one hell of a winning streak. Ten games in a row. And they're a Stanley Cup favorite. But that was before I joined the Assassins. That Cup is ours. I fall to the ice and stretch my hips. When I tuck my leg beneath me to stretch it, I look over to where the IceCats are warming up, and my brows come together. By the bench is that asshole who was with Shelli last night. His goalie helmet is hanging on his head as he laughs with one of the players.

You've got to be kidding me.

I feel myself glaring as I watch him move with such confidence. Like the most gorgeous girl known to man just did him real good. My blood starts to boil. I don't even know if they did anything, but I assume so by that shit-eating grin on his face.

"BB, why's your face like that?"

I look up at Boon and shake my head. "I hate that fucker."

He looks to where I am glaring and scoffs. "Nico Merryweather? He's a great goalie."

"He's a jackass."

"Well, tell me truly how you feel," he teases, and I glare up at him.

"Pretty sure he had sex with Shelli."

He shrugs. "So?"

"So—" I pause and shake my head. "Fuck it."

I get up and head off the ice, needing to clear my head. Once at my locker, I lean my torso on my thighs and close my eyes. I try meditating, and it works for maybe a minute before my anger gets the best of me. I want to go out there and beat that fucker's ass. What that will do, no clue, but I'll feel better.

Who am I kidding? I won't feel better until I talk to Shelli.

I try to pay attention to Coach's talk. I even try to be excited when they call my name for the starting lineup. I try to get in the game, but my gaze is on that bastard in goal. I know him. He's stolen plenty of my goals, and it only makes me hate him more. He's a Vezina trophy favorite, for sure, and Shelli smiled at him in the way I want her to smile at only me. He's basically the scum on my shoes.

The chip on my shoulder is real, and I find myself slamming my body into everyone with no cares in the world. I play the puck with urgency, but no matter how much I shoot, I don't score. Merryweather is everywhere. He's a brick wall, and it's pissing me off. When I head to the bench, going through the door, Coach smacks my shoulders. "Love the play, the aggression! Keep it up."

Oh, I will.

When my line is called, I rush the zone just as Sinclair passes it up to me. I take the puck into the zone and pass it off to Boon as I crash the net. I'm screening Merryweather, but somehow, he is making blocker saves like I'm not even there. When his stick comes into my back, I hit the ice.

"Move, fucker."

"Kiss my ass," I say, and I get back into position, closer to him but not in his crease. The goal will come, I know it. Reeves shoots a beauty, and I jump so I don't block it, but this dude somehow blocks it! But then, it's back in front of me. Without even turning, I backhand it between his legs.

Goal.

"Fuck yes!"

"Thataway, BB!"

"Way to be there."

"Let's go!"

"You're not shit," I hear him yell at me as my teammates hug me, tapping me on the head.

The boys break, ready to go tap gloves with the rest of our team, but I look back at Nico. "That's why I just scored on your punk ass."

He glares at me through his helmet. "And that's why I fucked your girl."

"Holy shit," Wes says, his eyes wide.

Boon presses his hand into my chest. "Come on, BB."

But I don't move. Blood is rushing to my head. "What did you say?"

"You heard me," he says, his eyes on me. "And she wanted it. All fucking night long, she rode my dick. She wants me, not you."

"That's enough, boys. Go on, Brooks!" the ref yells, but I feel as if something snaps.

I drop my stick and throw off my gloves at the same time he does.

And it's fucking on.

CHAPTER TWENTY

AIDEN

I wince as my trainer, Ryan Justice, tapes up the wound under my eye. I had to have it restitched since I busted the first set of stitches during the third period. After my ten-minute major penalty, five for fighting and five for unsportsmanlike behavior, I thought I would get my head in the game, but I didn't. Hell, I'm still pissed the fuck off. I'm pissed about what Merryweather said, the fact that I believe him, and that he landed two hard hits and all I did was bust his nose.

"Man, he got you good," Ryan says, spreading some cooling cream along my jaw.

I wave him off. "You should see him. Pretty sure I broke his nose."

He grins. "I don't think I've ever seen a player fight a goalie."

"Dafoe vs. Kolzig."

He grins. "I mean live. Did you know that they were each the best man at the other's wedding?"

I laugh. "Yeah, my dad always told me that when I watched the highlights of the best fights."

"Mine too," he says, knocking fists with me. "But for real. This is totally going in my highlight reel."

Not sure if it will make mine. "He's a dick."

"Is that why you chopped him in the groin with your stick?"

Not my finest moment, and I'm pretty sure a fine will come in the morning, but he smacked me in the arm with his goalie stick.

"Hey, he hit me first."

"Arm, dick. Which one is first?"

"He has a cup," I throw back, and he scoffs.

"I guess so." He sends me a grin before patting my leg. "You're good to go."

"Great."

I hop off the table and send him a wave before I head out of the training room. I'm almost to the locker room doors when a voice stops me.

Elli Adler.

Kill me now.

"Aiden Brooks, what in the world?"

I let my shoulders fall as I stop in front of her. "I don't know. He pissed me off. I let him get the best of me."

"You know they might suspend you for that hit to the groin."

"He hit me in the arm!"

She rolls her eyes. "It's an arm! It's his groin!"

"He wears a cup!" I complain, and she sets me with a look.

"What am I going to do with you?"

"I have no clue. I'm really sorry."

"I told you to keep that nose clean. I can't be playing games without my top center."

I nod. "I know."

To my surprise, she holds her arms out, and I go into them. She rubs my back, and I feel bad for this. I shouldn't be going to her for comfort when I treated Shelli the way I did. I bet Elli wouldn't be hugging me if she knew what happened. Nope, she'd probably be the one hitting me in the groin with a stick. "You seem off. Are you okay?"

"No, I had a crappy day."

She pats my face. "Shelli did too. Maybe we should throw another party."

My stomach sinks. "Please don't."

She laughs. "Then don't fight goalies anymore."

"Yes, ma'am."

She kisses my temple before pulling my face back. "What in the world did he say?"

I shake my head. "Nothing. It was dumb."

She clicks her tongue at me before tapping my nose. "Keep your nose clean."

"Trying," I say, and she hugs me once more.

"Go home and sleep it off."

"Yes, ma'am."

But I know I won't do that. Not when I need to get ahold of her daughter.

When I hit the hall, I turn the corner just as Merryweather is coming out of the locker room. His gaze meets mine, and then he shakes his head. "You're a real dick, you know that?"

"Says the dude claiming to fuck the girl I want."

"If you wanted her, you'd treat her better."

I glare. "Fuck you. Want to go again?"

"You're not worth it. I don't even know why she's so caught up on you. You're trash."

"You don't even know me!" I yell back, and he laughs.

"I know a dick when I see one. You watch—she'll get her head on straight and come back to the one who will treat her right."

He taps his hand to his chest, and I raise a brow. "If you're gonna treat her right, why isn't she with you?"

"'Cause she's caught up on you. I'm patient. I can wait."

"Don't. There is a reason she's caught up on me."

He rolls his eyes. "No clue why. It's obvious you don't give a shit about her."

"You don't know shit," I sneer, and he shakes his head.

"Fuck off."

"Right back at you," I holler as he heads out the side door.

His words bother me, though. Did Shelli tell him what I did? Is that what she thinks? Man, I really fucked up. I pull out my phone and dial her number. It goes straight to voice mail, though, and my heart sinks. She isn't going to talk to me.

And I can't blame her one bit.

⚜

WHEN THE ELEVATOR DOORS OPEN, I STEP OUT AS I TUCK MY PHONE back into my pocket. My phone has been ringing off the hook since I left the rink. My mom and dad are hell-bent on talking to me, but I don't want to talk to them. I only want to talk to one person, but she isn't answering. It just keeps going to voice mail.

Take a hint, Brooks. She knows you're trash.

I sigh as I pull out my keys. When I look up, though, I'm stunned in place.

Shelli is leaning on my door.

I pause midstep as my heart jumps into my throat. Her arms are crossed over her chest, bunching up her Assassins jersey. She's in a pair of black leggings with thigh-high purple stiletto boots. Her hair is up in a huge bun, and on her face is painted the number six. Her dad's number. She looks damn perfect.

"Hey," I say.

"Hey."

The tension is crackling around us as I take a step forward. "I tried calling you."

"My phone is dead. My charger is on your bar."

"Oh," I say as my shoulders drop. "So, that's why you're here?"

She shakes her head. "As much as I should say yes...no, it's not the only reason."

I move past her, unlocking the door. "Come in."

"Thanks," she says, walking by me, and I can't help but check out her perfect ass. Her heels click on my hardwood as she goes toward my bar and plugs in her phone. She pulls out the barstool and sits down, crossing those naughty boots over each other before setting me with a look. "Did you fight him because of me?"

I lay my phone and keys beside her phone as I nod. "I did."

She shakes her head. "What am I supposed to do with that?"

"I don't know. All I know is I'm sorry."

I try to meet her gaze as she looks away. "For what?"

"Everything."

She presses her glossed-up lips together as she laces her fingers. "You aren't a fighter. You're a scorer. What the hell got into you? I mean, shit, Aiden, look at your face. He got you good."

She reaches out, touching my jaw and wincing. I lean into her hand, my eyes meeting hers. "Figure since I don't have tattoos, it would help my man-bun look."

I was hoping she would at least smile, but she doesn't as her hand drops. "Aiden, come on. Stop being cute."

I take a step toward her, moving my hand onto hers. "He said he fucked you, and I went crazy."

She rolls her eyes as she moves her hand from underneath mine, crossing her arms again. "Have we slept together? Yes, but we stopped sleeping together before Christmas. It was a short thing, nothing big. He wanted more. I didn't."

I look down at the floor as I nod. "So, you didn't sleep with him last night?"

"No, Aiden. Not that it matters. You made that very clear."

"But it does."

Our eyes meet as she shakes her head. "Funny way of showing it."

"Shelli, I'm really sorry. I didn't mean to say what I did or even imply it."

"I've heard this apology before," she says matter-of-factly, her gaze locked with mine. "I honestly don't know why I am here. I shouldn't be. You've practically screamed in my face that I don't mean shit to you."

"You do," I stress, taking her hand in mine. "Shell, I promise you do."

"Then why are you such a dick about stuff? Yeah, maybe it was a little weird I helped with the house, but you didn't have to say I was just a fuck. My mom says I romanticized our situation and rushed into it, and maybe I did. But I thought—"

I cover her lips with my fingers. "I didn't mean to say that. I just got really overwhelmed. It was all so much at once, and it made me uncomfortable. These feelings... I don't know what to do with them," I say, moving my hands along my chest.

She shakes her head. "I'm unafraid to make you uncomfortable, Aiden. I want you to feel things only I can make you feel because you do the same to me."

"Well, you're doing a great job."

"What does that even mean?"

"I don't know," I say, and by the way her face scrunches up, I know it wasn't the right thing to say.

"You know what? You were better off as a crush."

"No, don't say that."

"Oh, I'm not done!" she yells, getting up, her chin tipped up at me. "I wish I hadn't ever met you because, damn it, you're too hard to forget." She's frantic and angry. Gorgeous.

"You're so beautiful."

"Aiden! Really?"

"You want me to say what I think? I think you're beautiful."

"No, you don't even know what you want, and it drives me crazy!"

"You think it doesn't drive me crazy?" I ask, pressing my hand to my chest.

"It's bullshit. I don't want this. I don't want all this," she says, moving her hands over her heart, her eyes wild. "Yet, the feelings are there, and I can't shake them."

I move to her, but she holds up her hand, stopping me. I reach out, taking her hand and lacing our fingers together. "You think I do? Do you think I wanted to wake up next to you? A fucking beautiful angel who is not only gorgeous but also witty, sassy, and someone I want to have smile at me? Not only all that, but my boss's daughter? I mean, shit, Shell. I wanted a fucking one-time whore, and what I got was a fucking angel! So yeah, the situation sucks, but you don't. You're amazing, and while I know I need to get you out of my head, I can't."

Her eyes are wild, wide as she stares up at me. "And what do we do about it?"

"Fuck, I don't know, because as much as I want you, I know it can't happen. That's what's holding me back, Shelli. I have all these feelings,

feelings I don't even understand. Don't you understand? I've never been with anyone more than once. I've never been in a relationship because no one has ever made me think about one until you. I don't even know what that means or what I'm feeling. It's fucking crazy."

Her eyes are filling with tears, gutting me. "So what? You're just gonna push me away?"

"I don't want to, but I don't know how to tell you what I am feeling."

"It's easy. You open your mouth and tell me the truth."

"I feel like every time I do, I fuck up."

She shakes her head. "No, you come at me with some other bullshit. Instead of just telling me what you're feeling, you jump on the defensive. Push me away. If you'd told me it freaked you out that I touched your stuff and fixed this place up, I wouldn't have gotten so upset."

"It didn't freak me out," I say quickly. "It just felt very intimate. Like we were a couple."

"Because I thought we were! Or at least heading that way."

"I couldn't think like that."

"Why? Aiden, that's insane. I get the whole never having a girlfriend thing and not understanding what you're feeling, but don't push me away. Talk to me."

I look away, shaking my head. "It's hard when I really don't think this can happen."

"Then why the hell are we standing here talking about this?" she yells, tearing her hand from mine. "Why touch me? Look at me like I'm important—"

"Because you fucking are important, and I can't not touch you. I need to," I say, snaking my arm around her waist and pulling her against me. She presses her hands into my chest. "I do want you. I want you so bad. More than a fuck, so much more."

Her brows are almost touching as she gazes up at me. "Aiden, you're making no fucking sense."

"You deserve someone better—"

"Oh, for the love of Pete, I know what I deserve. I am well aware, so please tell me the fucking truth."

I swallow hard as I gaze down into her beautiful face. "No matter how much I want you, crave you, I know your parents won't let this happen."

"Why?" she asks incredulously. "Yes, my dad has the angina, but it's all dramatics. They love you. I think they would be happy."

"No, Shelli."

"Why?"

My grip on her waist tightens. "Because of the fucking allegations against me."

Her shoulders fall along with her hands as her eyes fill with compassion. "Aiden, you know that none of us believe that, right?"

"It doesn't matter, Shelli. They know that I was accused of basically abusing that girl—"

"But you didn't do it."

Her faith in me is surprising but refreshing. "I didn't. But they saw the bite marks on her, they saw the handprints on her throat—"

"And they've seen the ones you had, Aiden. It was rough sex gone wrong. She wanted more. She wanted to trap you. I know this, and so do my mom and dad."

"But that's not what Elli said. Your mom told me I had to keep my nose clean, trust the woman I'm with—"

"So you don't get fucking screwed. Aiden, she wants to help you. No one believes you did those things. That girl said you peed on her. Bless, you shut the door when you go to the bathroom. Pretty sure you wouldn't just piss on someone," she stresses, and then she grabs my face. "Aiden, I know you didn't do it. I get it. My parents make you nervous, but don't let all that, the fact that you can't deal with your feelings and your general fight-or-flight sense, ruin a good thing. We can be real good together if you give me a chance."

I scoff. "I don't have to give you a chance. You gotta give me one." I cover her hands with mine. "I fucked up. I was a dick. But I promise, I'll never hurt you again."

She licks her lips as she gazes into my eyes. "I should say no."

"You should."

"But I don't want to."

"I don't want you to either, but you have reasons."

"I do," she agrees, her eyes burning into mine. "But I know you. I know how you were raised. I know that you've never had a girlfriend, that you've never made time for one. I feel like you want to make time for me, you just don't know how."

"I don't, but I want to. For you."

"I know you do, Aiden. I also know you've had a rough year. It hasn't been easy, and then I came into your life. With how amazing and hot I am, it's easy to say I turned your world upside down."

I take a deep breath in and nod. "Completely." I cup her jaw. "Seeing you with him made me crazy."

"I know."

"I don't have a clue what I'm doing here with you."

She shrugs. "Just do what you feel."

I nod. "I feel if I don't kiss you, I might fucking die."

Her lips curve. "I guess a kiss wouldn't be too bad."

"So you forgive my dumb ass?"

"I do because you're not dumb. You're scared, and I get it. If you've never done this before, I can understand the fear."

I grab her, wrapping my arms around her tightly. "I won't ever hurt you again, Shelli. I promise."

"Good, because next time, I'll be the one jabbing a stick in your groin."

As our mouths meet, I know she's not playing.

And it turns me on beyond belief.

CHAPTER TWENTY-ONE

SHELLI

My ass is hanging off the couch, but there is no way I'm moving.

Once Aiden and I started kissing, I assumed we were heading to the bedroom, but instead, he laid me down on the couch. We're facing each other, my feet at his knees as he holds my waist with one hand and his other trails along my jaw. His lips are sinful against mine and I'm burning from within, but I like this. I like the closeness. He smells divine, and he hasn't shaved, giving him a rugged look. His eyes are so gray, his lashes so dark, and I feel right. Good.

"I have a question."

I open my eyes to meet his. "Yeah?"

"What's going on with that fucker, Nico?"

I laugh softly. "That fucker, huh?"

"I wouldn't mind slamming my fist in his face. Again."

I shake my head as I trace along the bruise on his jaw. "I don't think that would be a good idea. He kicked your ass."

"Shelli! What the hell? My pride."

"What? He did. You flew off the handle when you went to swing on him after he jabbed you in the jaw."

"You weren't supposed to see that."

I giggle. "But hey, look, you're with me right now."

His face changes instantly as he gathers me closer, touching his lips to my bottom lip. "You're right."

"I am," I say, moving my nose with his. "The thing with Nico is nothing. It was always just supposed to be fun. I never wanted a relationship with him. I just wanted to have sex and hang out. He's funny and very nice, but he's so obsessed with himself, it's pathetic. We hardly ever talked about me. It was always him. Even when you walked away after we got into it at Brooks House, he didn't ask what was wrong, why we were fighting. He asked why didn't I just forget you and be with him. That he would be better for me. He never cared about what I was feeling. Only himself. I told him that, and he didn't like it. Which is why I think he said what he did to you. Though, I haven't talked to him."

Aiden's eyes search mine, and he looks worried. "I'm self-absorbed."

"No, you're not," I say quickly. "You took care of me when I was drunk. You made sure my mom wasn't worried. You like to talk to me about things that don't concern you. You care about what I think."

"Well, yeah."

"You're different."

He presses his nose into mine as his lips move along the side of my mouth. "He said you're caught up on me."

"So?"

He grins. "So, it's true."

"Obviously, Aiden. I'm here, aren't I?"

His eyes soften. "I'm glad you are."

"Me too."

"I'm sorry I'm an idiot."

"It's okay," I say, kissing his nose. "You're super hot, so I go with it."

His face breaks into a grin, and I smile back. "You're really beautiful, Shelli. Really. So damn gorgeous."

"I like this saying what you're thinking thing," I inform him, and his grin grows.

"It's kind of freaking me out."

I giggle. "But doesn't it feel good?"

He shrugs. "Nope, it's terrifying."

I laugh. "At least you're honest."

"I don't want you to think I'm dumb."

"I don't," I stress, kissing him. My eyes hold his as I cup his face. I move my thumb along the hair on his chin and whisper, "I promise."

"Okay," he says, nuzzling his nose against mine and closing his eyes.

We lie still for a moment, neither of us saying anything as my mind goes wild. I have so much to ask. Since I never beat around the bush, I jump right in. "Hey, Aiden. Can I ask you something?"

"Yeah," he says with his eyes still shut.

"Did you know her?" I ask, and his finger stops at my chin.

He pulls back a bit so our eyes can meet. "Who?"

"That girl in New York. What was her name? Trish or something?"

"Trisha." He swallows hard as he nods. "I didn't *know* her, know her. But I met her at a bar, we hit it off, and we went back to my place."

I watch him intently as I ask, "How did it go so wrong?"

He shakes his head, disdain making his face rigid. "I don't even know. I think I messed up asking her back over the next day. She left her number on the counter. And I thought, hell, why not? I should have known better, but I enjoyed her, and I didn't want to find someone else to sleep with."

"Because going a day without sex is completely out of the question," I say dryly, and he grins.

"You love sex just as much as I do, thank you very much."

"I don't have to have it every day."

He shrugs. "We'd lost in the play-offs. I was pissed and wanted to blow a load or seven." I snort, and he grins. "It was a mistake. I shouldn't have let her come back."

I slowly move my fingers into his hair. "So, what happened?"

He inhales deeply, letting it out through his mouth. "When she got there, I think I knew something was up. She was asking questions about my friends and my family, and I remember thinking, this is weird. Especially when she knew my mom's and dad's names. I know it's a simple Google search, but why would she have done it? We were just fucking. I don't know, it was weird. We started going at it, and she wanted it harder. Harder. I swear she said it over and over again, and not in a hot way but in a demanding way. At first, I was hesitant, but then she bit me, and I didn't think it was so bad. I sort of liked it."

"You did?" I ask, my brows coming in.

"Yes, at first. But then she really started biting me, and then she choked me out. When I came to, I was in a panic. It was all so weird and off. I was drunk, of course, but then she asked me to do the same. So, I did. I hadn't done it before, and she promised it would get me off, but it didn't. It freaked me out even more." He shakes his head as his eyes fall shut. "I couldn't even do it long enough for her to pass out. I panicked and then asked her to leave. She got really mad and started throwing things at me. I had to call security to get her out of there. I thought I would never see her again, but then the cops came the next morning because she claimed I raped her and beat her up."

"Man, that's insane."

"It was absolute hell."

"And wasn't she stalking you?"

"Yeah." He rolls his eyes. "One of the guys on the team told me he had seen her around me a lot while I was at the rink and hanging around my place when I had parties. He thought something was fishy. I hired a PI, and he found evidence of her stalking me. He hired one of her friends to spy on her, and she brought in pictures of the girl's apartment. There were hundreds of pictures of me and notebooks of things about me. Super-crazy shit."

"So crazy," I marvel, shaking my head. I saw the pictures online; the chick was seven shades of nuts. "Are you worried she'll come back?"

He shakes his head. "No, not really. I dropped the charges as long as she would. I haven't seen or heard from her in over ten months. I'm not worried the least bit about her."

"Why did you drop the charges? Didn't you want her to go to jail for what she did?"

He looks away, biting his lip. "I didn't want to ruin her life for a mistake, even though she was ready to ruin mine. I don't know. I felt bad for her. I just wanted the whole mess to go away."

I smile. "And you say you're self-absorbed."

He looks away, a small shrug of his shoulders. "I don't know."

"Either way, I'm glad it's in the past."

"Yeah, it was a load of shit that I didn't need," he says, moving his hands along my hips. He stops to press his lips to mine, and my eyes drift shut. I feel awful for him, how the whole thing went down. I know he isn't that person. Does he like sex? Sure. What man doesn't? But Aiden isn't the kind of man to hurt someone intentionally. He's gentle and cares what I want. Sometimes, he doesn't even ask what I want; he just knows and does it. I, for one, am a fan.

"I'm sorry."

"Not your fault."

"I know," I say, and then I look down. "I'm not a stalker."

He laughs. "I know, Shelli."

"I feel like maybe that's why you freaked out on me."

He shakes his head. "I actually didn't put the two together until now."

"Wonderful. I'll show myself out," I say, starting to get up, but he doesn't let me. He traps me in his arms, pulling me on top of him as a giggle falls off my lips. "I think I freaked about the unpacking because it did feel like something a girlfriend would do, and I didn't want to accept that this was going that way."

"Have you accepted it yet?"

He grins. "Working on it."

I roll my eyes. "For someone who doesn't want me with anyone—"

"I will legit fight anyone who tries to touch you."

I grin. "I didn't know you were so jealous."

His grip tightens around me. "Not jealous, just protecting what I want."

Swoon. I purse my lips, and he presses his to mine. When he drops his head back, he looks up at me. With a little tip of my lips, I ask, "Why hadn't you unpacked?"

He draws his lip between his teeth. "I sometimes feel like this isn't real. Like it's all going to be taken from me."

"Why?"

"It's too good to be true. I've wanted to play for the Nashville Assassins my whole life, and here I am. I rushed here, got started, and I'm worried that if I unpack, I'll lose it all."

"But you belong here."

His eyes darken. "I'm starting to realize that."

"Good, 'cause it's true."

He kisses the side of my mouth. "I think your mom scared me with her speech, and then after what happened in New York, I think I was waiting for the other shoe to drop. Add in the fact that I have a real hard time staying away from you, and I knew it would only be a matter of time before I got canned."

"I mean, I am irresistible, but I wouldn't let that happen."

He grins, his eyes flashing with desire. "No?"

"Nope. I'd take the fall and say you couldn't resist me."

"Oh, really?" he says with a cheeky grin.

"Yup," I say proudly.

"I wouldn't let you do that."

"Why not?" I ask, my brows furrowing.

"Because I take responsibility for what I do." He moves closer, pressing our noses together. "I want to try this. I want to promise that I'll do it well, but I don't think I can. I'm usually pretty confident in life, but you completely terrify me."

I feel my face fill with color as I press my lips together. "I do?"

"Yeah. I can't control how you make me feel."

"Good. Welcome to my world. Been this way since I was eleven."

He shakes his head. "I can't even imagine. Why didn't you tell me?"

"Because you're Aiden Brooks." I laugh, shaking my head. "Coolest guy ever. You wouldn't have time for me. Plus, what would you have said? 'Run along, Shelli. Go play with your dolls.'?"

When I laugh, he grins, a little bashful. "No, not at all."

"Whatever."

"Hey, I remember a time when I was checking you out. You were like sixteen or something."

"Yet, you wouldn't talk to me. Or even look at me."

He holds my gaze. "Maybe I knew you were dangerous even then?"

I cup his jaw. "You really do think you're cute, don't you?"

He laughs, but it stops when I press my lips to his. His arm comes up around my neck, holding me close, as his other hand grips one of my ass cheeks. I hold his face in my hands as our kiss deepens, and my heart nearly explodes in my chest. I pull back, running my fingers through his coarse hair as he gazes at me through his half-lidded eyes.

"I wish you had told me."

I scoff. "No way." I shake my head, the laughter bubbling in my throat. I'm pretty sure he's gonna think I'm crazy, but I want to tell him. "There was this time, you had this amazing Willie Nelson shirt on. I was learning 'Georgia on my Mind,' and I wanted so bad to play it for you so you'd think I was cool too. I even begged my mom to buy me that shirt."

"Which one?"

"It's the one that says 'Have a Willie Nice Day' with him on it?"

He thinks for a minute and then rolls me over and gets up. He goes into his room, and when he comes back a few seconds later, he has it in his hands. "This one?"

"Shut up!" I exclaim, jumping up and walking to him. I stumble from the excitement to get to him and the shirt. "You still have it?"

"Hell yeah. It's one of my favorites."

"It's amazing!"

He holds it out to me. "Here, wear it."

"Shut. Up."

"No, really," he urges, and then he's pulling off my jersey. "Wait, is this a Shea Adler jersey?"

"Yup, vintage. Circa his first season as an Assassin."

"Nice."

"For sure," I say quickly as I lift my arms and then grab his shirt, covering the tank I had under my jersey. Of course, the shirt drowns me, but I don't care. It smells like him. It's super soft from being so old, and I swear, I can still see him in it.

When I look up at him, my eyes wide and my face warm, he's grinning down at me. "Perfect fit."

He pulls out his phone and holds it up for me to pose. I give him a cheeky grin with my arms up, and I feel every bit like I'm eleven again. That fluttering feeling in my gut. That overwhelming need to touch him, to talk to him and make him see how amazing I am. I don't think I have to try so hard. I think he sees it now.

He sees me.

CHAPTER TWENTY-TWO

AIDEN

"No way."

Shelli's face is drop-dead serious as she holds out both palms, nodding. "Aiden, hear me out."

"You're insane."

"Never!" she stresses before taking a bite of pancake. She chews quickly, swallows, and I can't help but smile. She is going to make me agree with her. "I love Jensen as much as anyone else on this team, but he isn't our Jensen anymore. He's older, ready to move on. We need to bring up our talent. Gallagher needs to move up into the backup spot. We need to send Mansor back down at least for the rest of the season. Get Gallagher's feet wet, and then after we win the Cup, Jensen retires, Gallagher is our dude, and we make a trade for Peca."

My jaw drops. "Isn't he a first-round draft pick? No one will come off him."

"They will. No one needs a good goalie right now. Everyone thinks they're fine. It's all about scoring at the moment, which is how we swoop in and snatch him up. We can let go of some of our young talent, especially our forwards. Mom went crazy a couple years ago, but

I'm telling you, if Jensen goes, we need to strike now for our goalie team."

I shake my head. "I don't know."

"Seriously, ask Tate. I told him my plan, and he looked at me the way you are right now," she promises with a little grin and a forkful of pancakes. Her hair is up in a topknot, and she hasn't changed out of my tee yet. It's almost two in the morning, but I don't think either of us is tired. We've been talking and kissing since she got here. It's been pretty outstanding.

She takes a bite and nods. "It's starting to make sense, isn't it? You're getting past letting go of Jensen."

I narrow my gaze as I pull my hair up into a bun. "You're too damn hockey smart for your own good," I say, leaning over the bar and holding up a strawberry for her.

She leans over, taking it in her mouth before batting her eyelashes at me. "It's part of my charm."

I chuckle as I eat a strawberry. "How do you know all this?"

"It's a passion."

I eye her. "You should have been a coach or something. Played or been a scout. All that knowledge is going to waste."

She shakes her head as her brows come together. "No, I get to talk to my mom and dad, all the guys at the rink, and then you. I love it."

"Don't you want more?"

She shrugs. "My time will come. Right now, I'm enjoying singing at the bar and talking with people who love hockey as much as I do. I also love interning, even though I just update social media right now."

I point at her with my fork. "That's right. Why are you doing that? Your mom owns the team."

She nods and purses her lips at me. "You know my mom. You work for what you want. I decided a couple weeks ago I want the team. Well, no, that's not right. I've always wanted the team, but I thought she'd give it to the boys."

"Why would she do that? Anyone who talks to you knows you are basically an updated version of her."

"Updated?" she asks with a sly grin.

I nod as I count on my fingers. "Smarter, bolder, more cutthroat.

You won't think with your heart. You'll go toe-to-toe with anyone, and you'll win. No one would be able to shut you down. Not that your mom can't hold her own, but she cares too much. You'll get what you want. You've got a really great ass, spectacular eyes, and I think you rock the heels better than your mom."

Her lips curve. "All that makes me an updated version?"

"All that makes you Shelli Adler, the next owner of the Nashville Assassins. I hope I'm playing when it happens."

She looks up at me coyly through her lashes. "I don't know. It could be very unethical for you to be sleeping with the owner."

The thoughts swirling in my gut scare the hell out of me. As much as I can feel it, I can't see it. I don't want to ruin what we have going here, though. This is nice. It's special. "Your dad did it."

She grins. "He did."

I take a bite of my pancakes as she watches me. "Hopefully I'm still playing then."

"You will be. You're just now going into your prime. You're finding the confidence you've always had but didn't use 'cause you had talent. Now, your talent with your confidence? Shit, you're gonna be unstoppable in no time."

"Wow. You know my stats, don't you?"

She looks up at me, certainty on her face. "In the last five games—six goals, nine assists, plus/minus twelve, time on ice average about twenty-one minutes."

A wave of lust comes over me. "Wow, that's a turn-on."

She nods. "You're not the first to tell me that."

"I want to be the only." *What in the hell did I just say?*

She raises her brows. "The only, huh?"

"Yeah." *What the fuck? Am I not in control of my mouth?*

Shelli's lips curve. "I can make that happen."

Why does that make my stomach turn upside down? I lick my lips free of syrup as our eyes stay locked together. I put my fork in the middle of my plate and walk around the bar. She watches me, her blue eyes getting darker. I come up beside her, taking her by the knee and turning her so her legs are in front of me. "So, are you sure you want to stop singing?"

She looks down at where I'm grabbing her leg, unzipping those naughty fuck-me-stupid boots. "In favor of the Assassins, yes. Don't get me wrong, I love to sing, but I love hockey more. Plus, I can write and play in my free time."

I nod as I drop a boot to the floor. "True, but don't you love performing?"

She shrugs as I grab her sock, tossing it on the floor along with her boot. I take her other boot and unzip it as she says, "By the time I get the team, I'll be older and done with the performing stuff."

I drop the boot along with her sock before I hook her leg over my hip, bringing myself in closer, and cup her face in my hand. "Do you want to do another play?"

She swallows hard as she looks up at me. "I don't know. I didn't like the play I was in."

I nod as I move my thumb along her lip, catching some of the syrup she left behind. "I mean, singing to a snowman can get old."

"Exactly."

"I don't think you're done."

"No?" she asks, and I notice the breathless tone to her voice.

"No, I think you were born to be onstage."

She moves her mouth over my thumb, licking the syrup off it. My breath catches as those naughty eyes don't leave mine. She kisses the tip of my thumb. "You think so?"

"Yeah," I say as I thread my fingers up into her hair. "I really love to listen to you."

Her eyes burn into mine, her breathing picking up. "I need to ask you something."

"Funny, I need to ask you something."

We smile. "Go first."

"Stay with me tonight? I don't want you to leave."

She moves her hands up my chest and around my neck. "Don't you have a flight to catch in the morning?"

"Yeah."

"Won't I be a distraction?"

"Yeah."

She grins, and my stomach clenches. My cock is pressing into my slacks, and fuck, I want her. With a sneaky grin, she says, "You won't hear me say no."

"Good." I drop my mouth to hers, unable to hold off anymore before I take what I want. Which is all of her. She tastes sweet as all hell, and when she wraps her other leg around my waist, I can feel the heat of her against me. My fingers bite into her ass as I press into her. If the damn counter weren't so full, I'd throw her on it and do her right there.

Fuck it.

I push the plates off the counter. As they go crashing to the ground, I lift her and put her sweet ass on there. She smiles against my lips, and I yank at her leggings, needing them off.

"You really hated the plates."

I pause, pressing my forehead into her chin. "No, I'm sorry. Just really want you, and I wasn't thinking."

Her giggles make me harder. "It's okay."

I look up at her. "It's not. I'll replace them. You'll just need to show me where to get them. I'll even buy you something slutty so I can take it off you."

Her lips turn up. I'm pretty sure I just asked her to take me shopping. Again, a very intimate thing. It's like I have no control over myself around her. With her eyes dark and naughty, she says, "Slutty, huh?"

I nod, breathless. "Something strappy and see-through, for sure."

"Crotchless."

I groan against her mouth. "Well, of course."

I capture her mouth with mine as she lifts up so I can yank her leggings and panties down. I grab her butt as our tongues tangle together. She moves to the edge of the counter, wrapping her legs around me as she pulls my shirt up and over my body. She tears her mouth from mine, licking down my jaw, my throat, driving me absolutely wild. She sucks on the base of my neck, and my head falls back as I run my fingers down the crack of her ass. Her fingers move up the back of my head, threading through my hair as she nibbles and sucks, making me feel as if my cock will break off from being so goddamn hard. Her mouth feels so good.

I take her face in my hands, tipping her head back so I can feel her lips on mine. Her eyes are open, meeting mine for a second before they fall shut. Her lashes kiss her cheeks in such a beautiful, sweet way. I've never watched a girl as I kiss her, but I don't want to do anything but that now. Not just any girl either, only Shelli. Her thighs squeeze my waist, and I find that I'm shaking with need.

But then I remember something.

I pull my mouth from hers, and she mumbles for more. "You had a question."

She opens her eyes and blinks. "What?"

"You told me to go first."

She blinks once more. "Really? I think we have more important things to do."

I capture her bottom lip with my teeth. "Tell me," I say, and she shakes her head.

She hooks her thumb to the piano. "Do you play that, or is it for show?"

I'm offended. "Do I seem like one of those guys who would have that for show?"

She looks up at me with a straight face. "Yes. That's why I'm asking."

"Wow. Rude!"

Her laughter tickles my soul. I lift her off the counter and carry her to the piano.

"The bedroom is the other way."

"Ha. I have something to prove!"

God, I love the way she laughs. I put her on the top of the piano and pull my slacks up as I sit on the bench, opening the lid over the keys. I realize I'm still shaking, but I don't care. I will show her that I can do this. I press my fingers into the keys and start playing Niall Horan's, "Too Much to Ask." It's one of my new favorites that I've just learned. When I look up at her, her eyes are wide and her lips are turned up in a radiant smile.

"Shut. Up."

I love her reaction. I don't know why, or even what brings me to do it, but then I'm singing. I want to impress her, and my mom always said I have a nice voice. When I look up at her, her jaw has fallen as much as her topknot.

"No. Freaking. Way."

I close my eyes as I sing, nowhere near as great as her, but I'm decent. When she joins in with me, I open my eyes, and my heart stops dead in my chest at her beauty. She's let her hair down, and she's lying on the piano as her voice blends with mine. She could sing me under the table, but right now, she's only adding where she wants. It's beautiful, sweet, and when I finish, looking up at her, I feel like she's knocked me straight on my ass.

"Where the hell did you learn to sing like that?"

"I have no clue. My mom loves it."

"You're so good!" she gushes, and I feel heat creeping up my neck. "Though, I think we have a problem."

My face breaks into a grin. "I'm a better singer?"

She grins back. "That, and I might have to do you right here."

"Right here?" I ask as she moves herself down the piano, her feet lowering to the bench and giving me one hell of a view of her slick, wet center. "Oh, like right here."

"Yeah, I'm not joking," she says, leaning forward and taking my mouth with hers. Our tongues meet as I pull my wallet out of my back pocket, getting the condom I put in it to replace the one we used the other day. I pull away, nibbling at her bottom lip. "Stand up."

She arches a brow, but she does what I ask, standing above me, her pussy right there as I push my slacks down my thighs. I run my tongue up her center, and I'm met with the most amazing moan known to man. It should be the sound everyone hears when they look up passionate moan. I grab my cock as I lick her, and I slowly put on the condom. I love the sounds she's making, but I also know I can't wait much longer. Once I'm sheathed, I grab her by her hips, and she lowers down on my cock until she hits the hilt. She brings her arms around my neck as our eyes meet, and our cries of relief mingle together. I move my arms up under her knees and slowly lift her so she moves up my cock. Her head falls back as I bring her back down, my cock disappearing inside her. She's flushed everywhere, and I want to lift her shirt and bury my face in her breasts, but she loves the shirt.

And I love it on her.

Her pussy tightens around my cock as I pick up the pace, needing to come so damn bad, I can't see straight. It's torture, moving her up and down my body, but I love the color she's turning. Her face is red, her hair is wild, and those eyes are blazing.

When she cries out in frustration, lifting her head, her eyes meet mine. "I can't. This is too slow."

"Too slow?"

"Too fucking slow," she insists before smacking my hands away, my cock going deep inside of her from her ass landing on my lap. Before I can enjoy it, though, she's up and out of my lap, leaning on the piano, her ass up in the air.

Again, one of the greatest sights I've ever seen.

She looks over her shoulder at me. "Fast."

"Fast?"

"And hard."

I take hold of her hip in one hand and push my cock into her. "Oh, believe me, it's going to take some restraint not to go as hard as I want."

She looks up at me through those long, sexy lashes. "Fuck restraint."

I think I just came.

I take her by the knee and lift it up into her ribs as I move into her. She's moaning my name in a way that has my knees shaking as I start to slam into her. There is something about the sound of her ass against my thighs that gets me so hard. Or maybe it's the throaty way she screams my name as she shatters. Her head falls forward onto her arms, and I'm thrusting so hard into her, I can't breathe. Her body squeezes mine as my fingers bite into her skin. When I come, I feel it everywhere. And I mean everywhere.

My fingers, my toes, my knees, but most of all my heart. It's fucking exploding in my chest. She lets her head fall back as mine presses into her shoulder, our breathing audible and uneven. I jerk into her as the last shocks of my orgasm run through me. Soon, we still, our breathing still a bit out of sorts, but I can finally breathe and see again. I move my hands up to her waist, her chest, before cupping her throat and then her jaw. I turn her face so that I can take those lips with mine. I don't want to stop. I'm completely captivated by her.

When she breaks away so she can breathe, I sit back on the bench, pulling out of her. I drag her down into my lap, and she looks up at me with a naughty grin on that sweet, flushed face of hers.

"What?"

Her lips purse as her face fills with more color. "I don't know what I liked more. Your singing or having sex with you."

I chuckle loudly. "So, what are you saying? If I sing, you'll want to have sex with me? This could be a dangerous game. I'll start singing in the middle of a gas station."

She gives me a look, her face scrunching up as she snorts. "Hell, all ya gotta do is look at me and I'll want sex with you." Something moves in my chest as I gaze down at her. I search her blue depths, taking in her beauty. Her brows come together. "What are you doing?"

"You said all I gotta do is look at you, and you'd want sex!"

Her face goes from confusion to hilarity in seconds. She curls up in my lap, laughing so hard that she's shaking, and just like that, everything stops.

Because I know I'm in over my head with this girl.

CHAPTER TWENTY-THREE

SHELLI

"I'M GLAD YOU'RE NOT PLAYING TOMORROW, BECAUSE YOU'RE GONNA be useless. You know this, right?"

Aiden shrugs as he nuzzles his face between my breasts, caressing my back with his palms. "Eh, I'll sleep on the way there. Toronto is a long trip."

"True, but I'm worried it will throw off your groove."

He shakes his head as he kisses my breastbone. "I'll be fine. Promise."

I thread my fingers through his hair, moving it out of his face as I gaze down at him. While it's almost four in the morning, I, for one, am not the least bit tired. I can't believe how this night has gone. I thought when I got here that we'd get into it, and then that would be that. While I wanted to assume he had fought Nico because of me, I kinda thought it was because of his pride. After the way he looked at me, though, and touched me, I feel it was more. I feel he really wants to be with me, and Nico was in his way. That alone has a grin on my face.

But then tonight happened. We've talked. We've laughed. We've kissed, broken plates, and made love. I mean, we go at it and it's hot, but the way he looks at me, the way he cups my face, it just feels like more. It feels special. I don't want to be "romanticizing" anything, but it feels different to me. He feels different. I know it's all freaking him out, but he looks pretty satisfied right now.

Aiden tips his face up, his mouth against my boob as he says, "You've gone mute. What's wrong?"

I smile, braiding his hair. "Nothing. Just thinking."

"That can be dangerous with you."

I snort. "What does that mean?"

"That mind of yours is lethal. I may need to put a stop to this thinking to spare the world from your domination."

I giggle as he turns his face, nibbling at my nipple. I cup his head and tilt it back to press my lips to his. "I'm just thinking how great this has been."

He's heavy-eyed, bless him, as he gives me a sleepy grin. "It's been really great."

I move my fingers along the stitches under his eye. "I'm sorry about this."

He opens his eyes more before he narrows his gaze at me. "You didn't fight me, so why are you apologizing?"

"Because you fought over me."

"So? That's my choice."

"You don't regret it? That's a nasty cut."

He shakes his head. "I'd do it again."

I kiss his nose, but his hand comes up, clutching the back of my head before he presses his lips to mine. I get lost in the kiss, savoring it since I won't see him for over a week. When he pulls back, his eyes meet mine as he kisses me once more. Little kisses. Sweet ones that curl my toes. He nuzzles back into my chest, and I hold him close.

"Can I text you when you're gone?"

I feel his lips turn up. "You better."

"Really?"

"Yeah," he says, kissing the side of my boob. "Why wouldn't you? I'm going to text you."

"I don't know. Don't want to freak you out."

He chuckles. "I'm a walking ball of anxiety right now, but if I don't hear from you, I'm pretty sure it will get worse. I'll stay up thinking, 'Did she use me?' 'Was I not good enough?' 'Is she really pissed about the plates?'"

I laugh out as we tangle our legs. "Fine. I'll text."

"And call."

"And call."

"FaceTime me too, especially if you're naked." I sputter with laughter as he bites my breast lightly. "You're supposed to say, 'Yes, Aiden. I'll do just that.'"

Still giggling, I say, "Yes, Aiden. Only when I'm naked."

"That's right, angel."

A shiver runs through my body as I wrap my arms around his neck, closing my eyes.

"Hey, did you text your mom?"

I smile without opening my eyes. "Yeah, she knows I'm staying the night with someone I'm seeing."

"So she doesn't know about us?"

"No." A silence falls between us, and I wait for him to say something. When he doesn't, I ask, "Do you want me to tell her?"

"See, the issue is, I think that's something we need to do together. I respect and love her, and I think it's something I should tell her. But I am not ready for that because I can't even really accept that something has happened here."

"That shouldn't piss me off, right?"

He turns his head, putting his chin on my breastbone. "If you were to say it to me, I'd be annoyed. So I know it's bullshit, if that helps."

I nod. "It does help a bit."

"I'm sorry. But I can promise you I don't want anyone else."

My lips quirk at the side. "I know. I'm pretty great in bed."

His eyes darken. "And you're smart, beautiful, and know all my stats. So, I need you around."

I fight back my grin. I love his sense of humor. "Such a smooth talker you are."

He winks, and my stomach goes nuts before he lies back down. I can't sleep. I'm too amped up. This is exactly what I wanted, and it all seems like it could go real wrong at any second. "I don't want to tell my parents yet. Or yours. I really don't want to tell anyone."

He opens his eyes but doesn't look at me. "Okay?"

"I think we need to navigate this ourselves before we involve everyone else."

"And what are we navigating?"

I roll my eyes. "A relationship, Brooks."

He acts as if he's choking. "I was afraid you were going to say that." I yank on his hair, and he laughs as he looks at me, his eyes still so heavy. He's exhausted, and I'm such an asshole for keeping him awake. "Yeah, the R-word. I like the idea of navigating that with just you for a while. Especially since it freaks me the fuck out."

I ignore the last comment and go with my first thought. "Because you know if we get everyone involved and it goes to shit, my parents will hate you and yours will hate me."

He nods. "You're right."

"So I think it's best we just enjoy this. Us."

"If you're okay with it, I am."

I bite my lip. Am I making the right decision? "Let me ask Amelia."

"Who's Amelia?"

"My cousin. Ryan Justice's sister."

"Oh, that's right," he says, and then he sets me with a look. "What happened to not telling people?"

"Amelia isn't people."

"Then Asher isn't people."

"That's fine," I agree, and then I smile. "So, you're gonna tell your brother about me?"

"He already knows about you."

I flutter my lashes at him, and he rolls his eyes. "Aw, that's sweet."

"Are you done?"

"You like me," I sing, and he laughs, covering my mouth with his. I wrap my arms around his neck as he holds my jaw in his hands. His hands are so big, so comforting, and I've never felt so good in my life. When we part, he kisses my jaw and then my neck.

"I do."

"Do what?"

"I do like you."

I smile against his temple. "You're damn right, you do."

He squeezes my hip, and I close my eyes with the biggest damn grin on my face.

☙❧

I'M AWAKENED BY AIDEN'S PHONE.

It's ringing. Loudly. I feel the weight of him on my chest, and with one eye, I see him there. I smack his side. "Aiden, your phone."

"Ugh," he groans as he cuddles deeper against me. "Let it go to voice mail."

"Isn't it your alarm?" I ask, still smacking his side.

When he whips up onto his knees, my eyes fly open. "Fuck. What time is it?"

I sit up. "I don't know!"

He hurries off me as I rush the other way to grab my phone. We look at each other, both wide-eyed.

"Oh my God!" I yell.

"They're gonna kill me." He answers his phone. "I overslept. I don't know what happened. I had four alarms! Fuck! I'm coming."

He hangs up and throws his phone on the bed as he rushes through the room, pulling off his boxers before going to the bathroom to brush his teeth. I want to follow him, I want to apologize since I kept him up all night, but I stay where I am. I don't want to get in the way. When he rushes out of the bathroom, I bite my lip. "Can I do something?"

"No, I'm packed. Just gotta get dressed." His words are clipped, and I know not to take it personally. I'm freaking out for him. You can't be late for the plane. There is a fine, and Coach will rip you apart. Then there'll be a call from my mom about the importance of not wasting anyone's time. The guys get bitched at, and usually, there are extra laps on the ice. Which, in return, makes you public enemy number one, and the guys put Bengay in your cup.

I really like Aiden's balls.

Ah, I feel awful.

I throw up my hands. "Hide your jockstrap!"

He doesn't laugh, not that I expect him to, but I was kind of hoping he would. "Oh, I'm never taking it off."

"Good man." I nod as I get up, making his bed as he comes out of the closet in a nice three-piece suit.

"Babe, can you grab my toiletries bag?"

I basically fall over myself to get to the bathroom to grab it. I see it on the counter, and then I see a pen and Post-its that I left in here when I was organizing. I pick up the pen and write a quick note before stuffing it into his toiletry bag. I come back as he snags his bag from beside the closet and then his charger. I hand it to him as he stuffs both in his bag.

He looks around frantically, patting his jacket. "Where is my wallet?"

"By the piano."

He pauses, and then a sinful grin pulls at his lips. He drops his bag and closes the distance between us. I hold my breath as he comes for me. His eyes are so dark and only on me. His body slams into mine, pulling me close to him before tipping my jaw up so he can look into my eyes. His lips curve, causing mine to do the same. "I had a great time last night."

I bite my lip. "I did too. I'm really sorry for keeping you up."

"Don't be," he urges before pressing his lips to my nose. "I wanted to stay up with you."

I go onto my tiptoes, and our lips meet in a heated, wanton kiss. His fingers tangle in the back of my hair as he squeezes me to him. When he pulls back, it's because his phone is ringing again. He shakes his head before pressing his forehead to mine. "I'm sorry. I gotta go."

I move my hands into his jacket, hugging him tightly. "Be safe and keep that point streak going."

The biggest, brightest grin covers his lips. "Will do." He kisses me once more and then says against my lips, "You better text me."

"You text me so I know you're not sleeping."

"Okay," he whispers, and then he kisses me once more. "There is a key on the counter for you to lock the door on your way out."

"Okay. I'm gonna take a shower."

He groans. "Rude."

I grin. "We can take one together when you get back."

"Promise?"

"Promise," I say, kissing his chin. "Now, go on."

"Okay, yeah, I guess I better go."

"Yeah," I say, but he doesn't move. His fingers stroke along my bare ass as his eyes burn into mine. "I'm so dead."

"Why?"

"'Cause I want to stay right here with you."

I giggle and then press my lips to his before pushing him away. "Bye."

He shakes his head. "Bye, Shelli."

He grabs his bag and then quickly leaves while he answers the phone, telling whomever that he's in the car. I want to say I'm smiling so big because of the lie, but it has nothing to do with the lie and everything to do with the fact that I am completely smitten with him.

When my phone sounds, I look down to see a text from Aiden. I fall onto the bed, stomach first, and grab my phone from the night-stand. I open his text, and my face hurts from smiling so hard.

Aiden: Keep the shirt. It looks better on you.

I close my eyes as I hold my phone to my chest. I've wanted this for so long, and while I want to believe we're good, I know he's not where I am. I have to remember that. I have to take this slowly, help him through this, or I might lose him. On an exhale, I dial Amelia's number.

"Hey."

"Hey, what are you doing?"

"Growing a baby. You know, nothing important."

I smile. "How are you feeling?"

"Sick. All the time. But my man is being good to me."

"Good."

"What's wrong?"

"Huh?"

"You sound like something's wrong. I have a feeling it has to do with Aiden since I watched him fight Nico."

I shake my head. "I gotta call that asshole."

"Why? What happened?"

"He told Aiden he was fucking me, and Aiden lost his shit."

"Oh, how very jealous of him."

"Right?" I say with a grin.

"So, things are happening."

"Yeah," I say as I cuddle with Aiden's pillow. "I told him I didn't want to tell anyone."

"Well, that's for the best since from everything you tell me, it seems he's terrified of commitment."

"He is," I agree, and I bite my lip. "Am I stupid?"

"What do you mean?"

"Am I wasting my time?"

"Do you feel like you are?"

"No, not at all."

"Then you're not. You're not a dumb girl, Shelli. You know what you want. He's obviously important to you, and you believe in this. So, do you."

"You don't feel the same, do you?"

She clears her throat. "I want you to be happy, but no, I don't think it will work."

I thought she'd say that. "Why not?"

"Because someone like him doesn't settle down. He's set in his ways. But then, you never know. He may change for you, and if so, that's awesome. I'm just being honest in saying it doesn't happen often."

"I hear you." And I do. I just wish she were saying something else. I wish she believed in him the way I do, but then, she wasn't here with him last night or this morning. She wasn't under his gaze. I was. I feel good about this, but I'm not being naïve. I know there is a good chance of failure, which is why I need to proceed cautiously. "I'm gonna take it slow. I don't expect him to profess his love for me and marry me tomorrow."

"Well, that's good to hear, because after you unpacked his place, I thought you did."

"I may have jumped the gun on that."

"Just a bit," she teases. "But hey, that's you. You do what you want, and everyone either gets on board or they get left behind."

I smile. "Yeah."

"You sound happy, though."

"I am."

"Good. That's all I want."

"When will I see you?"

"Next month. We're coming in for the weekend since the IceCats have three days off. I gotta tell everyone I'm growing a child."

"I can't wait. It's gonna be awesome."

"Or a shitshow. So, we'll see."

I snort as I shake my head. "Don't worry. I'll be there."

"Thank God." We both laugh together, until my laughter falls off. I bite my lip as I inhale thoughtfully, getting drunk off Aiden's scent.

"Hey, Amelia."

"Yeah?"

"Do you think he will love me?"

"Oh, Shelli," she says softly. "If he's smart, he'll fall head over heels for you. You're perfection in my eyes."

I smile. "Same here. I love you."

"I love you."

After we hang up, I cuddle deeper into his pillow, and I remind myself to be patient.

I've waited ten years for him to notice me.

I just hope I don't have to wait that long for him to love me.

CHAPTER TWENTY-FOUR

AIDEN

I LEAN ON THE BATHROOM COUNTER, LOOKING DOWN AT THE NOTE Shelli put in my bag for me.

> *Go kick some ass. I'll be thinking of you.*
> *Love,*
> *Shelli*

I read it again and then again. This isn't the first time I've done this. Every time I open my bag, I read it. Every time, the warning bells go nuts in my head, but the weird thing is, the note makes me feel good. It makes me smile. She didn't have to leave me a note or even let me know she'd be thinking of me, but she did. I didn't want to leave her, which again, should set off some warning bells, but it doesn't. I wanted to stay. I wanted to hold her and sleep a little longer. If I'm honest, these last few days have been pretty damn lonely. It makes no sense at all since I'm surrounded by my teammates, but then, I want to be with Shelli.

I think I miss her.

Weird.

And there are more warning bells.

I pull my phone out of my pocket just as Boon comes into the bathroom. "Hey, bro. I gotta shit."

"My bad," I say, tucking the note into my back pocket and walking out into the hotel room. I hold my phone up to my ear as I wait for Asher to answer. When he does, I say, "I have an issue."

"An issue, you say?"

"Yeah."

"Well, before you hit me with your issue, I want to let you know I'm coming into town next week, and I'm staying with you. No way in hell I'm staying with Mom, Dad, and the girls. So make sure you leave my side of the bed open."

I shake my head. "No way."

"Guest room, then."

"Don't have one. I have an office. I don't want guests."

"Where will I go, then?"

"The couch."

"You're gonna put your favorite brother on the couch?"

"You're my only brother."

"Exactly, so scoot your big ass over and let me in the bed."

I scoff. "What if Shelli is over?"

"You can sleep in the middle."

I pause. "I'm done with this conversation, but yes, you can stay."

"You're right. We can discuss this when I get there." He laughs at my groan, and I roll my eyes. "So, what's the issue? I assume it has something to do with Shelli."

"Why do you say that?"

"'Cause you don't call unless it does."

I shrug. "While that's untrue, in this case, your assumption is right. I think we're in a relationship. Actually, I know we are, I just don't want to think of it that way. But I think I miss her. That's weird, right?"

I'm met with silence. "You really need help. Go see Emery's therapist. Please."

"Ash, come on. Tell me what to do."

"About what?"

"This. These feelings. What do I do?"

"Embrace them?"

"How?"

More silence. "I don't know what you want me to say here. It makes no sense to me whatsoever. I honestly didn't realize how fucked up our parents made you. Or was this Audrey's fault? We all know she wasn't normal until she got with Uncle Tate."

"It's no one's fault. I'm just... It's weird."

"Whatever, dude. Do you want to be with Shelli?"

"Yeah."

"Then shut up and be with her."

"I appreciate our meaningful conversations," I say dryly.

"Me too. Very productive. Listen, my girl just walked in. I gotta go."

I pause. "So, you just let it happen with her? You aren't freaked out by her?"

Asher groans loudly. "Of course, I'm freaked out by her, but I'd rather be with her than without."

That makes sense, but before I can say that, the asshole hangs up on me.

Boon sits down on the bed across from me and lets out a long breath. "I think we should go out, find some lady friends tonight. Wes is down."

I shake my head as I lie back on the bed. "I'm good."

He gives me an incredulous look. "Really? We're single dudes with the night off. I don't want to go to dinner with the married or in-relationship folks. They're boring."

I chew on my lip as I look up at my phone, seeing my lock screen of Shelli in my shirt. She has the goofiest grin on her face, but I still find her beautiful. "Yeah, I'm good."

"Why? Come on. It will be fun. I'll even let you have this room, and I'll go back to whoever's place."

As I stare at Shelli, her blue eyes shining, I know I don't want to do that. "I'm actually with someone."

"What? How? When were you dating?"

"Huh?"

"If you're with her, that means you're done with dating. I didn't even know you were dating anyone."

I look back down at my phone and text Asher.

Me: I moved past dating already!

Asher: Yes, because you've known her for her whole life. Jesus, loosen the man bun and think here.

Me: Do you even love me?

Asher: Eh. That's still up for debate.

"Oh yeah, I guess I am."

"Really?" Boon asks, and I nod before looking over at him.

"Yeah."

There is a knock on the adjoining door, and Wes comes in. Boon looks at him and announces, "BB is with someone."

Wes's eyes widen. "No way."

"That's what I said. He's famous for his whoring ways," Boon teases, and I flip him the bird.

"I am not."

He ignores me. "Did you even know he was dating?"

"I think you might, in fact, be famous for those whoring ways," Wes says with a shrug. "And no, I hadn't. But that's cool. Who is she? Do I know her?"

"No," I say quickly, shaking my head and shutting off my phone.

"When can we meet her?"

"I don't know." I don't want to share her with them. I don't want them judging us or making fun of us. I like us.

Boon makes a face. "Well, whoever it is has stolen our wingman, and he is now boring."

I glare at him. "What do you mean? I'm not boring."

Boon gets up, picking up his phone from the side table. "When you're in a relationship, you don't want to do anything fun unless you're with that person."

Hm, so that's what a relationship is? "That's not true. I'll go to dinner with you guys."

"Boring. I want to find someone to go home with."

"You can go home with the waitress."

Wes shakes his head. "Don't listen to him, BB. He's still bitter because his girl left him."

"I am not!"

"You are," Wes says, shaking his head. "I think it's cool. I'd rather be with someone than trolling for females."

"Because you're into that relationship shit!"

Wes sets him with a look. "And you were too until what's her name left you."

Boon rolls his eyes. "Fuck off. Trolling is fun," Boon insists. At one time, I agreed. I don't want to troll when I know there is a girl who's thinking of me. Only me.

Wes looks back at me. "Sure, but knowing there is that one girl who wants only you feels way better."

"Until she leaves you and breaks your heart."

It's as if I am watching the angel and devil argue on my shoulder.

Wes looks back at me. "And this is why we don't listen to Boon. Bitter."

"Fuck off!"

Wes laughs, but I feel what Boon is saying. Crazy thing is, I feel Wes too. Jesus, I'm a mess.

"Do you, bro. We're gonna go out, though," Wes says as he stands up.

"We sure are," Boon agrees, and then he goes to the door as Wes pats my shoulder.

"Wanna go?"

"No, I'm gonna order in."

"Cool. See ya."

"Have fun," I call at them as they walk out.

A part of me wants to go. I don't want to be boring, but I don't think Shelli would appreciate that. I wouldn't want her going out to troll for guys, and I sure as hell didn't like seeing her out with that fucker, Merryweather. I'm doing the right thing. I'm not boring. Especially when I know I can call Shelli. When my stomach rumbles, I sit up and order some food. It's going to be a while, so I sit back in the bed, opening my text thread with Shelli.

Me: wyd

Shelli: Nothing. Just sitting around. I'm hungry, but Mom isn't cooking, and I'm lazy.

Me: LOL. I just ordered food.

Shelli: Don't y'all go out on no-game nights? You didn't want to go?

Me: The guys are going to the club. I didn't think it was appropriate.

Shelli: Why?

Me: Cause they're going to find women.

Shelli: So? Doesn't mean you have to. Unless you want to.

Me: I don't, which is why I didn't go.

Shelli: Don't trust yourself?

Me: No, it's not that at all. I just didn't want to upset you.

Shelli: While I appreciate that, I trust you. You haven't done anything to make me think otherwise.

We shouldn't have skipped the dating thing. Or did we?

Me: Did we skip dating?

Shelli: I mean, I guess. We have known each other my whole life.

Me: Okay, true. So thinking I was doing the right thing is right, then?

Shelli: Did you want to go?

Me: No, I actually wanted to talk to you.

Shelli: Then you did the right thing.

A grin pulls at my lips.

Me: You should get something to eat, and we'll FaceTime. Eat together.

Shelli: Well, now that sounds like a digital DATE.

I know she said it to be funny, and while I am grinning, I'm hesitant to agree. I'm still thinking of what the guys said, and it's weighing heavy on me. I don't understand the way I'm thinking, but I know it's because of what Asher said. I want this, but I'm terrified of it.

Just do it. Just jump in. I swallow hard as I type back.

Me: Yeah, go get something. My food will be here in forty minutes.

Shelli: Okay, let me go whip something up.

I send her a thumbs-up and then lean back on the bed. I switch on GameCenter, but just as I set down the remote, I get a text.

Mom: Asher said you need Emery's therapist's number. I didn't know you were having problems. Do you need to talk?

Why does my brother love fucking with me?

Me: Mom, I'm fine, but I may kill Asher.

Mom: Are you sure? I love talking to you.

Me: I'm fine, plus Asher is staying with me while he's in town.

Mom: What? I didn't even know he was coming into town!

Ha.

Asher: I hate you.

Me: You're a jackass.

Asher: Hey, someone needs to help you before you ruin this.

Me: I'm not going to ruin it.

But even I'm not confident in my words. I want to say I feel good about all this, but I don't. I'm constantly freaking out and unsure of myself. Maybe I should have gone out, but I know I'd be bored because the only person I want to talk to is Shelli. No one can hold a candle to her. But should I worry that she'll find someone who's better than me? This relationship crap is wack. Why am I doing this again?

Asher: You better not, because Shelli is a super cool chick.

That's why. Because Shelli is a super cool chick, and I really enjoy her.

Before I can type back to my brother, my phone rings. The picture of Shelli and me from that shitshow of a party comes up. While the party was embarrassing, this picture isn't. I don't answer Shelli right away. I stare at us for a second, thinking how great we look. How perfectly beautiful she is.

I slide over to answer and hold the phone to my ear. "Hey."

"I'm bored. Talk to me."

I grin. "Okay. Whatcha making?"

"Grilled cheese. The reason we have no food is because Mom and Dad went out for dinner, leaving us offspring to fend for ourselves. I asked Posey to cook, but then Maxim said they should go out, so they did and took the boys."

"You didn't want to go?"

"I figured you might call, and I'd rather talk to you than watch my brothers burp and fart and Posey lust over Maxim while he completely ignores it because he doesn't see her like that."

I cock my head. "What's that about? Why doesn't Posey just say she has a thing for him?"

"Who knows. She's shy when it comes to that kind of stuff."

"Weird, since you are not even a little bit shy."

"Nope, I go for what I want."

I grin as I lick my lips. "Yeah, you do." Her soft laugh makes my body burn. "So, what did you do today?"

She lets out a long sigh. "Well, my intern supervisor says I'm too good to be an intern, so she's gonna talk to my mom. Before Mom left, she said I need to come in for a meeting."

"Too good to be an intern?"

"Uh, yeah. I'm amazing. I'm basically running the social media, and I can do that with my eyes closed. I need a challenge."

"I think it's funny your mom is making you start at the bottom."

She laughs. "Yeah, I don't know. But I do appreciate it. I want to start at the bottom so if Posey or the boys bitch that Mom gave me the team, I can be like, whoa, I worked for this shit."

"Absolutely. I admire that about you."

"Well, thank you." I hear the ding of the microwave before she says, "What did you order?"

"Steak, potatoes, and pasta."

"Jealous."

"Hey, come here, and I'll share."

She scoffs. "Don't tempt me. I have a plane, and I'm not afraid to use it."

I laugh. "You wouldn't find me complaining." Even though I can't see her grinning, I know she is. "Maybe when I get back, we can go have some steak."

"I do love steak."

"I do too, and if we need a cover, Asher is coming into town."

"Is he? For what?"

"No clue. To drive me crazy?"

She laughs. "I love Asher. He's so funny."

"He's a pain in my ass."

"Right? It's so funny how he picks at you."

I roll my eyes. "Yeah, he told me today that I can't mess this up because you're a super cool chick."

"I mean, he isn't wrong. Though, I kind of hope you know that and that you don't want to mess this up."

"Well, for your information, that's what I said."

"Oh, that's good to hear."

"I thought you'd like that." The grin on my face hurts, but it's there because of her. I know she's smiling too. "I want to see you."

"Give me a second. I'm bringing everything into my room."

"Okay," I say, though it isn't okay. I want to see her now. "Do you think I'm dumb for not going out?"

"Not at all," she says quickly. "I just don't want you to feel like you can't do what you want even though you're seeing me. Do you want me to stay at home and wait for you?"

"The answer should be no, right?"

She laughs loudly. "You're silly. I trust you. Trust me."

"Trust is a big word."

"It is, but the thing is, if you want to be trusted, be honest. We have no problem being honest with each other."

I nod. "We don't."

"So don't overthink it. Just do what makes you happy."

You make me happy.

I press my lips together. "It'd make me real happy if I could see you."

"Fine, fine. Jeez, impatient Pete."

"You don't want to see me?" I ask, and she laughs.

"Yes! Hush!"

My phone rings with FaceTime, and when I answer it, she's there. Naked.

Her hair is down along one shoulder, and she's wearing no makeup. I want to say I see a plate of food in her lap, but it's not what I'm looking at. It's the curve of her wonderful breasts and those lips that have my full attention.

I struggle with my next breath as I ask, "Did you lose your clothes along the way?"

She grins, her eyes narrowing a bit. "Yup. Is that a problem?"

"Not at all."

"Good. So when is your food coming?"

"No clue, but I don't want that food."

"No? Hungry for something else?" she asks, moving her hand along her breast, a sparkle in her eyes.

"Yeah, you."

With a wicked little grin, she licks her lips, and I swear I've never seen a more beautiful sight.

"You are trying to kill me."

She lifts her arms, her breasts so perky. "Just a bit."

"You're a mean, mean woman."

"And you love it," she says, her eyes twinkling mischievously.

Oh, this is a dangerous game. Real dangerous. But fuck if I don't want to play her game.

CHAPTER TWENTY-FIVE

SHELLI

"You know exactly why I did it. I want you to be with me."

I roll my eyes as I turn onto the interstate to head toward Luther Arena. I have a meeting with my mom, but first, I had to speak to Nico. I've had plenty of chances to call him since what happened between him and Aiden, but I wanted to sit back on it. I was too emotional before. I was mad he would make Aiden assume something and ultimately ruin a relationship I truly want. While I know Nico wants to be with me, I thought he cared enough for me not to hurt me. Breaking up Aiden and me would crush me.

"It's not the same for me," I say as calmly as I can. "I told you that back in Carolina. I told you the same thing at dinner. I don't want to be with you, Nico, and I don't say that to hurt you. I'm just being honest."

"That's shit, though. I know you want me."

"No, I don't," I stress. "From the rip, we were just fucking around. You knew that. I told you that—"

"But I love you."

I want to groan with annoyance. "No, Nico, you don't. I promise you don't. You just think you do because you like the way I make you feel. Sexually, not emotionally."

"Whatever. I love how you make me feel emotionally."

"For that to be true, you'd actually have to listen to me."

"I do!"

"What's my sister's name?"

He pauses. "Which one? Don't you have four?"

I sigh heavily. "No, I have one sister and three brothers. That's what I mean. You know nothing about me except I give great head and make you squeal."

"Shell, that's not true. I know you have a wicked left hook."

"But can you tell me the name of the last show I was in?"

He pauses for another second before he laughs. "It doesn't matter. It's all in the past. I want a future with you."

"We don't have a future," I say, shaking my head. "And I would appreciate it if you wouldn't ruin what I have with Aiden."

"You have nothing. He's a jackass. He doesn't even treat you right."

"Yes, he does. Maybe not at first, but that's because he was being an idiot."

"He's still an idiot."

"You don't even know him, and I can't believe you told him you fucked me."

"I did."

"You know what I mean. How you implied it."

"Whatever, Shelli. This is bullshit, and you know it."

"It isn't," I try, but he isn't having it.

"Whatever—"

"Nico, I care for you. You're a wonderful guy, and you're going to meet someone someday who will make you forget me completely. But when you do, ask her about herself and learn from this. Make her happy because you care, not because she can please you."

"Whatever," he says again, and then the line goes dead. While I feel like that had to be done, I didn't want it to end like this. I truly care for Nico, and he's also my cousin's fiancé's best friend, so I'm sure I'll see him again. I don't want bad blood between us, but more than that, I don't want to mess up what I've got with Aiden. He's so wary when it comes to what we're building. A lesser woman would give up and run, but I believe in this. I know he's still figuring it out. While I am hopelessly and unconditionally in love with him and I'm sure how I feel, I know Aiden will get there. I just need to give him time. I need to be patient because I truly believe we can have the kind of love our parents all have.

The thought of having that makes me grin and gives me that little fluttery feeling in my belly. I want it. I've watched my dad love and worship my mom my whole life. The same with Lucas and Fallon. They've all had such beautiful love stories, and I want Aiden and me to have that. I want him to realize that he can have it with me because I know I have it with him. No one has ever come close to how he makes me feel, and it's not because I have some fantasy version of us. I have truly loved him my whole life. I believe I was made to love him. I just hope he was made to love me back.

I bite my lip as I pull off the highway and head downtown to the arena. I'm not sure what my mom has in store for me, but I'm hoping it's not something boring. When I turn onto the road that holds the arena, my phone sounds again. I look down to see that it's Posey.

"Hey, what's up?"

"I need some advice."

"Okay?"

She hesitates, but then it's like she's speaking all her words at once. "Should I get something for Maxim for his birthday?"

My mouth quirks at the side. "Do you want to?"

"I do. I saw this amazing stick that I know he'd love but can't afford, and I thought if I get it, he'd like it."

I shrug. "I mean, if you want to, do it."

"You don't think that's dumb?"

"Why would it be?"

"I don't know. Like, it makes sense that Mom and Dad get him something, but I'm just me."

I hate that she feels like that. She's always so reserved. So self-conscious when she doesn't need to be. She's absolutely stunning and smart as a whip. Maxim would be lucky to be with her. "Yes. You're the girl in love with him."

"Shelli."

"What? You know what I think. I think you should get the stick and write on the blade that you're totally in love with—"

"Goodbye, Shelli."

The line goes dead, and I laugh. That's a first, being hung up on twice in one day. I follow the road through the parking garage up to the top where the players and employees park. I hope Posey takes my advice. She should tell him. They'd be cute together. As I get out of the truck, I'm excited I get to see Aiden soon. The guys had a great road trip, winning all three of their away games. They should be coming home today, but I haven't heard from him yet.

Not that I'm watching my phone or anything.

When it sounds, I rush to look at it, but it's only an email from a casting director up in New York. I open it as I walk toward the elevators. Before I can finish the email, though, my mom's voice startles me.

"Jumpy much?" she teases as she hits the button. My mother is by far the most beautiful woman I have ever seen. She's so classy and powerful in her pencil skirt and flowy blouse. She wears heels that are sky high and make her seem way taller than she is. Her hair is down, matching mine in big, wide curls. I grin as she hugs me from the side. "What has your attention?"

She looks over my shoulder at the email as we ride down. "A casting director wants me to audition for *Chicago*."

Her green eyes blaze back at me. "The one you always wanted to do."

"Yeah," I say softly.

"You should go."

"You think?"

She nods as we ride down to the offices. "I do. I know you think you're done, but maybe one more?"

I shrug as the doors open, and I tuck my phone into my pocket, deciding to write them back later. "I don't know. I'm happy here." But as soon as the words leave my mouth, I know I shouldn't think like that. While I love being home, the main reason I don't want to go back to New York is because Aiden wouldn't be there. This could all go to hell, and I would have missed out on an opportunity to be in a show I have wanted to perform in since I saw it at thirteen.

"But it's your favorite. At least go, try out, and then decide after they offer you the lead."

I scoff at her confidence in me as she wraps an arm around my shoulders. She kisses my temple as we head to her office. When the door shuts behind me, I look around at my life on display. Photos of my mom and dad together from when they were dating to the day they got married tell their story in front of me. There are photos of my siblings and me growing up too, but my eyes fall on the photo right above her desk. It's the one of my mom singing to my dad after a game, when she knew she had to win him over.

Her big gesture to get him back, after not singing live for so long. It's one of my favorite pictures and, for sure, one of my favorite stories she retells. I fall back in a chair, and I point up at the photograph. "I wish I had a chance to do *Funny Girl*."

My mom's face fills with such admiration as she gazes up at the photo, my dad holding her face as she holds the mic at her side. She looks back at me and says, "Oh honey, I would love to see you do that."

I grin. "Though I doubt I could ever sing 'My Man' the way the great Eleanor Fisher did," I say, using her maiden name.

She waves me off. "You'd sing it way better."

My heart swells in my chest. She is by far my biggest fan, as I am hers. We share a small smile before she opens up her laptop. I have never thought I couldn't do something. She always urged me to follow my dreams and never give up. While my dad is my hero, my mom is a role model. I strive to be her, to make her proud. "I love you, Mom."

Her loving gaze holds mine. "I love you too, honey." She winks at me, her lashes kissing her cheeks before she says, "So, let's get started."

I nod as I cross my legs, opening my tablet and taking out my digital pen. "All right, I assume this is to move me. So where am I going?"

"I want you to work with the foundation."

My brows come in. "The foundation?"

"Yes, the Assassins Foundation for Veterans."

A big grin pulls at my lips. "Really?"

"Really," she says with just as wide of a grin. "I want you to work with our new boys to get them involved in the foundation. I want you to plan some events for the guys to take part in. I think you should do a team fundraiser and then a gala to raise money for a new shelter I want to build for our veterans who need it."

My mind is blown. I've always admired the Assassins Foundation, and this is something I am super passionate about helping with. A new shelter? That's bomb. "Yes, I am so down."

"Wonderful."

"Which new guys?"

"Wesley McMillian, Boon Hoenes, and then Aiden, of course."

The last name sets my core on fire. "Great. I can do that."

"You'll need to really pin the boys down and make them work. They're all a bit squirrely. Gearing up for the play-offs."

"I know, but Wes and I are super cool. Boon is nice, and Aiden is Aiden," I say offhandedly, but Mom sets me with a look.

"You still have a thing for him."

"No, I don't..." I try, but she sees right through me.

"Shelli Grace, I know you, and I know it to be true. I don't blame you. He's handsome as all get-out, but remember, that boy has made some bad decisions."

I shrug. "That he's learned from, I assume, of course."

Her eyes burn into mine. "Maybe so. He has been on his best behavior. Nothing like what the GM of the Rangers made him out to be. He's always on time to practice, minus that time he overslept for the plane ride, and he's a team player. Everyone loves him, he works hard, and he shines on the ice."

While I think all the good could be because he's with me, I don't know that it is. I really think he was lost in New York. The shit with that crazy chick messed him up. Being home, finding his own way, and then me—I think it is all clicking for him.

Since I have nothing to say about that without giving away that I'm totally in love with Aiden, I save the document I have been taking notes in and nod. "I won't let you down."

"I know you won't." I look up at her, and she smiles as I get up. "Have you thought about asking him out?"

I furrow my brow. "Who?"

"Aiden."

I press my lips together, and I know this is the perfect moment to come clean. I tell this woman everything—she's one of my best friends—but I'm not ready to let her in on this. I don't want her to get her hopes up for me. She knows how badly I have wanted to be with Aiden, and if something goes wrong, she'll legit want to kill him. Then she'll get my dad and his angina involved, and I really don't need that.

"No, I don't think he sees me like that."

She narrows her eyes. "I think he may."

Her words make my heart pray she is right. "I don't know."

"See how it goes working with him. Maybe something will blossom?"

I wave her off. "I don't know. He seems pretty focused on his job."

She shrugs. "Maybe he doesn't have the right distraction?"

Oh, he does.

I have to hide my grin to make sure she doesn't see that I am it. "I'm gonna head out. I gotta get to the bar for my shift tonight."

She nods. "Please consider going to the audition."

"I will," I promise as I step around the desk to hug her tightly. "Thank you for this opportunity. I'm excited to do it."

"I know. You're going to do great. Call Aunt Grace if you need help."

"Duh. She's gonna be my planner."

She kisses my cheek. "Good thinking. Love you, honey."

"Love you," I say as I walk out of her office. When I shut the door, I lean against it as I exhale. I have admired this foundation for a really long time, and I finally get to help do something great for it. I'll be working on it, side by side with Aiden.

I really don't know how this day could get any better.

BROOKS HOUSE IS PACKED TO THE BRIM. I'M NOT SURE WHAT'S SO special about this Thursday, but everyone is out. There is a wait for a table, and my tip jar is overflowing. It's been a great night. Everyone has been really receptive to my playlist, and the requests that have come in have been fun to perform. The only downside is I haven't heard from Aiden. Like, at all. I wasn't sure if I should text him, so I just let it be.

Which is driving me crazy.

With my eyes closed, I let my voice fill the room as I move my fingers along the piano. "Total Eclipse of the Heart" is one of those songs that isn't done well without the all-out passion coming from the heart. I remember when I was nine and my mom taught me this song. We'd sing it while we did dishes, cleaned my room and the bathroom. It brings a smile to my face because I can still see my mom pressing into my gut and telling me to sing out into the world. I still use that advice to this day. Especially when I'm onstage.

When I finish the last lyrics, my pinkie hitting the final note on the piano, I open my eyes as my voice drops off. The room erupts with applause, and I sigh softly before reaching for a drink of my water.

That's when I see him.

Aiden sits at the end of the bar, one foot up on the lower rail, while his other is against the floor. He's wearing a fitted suit, a powder-blue color that makes his eyes seem blue instead of gray. His hair is down, tucked behind his ears, and his eyes, well, they're on me. A small grin pulls at his lips, and my breath catches. I want to close the distance between us. I want to wrap my body around his and kiss that naughty mouth of his. Only problem is, not only is Stella here, but so is Fallon.

Speaking of Fallon, she comes around the bar, hugging him tightly, and I know I have to look away. Or she'll see me with stars in my eyes only for him. Everything around me is crackling. I've missed him terribly. I look down at the piano, and something inside me wants to play Taylor Swift's "Sparks Fly." I move my fingers along the piano, and when I start to sing, I feel his gaze on me. Unable to keep my eyes closed, I open them to find I am right. Aiden is watching me, his eyes so intent on me as I sing the song that reminds me of him. Of us.

Fallon comes over to him with a plate of food, setting it down in front of him, and she looks over to me, a big grin on her face. Aiden says something, and she agrees, her eyes bright as she looks down at her firstborn. You can't deny how much she loves Aiden. Sometimes I think he's her favorite, and I can't blame her. He's absolutely amazing. When she walks away, his gaze moves over me once more, and the look in his eyes leaves me completely breathless.

I tear my gaze from his—or at least, I make it seem that way for the simple fact that I know people could be watching. When I finish the song, I notice he gets up as the crowd claps and cheers me on. But all I see is him, and all I hear is my heart pounding in my chest. He comes up to the piano and leans on it before sliding a napkin toward me.

"Stella and my mom think I'm up here requesting a song, but really, I wanted to ask if you'd come over tonight."

My lips quirk. "I would really like that."

"Good. See you when you get off?" I nod, and then he taps the piano. "Also, sorry I suck. My phone died, and I left my charger in Calgary. I would have used someone else's, but no one would give up their chargers. I may have a bit of a reputation for stealing them."

"Likely excuse," I tease, and he grins.

He taps the napkin and then winks before walking away. I watch his tight ass in those slacks, and I can't wait to meet him back at his place. I've missed him so damn much. I look down at the folded napkin, and when I open it, my heart explodes in my chest.

I missed you. A lot. I really want to kiss you and hold you in my arms. Don't make me wait long. It's already been long enough. Bring a bag, because you aren't leaving.
-Aiden

I look up just as a sexy grin moves across his lips, and I swear I fall for him all over again.

And I thought my day couldn't get any better.

CHAPTER TWENTY-SIX

AIDEN

My back hits the wall as I hold Shelli in my arms, our mouths in a fiery embrace of need. God, she feels good in my arms. Her thighs squeeze my hips as her mouth tortures mine. She threads her fingers through my hair as I draw out her soft and sexy moans. I squeeze her ass as I hold her, wanting her closer. Wanting her naked. I try to make it to my condo, but I'm too lost, and fuck it, I don't want to be found. Not when I'm with her.

When I finally get us to the front door, I fish out my keys as she continues to kiss me, raking her teeth along my jaw and neck. She's driving me out of my mind. Completely. I was a little hesitant leaving her that note. I was worried that it was silly to say those things, but if this is the response I get when I tell her I miss her... Well, damn it, I'll tell her every second. Especially since it's the truth.

I missed her like crazy these last few days. The phone wasn't enough. I wanted to feel her, touch her. Kiss her, taste her. I want to consume her. I missed the way she smelled. The way her thighs squished against my legs when we lay in bed. I missed her hair. I missed her eyes—fucking hell, I've missed all of her. It's odd and something I don't do, but I counted down the seconds every day until I could get back to the hotel to talk to her. There were warning bells, but I ignored them, especially when Shelli smiled. Or laughed. Yeah, her laugh gets me.

Who am I kidding? She knocks me on my ass, and I don't even want to get up because I know she'll get on top of me.

I shove the key in the lock and turn it before pushing the door open. I take only one step before my brother's voice fills the room. "Please don't fall on me and start having sex. That would be really awkward."

Shelli tears her mouth from mine, and her face turns beet red. "Oh!"

Annoyance rattles me. "Asher, what the fuck?"

He looks up at me innocently. Like me, he's huge, taking up the whole couch. Wide shoulders, tall as hell, and thick. He works out, a lot, which I tease him about since his whole look is that of a total dork. He wears these thick, black-framed glasses, and his hair is always a mess, but then, he's jacked. It's really comical. He's like the one genius who doesn't get thrown into lockers. Hell, he might do the throwing. His eyes are a weird combination of green and gray, but all I see is my dorky baby brother. I haven't seen him in a couple months, and don't get me wrong, I love the guy, but I really don't want to stop kissing Shelli.

Unfortunately, she's already climbing down my body. "Asher! Oh my God! I haven't seen you in forever."

A happy grin covers Asher's face as he gets up to hug Shelli.

"Please, don't stop your assault on my brother's mouth for my sake."

She smacks him. "Shut it. How are you?"

"I'm good. Great, even."

She gushes, her eyes bright. "Aw, wonderful! How's Jasmine?"

She knows my brother's girlfriend's name? "She's great, thanks for asking. She's actually out of town on a lacrosse trip. Figured I'd come home, visit while she's gone."

Shelli holds out her hands. "She is such a beast. I love watching her play."

She's watched the girl play? "I didn't know Jasmine played lacrosse."

They both look at me, and Asher scoffs. "Since that's the first time you've ever said her name, I wouldn't think you did."

Shelli gives me a disapproving look. "I thought y'all talk?"

Asher scoffs. "Yeah, about you."

Another disapproving look, and even with those stunning blue eyes, I feel like a jackass. "Aiden, you should know this stuff—"

But Asher waves her off. "It's fine. He didn't recognize relationships before you came along."

I really don't need a brother.

But then Shelli's lips curve as her eyes meet mine. "Oh."

"Thanks for that, by the way," he says, hugging her tightly, and she laughs.

I don't like him hugging her, and I really don't like his hand at her hip like that. He already thinks she's hot. Does she think he's hot? Why do I sound like an insecure fourteen-year-old going through puberty? I am a man. I am hot. She wants me. And fucking hell, I want her. "Hey, too close."

They laugh at me. She pats Asher's chest as she looks up at him. "When are you heading out?"

"Sunday night."

"Nice," she says, and then she looks over at me. Her brows pull together before she glances up at Asher. "Is this jealousy thing new?"

Asher rolls his eyes. "Another new trait that came along with you. I think it's adorable. Look at his little nostrils flaring. Isn't he sweet?"

"Right? And his vein. That's a hot vein."

"Yeah, laugh it up, Chuckles. I'll get your ass," I say, pointing to Asher. I turn back to her. "And I'll spank yours."

Asher snorts. "I should go before that happens, huh?"

She shrugs. "Probably. He's ready for bed."

"Sure, if that's what we're calling it now," he teases as he hugs her one last time. She laughs as Asher comes toward me. "I'm going out with Rocko and the boys. I'll be back."

"How did you even get in here?" I ask as we hug tightly.

"Mom."

"Wonderful. Couldn't call me?"

"Your phone kept going to voice mail, dumbass."

"Oh, it's dead," I say, and then I point to him. "Can you stop and get me a charger?"

He rolls his eyes. "Give me your car, and I will."

I drop the keys in his hand reluctantly. I just need him the hell out of here. "Please leave."

"Gone," he says, and then he waves to Shelli. "See you in the morning?"

She blushes. "Yeah."

He just grins back at me. "Aiden has a girlfriend," he sings, and I go to punch him, but he runs out the door, slamming it behind him.

I look back at Shelli, and her face is so bright, so pretty. "I'm sorry. I didn't remember he was going to be here."

"It's totally fine," she says, coming back to me and wrapping her arms around my torso. "I'm surprised you didn't run out of here with him."

I scrunch up my face. "Why would I? You're here. I want to be here, not with him."

She giggles as she slides her hands up the front of my shirt, unbuttoning it. "Because he said you have a girlfriend."

I lick my lips as she slowly exposes my chest. "I do."

Her eyes meet mine as her face lights up, her eyes brighter than the sun. "Really?"

"Yeah, if you want that."

"I do," she says, almost automatically. "Just wasn't sure how you felt about it."

"I feel good."

"Not terrified?"

I laugh. "Always terrified when it comes to you."

She rises up on her toes, kissing my jaw. "Let's go to bed, Aiden."

"We were already heading there."

I lift her into my arms, and hers go around my neck. Her eyes burn into mine as a small grin tugs at her lips. I glide my nose along hers before capturing those lips with mine, and as I kiss her, I let the whole girlfriend thing sink in. I wait for the warning bells, the need to run. But I realize the only place I want to run is into her arms. I lay her down on my bed and fall between her legs as our mouths continue to move together. Her leg slides up my thigh to my hip, hooking over it as she rubs that sinful center against my rock-hard cock. But all I'm thinking about is that Shelli Adler is my girlfriend.

And I'm her boyfriend...

And...there are the warning bells.

Shelli pulls back, her fingertips stroking along my jaw as I look down at her. Her eyes are so damn blue, they glow. Slowly, a grin takes over that beautiful face, and gone are the warning bells.

Gone is everything but her.

I only see her, my girlfriend.

WHEN I WAKE UP THE NEXT MORNING, I'M IN MY FAVORITE SPOT.

Right between Shelli's breasts. I nuzzle my nose in the curve, and her hand moves up and down my back. When I hear a clicking noise, I open an eye to see that she's typing on her phone.

"You're awake?"

She kisses the top of my head. "Yeah, I've been getting up early to work out since you've been gone, and now I also use the time to work on the foundation stuff."

"Or what you really mean is, I didn't work you hard enough last night?"

She snorts. "Not at all. I'm pretty sure I won't walk right today."

"Well, that's gonna be fun to watch."

She laughs softly before wrapping her arm around my neck, pressing her cheek into my head.

"What are you doing?"

"Looking at scores, stats, and news."

My lips curve teasingly. "Why?"

"'Cause I want to know," she says, smacking my shoulder. "Leave me alone."

"Never," I say before biting her boob.

"Oh, my mom put me in charge of the Assassins Foundation's spring fundraiser and gala."

"Of course she did. You were too awesome for the intern stuff."

She grins against my temple. "True, and this gig comes with perks."

"Perks?"

"I get to work side by side with the undeniably hot Aiden Brooks."

I turn my head, pressing it into her breastbone. "Oh, really? How does that make you feel?"

"Pretty damn good."

"I can be hard to work with," I say, my eyes drifting shut a bit, but she just grins.

"Don't worry, I know how to work ya," she says, grabbing on to my ass and squeezing hard. I jump slightly, but then our lips meet and I find myself grinning. When she pulls back, she runs her thumb along my bottom lip. "You need to brush your teeth."

I laugh out loud. "Seriously?"

"Seriously. Your breath is kickin'," she says, her eyes playful.

I smack her thigh. "In romantic movies, the girl never says that. She just goes down on the guy."

As I get up, she laughs. "Don't confuse a romantic movie with porn, Aiden."

I laugh as I head into the bathroom. As I put my toothpaste on my brush, my phone rings.

"It's your mom."

"I'll call her back."

I brush my teeth and then wash my face before coming back to bed. I take Shelli's phone and put it on the nightstand before covering her body with mine. "Maybe we should act out our own porn?"

She giggles as our lips meet. "That's exactly how I want to start my morning."

I close my eyes as we kiss, and I fall between her naked thighs. I move my hand down her chest, taking her breast in my palm as I press myself against her wet center. I groan against her mouth, and she does the same.

But then, Asher is knocking at the door.

"Hey, Aiden."

I tear my mouth from hers and groan loudly. "Die, Asher."

He laughs. The fucker laughs. "Dude, I'm just trying to help you out. Mom is downstairs and on her way up."

My eyes fly open just as Shelli's do. "Oh shit." We scramble out of the bed and hurry to get dressed. She kicks her bag under my bed and then rushes out of the room with her laptop and notebook. For what reason, I don't know.

"I was going to throw you in the closet."

She gives me a dirty look. "No one throws me in the closet."

"But you can throw me?" I toss back at her, but she's already out of the room. When she sets up her laptop, she crosses her legs, but then she looks at me with a panicked expression. "My hair? Do I have sex hair?"

"Totally," Asher says, and if looks could kill...

"Dude, shut the hell up!"

"What? She does, and FYI, I feel for your neighbors. I heard y'all down the hall."

Shelli's eyes widen, and I shake my head as she tries to do something with the mess that is her sex hair. "He's lying. You weren't even that loud."

"But you were," he says, and lucky for him, there is a knock at the door.

I go open the door to my mom. "Hey, I didn't expect you."

She gives me a dry look. "Well, you would if you would answer your phone."

"Oh, I didn't hear it," I lie.

"We're working," Shelli says then, and Mom's brows pull together.

"Shelli? Honey, I didn't expect you here." She goes to Shelli, hugging her tightly. "It's early."

"I know. We're working on the Assassins Foundation's spring fundraiser and gala. I'm an early riser."

Mom smiles. "You must be. How'd you get him up?" she asks, hooking her thumb toward me.

With a straight face, Shelli replies, "He's scared of me."

Mom and Asher laugh. "Well, you are your mother's child."

"I am," she agrees with a grin.

"I can't wait to see what you put together."

She grins. "Thanks. I'm hoping it's great."

"It will be," she says before handing me a plate. "I'm only here to drop off these cookies I made. They're vegan."

I put them on the counter, already planning to toss them. The last time she made these crap cakes, I almost puked.

"Please eat them."

"Mom, they taste like dirt. Like you literally pulled them out of the ground like a carrot. I'm good," I complain as Asher comes over and grabs one.

He takes a big bite. "Best cookie ever."

She pats his face, and I want to call him an ass-kisser, but I don't trust him. "My sweet boy. You two will be over for dinner, right?"

Asher throws his hand over my shoulder. "We sure will. Shelli and Aiden have a lot of vigorous work to do, though. They're working on it constantly. It gets loud too, but they're really passionate about it."

I twist a piece of his skin, and he cries out, smacking my hand. "Mom—"

But before he can finish, Shelli's phone starts to ring.

In my room.

Silence falls over us all as Shelli looks at me in utter panic. Mom glances toward my room and then back at me. "You gonna get that?"

"I sure am," I say, rushing to get it. I hit decline on a call from Elli Adler and tuck it into my pocket. "Sorry."

"I didn't know you were a Taylor Swift fan," she teases, and I plaster a huge grin on my face.

"Yup, Swiftie for life."

Asher is practically falling over himself laughing, but Shelli, she's beet red, and I'm pretty sure she wants to die.

"Well, I'm leaving. I'm actually meeting your mom," she says to Shelli, and she smiles brightly.

"For brunch?"

"Yup. Mimosas. You know..."

Shelli grins. "I do."

"So what's your plan for the fundraiser? I'm sure you're hiring Grace Justice for the party."

"I am. She's basically the best, and I'm not partial since she is my aunt." They both share a laugh as Shelli leans back in the chair. "But for the fundraiser, I think I want to do a calendar of the guys with puppies."

"Puppies?" I ask, and she nods.

"Women love hockey players and puppies. The calendars will sell out. I guarantee it."

Mom taps Shelli's forehead. "You're one smart cookie, Shelli Adler."

"Thanks, Fallon, I've learned from the best."

Mom gives her an indulgent smile.

"You're too sweet." But then Mom cocks her head to the side before she lowers her voice. "Honey, you do realize you look like you just rolled out of bed?"

I didn't know Shelli could turn another shade of red. Huh. Learn something new every day about her. I love that. "I worked out before I came over. I'm getting lazy."

Mom laughs. "Doubt that. Okay, I'll see you two later," she says, heading for the door. She then looks to Shelli. "Bye, honey."

"Bye, Fallon," she calls, and as the door shuts, she drops her head to the table.

"Well, that was fun," she groans, and I push Asher away and flip him the bird.

"You like fucking with me, huh?"

"Oh yeah, that was a blast."

"I might kill you."

"Eh, won't be the first time," he says, and I shake my head.

"Babe, your mom called," I say, and I dig Shelli's phone out of my pocket. I head toward her with it, but then I notice she has a text.

From Nico.

I pause in the middle of passing it to her, and she looks at me in question. "What's wrong?"

I lick my lips and try to keep the rage inside. "Nico doesn't like how you guys ended things and wants to meet up to talk about it because he doesn't believe you two are done."

She takes her phone from me and looks down at it, shaking her head. "He's so dumb."

"So you're still talking to him?"

She looks up at me. "I told him he and I were done and I thought it was shitty how he handled the situation."

"So why are you answering him?" I ask as she types back quickly.

She looks up at me, her brows meeting in the middle. "Aiden, I can't just cut him out. He's my cousin's fiancé's best friend."

"Whom you'll never see."

"But when I do, I don't want it to be weird. He is a nice guy."

"Who wants you."

"So? I don't want him."

"Whatever. I don't want you talking to him."

"That's ridiculous. Do you not trust me?"

"That's not the point. I don't trust that fucker."

"Again, do you not trust me?"

I shake my head. "Whatever, Shelli."

I should have known better than to say that. She gets up, throwing her phone down and going toe-to-toe with me. "No, tell me. Do you not trust me?"

"Of course, I fucking trust you, Shelli. But what if you decide you want him over me?"

"Aiden, abort! Disembark the crazy train!" Asher hollers at me, but Shelli's voice fills the room.

"Ash, shut up," she yells at him, and somehow, my brother's mouth snaps shut. "Get out."

But of course, needing the last word, he mutters, "Jeez, you're scary when you're mad."

I don't even see him go into my room because Shelli's eyes have locked in on mine. "Why would you say that?"

"It doesn't matt—"

"It does," she stresses.

"I don't like the guy."

"No, please tell me something I don't know," she says, her eyes searching mine. "Aiden, am I your girlfriend?"

I hold her gaze, but I don't answer.

"Last time I checked, I was. I'm yours. Not Nico's. Not anyone else's. I'm with you. I don't cheat, I don't lie, and what you see is what you get. You can either trust me or let me go. So you need to decide right now."

"I hate that guy," I say, and she nods.

"Again, I'm aware. But he isn't even on my radar." She slowly moves into my arms. "You are. Only you."

"Okay," I say softly. I hate how vulnerable I feel.

"Believe me, this jealousy stuff is really cute, but don't let it become a habit. I'm not going to hurt you, Aiden. I'm totally—" She wants to say more, but she shakes her head. "I'm not going to hurt you," she repeats, and then she rises onto her toes to touch her lips to mine. As I hold her, I want to believe her. I want to know she wouldn't, but it freaks me out. It's all so uncertain, and I hate that. But I'd rather be with her than without, so I fall into the kiss, ignoring all the warning bells and vulnerable feelings.

Because I want her.

CHAPTER TWENTY-SEVEN

AIDEN

"So."

I don't spare Asher a look as we drive to our parents'. For one, I'm still pissed at him for what he said to my mom about Shelli and me. For two, he gets on my ever-loving nerves. I just want to get this dinner done and go home so I can call Shelli. She had tasks to do for the fundraiser and forgot some things at her house. I promised to call when I got done at my parents'.

"What?" I snap, and he must think I'm hilarious by the way he laughs.

"You're still mad at me?"

"Yup."

He doesn't care. "That's fine. I need to say something to you before we go in there," he says just as we pull into my parents' driveway.

"Okay...?" I say as I put the car in park and shut it off. I finally look over at him. "What?"

"You do realize you are head over heels over ass in love with Shelli, right?"

My face twists up in disbelief as my heart stops. "What the hell are—"

"Fucking hell. You don't. Wonderful," he says, and then he gets out of the car.

I fumble over myself to get out also. "Why would you say that?"

"Because it's true," he says as we make our way up the driveway.

"No, it's not. We're together. There is no love."

Asher scoffs. "Aiden, you love her, and she's completely in love with you."

Shit, my mouth is dry. I can't breathe. "No. That's bullshit."

Asher sets me with a look, his weird-colored eyes burning into mine. "It's bullshit to be loved by someone? Do you know how many people beg for that daily? Crave it? You've got it, but I should have known you weren't ready for it. Which is going to make this awesome."

"Wait, what?"

He doesn't answer me. He just walks into the house as if he didn't just make my heart stop and my balls retract up into my body. What the hell does he mean? Do I feel something for Shelli? Totally. She's an awesome girl, and I really enjoy her—but love? I've never been in love. How would he know if I don't even know? Why can I still not breathe?

I walk into the house almost robotically. My limbs are stiff, and I feel like I'm about to pass out. *Do I love her? Shit, wait, does she love me?* She has had a crush on me since she was a kid. Did she fall in love with me? Wait, none of this matters. I can't let this ruin what I've got, and I've got it good with Shelli. I can't overthink this. I hate Asher. I hate him so much.

I fall down into a chair in the living room, a bit frantic and needing to breathe. I lean forward, dropping my phone and keys to the table before falling back and kicking up my feet. I close my eyes as I listen to my family in the kitchen. I need them to stay in there for a minute because my head is all over the place right now. If she does love me, what does that mean? Does she assume I love her? Why hasn't she told me? What would I say? Fuck. The ringing in my head is giving me a massive headache.

"Is this Shelli?"

My eyes fly open to find Stella with my phone in her hand, her eyes wide and her mouth hanging open. "It is! Why is Shelli—" Before she can finish, I'm up and out of my chair with my hand over her mouth and holding her to me.

Her eyes are like saucers, and my heart is in my throat as I stare down into her gaze. "Shut up." She mumbles something against my hand, but I refuse to move it. "I will give you all the money in my wallet—ow! Fuck! Stop hitting me!"

I look over my shoulder to see Emery beating me in the back. "Let go of her!"

When she kicks me in the back of the knee, I hit the floor with my hands up. "What the hell is wrong with you? You tried to kill her last week!"

Emery shrugs as Stella goes to stand beside her. "I can hurt her, not you. What's your issue?"

Stella holds out my phone. I try to reach for it, but she keeps it out of my grasp. "It's Shelli."

Emery's eyes widen, and I cover my face. "Give me my phone."

"She has, like, no pants on," Emery whispers, her eyes about to come out of her damn head. "Why doesn't she have pants on? Are you sleeping with her?"

"You know about sex?" I ask incredulously, and then both of them just stare at me.

Stella whisper-yells, "She's fourteen," just as Emery says, "I'm fourteen!"

"Touché," I say, and then I snatch my phone, much to their dismay. "Stay out of my shit."

"Are you?" Stella asks, and then a smile spreads over her face. "Wouldn't that be so sweet? She's been in love with you for, like, ever!"

That damn L-word!

"Shut up," I say, moving my hands frantically in front of my face. "Stop. Like, for real, stop."

Obviously, these two don't know what stop means.

"Does Mom know?" Emery asks, and her eyes go wider, much to my surprise. "There is no way because we'd all know."

"Oh my God, are y'all like hiding it? Like Romeo and Juliet?"

When they both *aww*, I cringe. "No, nothing like Romeo and Juliet. Our families love each other."

Stella laughs. "But Shea will kill you dead."

I swallow hard. "Which is why you guys can't tell anyone!" I snap, but apparently I'm dead wrong.

They both look at me with such mischievous expressions.

Emery looks like a cat with a canary in her mouth as she says, "Actually, we can."

Stella nods, looking more like Emery than the sweet girl I love. "We so can."

"But that money in your wallet could buy our silence," Emery says, and when she holds up her hand, Stella high-fives her.

Thick as thieves, these two.

It's easy to say when I enter the kitchen, I'm out four hundred dollars and my heart still hasn't slowed down.

"Aiden, baby, why do you look so pale?"

I shake my head as I sit down. "Your daughters are criminals," I mutter, and my dad laughs.

"Especially the younger one."

I shake my head. "Because the older one trained her."

Dad laughs harder as Mom looks back at the girls, who are talking about how they're gonna spend the money. Little assholes. Extorting their older brother. Way smarter than I was at that age. I was too obsessed with hockey to even know to do that. I was too obsessed with hockey to do a lot of things. I missed my whole senior year to go to college early. I don't regret it. I wanted it. I didn't need homecoming or prom or senior year crap. I wanted to go into the NHL, I wanted to be successful, and I did it. Because of that, I missed out on the whole having-a-relationship thing. Which is proving to be a bit of an issue now.

While everyone sits, ready for the meal, I feel as if I have a billion Minions in my head, tearing up Gru's laboratory. It's a mess up there, and I don't know what the hell I'm feeling. I'm freaked to the max, though my family has no damn clue whatsoever. We eat dinner as we've been doing for most of my life. Stella and Emery steal the show; they're funny and witty. My mom loves it and jokes with them. Asher doesn't say much, but when he does, everyone listens. I stay mute, and thankfully, no one notices. But I do notice that my dad looks happy.

"What's the grin about?" I find myself asking, and he squeezes my shoulder.

"It's good to have everyone home," he says proudly, and my heart swells. It is nice, even if Asher is an asshole and Stella and Emery should be starring in their own episode of *Law and Order*. I love my family. They're my rock, and Dad's right, it feels good to be together.

When dessert is served—my favorite, key lime pie—we're arguing about how much skin Stella can show in her prom dress. Dad and I are pretty much on the same page—none—while Mom and Stella feel the stomach should be allowed.

"You can just not go," Dad says then, and Stella pouts.

"That's unfair."

"Life isn't fair, sweetheart, and while you live under my roof, you'll stay covered up." He points his fork at her. "A guy won't want the milk if he can see the cow's udders."

I snort. "What the hell?"

The fork comes at me next. "Shut it, you."

Asher gives Dad a look. "But Dad, I think we all know guys want the milk no matter what."

Dad slams the fork on the table as we all laugh. "Not my baby's milk!"

"Wow, okay, this conversation is done," Mom announces loudly, shaking her head. When Stella starts to complain, Mom presses her hand into hers. "I'll talk to him."

Dad leans in. "And I'll still say no."

Mom gives him a look that says otherwise, but I don't think anyone was supposed to catch that. That's my mom and dad though, secret looks and sweet touches. When I notice a huge bouquet of red roses on the counter, I cock my head.

"What are the roses for?"

Mom grins over at Dad before he looks at me. "Just because."

"Just because?"

He nods. "Yeah, because I love your mom. I wanted her to smile."

Oh. I want to make Shelli smile.

Does that mean I love her?

I lean on my hand as I eat my pie. I wish pie could tell me what I feel. Asher pushes his plate away. I watch as he leans on his elbows and clears his throat. Stella, Dad, and Emery keep eating, but Mom and I look to him.

"What's wrong, baby? Did you not like it?"

"Mom, the plate is empty."

She grins. "Then why are you clearing your throat for my attention?"

He crosses his arms over his chest. "Because I need it."

Dad finally looks up, and with his mouth full of pie, he says, "Well, you got it. What?"

Asher runs his hand along his mouth, and I notice he's nervous. What's wrong with him? "I didn't just come home because I missed you guys."

"Please don't spare our feelings," I say, but he doesn't laugh.

"Yeah, plus, none of us miss you anyway," Emery teases, and I snort as I point at her. Though, Asher doesn't find any of us comical. His eyes are on Mom, and he seems pretty serious.

My smile drops as I ask, "What's going on?"

He doesn't look at me. "I came home to get the family engagement ring."

A silence falls over the table. Through the years, my dad has bought my mom many upgrades to her wedding set. The engagement ring Asher speaks of is the very first one. I remember picking it out with my dad. It's a huge heart-shaped single diamond that is set on a band engraved with "I love you and you love me." It almost exactly matches the tattoos on Mom's and Dad's wrists.

Asher looks so damn sure of himself as he says, "I'm very much in love with Jasmine, and I want to ask her to marry me."

Along with the rest of the table, I just blink. I don't believe what I am hearing. I'm envious of him for knowing what he wants, but he's a kid! Mom is the first to recover. "Asher, baby, I'm so happy that you're in love, but you're only nineteen."

Thank you, Mom!

"I'm aware, but she's all I want. And like Dad always says, when you know, you know."

I look back to Mom, who nods slowly. "Well then, wow, that's so amazing. Jasmine is wonderful. I adore her."

"She is great," Stella says, and Emery nods.

"She's crazy strong."

"I'm sure the more we get to know her, we'll fall in love with her too," Dad says, and I make a face. Am I the only one who hasn't met her?

"Yeah, I've got nothing. I haven't met her, but congratulations. I'm sure she's great if you like her."

Asher looks over at me. "Love her."

I nod. "Yeah, that."

He shakes his head and doesn't look excited as he holds my gaze. He looks kind of pissed. "I've wanted you to meet her plenty of times, but you never made the time."

Oh, so he is pissed. "And I regret that. I hope I can meet her before the wedding."

Asher shakes his head. "None of that matters right now. You're supposed to get the family ring."

I blink, unsure where he is going with this. "Okay?"

Stella makes a face. "But I want that ring!"

"Me too. It's the prettiest and means the most!" Emery says, but Dad shakes his head.

"That ring is for Aiden. He helped me pick it out."

Mom nods. "Daddy has updated my ring four times. There is one for each of you. You know that, Asher. I have yours if you want it."

He shakes his head. "I wanted the first one. Like Emery says, it's the one with the most meaning."

Everyone then looks at me. "What?"

"I want the ring," Asher says, and I shrug.

"Okay?"

"Okay, I can have it?"

"Okay, good for you. But, no, it's mine."

Asher's face fills with color, and his eyes narrow to slits.

"I don't know why you're so upset. We all know who gets that ring. I was there. I picked it out."

"Why? You won't use it. Hell, you won't even admit to loving her!"

There are audible gasps from my sisters, and I feel everyone's stares as I glare at my brother. "Shut up."

"No, it's not fair. You won't use it, so let me."

"No," I say simply. "I may be a little confused now, but if I decide one day to use it, I want it."

"Why? You don't even believe in love, Aiden. They fucked you up!"

Dad's voice fills the kitchen. "What the hell is going on?"

"Asher, what in the world?" Mom asks, her gaze flicking between us. "Are you dating someone?"

I watch as Asher looks away, shaking his head. "It's nothing. Just let it go. Give him his ring, and let it be."

"It's bullshit, and you know it."

"Ash, let it go," I warn, but his eyes meet mine once more.

"If you could look at me and tell me you'd honestly use the ring, I'd believe you. But you've been with her for months now, and you won't even accept that you love her—and she sure as hell loves you. You have no plan to commit to anyone. Right now, it's easy 'cause no one knows, but when they do, you'll bail."

"That's bullshit. You don't know shit."

"I know you. I know what they've done to you."

He jerks his thumb at my parents, and Mom smacks her hands together. "What the hell is going on? Why do you keep saying we've done something? What have we done?"

I don't say anything, and neither does Asher. But then, there's my father. "Please say this has nothing to do with she-who-must-not-be-named?"

I close my eyes as another gasp comes from the girls.

"Aiden, really? You've got to be kidding me. You're not an idiot. Come on!"

Mom's annoyance rings in her voice. "If someone doesn't tell me what is going on, I'm going to flip this table."

"And we wonder why Emery is the way she is," Asher snaps, and Emery glares.

"Hey!"

Silence. I know I've gotta get out of here. There are four too many people who know what is going on. My mom can't know; she'll freak. I push back my chair. "I'm out of here."

"The hell you are!" Mom yells, and when I look at her, her eyes are wild. "You tell me right now what the hell is going on."

"Mom, please. It's nothing."

"Are you going to give me the ring?" Asher asks, and I shake my head.

"No, asshole. Let it—"

"He's dating Shelli Adler," Asher announces, and he doesn't spare me a glance.

My jaw drops. "Wow. All over a ring that isn't even yours. That's real rich!" I yell, and the girls cower in their chairs. Dad is looking down at the table, and I refuse to look at my mother.

"May be an asshole move, but if I can't have it, then you better fucking use it," he snaps at me, and I think I might hit him.

Before I can snap back at him, my mom says, "Shelli Adler, as in the girl we've known since she was born?"

Everyone nods except me.

"The same girl you held and said she had a tomato head when she was born?"

I want to laugh. Shelli would get a kick out of that. I don't answer, though; I just move my fork through my whipped cream.

"The same girl who was at your house this morning with sex hair?"

Well, I guess she did have some serious sex hair. I love it, though.

"That's her," Asher says with no problem whatsoever.

Mom's voice is low and angry. "Asher, Stella, and Emery, get out now."

I swallow hard, and even though my name wasn't on the list to leave, I'm twenty-seven years old. If I want to leave, I will. I start to get up, only to stop at my mom's voice.

"Aiden James Brooks, you better sit that ass down right now."

At least I like to think I'm a man.

As the room clears out, I sit down, staring down at the table.

"You've known?"

I look up to see my dad nod. "I thought he was going to break it off."

I feel my mom's gaze on me. "How long?"

I shrug. "Not too long—"

"Over three months," Asher calls from the other room.

"He has a picture of her with no pants on his phone, Mom. I think they're sleeping together," Emery calls.

"Y'all are so dead," Stella laughs, and I'm vibrating with anger.

"Fucking traitors," I mutter, and when I lean back, my mom's eyes are on me. In slits, those green eyes are piercing as she shakes her head.

She swallows hard, and my stomach clenches. My mom is scary as fuck. "You know, if you'd told me, I would have said it's great. I love Shelli, she's a wonderful girl, and I think she'd be great for you. Will her dad freak? Hell yes, but he loves you and would support you. While this does have the potential to mess up our friendship with the Adlers, we are all adults and can handle it. But not when we're being lied to."

"It's my business—"

"That apparently everyone knows but me."

"I didn't want them knowing either!" I yell, holding my palms up. "Your daughters extorted me, and I thought Asher was my best friend, but that's been revealed as a lie." I look toward the living room. "All over a ring he's not fucking getting!"

"Aiden James, if you don't watch your mouth, I might wash it out with soap."

I snap my mouth shut. I'm twenty-seven; why am I being chastised right now? "I don't see what the big deal—"

"Oh, the big deal, you say? It's the fact that you kept this from us. And then you're supposedly in love with her, but you won't accept that because of us, so please, explain to me how this is our fault."

"I never said I was in love with her."

"Asher seems to think so."

"Asher is a jack—" I let the word fall off when she sets me with a look. "Mom, it's nothing—"

"Fallon, you know why it's our fault," Dad says then, and I close my eyes. I don't want to do this.

"There is no reason for anyone to be faulted right now. It's done," I try, but it's as if I'm not there. Mom looks at Dad, and their eyes lock. This isn't the first time I've seen them look at each other like that, but nonetheless, it takes my breath away. They look at each other like no one else is in the room. In a way, it's how I feel when I look at Shelli.

"We've talked about it before. Unlike with the other three, I wasn't there from the beginning. He didn't get to see us in love when he was younger—"

"But we love each other more now than ever. He's seen that," Mom tries. "I refuse to blame us for his commitment issues."

"But it is our fault. Mine for not being there, and yours for being so jaded when it came to relationships," Dad says slowly. "I love you, Fallon. I love you more than I can ever express, but we did this."

Mom looks at me, and I swallow past the emotion in my throat. I don't want to hurt her. I love her. My mom is perfection in my eyes. She gave me a great life before Dad came along. She loved me enough for both of them, along with Audrey's help. They were great to me, and while it was a good change when Dad came along, I know my mom did her best.

"Are you in love with her?" she asks, and I shake my head.

"I don't even know what love is."

Dad holds out his hand to me. "Why is that?"

"'Cause I've never been with anyone to find out," I answer, and when I see the tears gather in my mom's eyes, I look away. "It's not a big deal."

"Aiden, it's a huge deal. We don't want that for you. You deserve to love someone. To be loved. Don't let what happened to me hold you back."

I look up, meeting her gaze. "That's hard when I heard you cry. When I saw you try and try to find someone to fill that hole he left you with. You'd lie in bed with me, and I could see the pain on your face. You were never complete, never happy—"

"Aiden, you were the light of my life. I was always happy—"

"Yes, with me. But when it was just you, or even with AA, you were sad. You were bitter, you were angry, because all you wanted was the love of your life. You wanted the man who completed you. And I'm sorry, I can't do that."

"Can't do what?" Dad asks, his hand slipping around my mom and scooting her beside him so he can hold her. "We are happy, Aiden. We are in love. This is a great life."

"But it doesn't erase the fact that she was miserable for a long time. Six years, to be exact. So you want me to just give in to that, feel that, and then have it go away?" Both of their faces are filled with such turmoil. "Don't you remember, Mom? Not everyone gets a happily ever after, so why should I even chance it?"

Tears stream down my mom's face, and I hate it. I didn't want to make her cry. She gets up and comes around the table. I don't move until she makes me, turning me in my chair before taking my face in her hand. "You chance it for this," she says, gesturing around the room. "For a family. A home. A love that will last a lifetime. Yes, your father broke me, but he also put me back together. He gave me the best life I could ever ask for—"

"But I don't want that pain," I tell her.

She blinks as the tears fall down her cheeks, and then she slowly lowers to her knees, cupping my face in both her hands. "The truth is, punkin', everybody can hurt you, but you gotta find the one worth hurting for. The one who may hurt you but will love you even harder. We're human. We make mistakes. It happens."

As I stare into her flooded green eyes, I find myself asking if Shelli is worth hurting for. I see her blue eyes, her quick grin, and I can feel her laugh in my soul.

Is she?

"Punkin', I found mine, and then I lost him. Did I do things wrong? You're damn right I did, but I was young, I was hurt, and I was mad. Dad and I both made bad choices, him with the drinking and me with keeping him away from you completely. I tried to stop myself from being hurt again, and I was miserable. I hurt him and he hurt me, but here we are. My heart belongs to him, and sometimes, if you're lucky, that's how it is. You find the one you belong to, the one you were made for, and that's it."

I swallow hard as I get lost in her loving eyes. "I don't want to get hurt."

She holds my face. "But is the fear of hurt enough to keep you from feeling complete?"

I look down at my hands as I absorb everything they are saying. "I hear you guys, but I honestly don't know what to say. I don't know what I'm feeling."

"Is it serious? You and Shelli?"

I swallow past the lump in my throat. "I don't... I think so. I miss her, a lot, and I love being with her."

She pats my face. "Ask yourself if you can live without her, and you'll know if it's serious or not."

It's serious.

I don't say that, though. I just nod as she kisses my temple. "Now we have to figure out a way to protect you from the wrath of Shea Adler when he finds out." She looks to my dad then. "I can't lose him. I love him the most."

A grin pulls at my lips at the sounds of distress from my siblings in the living room. But then it disappears when I realize my whole family now knows about Shelli. They know I don't know what I'm feeling.

But all I want to know is if I'll get hurt.

CHAPTER TWENTY-EIGHT

SHELLI

I'M A TAD BIT ANNOYED.

As I sit at the kitchen table, working on the scheduling and other details, I find myself looking back at my phone every minute or so. It's pathetic and I'm aware, but it's unlike Aiden not to text or call me. We haven't gone a day without talking since we started this, and I really don't know what is going on. Since I have my pride, I refuse to text him first. He said he would text me when he was done with dinner. That was twenty-four hours ago—not that I'm keeping up with it or anything.

What did I do?

When my phone sounds, I look down to see it's Amelia.

Amelia: You did nothing. Don't turn this into something it's not. He has probably just been busy.

But even so, he would at least text me. Tell me so. I don't know... Something seems off. Not that I tell that to Amelia. I don't want to seem needy or obsessed with him. I'm not... Well, maybe a little. But in my defense, he's absolutely wonderful. I love spending time with him. I love talking to him. I love laughing with him. I really love being in bed with him.

Who am I kidding? I love him. All of him.

Every single fiber of him. And I really want him to love me. I want him to look into my eyes, hold my face, and I want to hear him utter those words. So badly. A part of me wants to believe that he's getting there, that he actually does care for me, but the other part is telling me I'm delusional. It won't happen. Aiden Brooks, love me? Please, why would he? I may think I'm enough, but no one has ever been enough for him.

"Working?"

I look up as Mom comes into the kitchen. She's wearing her robe, as she should since it's almost nine at night. Meanwhile, I'm wearing jeans and a tee in the hopes that Aiden will call. Even if he does, I shouldn't go. I should stay here, even if I don't want to. I miss him, and he's leaving tomorrow night for a long road trip. That's the reason I thought I was staying the weekend with him. It's rare that they have a weekend off, but with back-to-backs in two different cities, I guess they thought it would be a nice break. It would be, if I were with Aiden.

"Yeah, trying to get a spot for the shoot."

She nods as she pulls out the chair. "You should do it at the arena."

I shrug, wrinkling my face at her. "That's so overdone. I kind of want to do it in a park or even a really rustic house. I don't know. I want it to feel homey, if that makes sense. Like the guys on the couch with the pups or even in a truck? Just something really down-home."

Mom nods. "Well, you could do it here."

My lips curve. "That would be free."

"What's free?" Dad asks as he pulls out a chair, sitting down across from me.

Mom leans into him, kissing his shoulder. "The house, for the spring fundraiser. A photo shoot with dogs."

"That would be cool," he says, wrapping his arm around Mom. They share a look, and I love how in love they are. I want that kind of love, and I want to believe I'll have it. But for that to happen, Aiden would have to love me. "So I guess you're liking this gig, then?"

I nod eagerly. "I am. I love it."

"Well, I don't think anyone could do it as well as you are. You're gonna make us even more proud of you, aren't you?"

I grin at him, nodding. "That's my goal."

He pats my hand as Posey comes into the kitchen. She falls into the chair beside my mom before Mom asks, "Have you decided what you're going to do about the audition?"

I look down at my hands. I haven't told Aiden about it, but I'm unsure what I want to do. I don't want to leave him, but I have always wanted to be in *Chicago*. It's one of my top three shows. I can't stay for a guy, I know I can't, and I also suspect he wouldn't let me. We're both too goal-oriented. "I don't know yet. I'm still considering it. I haven't emailed them back yet. I will by tomorrow."

"That's unlike you. Why haven't you decided?"

I bite my lip as I look down at my computer. "Just been busy."

"While I know you're working hard on your assignment, I also know that you haven't been sleeping in your bed." My eyes widen as I meet her gaze. What is she doing? Dad is at the table. *Hello?* Did we forget about the angina? She waves me off. "He knows."

I don't look at my dad. "But the angina?"

She snorts, and my dad chuckles lightly. "Still in full effect."

"I have to say, Dad, you're not even red," Posey teases. "You did hear that she's not sleeping in her bed? Which means she's sleeping in someone else's. A boy, Dad, or maybe even a man."

I glare at my sister. "Do you want me to stab you?"

She laughs at me as Dad swallows hard. "Mom says I need to relax. That you're not a baby anymore."

"But?" I supply, and he laughs.

"But I don't want to know about it, so I'm leaving."

He gets up then and heads out as we all laugh together. When we hear the TV come on, Mom looks at me all excitedly as she pats my hand. "So? Who is he?"

I shake my head. "I'm not ready to say."

She pulls her brows in. "Really? You tell me everything."

"I know," I agree as I look away. "But he's skittish, and we've decided to do us before we involve parents and stuff."

I feel as if I've said too much, but she doesn't seem to catch on. "So you know his family? Do I know him?"

"No, we're just taking it slow," I lie, but Posey sees right through me.

"Is it that guy AJ?"

My eyes widen as I look back at her. Aiden doesn't really go by AJ, but he did a bit in high school.

Mom's brows perk. "AJ who? Posey, do you know?"

Posey just shakes her head. "No, Mom. I just know she talks to AJ all the time, so I assumed it was him."

Our gazes stay locked, and in a way, it's nice that Posey knows.

"Is it serious?"

I smile. "For me, yes. For him, eh, not sure." When she makes a face, I hold up my hands. "I want to say it is, but like I said, he's skittish."

She shrugs. "I was skittish."

I raise my brow. "What? You love Daddy."

Mom grins as she nods. "Of course I do, but I was scared shitless of getting hurt, and I was terrified of commitment. It takes one bad relationship to ruin you."

I press my lips together. Aiden's never dated anyone. I really have no clue why he's afraid of commitment. "How did you get over it?"

She moves her head toward the living room, where I know my dad is sitting in his La-Z-Boy, watching the hockey highlights. "He never gave up on me. He loved me until I realized he wasn't going anywhere. Now, look at us. Five beautiful children, a home, and happiness."

My lips curve. "You guys are such relationship goals."

Posey nods. "Totally."

Mom smiles at us both. "It will happen for y'all too. Don't worry."

I glance at Posey, and she looks down, seeming unsure of herself. I know she's thinking of Maxim, and it bothers me. I want her to realize there are men out there who want her, but she's caught up on one guy. Just as I am. I didn't give up on what I wanted, and now I have him.

When my phone flashes with a call, I look down to see it's Aiden.

I lift the phone quickly and stand up. "Excuse me."

"Is it AJ?" Mom squeals, and Posey laughs.

I roll my eyes as I answer it before heading out of the kitchen and down the hall to my room. "Well, hey there, stranger."

"Hey. What are you doing?" His voice is soft, a little defeated.

I hold in my anger. "Nothing. Just working."

"Cool. Do you wanna come over?"

"For?"

He pauses. "To see me? I leave tomorrow. I wanted to spend time with you."

I nod, even though he can't see me. "Oh, so we're acting like you've been talking to me for the last twenty-four hours? You've been radio silent."

He doesn't answer for a moment before clearing his throat. "You haven't texted me."

"Because you said you'd text me when you were done at dinner," I throw back, and he lets out a long sigh. "So, what happened?"

He doesn't speak right away. I wait for an answer, and then he says, "Can you come over, please? I miss you."

I purse my lips. "Why? So you can do something cute so I won't be upset anymore?"

"Exactly," he says warily, and I shake my head.

"You're impossible."

"Please?"

"Fine, but I'm not staying."

"Yeah, you are," he says, and finally, a bit of his cockiness is back.

"No."

"Don't forget your charger. Your toothbrush is here."

"Whatever."

"Be careful. It's raining."

The line goes dead, and I shake my head, though I am grinning from ear to ear. I want to see him. I'm annoyed he hasn't called or texted, but by the way he sounded, I think dinner must have been a shitshow. I don't know why, though. He was excited to spend time with his family. I tuck my phone into my pocket and grab my charger. I already have a bag there. I head out of my room and down the hall just as my dad comes out of the bathroom.

"You leaving?"

I nod. "Yeah, I'll be back tomorrow."

I go to step around him, but he stops me. His eyes search mine, and I find I'm holding my breath. If he tells me I can't go, I won't. "Shelli, is he good to you?"

His eyes are so full of worry, they make my heart stop. "Of course, Daddy. You know me. I won't settle for anything less than perfect. Not with you as the example."

He nods firmly. "Good. You better not."

"I won't."

He wraps an arm around my neck and pulls me in. "I love you, darling."

And because of how he loves me, I know how I want to be loved. Completely.

❧

WHEN AIDEN OPENS THE DOOR, OUR EYES MEET. I GO TO SAY something witty, something a little bitchy, but he looks overwhelmed. He lets out a long sigh before he pulls me into his arms and hugs me tightly. He nuzzles his nose into my neck, and I close my eyes as I hold him. We stand in the doorway for what seems like hours, our hearts beating and our breathing in sync.

When he pulls back, he kisses my lips. "I missed you."

"Not enough to call me?" I ask, not able to let go of my annoyance.

He laces his fingers with mine. "Rough night, and then I had practice this morning."

"Still could have texted me," I remind him as he leads me in.

As he shuts the door, he says, "You're right. I'm sorry."

I throw my keys and charger on the table by the door before looking up at him. "What happened?"

He shakes his head. "Too much crap to even talk about." I go to ask what, but then I notice a mason jar of yellow daffodils on the counter. I look over at him, and he holds his hands up. "I swear, I got them last night. I'm so not trying to be cute about not calling. I really am sorry."

I walk to the counter, skeptical, but then I notice a card beside them. It's a narwhal that is saying "You're one of a kind!" I open the card, and inside, in his messy handwriting, it reads:

Just because...
They reminded me of you.
-Aiden

I press the card to my chest as I look over my shoulder at him. "They reminded you of me?"

"They're bright and make me happy when I look at them."

My heart explodes in my chest. Holy swoon, Batman. "And you bought these last night?"

"I picked them out of my mom's garden, and I bought the card at the gas station last night." I eye him, and he shrugs. "I have the receipt."

My face breaks into a grin. "This is very sweet."

He comes up beside me, wrapping his arms around my waist and kissing my jaw. "You're sweet."

"Will you tell me what happened?"

He hesitates. "I'd rather take you to bed."

I search his gaze. "Where is Asher?"

"Who cares? I don't," he answers as he nuzzles my neck.

"So Asher pissed you off?"

He nods. "But I don't want to talk about him either."

"Is he the reason dinner went badly?"

"Yes." He kisses my jaw. "Did you know I called you tomato head the whole first month after you were born?"

I smile. "I didn't, but since I came up, does the bad dinner have to do with me?"

"Yes."

My heart picks up in cadence. I press my lips together. "Do they know?"

"Yeah."

"But you don't want to talk about it?"

"No."

I move my fingers along his jaw. "Should I be worried?"

"No," he says fiercely. "Everything is under control."

I tip his jaw up so our eyes meet. "Are you okay?"

He leans his head into mine, his gray thundercloud eyes burning into mine. I feel so special under his gaze. So beautiful. So complete. In a gruff voice, he whispers, "I am now."

It's funny... So am I. I was waiting for the anxiety to come, knowing his family knows. That they'll tell my parents. But I don't care. For once Aiden's lips meet mine, nothing matters.

Only us.

CHAPTER TWENTY-NINE

AIDEN

I RACE ONE OF TAMPA'S DEFENSEMEN INTO THEIR ZONE FOR THE puck. I gotta get there before icing is called. Thankfully, I do, and they wave it off. What I don't expect is for the 900-pound Igor-looking motherfucker to slam me into the boards. My face goes into the glass, and yup, I'm going to feel that tomorrow. Maybe Shelli can kiss away the pain. That's the only good thing about tomorrow, seeing her. First, though, I gotta win this hockey game.

I push my ass into the guy to give myself some room as I fight for the puck against two defensemen. Thankfully, Wes has skated up and is fighting also. Somehow, he gets the puck and sends it up the boards. I push off the Igor fucker and crash the net just as Boon shoots. He misses the net completely, but in his defense, it was redirected. The puck stumbles over the line, and we all rush for a change so the next line can get on the ice. I fall into my spot between Boon and Wes before grabbing my water bottle and cheering the boys on.

"Pressure! Pressure!"

From beside me, Wes lowers his bottle. "What kind of dogs will be there?"

"Where?"

"The calendar thing."

"Puppies?" I answer before squirting the water into my mouth. I then grab the Gatorade, doing the same.

"You think there will be Boxers? I love Boxers."

I shrug, not the least bit worried about dogs and more worried about tying this game. "I don't know. Ask Shelli."

"Maybe there will be German shepherds," Boon says from beside me. "We're meeting at the Adlers' house, right? Man, that's gonna be awesome. Will there be food?"

I blink, unsure what the hell is happening here. "I don't know. Ask Shelli."

Wes gives me a look. "We all know you know, dude."

"What's that mean?"

"Means we *know*," Wes says, waggling his brows, and praise God, our line is called. We all three go over the boards, and thankfully, the guys are in game mode once their skates hit the ice. I go to center ice, waiting for Tampa to carry the puck in. I have my stick out, ready to block the pass, but they go the other way, wanting to hit their forward. But Wes is there, breaking the pass and passing it toward me. I rush after it into the zone, and I realize I'm on a breakaway.

Awesome.

I corral the puck and rush toward the net. The goalie sets, his eyes on me, and mine are on the back of the net. I deke left, but he doesn't follow, so I cross quickly, but I feel the defense coming up on me. I drop the puck behind me, skating over it before moving my stick between my legs back to the puck, where I wrist it up and over the goalie's shoulder.

Goal.

The red light goes off, and I swear, even Tampa fans are cheering. I turn, throwing my hands up as my teammates skate toward me, yelling and hollering as we wrap up in a tight hug. That was probably the sickest goal of my career, and damn, I hope Shelli saw it.

She'll be so damn proud.

We end up going into overtime and winning twenty-seven seconds in with a crazy slapper from Paxton. It was amazing and a great win. It feels good to be going home on a high note, especially when we only have nineteen games until the play-offs start. The three-week-long road trip was successful, only losing three games, but one thing is for sure... I'm ready to go home. I'm tired of living out of a suitcase, and I miss Shelli. So damn much.

While things have been great for me on the ice and even on the phone with Shelli, I haven't spoken to Asher in weeks. I'm still livid with him, and I can't bring myself to call him. I had to swear my family to secrecy, which means my mom is hardly talking to Elli. I told Shelli it was under control, and they promised they wouldn't tell. I feel like we need to tell Shelli's family, but at the same time, I like how we are right now. I don't know what to do. All I know is that Asher caused some shit for me. He's texted and even called a few times, but I have nothing to say. Even if he was trying to push me to feel things, he did it in a shitty, crybaby way. I'm not ready to forgive him. I will because I love the idiot, but not right now. Right now, I want to play hockey and spend time with Shelli. That's all. Everything and everyone else just need to leave me the hell alone.

"Yes, I saw it, you big dork. That was the best part of the game."

I lean back in my seat on my phone with a shit-eating grin on my face as Wes plays on his phone beside me. "It was a pretty badass shot."

"It was, but my favorite part was your face. You couldn't believe it went in."

"I've legit been practicing that for months. I'm stoked."

"You should be. It was awesome."

"Thanks. Too bad you weren't here to see it live."

"Right? Can you please do cool shit like that in our arena?"

"Will do."

"Thank you," she says, and I can hear the grin in her voice. "When will y'all be in?"

"I think around midnight. Wanna meet me at my place?"

"I can't. I have to sleep and be ready for tomorrow morning. The crew is coming at seven to be ready for y'all at ten. I have to make sure nothing gets fucked up."

"My little lady boss," I tease, and she scoffs.

"There is nothing little about me."

"Eh, you're short."

"And I could still kick your ass."

I grin as my heart soars in my chest. "What are you wearing?"

"Footie Harry Potter PJs."

I choke on my laughter. "No way."

When my phone rings with a FaceTime call, I switch over to see her, in fact, wearing what she said she was. As I put my earbuds in, I say, "I'm so jealous."

She grins. "Don't worry. I got you a pair too."

I fist-pump, much to her pleasure. "Yes, you've made my day!"

"I figured," she says, and then she falls onto her bed. "Thought we could have a marathon once y'all bring the Cup home."

"I love the sound of that."

"But we'll need to keep the air on. It's hot in these things."

I smile. "Take it off. I command it."

She laughs out. "No way. I'll leave that to you."

I groan softly. "How about you leave your window unlocked?"

She snorts. "So Shea Adler can murder you? No thanks."

"Cockblocker, that man."

Now she's laughing hard. "I never thought cockblocker and my dad would be in the same sentence."

I can't help it, I laugh too. She's so pretty when she laughs. "I miss you."

Her lips curve before she moves a piece of hair out of her face. "Well, it's been nine years since I saw you last, so believe me, I miss you too."

"You better."

"You better!" she calls back at me, and my heart, it yearns for her.

"We just got to the airport. I'll see you tomorrow?"

She nods. "Yeah. Don't be late."

"I won't, not when I get to see you."

Her cheeks redden. "Bye, Aiden."

"Bye."

I hang up, a wide smile on my face, but then one of my earbuds is yanked out of my ear.

"Told ya."

I look over at Wes. "Told ya what?"

His voice drops. "You're dating Shelli."

I blink. "How do you know?"

He points to my phone. "I seriously just saw her on your phone."

"That was my sister."

He blinks. "I know I play hockey, but I'm not dumb." I look away as he moves his elbow into mine. "Don't worry. I won't tell anyone. I think it's cool. She's great."

"She's perfect," I find myself saying, and Wes just grins back at me.

I want to be embarrassed that I just said that, but I'm not. I'm good with it because Shelli *is* perfect, and she's all mine.

WHILE MOST GUYS WOULDN'T MIND WAKING UP TO SOMEONE kissing them—hopefully a girl, if they're into them—I do mind. My girlfriend made it clear she couldn't come over, so that must mean it's someone else. I pull back jerkily and blink a few times, trying to focus. It only takes seconds to realize whose eyes are staring into mine.

Shelli.

My lips curve as I wrap my arms around her neck and pull her on top of me before rolling us deep into the covers. Her laughter is music to my ears. She hooks her leg over my hip as our lips meet once more. God, she tastes good. When I pull back, her blue eyes shine into mine. It's dark in my room, so I'm a bit confused as to why she is completely done up with hair and makeup. She's also fully dressed. I move my lips along hers as I ask, "What time is it?"

"Five a.m."

I wrinkle my face at her as I kiss her once more. "I thought you couldn't come over?"

She moves her fingers up my jaw and into my hair. "I woke up at about three thirty and couldn't fall back asleep. I'm too excited for today. I got dressed and ready then had nothing to do. Figured I'd come bug you."

"I'm not complaining at all," I say as I squeeze her tightly in my arms.

"I figured you wouldn't," she says softly, kicking off her heels and throwing them over the side of the bed.

"Staying a while?" I tease against her neck while I nibble. I've missed her a lot. In my opinion, she shouldn't leave.

"Yup," she says, pulling the blankets up and sliding underneath them. "I should have just come over last night."

"I agree." I kiss up her jaw. "Can I mess all this up?"

"Nope," she says simply, kissing my lips. "I need to be perfect for today."

I scoff. "You're perfect all the time."

She flashes me a dazzling smile as she snuggles closer. A comfortable silence falls over us as I hold her tightly. She smells so damn good, but she feels even better in my arms. I could honestly lie like this forever. I kiss her nose. "So you got me a manly dog for today, right?"

She grins. "Yup. A pug."

I glare. "A pug is not manly."

"Ugh. All monarchs had pugs. They're regal."

I perk a brow. "Didn't you guys have a pug?"

Her face lights up. "Yes. Adler. He was my mom's, really. I only got to have him for three years before he passed."

"Didn't I go to his funeral?"

She nods, like that's totally normal. "Yeah, we all did. Mom was wrecked."

"I remember that. Crazy thing to remember. A dog funeral."

"He was a part of the family, and he was irreplaceable. My mom never got another one."

She looks so sad, and it knocks the air out of me. I move her hair out of her face. "You want me to get you one?"

"One what?"

"A pug."

She snorts. "Where would we keep it?"

"Here."

"We're busy!"

I shrug. "Wes has a dog and no girlfriend to love it. I have the girl-friend part."

"I don't know," she says softly. "Things can change."

"I don't know what these things are, but we can share custody of him."

"Or her."

"It," I say dryly, but she doesn't smile. Something is bothering her. "What?"

"I need to tell you something."

I hate the alarms that go off inside me. Is she not happy anymore? "Okay?"

With her eyes searching mine, she says, "I got a casting call up in New York for *Chicago*."

My face lights up. "You love that show. It's in your top three, right? This is awesome!"

"Yeah, it is."

I bring my brows in. "You don't look happy."

"Yet, you're really happy."

My brows are basically touching. "Because you want this. This is one of your dreams. I know you think you're done, but you can't turn this down."

She blinks. "I would need to live in New York again."

It's like it all comes together in my head. "Oh."

"Yeah," she says on an exhale, looking down at my throat. "What would that mean for us?"

Oh. Oh fuck. "Well, I mean, we're already playing the long-distance game as it is. We can try it."

"You'd be okay with that?"

I nod. "Yeah, because I'm not okay with this ending."

"Neither am I."

"Then we're good." I gather her up in my arms. "I'm so excited for you. When is the audition?"

"Three weeks, between two road trips."

I purse my lips. "Maybe I can come."

"I think you could, if you could get out of practice."

I shrug. "Let me see what I can do. I want to be there with you."

Her lips curve as her eyes sparkle. "That would be awesome." She cups my face as she moves her fingers along my jaw. "Have you talked to Asher yet?"

I wrinkle my face. "How did we get on this subject? Dogs, auditioning...no room for Asher."

She gives me a dry look. "You miss him."

"Nope."

"You do."

"Don't."

"You should. He's your brother." She sighs loudly as she lays her head against mine.

"He's a crybaby asshole. It's my ring. It's always been my ring."

She nods against my jaw. "I know, but he's in love and wants to give her the best."

"Yeah, well, go buy something. He's a jerk. He threw me completely under the bus."

I feel her lashes against my cheek. "I still can't believe they all know."

I turn my head, moving my nose through her hair. "They promised not to tell."

She doesn't say anything for a moment and then whispers, "When should we tell my parents?"

I shrug. "I don't know. I think I want to wait till we bring the Cup home."

I feel her stiffen beside me. "That's a long time."

"I know, but I don't want to piss off your mom and have her trade me or something crazy." I kiss her temple. "And I really need my legs to play, so I can't tell your dad yet."

She snorts against my cheek. "He won't hurt you."

"Yeah, okay," I laugh, and she smiles. I turn my head to look at her, and her eyes meet mine. "Is that okay?"

She shrugs. "Yeah, I guess. I don't want you feeling what I am. I have no clue how to act around your mom now."

I hold her gaze. "Like the perfect, beautiful, smart, kick-ass woman you are."

Her lips curve. "Wow. You don't have to suck up to get me naked."

"I really do, because then, maybe you'll let me mess all this up."

I press my lips into hers, stopping her laughter. And as with every single time our lips meet, things start to burn. She feels too damn good in my arms, and when I cup her breast, I know I'm going to be unable to stop. Just as I roll on top of her, though, her phone rings. I groan loudly as she digs between us for her phone.

"It's my mom."

"Now your mom is a cockblock."

She giggles as she answers, and I watch as her face changes. "No, I didn't know that. I thought they said seven. It's only five forty-five. Ugh. No, they said seven, not six! I'm out. Yes, out at this time of the morning. Um. Ugh. I don't know. Why? No. Okay, Mom. I'm on the way."

She hangs up quickly and looks up at me as I hover over her.

"Don't tell me you have to leave."

"I have to leave."

"Shell, I've missed you."

"I know," she says, trying to roll out from underneath me, but I won't let her go. "Aiden." I look around frantically, playfully, and her brows pull together. "What are you doing?"

"I can't remember where my wand is!"

"Your wand?" she laughs as I reach over into my nightstand and pull one out. "You keep a wand in your nightstand?"

"Among other things," I tease, waggling my brows at her. She laughs hard as I lean back on my haunches, pointing my wand at her. "Imperio."

Her eyes light up. "One of the unforgivable curses. How naughty of you."

I run the wand down her chest. "Now I'm in control, and you can't leave."

She grabs me by my shirt and pulls me down so our lips touch. "You think I want to leave? Do you know how hard it's gonna be to be around you and not touch you? And today, I have to watch you with puppies? That's totally unfair. How am I supposed to resist that?"

I grin. "And I'm supposed to resist you walking around in those fuck-me purple heels?"

She kisses my jaw. "I'll wear them tonight."

"At dinner."

Her eyes meet mine. "Dinner?"

"I want to take you out."

"Okay, that sounds fun. Should I wear a dress?"

"Yes. The tighter, the better."

Her eyes darken. "I'm sure I can find something."

I grip her ass as I lay my wand on the bed. "I can't wait."

Shelli's lips meet mine, and I can't handle her. I've wanted to take her out for a while. We've just been busy. I don't want to go out for business either. I want to sit across the table from her and just admire what I have. As our lips embrace, I know I need to take advantage of the time we have because she'll get the part, and then I'll be fighting for time to see her. I can't waste the time we have. I have to seize it, because I need it.

I need her.

CHAPTER THIRTY

SHELLI

"I HAVE NO CLUE HOW I FORGOT ABOUT THIS DINNER. AMELIA IS gonna kill me," I say frantically as Aiden drives toward my aunt's house. He's dropping me off and heading back to his place. We've spent the last couple days together. We had the photo shoot, and it went amazing. The guys and the puppies were awesome. The only thing that might have been an issue was Fallon and my mom. They were whispering to each other and looking at us funny all day. A part of me thinks my mom is onto us, but that can't be. Fallon promised not to tell. Even with the stress of my mom maybe knowing, the day was perfect. And today has been even better. We went shopping for his apartment and had a really nice lunch at my favorite sushi place. It's been a great day. I hadn't even realized it was the day Amelia got in until she texted me, asking what time I would be at her mom's house.

"It's not a big deal. It's not like you're late." He holds my hand in his lap as he turns onto my aunt's street.

I look over at him and smile. "Yeah, but I forgot, which kinda makes me one of those girls too engrossed in my boyfriend to remember when my cousin is coming into town."

He shrugs. "I won't tell if you don't," he says, and then he winks, sending a rumble through my guts.

"Deal."

We leave tomorrow for New York. My audition is in the afternoon, so we'll only get one day in the Big Apple. He apparently has a romantic little something in the works from what he tells me. I'm sorta crazy excited for it. I'm nervous, though. As much as I want to get this part, I hate the thought of not being with him. It totally blows, but he's being so damn supportive, it's hard not to be excited. He helped me choose my music and has been practicing with me a lot. Apparently the guitars on the wall aren't just for show either. He can play them—and not just okay, but really well.

He blows me away.

"Are you going to get a ride home with your mom?"

"Yeah, or I'll skip out early and get an Uber to your place."

He nods. "Cool. Text me when you leave."

"I will," I say as he pulls up behind my mom's truck. I lean over, kissing him quickly on the cheek. "See ya."

"Bye, baby," he says as I fling open the door and get out. When I go to shut it, though, my mom is standing up from her truck holding a cake stand with a cake on it in her hands. Everything stops. Did she see me kiss him?

Mom's intuitive eyes go from me to the car before she bends a bit to see who's inside. "Aiden Brooks, is that you?"

Aiden throws his door open and gets out. "Hey, Elli. How you doing?" he says nervously, and I swear I'm biting a hole in my lip.

"Good. What are y'all doing?"

"We went to lunch with Wes and Boon. We have that jacket drive next week, and she's making me do stuff at the gala. You know Shelli. Such a stickler for details."

God bless this man. I nod quickly. "Yeah, he had picked me up at the house, and I sort of forgot about this, so I just had him drop me off here."

"That's nice. Thank you, Aiden."

"Anytime," he says happily as he waves her off. "I'm gonna go—"

"Do you have dinner plans?"

Aiden blinks and tries to look at me, but my mom has him in her gaze. "Um... No, ma'am. A Hot Pocket and Netflix was my plan."

"Well, come on in. Grace has plenty of food, and Ryan is here, along with his beautiful wife, Sofia, as well as Amelia and her fiancé. Oh, and Shea. It's gonna be a great time."

He swallows visibly. "Um, are you sure? I don't want to intrude."

"Nonsense! Come on."

"Okay," he says, and my eyes are as big as saucers as he shuts off his car and then locks the door.

She waits for him to come to her before she wraps her arm around his bicep, being careful with the cake stand in her other hand. "I thought Shelli would have brought her boyfriend. Do you know him? I haven't gotten the pleasure yet."

"Uh—"

"He's busy tonight," I say quickly, falling into step with them. "Plus, I forgot I was coming."

"Oh, well, true," Mom says simply as we head up the walkway of my aunt's humongous house. It was massive before my uncle passed, but since then, she keeps adding on to it. I don't know why she needs all these rooms, but she is happy, which is all that matters. "How does he feel about you spending time with these adorable men? I'm surprised he lets you hang out with Aiden here."

Aiden lets out a nervous laugh, and I scoff. "Lets? I do what I want."

"That's the damn truth," Aiden says then, and Mom gives him a look, her eyes narrowed. "I just mean, she's very bossy and does what she wants," he says quickly, and I roll my eyes.

"You're right on that one," she says, letting him go and heading inside.

I smack him on the arm. "I'm not bossy!"

He rolls his eyes. "You legit made me unpack all my dishes into the dishwasher before we could go to lunch. You're bossy." He then leans in, his lips by my ear. "But don't worry... It turns me on."

When he leans away, I fight back the grin that wants to show. "This is not good."

He shakes his head. "It's fine. We'll eat and go."

"Seriously, they can't find out we're together. Not when Amelia is telling everyone she's pregnant."

He moves my hair off my shoulders. "Shell, no one will know. I can resist you. It's not hard." I glare as he flashes me a huge grin before he holds his hand out toward the house. "Go on, I like watching that ass of yours."

"And grab it, I'm sure."

"No one is around," he teases as I step in front of him, shaking my head.

When he shuts the door behind us, I look up to see my stunning cousin coming toward me. She's always been super lean from being a hardcore gymnast, and anyone else might not notice, but I can see the bump that shows when her dress pulls against it. My eyes light up as we embrace, and I feel this sense of completion. She's always been my very best friend.

"I've missed you," she whispers, and I hug her tightly, feeling her little bump against my own stomach. My siblings are scattered around the living room. The boys are on the couch, playing on their Nintendo Switch, while Posey has a book on her legs, reading. I'm not sure how long everyone has been here, but it doesn't matter. I have missed Amelia.

"I can't believe you're showing," I say so no one hears us.

"I know! It's insane. No one has said anything yet," she says in my ear.

"No one can tell but me."

"You brought Aiden?"

"No, Mom invited him in when he dropped me off."

"Do they always hug like that?" I hear Aiden ask, and my mom laughs.

"Yes. We ignore them. Come on in here. Shea is in the kitchen being all scary dad-ish on poor Chandler. Have you met Chandler?"

Amelia and I don't move. "Do they know?"

"Nope, and they won't know. Not until after the season is over, according to him." I kiss her cheek. "But he's terrified of Dad, so let me go be there."

She kisses me back. "I'm terrified to tell them."

"Don't be. It's gonna be awesome!"

I pat her belly sweetly and then head to the kitchen where my dad is standing in the middle of Aiden and Ryan.

"I don't like that guy—or his friend."

Aiden looks up just as I do. "Friend?" he asks, and my dad nods, his face scrunched up as if he smells something awful.

"Yeah, Nico Merryweather. Full of himself, that kid is."

Aiden looks back at me, but I'm currently not breathing.

What the hell is Nico doing here?

Ryan, my older cousin, shakes his head. "Chandler is awesome, but the jury is still out on Nico."

"He called me old man. I'm not old," Dad pouts, and Ryan scoffs.

"Nope. Fresh spring chicken."

"You've always been my favorite," Dad says, knocking knuckles with him, but Aiden is just looking at me. His eyes are dark and dangerous. This is not good. I try to tell him with my eyes that it's okay, no big deal, but I know he doesn't believe me. Hell, I don't believe myself. Aiden hates Nico. Nico hates Aiden. Nico could blow our relationship wide open, which would piss off Amelia because she needs to be the center of attention since she is carrying my niece or nephew. I don't care that the baby is technically my cousin; I'm gonna love on it just as hard.

"Hey there, Shell."

I look to the doorway of the dining room to see Chandler Moon—the prince who was sent to save my cousin. A smile takes over my face as we hug tightly. I want to be happy to see Chandler, but I'm annoyed. "Why the hell did you bring him?" I ask low and angrily.

"Didn't have a choice. My mom invited him for the weekend, and he insisted on coming to see you." I pull back as he does, and our eyes lock. "I know. I'm sorry. Amelia already lit into him."

"You warned him. He can't ruin this for y'all."

"I did." But by the look in his eyes, I know he knows it doesn't matter.

Like me, Nico does what he wants. I'll just ignore him. "I need to talk to him."

Why did I say that?

I can feel Aiden's anger coming off him in waves. "I might head out."

Ack. This is a clusterfuck. I just wanted to be here for my cousin as she revealed her news. It had been such a great day. Should have been an even greater day with Amelia's news.

"Wow, Shelli. Gorgeous as always."

Damn it.

Nico comes up behind Chandler, his dark eyes meeting mine.

"Hey, Nico."

"Hey," he says sweetly, and yes, he is handsome and charming, but he is not Aiden Brooks. He is not the man I love.

My mom walks into the kitchen along with my aunt, just as Amelia comes out of the bathroom. Amelia looks around, her eyes wild as she moves them from me to Nico to Chandler and then back to me.

Aunt Grace throws her arms around Amelia. "Isn't it wonderful having everyone home?"

"So wonderful," Mom says happily. "You remember Aiden, right?"

"Of course. So glad you could come."

Aiden looks as if he's getting an enema. "Thanks for having me, but I don't know if I—"

I clear my throat. "Can I talk to you real fast? Privately, please?"

Aiden looks at me, but then Nico says, "Can I talk to you after him?"

"No," I say at the same time Aiden does. Everyone looks at us, and I can feel Aiden about to hightail it out of here. "I have nothing to say to you, Nico."

"Shelli Grace, be nice."

I ignore my mom, as does Nico. His eyes hold mine as he says, "You won't answer my texts or my calls."

I feel my dad's gaze on me as I sneer, "Because I don't want to talk to you."

"That's not fair. We're good together—"

"Nico! Shut the hell up," Amelia yells, and she crosses her arms over her chest.

Chandler comes up beside her and wraps his arms around her. "For real, dude, be quiet."

"You guys saw it!"

Mom looks back to me. "Is he your boyfriend?"

"For the love of God," I mutter.

"No, I will not accept that. He's a dick," Dad yells. "Damn it, my chest is burning. He called me old, Elli!"

Ryan presses his hand into my dad's chest, his brow furrowed with worry. "Is it the angina?"

I throw up my hands. Why can't we just have normal dinners? "I am not dating Nico."

Nico glares. "Nope, she's dating that scum—"

Before he can even finish or point at Aiden, I yell, "Amelia! Don't you have something to tell everyone?"

"Scum, eh?" Aiden asks, and he takes a step forward, but I step in front of him.

My gaze meets Amelia's wide-eyed one. Probably wasn't the moment when she wanted to say anything, yet here we are. "Amelia, what do you have to tell us?"

I'm thankful when all eyes turn to Amelia. I press my hand into Aiden's chest and look up at him. His eyes are wild and angry, but he stays put. Thankful, I turn my attention to Amelia when she looks up at Chandler as he grins down at her. "Um, well—" She pauses when he laces their fingers together before resting them on her little growing bump. "We're pregnant."

The silence is deafening.

"What do you mean?" Grace asks. "You're not married."

"And we won't be until after the baby comes," Amelia says. "I want to look perfect in my dress."

Chandler grins down at her. "You'll look perfect no matter what."

She cups his face, but Grace is still gawking at them. "But the baby will be born out of wedlock."

"Um, Mom, I was born out of wedlock," Ryan says with a grin.

Dad snorts. "Way out of it."

Why isn't anyone hugging Amelia? "Well, I think it's wonderful. I'm so happy for you guys," I say, and I hug them tightly. "I love you both, and I can't wait to be an aunt."

"Congratulations, Amelia and Chandler," I hear Aiden say as Amelia gives me a thankful grin and Chandler squeezes my arm.

"It really is," Ryan says, walking over and hugging his sister. "I'm jealous. Sofia won't have my baby."

Sofia, his gorgeous and very quiet wife, smacks his arm. "I just opened a business, and you're gone all the time. Relax."

They share a loving smile before everyone finally starts to follow suit. I back off so they can get to the lovely couple, when Nico takes my arm. He pulls me to the side, despite me pulling my arm out of his hold.

"Stop."

"No, really, Shelli. We'd be great together. I can love you right, I swear. I know your sister's name is Posey, and you have twin brothers, Evan and Owen, and then your baby brother is Quinn. You've starred in *Frozen, Cats, Les Miserables*—"

"Nico, stop," I demand, shaking my head. "I don't want to be with you."

"But I would actually love you." Man, he knows what buttons to push. "He doesn't love you," he stresses, but I throw my hands up.

"Stop, for real. I don't know how else to say I don't want to be with you." When I hear the door slam, I look back to see that Aiden is gone. "You've got to be kidding me."

I turn to head after him, but Nico grabs my arm. My eyes are narrowed to slits as I look back at him. "I swear, I will break your nose if you touch me one more time."

He lets me go instantly, and I rush to the front door. When I hit the porch, Aiden is rounding his car. "Aiden!"

He glances over at me, and he just looks so defeated. "Go back inside. I don't want to ruin Amelia's night, but I need to go."

I kick off my shoes and run through the lawn toward him. "What is wrong? I'm not even speaking to him."

"I don't like him!"

"I'm aware. But, Aiden, I don't want anything to do with him!"

"But he thinks he can get you. How he keeps coming for you—"

"I am yours, remember? I deflected him left and right, and I don't want anything to do with him. I really don't understand why you're upset. Yes, I get being pissed at the guy, but that shouldn't ruin the night with my family."

"For now."

I bring my brows in. "For now, what?"

"You deflect him now, but what happens when you don't?"

I take a step toward him, my heart pounding in my chest. "I'm sorry, what? How many times do I have to tell you I don't want him for it to sink into that thick skull of yours and you believe me?"

"For him to be so confident, there has to be a reason."

I glare. "Because he's a self-absorbed crazy person. I don't know! I don't want him. I want you."

I poke him square in the chest, and he just looks down at me. "Yeah, but what happens when you don't?"

I blink. "What the hell is wrong with you? We've had a great day. Everything was awesome, has been awesome. We're great! But this is going to trip you up? I get it. I didn't want him here either, but this isn't about him because he doesn't matter. We matter." Why does he look so overwhelmed? So unsure of himself. This isn't my Aiden. My Aiden is confident and knows what he has. Why does he get like this? "Aiden, what the hell, babe? This isn't you."

He won't look at me. "You think I like this? Like feeling like this? I don't, but I swear, he's completely convinced he can get you. There has to be a reason. There has to be something you're doing to urge him on."

My jaw drops, and tears are starting to burn my eyes. "You're accusing me of entertaining that craziness?"

"I just don't know. Why is he so convinced? What are you doing to fuel that fire?"

"I'm not doing a fucking thing, Aiden. Do you think I would really fuck this up? I've wanted this, *you*, since I was eleven. I am doing nothing. I don't want him. It's his own delusion. I don't answer his calls or his texts because I respect your wishes. I don't even think of him. I only think of you."

"I just don't trust him."

"Don't. It's nothing off my back because he doesn't fucking matter! *We* matter."

"It freaks me—"

That's it. "Damn it, Aiden. I don't fucking love him—I love you."

He looks up then, his eyes wide and his jaw hanging open. I hate that tears start to fall down my cheeks, but damn it, here I am. "I have loved you my whole entire life. I put you on a pedestal and admired you up there. When you finally saw me, I knew, from that moment on, there was no way in hell I was letting you go. I know I am hard to deal with. I may clean a lot, and I've got one hell of a mouth, but I would never hurt you. I would never ruin this. Not with how much I love you."

He draws in deep breaths, his gray eyes dark and wild as he holds my gaze. I wait for him to say he loves me too, but he just stares at me. He looks absolutely terrified, and it knocks the air out of me. Why isn't he saying he loves me too?

Defeated, I look down at my feet. "But if you can't see that, if you can't trust me or even love me, then what the fuck is the point, Aiden? I don't deserve that, not with how loyal and patient I've been with you."

I wait for him to stay something, but he's just staring at me, his jaw hanging open. I don't understand; I don't even know what is happening. How can he not realize he loves me? I know he does. I feel it. Damn it. I turn around and head back across the lawn. He doesn't call my name or even stop me.

Maybe he *doesn't* love me.

"Are you okay?"

"Fine," I say simply as I lean back in my seat on my mom's plane. "He didn't call or text me last night, so I'm pretty sure we're over. Which is fine since I am going to get this part and move back to New York."

"Wow. You sound very detached, but I can hear the tears in your voice," Amelia says, and I wipe away a stupid tear. "You're not okay."

"I'm not, but it is what it is."

"Shelli, call him."

"No. I put it all out there, and he just stared at me."

She lets out a long breath. "Shelli, you've been telling me since the rip that he's skittish and is terrified of commitment. What did you think was going to happen?"

I close my eyes. "I was hoping, by now, he had figured out we have a great thing and he loves me."

"Oh honey, I wanted that too. But maybe he isn't ready to accept it. He's been single his whole life until you."

"Which means I should be enough. He settled down for me, yet he won't admit it."

"Shelli, you're more than enough, and I honestly think he knows that. I saw the way he looked at you, and I saw how he wanted to rip Nico's head off. He's scared."

I hate that word. I hate that he feels like that. "Which is fine, but haven't I done enough to make him comfortable?"

"Shelli, this isn't you. It's him."

"So, what do I do?"

"Call him."

"No way. The puck is in his zone." I know that's my pride talking, but I refuse. I've done everything thus far; it's all on him now.

She snorts. "So corny."

I can't even smile. I just feel empty. I hate not talking to him. I hate that he allowed Nico to come between us once more. I never even loved that guy. I've only ever loved Aiden, and I don't understand how he doesn't realize that.

"In other news, my mom is dead set on us getting married before the baby comes."

I roll my eyes. "She's insane."

"Right? But she's happy. She told me she was proud of me last night."

I smile. "You're going to be an awesome mom, Am."

"And you're gonna be the best aunt."

"Damn right. That baby is gonna be spoiled rotten."

Amelia laughs. "Between the Adlers, the Justices, and the Moons, I'd say so."

"For real, and the baby will be super loved."

"So loved," she agrees just as the flight attendant stops beside me.

"Ms. Adler, there is an issue with takeoff."

I scrunch up my face. "Am, let me call you back." I hang up and then stand. "What's wrong?"

"There is a gentleman outside who says he needs to speak to you, but he isn't on the manifest, so I can't let him on."

"Huh?" I ask, and then I walk past her to the entrance of the plane.

When I look down the stairs, I see Aiden standing at the bottom. His bag is hanging on his shoulder, and he's wearing a nice blue suit that hugs every inch of him. His hair is down, tucked behind his ears, but all I see are those gray eyes that are swimming in despair.

"They won't let me on."

I shrug, crossing my arms. "I didn't think you were coming."

"I am," he says, sending my heart into a frenzy.

"Why?"

"'Cause I want to be with you. I want to watch you get this part, Shelli. I fucked up. I should have called you last night, but you dropped a hell of a bomb on me and I didn't really recover. Still not sure what I am doing."

I bite my lip before looking at the pilot, who has come out of the cockpit to stand beside me. "Can you add Aiden Brooks back on to the manifest, please?"

"Yes, ma'am." He then turns to Aiden. "Can I see your ID, sir?"

With his eyes on me, Aiden pulls out his wallet and hands over his ID.

"You're good to go."

Aiden takes his ID back and then heads up the stairs as he tucks that and his wallet into his pocket. When he stops before me, two steps down so our eyes are on the same level, I find I'm holding my breath. He reaches out, snaking his arm around my waist before pulling me closer, our noses almost touching.

"I'm sorry about yesterday." I bring my lip between my teeth as he speaks. "It isn't fair to you, but I was overwhelmed and I was jealous. So jealous." He leans his head into mine, and I take in a deep breath. "I don't want to lose you."

"Then stop acting like an idiot."

He smiles. "Noted." He opens his eyes to meet mine. "I couldn't sleep last night. I was a wreck. I swear, Shelli, I feel something great for you. I may not know what love is, but I feel something."

I roll my eyes. "You know what love is, Aiden."

"How do you know?"

"Because I've seen you with your family, with mine. You're being stubborn, but as long as you want me—"

"Shelli, I need you," he says softly, and then he kisses my bottom lip. "I feel like I'm fucking up left and right, and damn it, you deserve better. Someone who knows what they're feeling and what they want—"

"I want you." I move my fingers down his jaw, and I watch as his lashes kiss his cheeks.

"I never wanted to be wanted by anyone—until now."

That's all I need to know.

Because by the way he's looking at me, he's there.

He just doesn't realize it yet.

CHAPTER THIRTY-ONE

AIDEN

"GOOD THING YOU HAVE YOUR OWN PLANE."

Shelli looks over her shoulder at me as she opens one of the guitars that a friend of hers brought over for her to take back to Nashville. Apparently, she leaves guitars everywhere. "I didn't expect to see her today, and of course, I totally forgot she had these."

Shelli is still in her dress from the audition. It's a dark green satin ballgown that is floor-length but with a completely open back. The front has a high neck with straps that wrap around her neck and are studded with stones. She wore her hair down in wide curls, and her makeup is dramatic and stunning. I didn't know I liked her eyes with winged eyeliner as much as I do until now.

She was absolutely mesmerizing at her audition. She sang "All that Jazz," but a slow, haunting piano version we've been working on for weeks. We weren't sure if we should do it on the piano or guitar, but I'm happy she went with piano. It was different and classy in my opinion. Everyone else came dressed in their best *Chicago* attire and singing the songs the way they would be in the show, but I think Shelli stood out. I think she sparkled, and I was pretty fucking proud to be in the audience, knowing she was all mine.

And to think, I almost blew it. I don't know what it is about Nico Merryweather, but he is a thorn in my side. I don't like the way he looks at Shelli, and I sure as shit don't like how he thinks she wants him. I hate how insecure he makes me—in myself and in her. I know she doesn't want to be with him, yet I get these irrational thoughts in my head that make me want to rip him limb from limb. I refuse to allow him to come between us. I'm not saying I'm completely confident in us, but I'm opening my eyes. I don't want to lose her, and I wasn't lying when I said I felt something for her. I do. I feel it deep in my chest, but I'm afraid that it isn't the love she feels for me. I'm worried that I don't know how to feel that.

She moves her hair off her shoulder and gathers it on the other side. She's crouched down on the floor, her dress pooling around her as she wipes off her guitar and pulls it out of the case. "I bought both of these after my first standing ovation in *Frozen*."

She stands as she brings the guitar to her stomach, strumming her fingers along the strings. As she tunes it, I lift the other case and put it on the coffee table before opening it. "Why didn't you bring them home?"

"I totally forgot about them. I brought them over to Essie's house for a party, and I got trashed. Forgot them."

I lift the Echo acoustic up to my chest and strum it. "Well, since you don't want to care for them, I'll be happy to take them home with me."

"Please, I love these guitars. Aww, she had them tuned for me. She's so sweet."

I nod. "This one needs to be cleaned."

"Yeah," she says, and she then grabs a rag off the sink. As she wipes them down, she looks over at me. "Was it weird seeing Chris?"

When I saw the guy who had ultimately fixed us up, I thought I would still be pissed at him, but I wasn't. I didn't care. "Nope. We hardly talked. Just pleasantries."

"Oh."

"Oh?" I ask. "What... Did you want me to fight him for your honor?"

She snorts. "No, not at all. Just thought you'd tell him about us."

Our eyes meet. "Shell, I told him about us like a month ago."

Her eyes widen. "You did?"

"Yeah."

"Why? What did you say?"

My lips curve a bit as I look down at the guitar. I guess I'm a bit embarrassed. "I said, 'Thanks for fixing us up. It was the best thing that could have happened to me.'"

"You really said that?"

I nod. "I did."

She sends me a dazzling grin. "Well, that's very sweet."

"Well, it's very true."

I want to take her in my arms and kiss that pouty mouth. Such tenderness is all over her face, and it's leaving me breathless. She bites her lip and then looks down at the guitar. "Wanna know the first song I played on it?" Her grin is the one she flashed when she finished her audition. I was two seconds from standing up and telling those casting people if they didn't sign her, I would. For what, I have no clue, but I was blown away by her. I find that happens a whole lot.

"What?" I ask, looking up at her as she plays nothing in particular, but still, I think she's beautiful doing it.

"'Free Fallin',"" she says happily. "I sang it at my third-grade talent show, and these guitars made me want to play it again."

I look down at the strings. When I start the song, she stops playing. I look back up, and her eyes are full of excitement.

"You never cease to amaze me, Aiden Brooks."

With a grin on my lips, I start to sing the popular, well-written song. She comes over to me, sitting on the coffee table in front of me, and starts playing along. "Oh, you weren't calling me a good girl earlier," she comments as I sing and she plays. "I do love my momma. Jesus too. Elvis is by far the greatest singer ever, and yeah, my boyfriend is okay." I wink as I continue. "Total bad boy, but you miss me all the time."

She isn't wrong.

Our eyes meet when she starts to sing. Her voice complements mine, making me sound pretty damn good. Or maybe it's just her. She looks so regal, so perfect. I lean closer, and her knees slide between my legs, our guitars almost touching as we sing in unison. I love how she sings, how her lashes kiss her cheeks when she hits those high notes. I let her take over, singing the second verse as her flirty eyes burn into mine, making me feel like this is all brand-new. Unable to handle it, I stop playing and lay my guitar down on the couch. I then reach for hers, setting it on the table before trapping her hips between my hands and bringing our mouths together. She leans into the kiss, and everything fades away.

I don't see her sitting across from me at the ritzy restaurant I took her to. Or how she laughed her ass off when the lobster flew out of my hand when I was trying to crack it open. I don't even see her onstage, where she absolutely belongs. As much as I don't want to be without her, I know she has to go. She has to do this. I run my fingers along her sharp jaw, and all I feel, all I see, is her.

I stand, pulling her up with me as she wraps her arms around my neck. I undo the tie at her neck before finding the zipper at the base of her back. Once I have her all undone, I step back, and the dress falls to the floor with ease. With only some stickers on her nipples and a barely there thong, my girl stands in all her glory. Her eyes are hooded as I take her by her ass, lifting her up as our mouths meet once more.

"You're so beautiful," I whisper against her lips as I carry her to the bed, laying her down as I cover her sweet body with mine. Her lips curve while she pulls my shirt up and out of my slacks as our kisses deepen. I sit back, unbuttoning my shirt with her before throwing it off. "Thanks for letting me be here today. I really enjoyed watching you."

Her eyes fill with such admiration. "Thank you for coming."

"I'm still really sorry for yesterday. I froze—"

"It doesn't matter now."

I press my nose into hers. "I'm an idiot. I shouldn't question you or even this."

A smile plays on her lips as she unfastens my pants. "It's part of your charm."

I laugh as I toe out of my shoes, kicking them off along with my pants. I pull her thong down as she removes the stickers from her boobs, flinching a bit but laughing too.

"These things suck."

"You don't need them."

"I didn't want my nips to be hard!"

"I would have loved it," I say before taking her breast into my mouth. Her fingers run through my hair as I hitch her leg up, digging my fingers into her thigh. I'm about to enter her slick center when somehow, in the lust cloud she keeps me in, I remember I don't have a condom. I pull back and kiss between her breasts. "One second. I gotta find a condom."

"Don't."

I pause and then meet her gaze. "Don't?"

She shakes her head. "I'm on birth control."

I lick my lips. "Seriously?"

"Seriously."

I look down at her center and then at my hard cock. It's right there. What's holding me back? I meet her gaze once more, and I know why. Because if I do it without a condom, then this is more real than I ever could have imagined it would be. I now know only people who truly trust each other should have sex without condoms. I learned that from her. I've learned a lot from her. I drop my head to hers. I've learned who I want to be, and it's the man she wants. I slowly enter her, inch by inch, falling into all-encompassing ecstasy. She felt good before, but now... Now, she is truly out of this world. She completes me.

She arches off the bed, my name falling from her lips, and my chin hits her breastbone. I'm lost. Completely lost.

I have a pretty good idea what that means.

And it terrifies me.

SHELLI MOVES HER FINGERS THROUGH MY HAIR AS WE LIE NAKED against each other. Her body is sweet, hot against mine, and so damn beautiful. We ate a midnight snack naked and drank a bottle of champagne I had brought up along with strawberries. It's over-the-top romantic, but I wanted her to feel special. I'm so proud of her, and I want her to feel that. The moon is shining in on us, along with the lights from the bright New York skyline, and I almost miss living here. Almost, because nothing is Nashville in my opinion. I kiss the side of her breast as I close my eyes. We have to wake up early because I have to be back for practice, but for now, I just want to lie here and not move. She hums a soft melody as I hold her, nuzzling my nose against her body.

"What song is that? I think I've heard it."

"'My Man,' from *Funny Girl*."

Maybe I don't know it. "Sing it."

So she does, the room filling with her angelic voice. As soon as I hear the lyrics, talking about how much she loves her man, I know it instantly. "Your mom sang this to Shea at a game. It's on YouTube."

"Yup. It's one of my favorites. Her big gesture to get him back."

"My mom stood in the rain and yelled at my dad to join her." A smile pulls at my lips. "They got into a fight over my aunt Audrey lying to my mom or something. Dad wasn't ready to stop fighting for my mom, but she gave up. Tried to give up. I don't know. It was a mess. My mom tried so hard to stay away from my dad, when it was obvious they belonged together."

A silence envelops us, but Shelli's fingers still slide through my hair. "Do you think that's why you are the way you are? So hesitant about feeling something for someone?"

Not someone. Her. I didn't care to feel anything before now. I bite my lip and then nod. "Yeah."

"It worked out for her, though."

"After a whole lot of pain," I answer, and then her fingers stop.

"Aiden, I won't hurt you."

"The thing is, I know that," I say, and then I lift my head to look at her. "I know that deep inside myself, but then I get freaked out at the thought of you finding someone better than me—"

"There is no one better," she says softly, her eyes holding me captive. "Not for me."

I want to feel high from that thought, but instead, I feel held down by my uncertainties. "But I can't shake it. I feel like you deserve someone better, like you're too good for me—"

"How would you feel if I left?"

"Devastated," I say quickly, without much thought. Then I pause. "But in a manly way, of course."

"Of course," she says with a smile. She reaches down, cupping my face. "I know love and relationships are uncertain, Aiden, but sometimes, someone is worth the risk you have to take."

"How do you know I am?" I find myself asking, and her lips curve more.

"Because I've loved you my whole life," she says unabashedly, with so much certainty and confidence. "I love your drive, how you worked endlessly to get into the NHL. I love how smart you are, how you were taking AP classes in middle school. I know I did the same because I wanted to be smart like you. I love how kind you are, how caring you are. You love and treat your sisters like princesses, and the relationship you have with Asher, pre-what just happened, is beautiful. I love how much you love your mom and how your dad is your best friend. I love how much you've changed over the last couple months. It isn't strictly about the game anymore or how to master it, even though you do just that. But it's also about who you can help. You're a great teammate. You'd do anything for the guys, and you're my favorite person to work with for the foundation. You're eager to jump in and to come up with ideas for what we can do." Her head falls to the side as she brushes my hair behind my ears. Her eyes are only on me, making me feel warm inside. "I love how you make me feel. I love how you make me laugh. I love how you'll listen to me talk about stats every morning and not get annoyed. You encourage me, believe in me. I love that you know my family and love them. I love that you don't judge my weirdness with cleaning—"

"I totally judge you," I say, needing to lighten the mood, but even with her grin and her laughter, this mood is heavy. Raw. Real. No one has ever said these things to me. My parents do, but they're my parents. They have to feel that stuff for me, but Shelli, she doesn't. She is choosing to.

"Not too bad though," she says softly, moving her fingers along my jaw. "But most of all, Aiden, I love you. All of you. To me, you're it. You fill my empty spaces, and no one comes close to you. So please, don't worry about me leaving or hurting you in that way. Worry about me talking your ear off or even cleaning something I shouldn't. Or eating something—I'll definitely eat that burrito if it's in the fridge again—"

I laugh hard and shake my head. I was so mad she ate it, but then I wasn't. Not when she grins at me like that.

"It was rude, Shelli Adler. The amount of guac in that burrito was the perfect ratio."

"Oh, I know, and it was fantastic."

"You have no guilt. None."

She shakes her head, her eyes playful. "None at all."

I gather her up and roll over so she's on top of me, her laughter filling the room. Her elbows fall to the sides of my head as she holds my face. I look into her blue eyes, getting completely lost but also feeling all those things she speaks of. If I accepted the L-word into my vocabulary, I would L-word all those things. She makes me laugh to the point I cry. She's witty and so damn smart. She's undeniably gorgeous but also kind and perfect. Talented? Damn, she's so talented. Fuck, she's perfect to me.

I think I do love her.

Oh shit, I thought the word.

Is it true?

"I know you care for me," she says, stealing me away from my uncertain thoughts. "I think you may even love me, which is why I can be patient. Some girls wouldn't be able to handle it, the not-knowing and all, but I can. Because I believe in us. I believe in you, Aiden. So, do me a favor. Believe in me and maybe realize what we have here."

"What we have?" I ask, my brows coming together. "I know what we have."

"What?"

"Happiness."

Her lips curve as she nods. "Yeah, and a damn good thing," she says boldly. "Be confident in us. In me. In yourself. The rest will come."

I search her gaze. "How can you be so confident?"

"Because you haven't said anything to make me think otherwise."

"Shelli, I said you were just a fuck. Like, twice."

"Did you believe it?"

"No," I say softly. "But you didn't know that."

She shrugs as she gives me a bashful grin. "I may have been a bit stubborn, but I always believed that you didn't mean it. That you were just scared, which may make me an idiot and might be setting me up for failure—"

"No," I say once more, gathering her closer. "You were right. You are right."

She cups my face, pressing her nose to mine as her eyes stare playfully into mine. "I also love, very much, when you say I'm right."

"Unfortunately, you're way smarter than me in the whole relationship zone. I would have cut you out and been lost."

She grins against my lips, and her eyes capture me. "See, it's when you say things like that, that makes me so confident in us. You don't even realize how important those words are to me."

I stroke my fingers along her hair, pushing it back behind her ears as my heart beats hard and strong in my chest. I love the rosiness of her cheeks and the gleam in her eyes. Her sex hair drives me wild, and I love how swollen her lips are. I especially love how she makes me feel.

I just used the L-word plenty of times and no warning bells whatsoever.

Man, *do* I love her?

CHAPTER THIRTY-TWO

SHELLI

I'M CHECKING MY MESSAGES AND EMAILS AS AIDEN DRIVES TOWARD the arena. We're in my truck since we're coming straight from the airport. He's gonna get a ride home with Wes since I gotta go to my parents' and act like I wasn't with him. I'm kind of over the whole hiding thing, especially since Fallon and Lucas already know. I get that Aiden doesn't want to upset my parents, but isn't he sick of keeping this a secret?

"So, the gala..."

He glances over at me and then returns his gaze to the road. "Yes, it's this weekend. I didn't know Amelia was going—or staying, for that matter."

"Yeah, she wants to come and enjoy the masterpiece I'm putting on. With Chandler going on a road trip, she figured she could have time with my aunt and go baby shopping."

"Fun," he says, getting off the highway. "So, the gala?"

"Can we go together?"

He looks at me out of the corner of his eye as a silly grin pulls at his lips. "You got someone else in mind?"

I flash him a dark look. "No, I want to go with you."

"Well, that was kind of a given. I don't understand." He doesn't have to say that; his face reads his misunderstanding perfectly.

"I mean I want us to go together as a couple."

He blinks twice and then glances over at me. "Everyone will be there. Your mom and dad."

"I know."

"And I like my legs, Shelli."

I roll my eyes. "My dad won't do anything to you."

"You can't guarantee that," he laughs and shakes his head. "I thought we said after the play-offs."

"You said that."

He ignores me. "They'll be so happy we won the Cup that they won't be mad."

"They wouldn't be mad anyway," I insist. "I'm tired of hiding."

"I know, but it's only for a couple more months. We know. Who cares about everyone else?"

I feel his gaze on me as I stare down at my phone.

"Okay, you do. But you get where I'm coming from, right?"

"Yeah, but I just want to tell my parents. I don't want to hide this. I like this," I say, gesturing between us. "And I know they will."

He nods, chewing his lip. "I hear you, and I do too. Let me think on it, okay?"

"What exactly are you thinking?" I ask just as I open an email from the casting director.

He parks. "Right now, I'm thinking, if I wear my gear, will it still hurt when your dad takes me out?"

I know he wants to make me laugh, but I'm too engrossed in the email. "'Ms. Adler, I was pleased and delighted to hear your glorious voice at the audition. You are the first I am emailing because even though you tried out for the part of Roxie Hart, I feel your voice is too powerful for that role. I know it's not considered the 'lead,' but it would be a great pleasure if you would consider the part of Velma Kelly. I happen to think you'll be the best Velma Kelly to date.'"

It's always a rush when I get a part, but in all honesty, even though I tried out for Roxie, I really wanted Velma. I think the only reason I tried for Roxie is because she was the lead. I've been the lead in the last four shows. I figured I had to, but it's kind of exciting to know they want me for the part I originally wanted.

I beam over at Aiden, and he has the most handsome look on his face. "I agree. I think you're going to be the best Velma Kelly. Ever," he says, and then he takes me by the back of the neck before kissing me hard on the lips. His nose smashes into mine as I squeeze my eyes shut. "I'm so proud of you."

A wide grin takes over my face. "I should take it, right?"

"Yes, without question."

"But what about us—"

"No way, Shelli. We're good. You have to do this, and I'll be there opening night, cheering you on."

My eyes search his. "I'll have to leave this summer."

"Well, you better make room for me because I'm coming too."

"To stay with me?"

"Yeah."

"That's like living together, you know?"

"So? We practically live together now."

"Do we now?"

He gives me a look. "Stop making this weird."

My lips curve. "So, no warning bells?"

He shakes his head, giving me a little smidge of a grin. "None."

"Okay."

"Okay." He kisses the back of my hand and then grins as he holds it. "Man, Shelli, I'm so proud of you," he says, kissing me once more. I savor his kiss, loving the feel of his lips and missing them when he pulls away. "Dinner tonight. Me and you, sushi. Celebration with wine."

I nod eagerly. "I will do extra cardio since I will be eating my body weight in tuna rolls, and I have to wear a bodysuit where my ass hangs out soon."

He kisses my nose. "You eat what you want, and if you want to do the cardio, do it. If you don't, I got you tonight," he says with a wink, and I giggle like a little girl. I want to scream in his face that I love him, but I don't want to make him uncomfortable.

Wait. No, fuck that.

"I love you, Aiden Brooks. So much," I say, kissing his top lip.

He holds my face close, kissing my bottom lip. He rubs his nose against mine, his fingers tangling in my hair before he deepens the kiss, his tongue sliding into my mouth, needy. When he pulls back, taking in a deep breath, his eyes meet mine. I know he isn't going to say it, but I almost feel like he wants to.

I can't take the silence, though. "You're gonna be late."

He doesn't move. His eyes just burn into mine, and I know he is struggling. He wants to say it, he wants to tell me he loves me, but he wants to be sure. "I'm really, really, really proud of you, and you blow me away."

It bothers me that he doesn't say it, but then, it doesn't. He's trying.

"Thank you." I grip his jaw. "Go to practice."

He kisses my nose and hands me the keys before getting out. He grabs his bag from the back and heads in. When he reaches the door, though, he looks back at me, tipping his chin at me in that sexy, manly way. Maybe I shouldn't have told him like that. Not when he has practice and he'll be thinking of my words constantly. But I want him to think about it. I don't want to be a distraction, but I want him to realize what he is feeling.

I scoot over to the driver's side, and I'm about to start the truck when my phone rings. It's my mom. "Hey, I just got in."

"Almost an hour ago."

I laugh. "Stalker much?"

"Maybe," she teases. "How'd it go?"

"I think it went great," I say without giving away my big news. I want to tell her in person.

"Wonderful. Hey, where are you?"

"Um," I say, looking around to make sure I don't see her. "I'm actually on the roof of the arena. I was going to go work out." Not a total lie. I am, and I was—but later. I wanted to go home and maybe take a nap first.

"So committed," she says proudly, and I smile.

"Ya know it."

"When you get done, can you swing by the office?"

"Your office?" I ask, and for some reason, the tone of her voice is throwing me off.

"Well, yes, sweetheart," she laughs. "I want to hear about the audition!"

Oh. Duh. "Yeah, I'll be about an hour. Just cardio today."

"Great. Gives me time to bitch at some of these players before you get here."

"What did the guys do now?"

"Oh, you know, normal player stuff. Whoring around."

Not my man.

"Get them, Momma. Use the Adler iron fist!"

She laughs, but it's not her normal laugh. "I'll see you in a bit."

As I hang up and gather my things to go do the workout I wasn't committed to, I feel like something is off.

I'm not sure what, but I know something is.

❧

I SHOWER AFTER MY WORKOUT AND PUT ON AIDEN'S WILLIE Nelson tee and a pair of sweats. It's all I have clean from our trip to New York. After packing up my bag and checking in on practice, which is in full swing, I head to my mom's office. I wave at the receptionist, and when she doesn't stop me, I go right in. To my surprise, though, my dad is sitting in one of the wingback chairs. A tight smile is on his face. "Oh hey, Dad!"

"Hey, baby," he says, getting up to kiss my temple. "How was New York?"

"Awesome. Since you're both here, I got the part."

They both light up, which allows me to breathe. "Not Roxie, but Velma."

"Oh, you're gonna be a great Velma," Mom gushes, and I nod.

"It's the part I wanted."

"No clue who these people are, but if you're happy, I am," Dad says as we both sit down.

"I am. Really happy."

I cross my legs as Dad glances at Mom. She's looking down at something, but when she looks up, it's as if she knocks the air out of my body with those piercing green eyes. I swallow hard as she holds up a paper, though I can't see it. "Shelli, are you aware how the plane works?"

I blink, confused. "Um, it flies in the air?"

Dad scoffs as Mom glares. "Yes, smartass, but I mean behind the scenes."

I furrow my brows. "Wait. I paid for gas, and it was clean. I didn't even eat or anything on the plane. That spot in the carpet is from Quinn! He—"

"Shelli," she says, stopping me, and I snap my mouth shut. "I know about all that. I mean with the manifest."

Manifest.

Shit.

"We got the manifest emailed to us yesterday after you landed in New York and again this morning when you landed here," Dad says, and I can't look at him. "Shelli Adler is on there, along with the pilot and crew, but also Aiden Brooks."

My heart jumps into my throat as I look up at my mom, who is watching me intently. Her face is set in stone, and my mind is going crazy. Do I lie? Do I make something up? Well, one thing is for sure, the cat is out of the bag.

"Um, yeah?"

She narrows her eyes, and still, I don't look at my dad. "So, Aiden went with you to New York?"

I swallow hard. "Yes, he did."

"He missed practice for charity business. I mean, I appreciate his dedication to the foundation, but I'm unsure what y'all could have been doing foundation-wise."

Absolutely nothing.

I take a deep breath. "We didn't do foundation stuff."

I feel Dad's gaze on me. "Then why did he go?"

I lick my lips as I look down at my phone. If I opened it, there would be a picture of Aiden and me at dinner in New York. He's looking at me with this goofy expression on his face, and I'm laughing. It wasn't supposed to be the picture we had taken, but the girl who took it took so many that I lucked out and got that shot. It's my favorite. He's my favorite. I turn my gaze to my father and exhale just as harshly as I inhaled. "He went because he wanted to see me audition, and he wanted to take me to dinner at his favorite place in New York."

Dad's face is stony. "Why would he do that?"

I bite my lip as I pray for my dad's angina. "Because we've been seeing each other since I left New York."

Yup, he's speechless. I look back to my mom, and she doesn't look surprised or speechless.

"At first, we didn't want to tell anyone because we wanted to make sure we were good. We know now, but he's worried Dad will kill him and you'll trade him, so he wanted to bring the Cup home to smooth that over."

"I would like a Cup, but I also don't like being lied to," Mom says, and I nod.

"I don't think we lied, just kind of kept it from you," I say, trying to go the least-guilty route.

"This is unlike you. You usually tell me everything."

I nod, and though I notice my dad hasn't said a word, he seems to be breathing, so that should mean he's okay. Ish. "I know, but with Aiden, it's different. You know I've liked him for a long time—"

"You have?" Dad asks, and I nod.

"Yeah, like, since I was a kid."

"Why? He's goofy as shit."

Mom laughs as I shake my head. "Because he's driven, gorgeous, and so smart. I love how he makes me laugh. How his smile hits me in the gut. He's really sweet—"

"Shelli, I love the guy. Don't get me wrong. But he has a reputation. It's not a good one either, even if it appears he's changed—"

Mom cuts him off. "You're right, Shea, but he also has worked hard to clear his name. He is a good kid, always has been, and got himself in a shit situation. If I remember correctly, you did the same."

He has? Dad gives her a dark look. "That's unfair. I was young, and that girl was trying to trap me."

"You just said the same thing Aiden said to me," Mom says, but Dad's comment steals my attention.

I look over at my dad. "What happened?"

"Girl tried to claim she was pregnant when I was on my way to the NHL. Real spotty. Aunt Grace beat her up."

I nod. "Sounds like her."

He throws up his hands. "But that's not the point. The point is, I don't want my daughter with someone with that black mark on his name."

"Doesn't really matter who you want me with, Dad. I get to choose, and I choose Aiden," I say confidently. "I love you, so much. You know that. You also know I'm smart. Aiden is a great guy, and he didn't do those things. He *wouldn't* do them. He treats me with such kindness—and respect. I love him, Dad."

Mom takes in a quick breath as my dad gawks at me. His brows come in, and he shakes his head. "He has a man bun. You're in love with that?"

I grin. "Yes. All of him."

Dad looks to Mom, and she's smiling. "Well, then, that's settled."

"What is?"

"This. Now we know. Even though I've known since the puppy shoot."

My eyes widen. "You have?"

"Oh yeah. Fallon told me, and to be honest, I was trying to hook you two up."

"I didn't approve that."

Mom sets Dad with a look. "When do you ever approve anything?"

He leans back. "She's right."

I meet his gaze. "Why are you okay with this? I feel like you're acting cool in front of me but you're going to kill Aiden."

He doesn't laugh; Dad just looks at me with the blue eyes I share with him and shrugs. "No, it's not that at all. I'm pretty sure I freaked out last night."

"He did," Mom says with a tilt to her lips.

"But we talked, and she already knew, so she calmed my crazy. The truth is, sweetheart, over these past few months, I've realized you aren't a baby anymore. You've grown into this amazing, headstrong woman, and I think I started realizing it after you knocked the shit out of Amelia's ex."

"Mom says that wasn't one of my finer moments," I remind him, but he shakes his head.

"Maybe not. But in my heart, I think it made me realize that you can take care of yourself. As much as I want you to need me, you don't. You're going to pick your person just as I chose your mother. Shelli, baby, you blow me away. You're amazing."

I don't know why I'm tearing up as I gaze into my dad's eyes. He reaches out, taking my hand. "I am so incredibly proud of you, and if Aiden is the guy you choose, then as much as I think I might die from the angina, I support you. You aren't some flighty girl. You know what you want. I mean, you just shot me down. Pretty sure no one can dim your shine."

I swallow past the emotion in my throat. "Thanks, Daddy. But I promise, Aiden is really great—though he is nervous about y'all knowing."

"No reason to be. I'm only gonna break his toes and fingers," Dad says, getting up and popping his fist into his other palm. "He can still play. I did it with a broken foot in the play-offs."

I look back to Mom, terrified, and she shakes her head. "He is not. But I do think we should go find him and have a little talk. I'll bring him in here. He'll be the one with angina."

I feel as if a weight has been lifted off my chest. I've wanted to tell my mom for a while. But now, knowing my dad is okay with it too, I feel so much better. It's as if all the pieces I needed to make this whole are falling into place, and Aiden and I are gonna be good. Great, even. I just need him to see it. To see how great we're gonna be at this.

I grin up at my dad. "How's your angina?"

He presses his fingers into his chest. "Hurts, but I'll ignore it if he makes you happy."

I stand up, wrapping my arms around him as he envelops me in his embrace. He kisses my temple and rests his head against mine as I let my eyes fall shut.

"He does. I promise he does."

CHAPTER THIRTY-THREE

AIDEN

"I DON'T CARE WHAT ANYONE SAYS. THAT GM IS TERRIFYING!"

I lean back in my locker, drying my face and chest free of the water from my shower as our new forward, Benson, complains. Everyone seems to disagree with him, but I don't. Elli Adler is terrifying. So is her hot-ass daughter. Hell, the whole family is! Well, maybe not Quinn. He's a sweet kid, but the rest of them—they could take you down with a look. One thing is for sure, I don't want to piss the lot of them off. I'm already worried that Shelli is upset. I know she wants to come clean to her family, but I'm not ready. I like what we have right now, and it's bad enough my family knows.

I sort of want to be sure when I step in front of her dad. I don't want him to see me as the punk-ass kid who's trying to get in his daughter's pants. I want him to see me as someone who is good for her. I think I am, but I want to be able to look at him and tell him I *L-word* her. Like, totally. Helplessly. Hell, I might already, but these feelings are totally up in the air. I don't know what is wrong with me. I hate how unsure I am. Or is it the fear? What if I tell her and she runs off? Who am I kidding? She could do that now, and I would be traumatized. There is a reason no one has been able to pin me down, and that reason is because they weren't Shelli Adler.

"She's awesome. So sweet," Wes calls out, standing beside me in all his nakedness.

I make a face and hold up my hand to guard my view of his schlong. "Dude."

He doesn't even care. He looks back to Benson. "You treat her with respect, you respect this team, you're golden."

Benson doesn't seem convinced. "Dude, she ripped me apart because there are pictures of me on Instagram at that orgy party I had last week."

I snort as I shake my head. "Yeah, that's a no-go."

Boon hooks a thumb toward me. "BB knows all about that. He came here and turned over a new leaf. He's a fucking saint now."

I flip him off. "Hardly."

"Maybe not with his girl," Boon says, waggling his brows at me.

"You got a girl?" Benson asks, and all eyes turn on me.

"Yeah," I say simply.

"But we've all heard about your fuck-'em-and-leave-'em philosophy."

I scoff. "I left that back in New York."

I'm not lying either. I think I did. Before I talked to Elli that first day, I only wanted to see Shelli again. That should tell me something right there.

Benson shakes his head. "So, one girl?"

I stand up, getting dressed. "Elli told me to get one girl and stick with her. It would keep my nose clean. So, that's what I did."

And I couldn't shake what I feel for Shelli even if I tried.

His dark eyes hold mine, and he looks as if I'm speaking German. "How does that even work?"

I shrug. "Great, in my opinion," I say, putting on my hoodie and grabbing my bag. "I'm good with it."

Benson isn't comprehending at all. "What about feelings? Don't they start falling for you and shit?"

I nod. "Yeah."

"And what do you do? Wait, don't tell me you feel shit for them! That's a recipe for disaster."

I used to think the way he does, but not anymore. I'm unable to say that, though. It will lead to more questions, and I already feel Boon's and Wes's gazes on me. I don't want people in my business, so I shake my head. "No, I just ignore it all and get what I want from her."

I meet Wes's and Boon's gazes and shake my head, which makes them both smile as I head out with a wave to the guys. "See ya—"

My words fall off when I see Shelli with Shea and Elli beside her, standing in the doorway.

One look into Shelli's eyes and I know one thing.

I'm so fucked.

My instinct is to hold out my hands, so I do because I have to calm the storm that is brewing inside her. But Elli and Shea are watching me. I drop my hands and inhale. "Um... Hey, guys. Um—" I'm stuttering like a fucking fool, and in all honesty, I probably am one. "Did you want to talk about that thing, Shelli?"

When a tear falls down her cheek, it wrecks me. I don't care that they are there; I don't care who the fuck is here. I take a step forward, holding up my hands, and she smacks them away. "Shell—"

Her eyes shut me up instantly. The roar of my heartbeat is killing my eardrums and probably breaking my ribs. "Really, Aiden?"

"No. I promise. No."

"Is that what you've been doing all this time?"

"No. Fuck no, Shelli. Can we talk over here?" I say, jerking my head to the side. "Please."

"I have nothing to say to you—"

"Shelli, for real—" She turns quickly, her hair flying with the turn, but I'm on her heels. I ignore the death glare coming from Shea—partly because I'm confused by it but mostly because I have to get Shelli to listen to me. "Shelli, no. Listen to me. I didn't mean that at all. Stop," I say, reaching out for her, but she whips her arm out of reach.

"I can't believe you! I'm so fucking stupid."

I finally get ahold of her and stop her. "Shelli, you're not. Baby, listen to me," I demand, my eyes trying to capture hers as I hold her in place, but she's got that fighter's soul. "I didn't mean any of that. I was just shooting the shit with the guys—"

"And mentioning the one thing I have an insecurity about?"

I raise my brows.

"Oh yeah, Aiden. I have insecurities too. I'm scared you're just with me for the fuck, but I ignored that because I believed in you, in us. But that's all in the tank now."

I look down the hall, terrified, to see both of her parents watching me.

"They already fucking know, Aiden! They've known since last night!"

My gaze snaps back to her. "Well, this is fucking great."

"Yeah, it is. Especially since I just sat in my mom's office and told them that you've changed. That you're a damn good man and you make me happy. That I love you, that I choose you—"

"That shouldn't change due to what I said in there, because it wasn't the truth, Shell. I looked at Boon and Wes and shook my head. I didn't mean it! I promise you, I was trying to protect us—"

She throws her hands in the air, more tears falling down her face. "Do you love me?"

I'm flabbergasted, stuttering like crazy. "W-Wait, huh? What? Why? You know I feel something. Why are you asking that? That's not fair. You said you're going to be patient with me. And the way you make that sound is that either I do or I don't, and that's not fucking fair."

"I also said I was in this till you gave me a reason to doubt it. That was a reason," she yells, her fingers jabbing at the locker room. "That is bullshit. How hard was it to say, 'You know, yeah, I got me a girl, and you know, we're navigating our feelings.'?"

I scrunch up my face. "'Cause I didn't want to sound like a fucking loser!"

"So being in love and caring about someone makes you a loser?" she sneers, her eyes narrowed to slits as they leak tears, and I feel helpless. She isn't the idiot; I am.

"What the fuck? No. Damn it. This is spiraling out of control. We need to calm down. Please. Let's go home—"

"Home? I have to mean more to you than a fucking fuck for that to be our home," she yells, her eyes wild and tear-filled. "We're done."

With that, she turns. I'm about to chase after her when a huge hand presses into my chest. I look up into Shea's eyes, and he shakes his head.

"Let her go."

"But I have to stop her."

"No, bud, you don't. You're right. She needs to calm down. You need to calm down. Give her some space. You knocked the shit out of her pride."

I shake my head. "No, no, I couldn't have. It's just a huge misunderstanding."

Elli squeezes my other shoulder. "I know, honey, but she can't see that right now. Your words hurt her—and pissed me off."

"Yeah, wouldn't mind ripping off your arm and beating you with the bloody end for making my baby cry," Shea says matter-of-factly. "I can't do that, can I?"

"No, we told Shelli not to hit people when she's upset."

"Bullshit-ass parenting on our part," he mutters, but I don't even care.

"But she said we're done—"

Emotion makes my voice crack, and I crouch down, covering my face as I suck in deep breaths.

She said we're done.

But we can't be done.

I squeeze my eyes shut as I'm struck by emotional hit after hit. I feel like I'm standing in the ocean and getting smacked in the face by waves and jellyfish. I'm feeling everything at once. I didn't mean what I said. I really didn't realize what I was saying until it was out of my mouth. I wanted to shut the guys up. She wasn't supposed to hear that because it isn't fucking true. There are feelings. There are so many feelings, and it's as if they're ripping me apart right now.

She said what I thought she'd never say.

We're done.

MY APARTMENT FEELS EMPTY WITHOUT SHELLI HERE.

Without her laugh.

Her ass always cleaning something.

Lying on me.

Kissing me.

Holding me.

Maybe it's not the apartment. Maybe it's me. I feel empty.

She hasn't answered any of my calls. My texts have been ignored, and I thought about driving by her parents', but I'm sure she'll ignore me there too. I know I need to give her space. The sympathy in Elli's and Shea's eyes told me that, but I don't want to. I want to find her, scream in her face that she has it all wrong, and show her that we aren't done. We can't be done. But I don't know how to do that when she doesn't want to speak to me.

The main reason I wanted to keep our relationship to ourselves was because of our families. They're very much in the know on everything. Shelli's and my fight is no different. Emery and Stella have already texted me, calling me a dumbass. My mom has called nineteen times, but I refuse to talk to her. My dad, though...radio silence. Which means one thing. He's disgusted with me. Fuck, I'm disgusted with myself. I shouldn't have said those things. I wasn't even thinking. But Shelli won't hear it. I did the one thing I didn't want to do. I hurt her. I beat up her pride, and now, I'm left feeling bruised and battered. I want to make it better. I want her to listen, but I don't know how to get her to.

I stare at my phone, willing it to ring and for it to be Shelli. Alas, it doesn't. It just sits there silent, a reminder of my stupidity. I reach for it and dial her number once more.

Her voice mail—again.

Fuck, I miss her. "Shelli, it's me. Again. Listen, this is bullshit. I didn't mean what I said. I promise you that. Please. Call me. Come here, or I'll come to you. Any way that works for you. We just have to fix this. I don't care what you say—we aren't done. Answer me."

I hang up, and I'm tempted to fling my phone into the wall. Since it's the only way for her to get ahold of me, I refrain. I let my head drop back, and I stare up at the ceiling. I'm going crazy not knowing what to do. I bring my phone up along with my head and dial another number. The only person I want to talk to other than Shelli.

Asher's voice sounds excited to hear from me when he answers. "Hey."

"Hey." Silence. I close my eyes and pinch the bridge of my nose. "I fucked up."

"I figured. What happened?"

I explain the situation, and as if we hadn't gotten into a huge fight, Asher listens and comments where he feels he should. I fall back into the couch, running my hand down my face. "I'm going crazy. What do I do?"

"You need to give her space, man. I know you don't want to hear that, but you do."

"I don't think space is what we need. We need to talk this through."

"But she isn't seeing it that way. She's hurt. You said things she's been worried about since the jump."

"But I didn't mean them."

"And I truly believe she knows that. But knowing her parents heard you say it, and then the whole team... Yeah, she's gonna be pissed."

I close my eyes. "You're right."

"I'm sorry, dude. That sucks."

"I just want her back. I miss her. I want her here." When he laughs softly, I roll my eyes. "Great to know my misery is hilarious to you."

"I'm laughing because you're so in love with her, yet you still can't realize it."

I sigh. "I get it. I'm fucked up—"

"You're not, though, Pity Party Pete. I get that I've said it before, but if you were so fucked up, would you be where you are? You're in a full-blown relationship, dude, and you love it. You love her. And I think when you tell her that, everything will fall into place."

I shake my head. "Sure, but I know for a fact that she wouldn't listen to me. She probably wouldn't believe me. She'd probably think I was saying it to get her back. I should have said it when she said it this morning. I wanted to, but I didn't."

"Why?"

I shrug. "I honestly don't know. The words were there. But I can't say it now. She wants actions, not words. I know her."

"Exactly, Aiden. You know her. So how do you get her back?"

"I have no clue, which is why I'm asking your ass!"

"You are really annoying, you know that?"

"Yeah, well, you're a dick."

"True. I'm sorry about that, by the way. Wasn't my finest behavior."

"Nope. Totally crybaby dick move."

"You're right, and I'm sorry."

"It's over and done with. Thanks for answering the phone."

"For you? Always," he says softly. "I do love your clueless ass."

I want to smile, but I can't. "Same here."

"And if you think really hard, you'll figure this out."

When my alarm sounds, alerting me that someone is coming upstairs, I rush to the screen in the wall, praying it's Shelli.

It's my dad and Shea.

"Great, it's Dad and Shea. Dad's probably here to lecture me as Shea beats me with the bloody ends of my limbs."

Asher laughs ruefully. "Sounds about right. I'm praying for you."

"Appreciate it."

"And don't worry, dude. You'll figure this out. Just like you'll figure out that you're head over heels in love with her."

I swallow hard and shake my head. "I don't need to figure that out. I know it. I think I always knew. I was scared to accept it because it meant she could hurt me. Yet here I am, not saying those words, and I'm empty. So, yeah, I'm winning at life over here."

"Totally. But here is a bit of advice."

"Am I going to like it?"

"Probably not," he says honestly. "But Mom always told me you have to love like there is no such thing as a broken heart."

I bring in my brows. "Pretty sure she got that from a song and didn't take that advice at all."

"Probably, but I like it."

There is a knock at my door. "It terrifies me, but I gotta go. Talk to you later."

"Stay alive," he yells as I hang up and open my door.

Dad and Shea are huge men. I'm the same height, but I feel small under their gazes. "Hey."

I move out of the way so they can come in. "We came to check on you," Dad says as he walks in and sets a six-pack of beer on the table. He grabs two, handing them to Shea and me before opening the bottle of water I hadn't seen in his hand. "To fucking up."

I shut the door, and for some reason, I clink my bottle to theirs before taking a long pull of my beer. "You guys fucked up?"

Shea scoffs loudly. "Elli's sister kissed me."

"I lied for your aunt, and when your mom found out, she lost her shit. That was the second time."

"Elli broke up with me for it."

"Yeah, Fallon did that too. Twice, mind you. First time was when she found me in her roommate's bed, drunk, naked, and passed out."

"Man, that sucks," Shea says, and Dad nods.

"Addiction is a bitch."

They tap bottles with each other, and then both of them sit on my couch.

I watch them for a moment. "So, is this like a pity party?"

They nod. "Yup," Shea says, and then he pats the couch between them. "You can come sit."

I don't move, though. "I thought you guys were coming to lecture me and beat me up."

Dad laughs as Shea nods. "That's after we make sure you're okay."

"You're not mad?"

"Oh, I'm pissed my daughter is at home crying her ass off. But I know it was a misunderstanding. I know you wouldn't speak that way about her to others."

His words gut me. She's crying? Over me? Damn it, why won't she speak to me? "How do you know that?"

"'Cause I know you. I was hell-bent on keeping her away from you when Elli told me you two were together, but then that wife of mine reminded me of my bad fortune when it came to women trying to take advantage of professional hockey players like us."

Dad nods. "They sure as hell do."

"Then I remembered all the times you helped my kids with

homework and hockey. How you've always treated me with respect—minus the last few months when you dated my daughter without telling me."

"He didn't tell us either. They wanted to be sure of each other before they brought us into the mix. Can't blame them," Dad adds, and Shea nods. "We're all a lot to handle."

That's the damn truth. I've got my dad and hers on my couch, throwing me a pity party.

I'm pathetic.

"You're right. See, I know you're a good guy. I'd love to beat the shit out of you for hurting my girl, but I won't. It won't help anything."

"It'd make you feel better."

"And hurt Shelli more."

I swallow past the lump in my throat. "She won't answer my calls."

"Nope, she shut off her phone."

I look down at my beer and shake my head. "How am I supposed to fix this?"

They both shrug, and Shea leans forward on his knees. "Give her time to realize she's partly wrong."

I give him a dry look. "That girl is beyond stubborn. That's gonna be a while, and— Wait. Partly? This is all my fault."

"And hers for letting her pride get in the way," Shea says. I never thought Shea would defend me. I thought he would want to hang me out to dry. "Don't get me wrong. You're an asshole for what you said, even if you didn't mean it. But Shelli is in the wrong by letting it play out like this. It's obvious it was a mistake."

"A mistake you gotta make sure you never make again—if you want her back," Dad says, and I give him a look.

"Of course I want her back. But shit, I never lost her. We're just in limbo right now, but if she answers the fucking phone, we'll be fine."

They both nod. "Let me know how that goes." Dad smirks.

"Yeah, because I tried to talk to Elli for about two months, wore her engagement ring around my neck, and she didn't give a damn." Shea grins at me. "You forget, I'm with the older, wiser, and more stubborn version of Shelli."

Dad leans on his legs, and then he points to me. "Do you love her?"

My mouth goes dry under their scrutiny. I look down at my bottle and slowly nod. "But she wouldn't listen to that now."

"Nope, not even kinda," Shea says.

"She'd probably laugh in your face," Dad says with a nod. "So you gotta talk to her in another way."

"You're the second person to say that to me, and I don't know what that means," I say, exasperated. "I just want to make this better. I hate being here without her."

Shea looks around and nods. "I'm gonna ignore the fact that my daughter's bra is hanging off your barstool."

Dad laughs, and I look at them longingly. I just want her here.

Shea meets my gaze. "Why do you think she got so upset?"

"Because I embarrassed her. I said the one thing she was worried about. And I can't seem to get my head out of my ass and scream in her face that I love her more than I love life itself."

Okay, so apparently I can tell my dad and her dad that I love her, but when it comes to actually telling the person it matters to, the words won't come out. I'm a real piece of work.

Dad nods. "What do you want to do?"

"I want to make her listen to me. I don't want to wait. I don't want to spend another second without her."

"You're gonna have to accept that you will. For at least a little bit, dude," Shea says. "But then there will be a perfect moment, and that's when you need to score."

I blink, completely confused. "Huh?"

"Jesus, he really does take after you," Shea teases, and Dad laughs.

"The gala, Aiden," Dad says simply.

"The gala?"

Dad shakes his head with a sigh. "Maybe he does take after me."

They both laugh, yet I'm completely in the dark.

I guess that's where I belong.

Alone.

But that doesn't sit right with me.

I want her back.

I *need* her back.

I'm going to get her back.

CHAPTER THIRTY-FOUR

SHELLI

"I'm not one to say you're overreacting, but I think you are."

I roll my eyes as I climb up the stairs of Mordor—also known as the StairMaster in the Assassins' gym. My mom has called me in for another meeting. I'm sure it's to make sure everything is good for the gala tomorrow, but I don't want to go. I don't want to do anything, really. I'm so upset with Aiden, I honestly don't know how to function. He's called nonstop, but I have absolutely nothing to say to him. I can't believe he said what he did. How dare he? If he didn't mean it, then why say it? I want to wring his damn neck and tell him he's an idiot, but I also want to hug him. It's really complicated up here in my head.

I glance back at where Amelia is lying on the weight bench with a package of Sour Patch Kids. It's her craving right now. "I don't think I'm overreacting at all."

"You are," she says simply. "Believe me, I don't want to defend Aiden since I've never figured out what you see in him, but he didn't mean it, Shell. You know he didn't."

"I feel like he might have."

She drops a piece of candy into her mouth. "Why?"

"He doesn't say things without thinking them through. Believe me, I know. If he did, he would have said he loved me a long time ago. But the fact that he has kept that in check makes me believe his words are true."

"That's dumb," she says, shaking her head. "He was trying to keep everyone from knowing about y'all. He wasn't trying to hurt you."

"I agree that he wasn't, but that doesn't mean he didn't do it."

"Shelli, come on."

"Come on, what?"

"I think you need to talk to him."

"I'd rather not. He's too charming. He'll get me to let it go, and then I'll be back with him when, really, I probably never should have gotten with him."

I feel her gaze on me. "You don't have to be so tough with me," she accuses, and I shrug.

"It's true."

"I don't believe you. I think you know it's all a big misunderstanding, but since he embarrassed the hell out of you in front of your parents, you're gonna torture him until you're not mad anymore."

I shake my head. "I'm not even mad."

"Lies."

"Whatever. He hurt me."

"And pissed you off."

I bite my lip as I continue to climb to fucking nowhere, but I'm doing it because I want to look good in my fishnets when I go to New York. Don't know why. I don't have anyone to impress anymore. As much as I think that, I also don't believe it. I don't want things to be over with Aiden. I love him, but I'm just so mad. I don't know why he had to say that. I know that Boon and Wes know about us, so what was his game? It doesn't make sense to me, and it guts me. I don't want to be just a fuck, and I really didn't think I was. I mean, we had just been talking about living together, and when I said I loved him, I swear I saw it in his eyes. I swear he loves me too.

So I really don't understand.

"Maybe instead of leaving your phone off, you could talk to him?"

I shake my head as my watch beeps that my workout is complete. "I can't talk to him and keep my emotions in check." I turn off the death machine and draw in a deep breath. "I miss him so damn much. And by talking to him, I'll get stupid and let it go."

"I mean, what is he supposed to do, Shelli? What do you want?"

"I don't know." I step off, gasping for breath. "I just want to forget it all."

"So you want to be done?"

"No, I don't," I say, and I hate the emotion clogging my throat. Or maybe it's the fact that I can't breathe. "I don't know. I just need some space." I wipe my face free of sweat and then start stretching. "It scares me, Amelia. What if his words were true, but he doesn't know it? Like how he doesn't know he loves me?"

"I don't get how you are so caught up on this when you know he loves you. You've sung his praises, and you've been patient as hell with him because you believe in him. You're the most confident person I know, Shell. Why is this tripping you up?"

I look down at my towel and shrug. "Because I *was* just a fuck at the beginning."

Her brows come in, and she nods slowly. "But from the way you speak of him, and how I saw him look at you at dinner with my mom, or even the picture you sent me of you two back in New York the other night, it doesn't seem like that anymore." She searches my eyes. "Maybe you weren't ever that at all."

My eyes itch with tears. I know I'm not. In my gut, I know it. But what if my gut is wrong? What if my heart is just taking over and I want so badly to be Aiden's world? For the last couple weeks, I've felt like his world, but all it took was for him to say what he did and it was like the last four months didn't even happen. The Aiden I know and love wouldn't say those things, so why did he?

"I gotta go get ready."

"Okay. Call me later?"

"Yeah," I say, and then I kiss her before heading to the showers.

After my meeting with my mom, I'll be working up at the piano bar since I have to take the weekend off. Hope everyone is ready for some really sad, depressing music since that's all I feel like singing tonight.

As I wash my hair and my body, Amelia's words play over and over again in my head. How is Aiden supposed to fix this? I won't give him the opportunity. But even so, what could he say to heal this hurt? He already tried to say that he didn't mean it, that he was sorry, and I blew him off.

We were so perfect, and now... Now, I don't even know. I miss him. God, I miss him, but I don't know how to get past what he said. I still can't believe he thought that was okay. He knew how I felt when it came to being just a fuck. I struggled with it so much at the beginning, but then I let it go. I knew we were good. But now, I don't know if we are, and that scares me. I am ready to give myself to him completely, and it sucks that I don't know if he feels the same.

After blow-drying my hair and curling it, I put on a tight black pencil skirt with a green tank and black blazer. I lace up my green heels before packing up my gym bag and making sure I look okay. I plan to put on makeup once I get to Brooks House. I'm not in the mood right now. After making sure I have everything, I head out of the gym and toward my mom's office. As I walk, my heels clicking on the floor, I can't help but think of Aiden. Everything about him makes me smile, but then I hear his words again, and tears burn my eyes. I'm pretty sure I said I'd never shed another tear over Aiden Brooks.

When I get to my mom's office, she isn't there. I check my phone and I'm early, so I'm confused. Maybe she's running late. I throw my bag on her floor before shutting the door and walking back to the receptionist. "Hey, do you happen to know where my mom is? Is she running late?"

Tanya shakes her head. "No, ma'am. She's waiting for you in conference room seven."

Conference room seven? What the hell? "Thanks so much."

I head toward the conference rooms, and I'm annoyed. I don't want to do this. I don't even want to go to the gala tomorrow. How am I supposed to face Aiden when I won't even speak to him? This is what I get for falling hopelessly in love with someone who wasn't ready for it. Who am I kidding? I couldn't stop myself if I tried. And damn it, he *is* ready; he's just being a punk.

Now I'm irritated all over again. Wonderful.

I turn the corner of the long hall where all the conference rooms are located, and coming toward me from the other end is the last person I want to see right now.

Aiden's eyes widen as he watches me. He runs his hands through his hair, but his eyes don't leave mine. I plan to ignore him, walk right past his ass, but he stops before I even reach him. Since I can't just slip into any old conference room, especially since they're locked, I keep walking toward him as my heart jackhammers in my chest. It's totally unfair how gorgeous he is. Especially when he's wearing athletic pants and a hoodie, not his usual slacks and nice shirt.

I swallow hard and try to ignore him, but his eyes burn into mine as he speaks. "It's really unfair for you to look that fucking good when I'm dying here."

Don't answer him. Ignore him. Even if he does look unlike his usually put-together self, he's baiting you. "Dying, huh? Funny… Didn't think you'd care about just some fuck."

Now he's glaring. "Shelli, it isn't like that, and you fucking know it."

"I don't know shit," I retort, glaring at him. "You don't say things you don't mean."

He throws his hands in the air. "I wasn't thinking. I was trying to get out of there, Shelli. I'm sorry. I didn't mean to say it or embarrass you in front of the team or your parents. I'm so sorry for that. I was just trying to keep us to us, and it all backfired. I swear, if you want me to scream from the rooftops that we're together, I will."

I shake my head. "Doesn't matter if there is no future."

"That's not fair. You know that's untrue."

"Or maybe not. Maybe I am just the girl you're using, ignoring your feelings so you don't have to feel them. I get it. It's easier that way and explains why you don't feel shit for me."

"That's not fucking true," he sneers, his eyes wild. "I feel a lot for you, Shelli. You don't just cross my mind—you fucking live there. And I'm not going to have you reduce what we have to nothing because I made a fucking mistake."

I blink back my tears as I look away, shaking my head. I'm trying to hurt him like he hurt me, which isn't right. I shouldn't do that. I'm just so mad, and my parents are against violence. "Whatever, Aiden. Excuse me—"

"I love you, Shelli." I meet his gaze, and anger ripples through me. "Shit, I shouldn't have said that now—I know I shouldn't have. But it's true. I do."

"Really? This is when you choose to tell me? Not the many times we were lying in bed or holding each other? Or when we were laughing so hard? Or, hell, any time other than this one where I am spitting mad at you? Really, Aiden?"

"I don't know what to do, Shelli. You won't listen to reason."

I shake my head. "Oh, so you don't mean it?"

His face is beet red, and I swear I can see his heart beating out of his chest. "What the hell? Yes, I do. This is not the way this is supposed to go!"

I can't breathe, my heart is aching so badly. Tears burn my eyes as I look away. "You're right. Just leave me alone, okay?"

"No, I won't. I won't give up. I do love you, Shelli Adler. I want you, and I refuse to allow you to let go of what we have."

"Aiden—"

"Tell me what I have to do. I'll do anything."

"Leave me alone," I say, and then I walk past him, fighting back my tears. He says my name, but I ignore him, opening the door to conference room seven. What I don't expect is for my dad, Fallon, and Lucas to be sitting with my mom. I look at all their faces and then behind me when the door opens again.

Aiden comes in, looking distraught, but when he sees our parents, he shakes his head. "What the hell is this?"

My mom stands, clasping her hands together. "You two need to talk, and we feel we should do it as a family."

You've. Got. To. Be. Fucking. Kidding. Me.

I turn and glare at him. I can't believe he did this. "Can't fight your own battles?"

"No, I had no clue about this," he snaps back at me, and then he points to our parents. "You guys are crazy if you think this is going down. This is why we didn't want to tell any of you. You guys always want to help, but we can figure this out. We're adults."

Okay, so he didn't know. "What he said."

"We just want you guys to be okay," Fallon says, holding out her palms to us. "You guys are beautiful together. Don't throw this away."

"Mom—"

"No disrespect, but what's happening is between him and me. And it doesn't matter anyway 'cause I'm leaving for New York to get away from all this crap. I never should have come home," I snap. I go to turn, but Aiden is blocking my way.

"There was never a question of you going back to New York for a little while, Shell. You know I support you one hundred percent, but you belong at home. You may be mad right now, but you know it doesn't matter because I am going with you."

I shake my head and push by him to get out the door so I don't break down crying. Does he really love me? Seriously, after all the crap he caused, he finally wants to admit it? He's infuriating! But nothing comes close to the anger I have toward our parents. I stomp up the hall, pissed the hell off. What the hell were they thinking? Did they really think butting in would get us back together? That's insane and just like them, but still! This isn't a business deal; this is my heart. His heart.

"Ugh!"

When I hear someone rushing up behind me, I pray it's not Aiden. But when I see it's my dad, I kind of wish it were Aiden. "Not right now, Dad."

He takes ahold of my arm, stopping me. "I'm gonna give you some unsolicited advice—"

"I'd rather you didn't."

He smiles, his blue eyes tender as he cups my face. "I know you don't want to hear this. But the truth is, baby, a long-lasting relationship comes with a lot of forgiveness and understanding."

I just blink up at him. "You want me to forgive him?"

"Yes, and I want you to acknowledge that it was a misunderstanding."

I'm flabbergasted. "You? You're the one telling me this?" I shake my head. "What happened to killing him?"

"He loves you, Shelli. I know that. And to be honest, after everything we talked about last night, I can see he's wrecked by this." I look away, the tears burning my eyes.

"Last night?"

"Yeah, Lucas and I went over to make sure he was okay. And baby, he isn't." I shake my head as he squeezes my wrist. "All that in there was your mother and Fallon. Lucas and I had no part in it, but I do agree that you need to talk to Aiden. Really talk to him."

I chew on my lip and then slowly nod. "I can't right now."

And at this moment, I don't know when I'll be ready to.

CHAPTER THIRTY-FIVE

SHELLI

I WANT TO BE PROUD OF WHAT I'VE DONE HERE.

The arena is decorated like the 1920s with an awesome *Great Gatsby* theme. Usually, my mom's themes are something purple, but I wanted to go bigger. While purple is the main color of the décor to honor our Assassins Foundation, I added sparkly golds and blacks to tie everything together. Lights, pearls, and feathers hang above us, while the tables are decorated with plumes of feathers and glitz. Flapper girls are walking around with champagne since there is no smoking, but I don't think anyone minds. Especially when the Gatsby-era jazz band I hired is killing it. They're freaking great, even if Aiden was the one to choose them.

I ignore that fact and try to smile at everyone as they enjoy themselves. Thankfully, the players were supportive of my request and are wearing the time-period-specific outfits I had ordered. I had their vests made with the Assassins logo and their numbers on the pocket. The vests are being auctioned off at the end of the night to fund the addition of a rec hall in the facility we're building for the veterans.

All the guests came dressed to the nines, and the photo booth is a huge hit. Along with taking pictures with the players, everyone seems pretty happy. People are bidding on the auction items and eating the wonderful food from Brooks House. We've already raised so much money, and the night is just getting started. It's all perfection, everything I wanted it to be. Yet I feel like utter shit.

I'd thought getting my hair done in a Roaring Twenties do, along with some fierce makeup, would have made me feel a lot better. It didn't. Especially when I had to put on my dress for the night. The dress Aiden had given to me. Of course, it has a sexy, plunging neckline with a scrap of tasteful sheer fabric in place to shield my breasts. The gold material hugs my body in all the right ways, stopping at midcalf. He bought me a thick strand of pearls to go with it, and the feather headpiece he picked out brings the whole outfit together. The only thing he didn't get me are my sparkly gold heels, but when I bought them, I'd picked them out just for him. The higher, the better is his motto.

A little grin pulls at my lips.

I miss him.

I stand by the stage as I people-watch. I haven't spoken to anyone, really. Only to give people direction on how to do their jobs and then to tell them to schmooze the folks with deep pockets. It's gone well for me, but I'm a bundle of nerves. This has to be a success. I can't leave for New York without having my name shine in this arena.

That's not the only reason I'm nervous, though. My stomach has been in knots since I arrived. I haven't seen him yet, but I know he's here. I can feel him here. All day, I thought about what my dad said. He's right; forgiveness and understanding are huge factors in a long-lasting relationship. If my mom hadn't forgiven my dad, or the other way around, they wouldn't be together. Same with Fallon and Lucas.

"This party is stunning, baby."

I look over at my mom, and she's dressed up perfectly. Instead of a flapper dress, though, she's wearing a billowing white floor-length gown. She is dripping with diamonds, and she looks as if she belongs in a film rather than at my party.

I beam as I nod. "It is. It's everything I wanted it to be."

"You did a wonderful job."

"Thank you," I say, and I bite the inside of my cheek. "I'm sorry for being disrespectful yesterday."

Mom scoffs. "Oh, love. I was probably in the wrong. I keep forgetting you're not a baby anymore."

"You *were* wrong." My lips curve.

She laughs as she cups my arm. "How are you?"

I shrug. "Living my best life."

I know she sees right through me. "Is that code for complete shit?"

I grin back at her. "Yup."

"Well, then, Aiden is doing the same."

I follow her gaze to where he sits with some of the guys. He looks stunning in his vest and newsboy hat. He's wearing an adorable purple bow tie that goes great with his whole outfit. He's pulled his hair back too, but it's typically messy and, of course, so sexy. Even with how good he looks, it's easy to see he's miserable. I swallow hard as I look away.

"Have you talked to him?"

"No, Mom."

She gives me a look. It's somewhere between pity and annoyance. "Can you stop being so stubborn?"

"Nope. Inherited it from you, so thanks."

She makes a face as she shakes her head. "You're a pain in my ass."

I smile and lean back into the stage. "Mom, let me be. I need to get through this."

She doesn't move, though, as her eyes burn into mine. With a small grin, she takes my arm in her hand. "Can I give you some advice?"

I groan loudly. "Please don't."

She ignores me. "You knew he was good before he did. Don't lose that, my love. Hold on to the love you want because, I'm telling you, he loves you something fierce." I meet her gaze, and she gives me a pointed look. "Remember, I was just as proud as you are being now, and all it did was bring me heartache. It wasn't until I knocked off the chip on my shoulder that I was happy again."

With that, she walks off, her dress flowing behind her. She's stunning, she really is, but she's also annoying as fuck. It doesn't matter. I only have to get through this party, and then I'm home free. I could even move back to New York now if I wanted. Not that I will, but I could. I don't want to. I want to go over and wrap my arms around Aiden.

My damn pride won't let me.

Since I know where he is, I keep my eye on him as I move around the room. I'm trying to be inconspicuous, but it's pretty obvious I'm staring at him. I hate how hopeless and upset he looks, even if it's exactly how I feel. It's kind of funny that we're both so bummed and apart, when I had asked him to come to this thing with me. If only we could go back to that time in the truck. Maybe then he would have said he loved me. Not during a fight... God, I can't believe he did that. He sure is handsome—and book-smart to boot—though, when it comes to relationships, the dude is a dud.

But he's trying.

When he looks up, our eyes meet, and everything around me just stops. Gone are the guests, the staff, the players, everyone. It's only him and me as my heart goes crazy in my chest. His eyes are so dark, so sad, and they gut me. He holds his beer by the neck, running his thumb along the top of it. He looks down, almost as if he is arguing with himself before looking back up at me, those gray eyes piercing my soul. When he starts to get up, I know I should probably go the other way, but I stay where I am.

It only takes a few strides before he's standing in front of me, intoxicating me with his ice-rink smell.

"I don't want to fight," he says then, calmly but sternly. "I just want to say that everything you've said is bullshit—"

I scoff. "If you don't want to fight, don't call what I say bullshit."

His eyes burn into mine. "Always got something to say, huh?"

"Always," I retort. "You hurt me, Aiden. Truly hurt me."

"I know, but that wasn't my intention. I really was just protecting us."

"But Boon and Wes know about us."

"They do, and of course, they know the truth. I even shook my head at them so they knew I was putting up a front. *We* know the truth. That's all that matters."

I slowly shake my head. "I don't know, Aiden. It's almost like I didn't know that guy who was saying that crap. You don't talk about me like that anymore, but then you did, and it hurt. It was a huge blow. Anyone who sees us together now will think I'm only the girl you keep around to fuck and not feel anything for."

He closes his eyes, and his head falls forward. "I don't give a fuck what they think," he says, meeting my gaze. "I only care what you think. Do you think that, Shelli?"

The tension between us is thicker than ice. Not even my daddy's slapshot could break it. "I want to say no, but I don't know if I can."

"You're not just a fuck," he says, coming closer and grabbing my hips to pull me into him. "You never were, Shelli. You were always special. From the moment I saw you and felt your lips on mine, I didn't want to let you go. Please believe me."

Tears flood my eyes as I look up at him. I take in a deep breath. I know he's waiting for an answer, but I can't give him one. "I have to go check on things."

"Lame excuse to get away."

"It's either that or the truth," I say, backing away even as his arms beckon me to him.

His shoulders slump. "What's the truth?"

"I don't know if I can get over it."

He shakes his head. "You're so fucking stubborn, Shelli."

"I know," I say, walking backward as I shrug.

"But I love that about you."

I stop midstride. His words are so strong, so confident, and they blow me away. Unlike before when I was pissed, now my heart takes a hit. Breathlessly, I ask, "You do?"

He nods. "I love everything about you." I blink, my heart in my throat as his eyes hold me captive. "I'm gonna prove it to you too."

I watch him for a moment until he disappears into the crowd. I don't know what just happened here, but hearing that he loves everything about me did something to my heart. Or better yet, my pride. My stubbornness. I've wanted to hear those words from his lips for as long as I can remember. Finally, he says them, and I just gawk at him. Why does he make me feel like a crazy person?

I shake my head and head toward the bar. I need a drink. Probably not the greatest answer to this situation, but I don't know what to do.

Do I just let it go? Do I forgive him when I'm worried it is true? I was so sure of us. Is this going to be what holds me back from having the guy I've always loved? I reach the bar and take a wine bottle out of the cooler, waving off the bartender. I pull the cork out with my teeth, spitting it into the trash, and then take a swig.

My mom would be so proud.

"Hey."

I have the bottle at my lips when I direct my gaze to where Wes is staring at me. Boon is beside him, nodding. "Man, you're a catch."

I laugh as I lower the bottle from my lips. "Y'all get to drink. Why shouldn't I?"

"Hey, no judgment here," Wes says, showing me his palms. "What are you doing?"

I wave the bottle at him. "Trying to get drunk."

He nods, and Boon grins. "I've got the strong stuff at my table. Come on."

"Okay," I say, following them but not leaving my bottle. I can drink the strong stuff and my wine. When they go to cut across the dance floor, I'm confused. I thought they were sitting in the back, but maybe I was wrong. Boon stops suddenly, and I run into him as Wes laughs.

"You already drunk?"

I give him a dry look. "Hardly."

Wes takes the bottle from me. "Good," he says with a grin.

He then backs away, as does Boon. No one is on the floor. Why isn't anyone dancing? I look up at the band to figure out why they're not playing, but then I see Aiden.

Only Aiden.

With a guitar.

"If I can have everyone's attention," he says, a guitar hanging around his neck as he brushes his hair back with his fingers. My heart jumps up into my throat as he ties his hair up and then grabs the mic. "My name is Aiden Brooks, and I want to thank everyone for coming out and supporting this amazing foundation. Isn't this party stellar?" The room erupts with applause as he takes the mic from the stand and then comes to the end of the stage, his guitar now on his back. I'm still trying to breathe because I think I know what he is doing. But surely not. "As a lot of you know, Shelli Adler is the one who put this shindig together, and I think she may have outdone herself."

More applause as he lowers himself to the stage and then hops off. I wave at the crowd with a curt smile, but my heart hurts, it's beating so hard. "I have witnessed Shelli plan this thing. She stayed up night after night, working hard to make sure it was a success, and I, for one, am very proud of her."

He comes toward me, his eyes only on me. "For those who don't know, she's very talented. But as all of you know, she is drop-dead gorgeous."

There are a few catcalls and laughter, but I don't hear it, I'm lost in his gray eyes. "I am also head over heels in love with her, and being the idiot I am, I made her question that, question how I feel for her. I never meant to do that, not when she is the best thing in my life. So I'm gonna speak to her in a way I know she'll listen to."

My eyes widen as Wes steps up with a mic stand for Aiden's mic. Some of the guys holler for him, but his eyes are on me, and this naughty little grin sits on his beautiful lips. I'm surprised I'm able to identify the beating noise as his hand against the guitar rather than my heart pounding in my ears. When he starts playing, the room goes quiet. Then the words are leaving his lips.

Oh, he's playing dirty.

"You & Me," by James TW is one of my all-time favorite songs. He learned this for me? Every time it comes on, I jam like no other, mostly because it reminds me of Aiden. Because all I've ever wanted was him and me. As he reaches the chorus, he really gets into it, his eyes falling shut as he sings so beautifully. I feel as if I'm flying. There are tears in my eyes, my heart is in my throat, and I can't believe this. When his eyes meet mine, the verse leaving his lips, the tears start to fall. I'm breathless as he plays with no cares and nothing holding him back. It as if it's just him and me in this room. This is the man I fell in love with.

When he pushes the guitar around to his back, he starts to clap, and the room joins in, leaving me utterly mind-blown. He moves past the mic stamd, coming toe-to-toe with me, before using his thumbs to clear away my tears. He cups my face in his large hands, his voice so perfect as he finishes the song just for me.

"That's all I want. I just want you and me," I say, and his lips curve.

"Well, that's what you're getting." He leans in, his forehead against mine. "Everyone will always know how much I love you. How you mean everything to me. How you and I are a two-person team in this world. I waited so long to fall in love for a reason, Shelli. I didn't know it at the time, but I was waiting for you."

"I've always been right here."

"Yeah, but remember, I didn't know what or who I was waiting for," he says, his lips curving, and I smile. "But I know now, and you aren't ever going anywhere."

"I'm not?"

"Nope," he says confidently, his eyes dark. "I'm sorry. Please forgive me—"

"It's in the past. We have a future to look forward to, apparently."

He grins. "Not apparently. For sure."

I cover his hands with mine, and at the same time, we both move in, our lips pressing together. The room erupts with noise, but I'm in my own world with only Aiden by my side.

My favorite place to be.

When he pulls back, I open my eyes to find him gazing down at me with such love in his eyes. "I know it took me forever to say it, but I swear, Shelli, I'll spend every waking moment telling you."

A tear rolls down my cheek.

"You will?"

"Yes, because I love you, Shelli. I love you so damn much." Those words have my world spinning. I've wanted them for so long. "I should have told you when you said it to me in the truck the other day. I wanted to, but I was so scared of losing you. I almost did, and now you can't stop me from saying it." He runs his nose along mine, his eyes beautiful and full of all things perfect. "I do, Shelli. I love you."

I gaze up at him, almost speechless. But I've been saying *I love Aiden Brooks* my whole life.

So naturally, as if I'm only taking my next breath, I say, "I love you more, Aiden Brooks."

EPILOGUE

AIDEN

Shelli is absolutely stunning.

She moves across the stage in a barely there flapper costume that has my mouth dry. I still can't believe they wanted her to lose weight for the part. Don't they see how gorgeous she is? Those curves are dangerous and have me squirming in my seat. Really awkward when Shea Adler is sitting right next to me, not that I care one bit. Not when Shelli is onstage. I watch my girl gyrating and singing her heart out, and I'm in awe of her. I love watching her live her dreams.

She was there with me at every round for the Cup. She was there when I was bruised and exhausted. She kept me going. She was there for every loss but also every win. And when I hoisted the Cup over my head in a Hollywood ending against the IceCats at the end of a seven-game series, in their arena, I looked up at the boxes, and I knew Shelli was there. Cheering for me. For the Assassins. When I went down the line, shaking hands with the IceCats, and I came to Merryweather, he didn't shake my hand. But I didn't care.

Not only did I win the Cup, I won Shelli's heart.

I don't think there's ever been a time when I've been this happy.

We spent the summer in New York for rehearsals. And when she had a week-long break, I flew her to Bora Bora since she'd never been. A lot of the guys went, and we had a blast. The best part was seeing the look of pure relaxation on her face. She works so hard, does so much, and it felt damn good to see her finally relax a bit. It's also funny watching her in the mornings these days. With no stats to follow, now she follows the moves the teams make. Her brain never stops, and boy, do I love it.

I love her. God, I love her.

It's funny how hard it was for me to tell her that. When I finally did, it was just like breathing. She completes me. No one gets me like she does, and no one can make me laugh until I cry. Everything seems perfect to me, and I wouldn't or couldn't change it for anything. Not when I get to be on the receiving end of Shelli's smile.

I'm going to miss that smile.

The apartment here is small, but it's only temporary. She'll stay for another four months, with both of us traveling to the other when we have time. It's gonna be tough, but if anyone can do it, we can. We have no choice, really, because the other option is being without her, and that isn't going to happen.

"Damn, she's amazing," Dad says from beside me. "Don't let her go, Aiden. Talented, smart girls like that, you keep forever."

"You forgot gorgeous," I add, and he laughs.

"Thought that would be weird."

We both nod in agreement, but beyond the last comment, he's right. I can't let her go. I won't. With the new season approaching, I'm nervous to be away from her. We have it so perfect when we're together, but I know we'll fall into a new rhythm. Lots of FaceTime and phone sex are in our future, but I wouldn't have it any other way. While she says *Chicago* is seriously her last show, I'm not sure she's done. She just wasn't happy where she was, and now that she has me, her biggest fan, I think she'll go on for a while. I could be wrong, though. She could come back home and hop right back in the saddle for everything to do with the foundation.

She could honestly do anything she wanted, and I'd be there.

Supporting and loving her.

Shelli moves across the stage, her voice carrying in such a mesmerizing way, and I can't stop smiling. It's crazy how quickly she's changed my life. I never thought someone could make me feel the things she makes me feel, but I do. I really never saw myself as someone who wanted a partner in life, but now I want that partner to be her. She makes me want things I never thought I could. I love living with her, I love watching her succeed, and I love that we cheer each other on.

Do we fight? Constantly. She drives me absolutely insane with her mouth. Always has to have the last word, and she sure as hell gets on me about leaving my boxers in the bathroom. Don't know why it matters. I pick them up when I remember, but it drives her to cussing at me. I've also learned that it doesn't matter if I put my name on my food...she'll eat it. If she's hungry, she's eating, and I don't know why it doesn't make me mad. Instead, it makes me laugh. *She* makes me laugh.

Shelli is it for me.

I thought it would be harder on us, with our parents knowing, but it hasn't been. They're annoying and think they know everything, but for the most part, they're very supportive. We have family dinners every damn week, and apparently, we're all going to Harry Potter world this Christmas. I'm not complaining since I wanna go, but it will be hard feeling Shelli up with my wand when Shea is right there. He's always right there, too. It's like he knows I want to touch her all the time, and he cockblocks like no other.

Shelli thinks it's funny. I don't.

But then, this is my life.

And what a life it is.

When the show ends with all the usual pomp and circumstance, my gaze stays on that girl I'm entirely in love with. I clap loudly, screaming her name as I stand to my feet. Her first show was a hit, and she was made for the role of Velma Kelly. Her sassy ass and sultry voice blew away everyone in the place. She was magnificent. She takes her bow when they call her name, and her eyes meet mine. She doesn't have to say anything for me to know she loves me. It's all over her gorgeous face.

And mine, I'm sure.

I gather with her parents and mine in the lobby. We're going to dinner once she comes out, and then we're heading back to our place. I'll leave tomorrow with our families, and while I'm bummed, I'm excited for the new season to start. Before I know it, Shelli will be home for the holidays, and we can start the next chapter of our lives. I'm excited, though a little nervous. I don't want to mess up. But if she hasn't left me for the constant pairs of boxers on the floor, I don't think she will.

We have to wait about an hour before she comes out, still glammed up from the stage. She's wearing a simple little black dress that fits her in all the ways I love. Her heels are high and sparkly, though she walks as if she's in sneakers. Such confidence and beauty. Her dad hugs her first and then her mom before she finally gets to me. I wrap my arms around her as she does the same to me, our mouths meeting in a heated embrace. I'll never get tired of kissing her. I swear it. I savor her kiss, the feel of her lips and the taste of her. She must have just eaten something sweet, making me feel as if I'm in heaven.

When I pull back, she gazes up at me. "What did you think? Be honest!"

I shrug. "It was okay. You missed a step in the second act and were off-key for most of the show," I say, all blasé-like, and her eyes narrow but she grins. "Totally joking! You were the best up there and blew me away completely. You should star in all the parts on Broadway. Can we ask for that? Who do I talk to?"

She wiggles as she squeals, and everyone laughs. She wraps her arms around me, and we kiss once more, this time a little longer and with tongue. When she pulls back, her cheeks are red, and she gives me a sultry look. It leaves me wanting to go back to our place rather than to dinner with our parents.

But we have to go.

I made the reservations months ago at the best steakhouse in New York to celebrate this night. Shea and Dad have been talking about getting a rib eye all week, but I don't give two shits about a steak. Nope, only my girl. She leans into me, kissing my jaw when I hold her close as I sit beside her. She's absolutely stunning and all mine.

"You were amazing tonight."

"You have to say that," she teases, kissing my nose.

"For real, Shelli, you were amazing," Mom says from across the table, stealing Shelli's attention from me.

My dad nods, and a huge grin is on his face. "Best I've ever seen. Seriously better than when you played that blond chick with the snowman."

She laughs. "Yeah, big change, huh? So much fun. It was perfect. Everything I wanted it to be."

Elli beams as she moves a pin back in Shelli's hair. "It was an honor to see you do that. Perfection, my love."

Shelli's eyes are starting to fill with tears, and I cuddle her close to me as Shea says, "Truly. You were spectacular."

"Thanks, guys. I wish that Amelia could have made it, but no, she's gotta be ready to have my nephew and niece."

I grin against her temple. Every time I think of that gender reveal, when both pink and blue balloons came out and everyone was shocked to hell, I laugh. I thought Chandler was going to puke. I think he did, actually. I don't remember. So funny, though. Amelia was crying and not because she was excited. Nope, she's terrified. Pretty sure Grace is moving in with them for a while since Chandler's season is about to start. We have a few preseason games against the IceCats, so we plan on checking in on Amelia, Chandler, and the kids. I'm excited to see who pukes more—the kids or Chandler.

My arm tightens around Shelli's neck as I kiss her temple once more. Sucks that, after tonight, we'll be apart for three weeks. She has so many shows, and preseason is about to start, but we'll be fine. I figure, if I tell myself that, I'll start to believe it and not be bummed that I won't see her daily. That I won't wake up to her gorgeous face and perfect lips. Man, I'm gonna miss her.

With my lips by her ear, I whisper, "You know we're about to do it all night, right?"

She pulls back and nods. "Oh, totally."

I kiss her nose, and she laughs as she leans into me. I feel our parents staring at us, but I really don't care. I only care about making this girl feel loved.

"So, what a year it has been for you two so far," Elli says, and I look over at her. "Getting together."

"Hiding it," Mom adds.

Dad nods. "And then breaking up—"

Shelli holds up her finger. "I wouldn't say breaking up. It was just an epic fight."

"But you said we were done," I remind her, and she shrugs.

"Technicality."

I laugh as Dad shakes his head. "Epic fight that led to one over-the-top and completely disgustingly sappy song performed by you."

Shea laughs. "Which then led to one amazing run that brought the Cup back to Nashville," he says, and we all cheer as if we're still at the Stanley Cup parade in Nashville.

"More really disgustingly sappy acts of love all over social media with the Cup," Dad adds, and we all laugh.

"Hey, you said we had nothing to hide."

Mom sets me with a look. "We didn't mean post pictures of you with your hands on her ass in her barely there bikini."

I look down at Shelli. "I love that bikini."

She nods. "So do I."

"I don't. Not at all," Shea says, and I snort as Shelli rolls her eyes.

It's obvious our parents do not love Shelli's choice of swimwear, but with a grin, Elli says, "And then after moving back to New York, you put on one hell of a show after saying you would never go back onstage. How does it feel?"

Shelli's eyes meet mine, and I lose all sense of time. "It feels perfect."

I kiss her nose as Shea asks, "What's next?"

"I think I hear wedding bells!" Elli gushes, and Mom bounces beside her.

"Could you imagine how awesome that wedding would be!"

Shelli laughs in my arms, shaking her head. "We're supposed to say Disney World!" she gushes, but our moms shake their heads.

"A wedding at Disney World?"

"We're hardly thinking of—" Her words drop off when she meets my gaze. She narrows her eyes as she searches my face. "Wait. Do you hear them?"

I shrug. "I wouldn't hate being married to you," I tease, and she looks surprised by that.

"You're kidding. After all this time, when you wouldn't even admit to loving me, now you want to marry me?"

I just smile. "It wouldn't be so bad."

"Come on."

"What? Seriously."

"Really?"

I nod, and then I get out of my chair as I feel my heart jump up and down in my throat. "Really."

I then fall to one knee while reaching for the ring in my pocket. My mom wanted me to get a box, but we both know it's not from a store. Shelli's hands come up to her mouth as she gasps loudly. I don't have to look at my parents and hers to know the cameras are out or even that Amelia is on FaceTime so she doesn't miss this. With shaky hands, I hold up the four-carat heart-shaped single diamond that's set in a band engraved with "I love you and you love me." I'm proud to give her this ring; it's special to me. It was the start of my parents' happiness, and now it will be ours.

She looks around and shakes her head. "That was all a setup?"

Our parents nod, and Amelia is already crying. "Yup. We planned this in June."

"June?"

"Yup. June 22, the day I met with everyone—our parents and our siblings—to ask if everyone was good with us getting married."

Tears flood her eyes. "Really?"

"Oh, hell yeah," I say, and then I clear my throat free of the emotion trying to choke me. "I knew the moment I said I loved you that I was going to marry you. If I fell for you, even with never having wanted that at all, it meant you were special. Perfect, even. You challenge me, you support me, you make me laugh, and you love me. I can't even begin to thank you for how much you've added to and changed my life. I love that we are each other's first love, but I want you to be my only."

Shelli lets out a sob as the tears stream down her sweet cheeks.

Damn it, I am too manly to cry right now. "I love you, Shelli Grace

Adler, and I want to love you for the rest of my life. Will you marry me?"

She doesn't even hesitate. "Yes," she cries, and just like that, my life is complete.

With a shaking hand, I put the ring on her finger before standing and wrapping her up in my arms, lifting her out of her seat. Her lips press to mine, as do her tears to my cheeks, and damn it, I won't cry. Okay, I might be crying. But in a manly way. When we part, we're both wiping each other's eyes, but I don't care. This is perfect.

"I love you, Aiden."

I press my nose into hers. "Shelli, I am completely and permanently in love with you, and I will be for the rest of my existence."

"You're damn right, you will."

I smile against her lips. "Between you and your dad, I don't think I have a choice."

She winks. "You don't."

We grin at each other before our lips meet once more. As I kiss her, I'm excited for what will happen next.

No matter what, it will be a surprise.

Just as every moment with Shelli has been.

THE END

Please remember that a review is like a HUG, and I love hugs!

ALSO BY TONI ALEO

NASHVILLE ASSASSINS

Breaking Away

Laces and Lace

A Very Merry Hockey Holiday

Wanting to Forget

Overtime

Rushing the Goal

Puck, Sticks, and Diapers

Face-off at the Altar

Delayed Call

Twenty-Two

In the Crease

Bellevue Bullies Series

Boarded by Love

Clipped by Love

Hooked by Love

End Game

IceCats Series

Juicy Rebound

Taking Risks

Whiskey Prince

Becoming the Whiskey Princess

Whiskey Rebellion

Patchwork Series

ACKNOWLEDGMENTS

Dear Reader,

I am so excited to read the reviews on this one! Usually, I'm a little terrified, but I absolutely LOVE this book. First, though, I want to thank you for reading Dump & Chase. I thought it would be hard to write D&C after Juicy Rebound, but it wasn't. Shelli and Aiden flew off the pages for me. Shelli had a story, and damn it, I was going to tell it. I want to say I have a favorite part of this book, but I don't. It's all just so perfect to me. Shea and Lucas cracked me the hell up. Elli was perfection in my eyes. Emery...that girl is gonna be so much fun to write down the road.

I LOVED IT!

Every second, I loved writing this book. I am proud of this book. If this is the way I'm going to write for my comeback year, I'm stoked. I have so much planned! I know people were curious about Jude and Claire, and they're getting a short story. The next Spring Grove is coming, the next IceCats, and then the Next Assassins: NG.

I AM SO EXCITED!!!

The first couple of months of 2019 have been good. I am handling the rough stuff and striving at the good stuff. I am getting control of my health, and my family is doing well. There have been a lot of changes, but I think it's for the best. Things will work out. They have to; I won't accept anything less.

I am thankful to my friends for always being there. My best friends have constantly had my back. While I've lost some friends this year, I am chalking that up to growth. Lisa continues to be just amazing and helping me when I ask. She is a wonderful friend and editor (if you happen to need a book edited.) My betas are perfection and are my biggest supporters when it comes to writing. I am beyond thankful for all of them.

Michael, Mikey, Alyssa, Gaston, and Winston, I love you. Thank you for giving me the love and strength I need each day. To the rest of my family, thank you and I love you.

Thank you again for reading Dump & Chase! Get ready 'cause I'm nowhere near done!

Love,
Toni

ABOUT TONI ALEO

My name is Toni Aleo, and I'm a #PredHead, #sherrio, #potterhead, and part of the #familybusiness!

I am also a wife to my amazing husband, mother of a gamer and a gymnast, and also a fur momma to Gaston el Papillion & Winnie Pooh. While my beautiful and amazing Shea Weber has been traded from my Predators, I'm still a huge fan. But when I'm not cheering for him, I'm hollering for the whole Nashville Predators since I'll never give my heart to one player again.

When I'm not in the gym getting swole, I'm usually writing, trying to make my dreams a reality, or being a taxi for my kids.

I'm obsessed with Harry Potter, Supernatural, Disney, and anything that sparkles! I'm pretty sure I was Belle in a past life, and if I could be on any show, it would be Supernatural so I could hunt with Sam and Dean.

Also, I did mention I love hockey, right?

Also make sure to join the mailing list for up to date news from Toni Aleo:
JOIN NOW!

www.tonialeo.com
toni@tonialeo.com

46898765R00200

Made in the USA
San Bernardino, CA
09 August 2019